Praise for **New York Times** *bestselling author*
Sherryl Woods

"Sherryl Woods gives her characters depth,
intensity and the right amount of humor."
—*RT Book Reviews*

"Compulsively readable…Woods's novel easily
rises above hot-button topics to tell a universal
tale of friendship's redemptive power."
—*Publishers Weekly* on *Mending Fences*

"Sherryl Woods always delights her readers—
including me!"
—#1 *New York Times* bestselling author
Debbie Macomber

Praise for bestselling author Sarah Mayberry

"Reading [*All They Need*] was like finding a
twenty-dollar bill in your coat pocket, then
unfolding it and finding a fifty wrapped inside.
It started out great and just kept getting better."
—*USATODAY.com*

"This very talented writer touches your heart
with her characters."
—*RT Book Reviews* on *Her Secret Fling*

SHERRYL WOODS

With her roots firmly planted in the South, Sherryl Woods has written many of her more than one hundred books in that distinctive setting, whether her home state of Virginia, her adopted state, Florida, or her much-adored South Carolina. She's also especially partial to small towns, wherever they may be.

A member of Novelists Inc. and Sisters in Crime, Sherryl divides her time between her childhood summer home overlooking the Potomac River in Colonial Beach, Virginia, and her oceanfront home with its lighthouse view in Key Biscayne, Florida. "Wherever I am, if there's no water in sight, I get a little antsy," she says.

Sherryl also loves hearing from readers. You can join her at her blog, www.justbetweenfriendsblog.com, visit her website at www.sherrylwoods.com, where you can also link directly to her Facebook fan page, or contact her directly at Sherryl703@gmail.com.

SARAH MAYBERRY

After several international moves, Sarah Mayberry now lives in Melbourne, Australia, her hometown, with her partner. She is the proud owner of a mini orchard, complete with quince and fig trees and raspberry canes. When she's not writing or thinking about all the jam she will make one day, she likes to shop for shoes and almost anything else. She also loves cooking, movies and, of course, reading. Visit her website at www.sarahmayberry.com.

BESTSELLING AUTHOR COLLECTION

New York Times Bestselling Author

SHERRYL WOODS

Edge of Forever

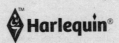

TORONTO NEW YORK LONDON
AMSTERDAM PARIS SYDNEY HAMBURG
STOCKHOLM ATHENS TOKYO MILAN MADRID
PRAGUE WARSAW BUDAPEST AUCKLAND

Recycling programs
for this product may
not exist in your area.

ISBN-13: 978-0-373-18057-8

EDGE OF FOREVER
Copyright © 2012 by Harlequin Books S.A.

The publisher acknowledges the copyright holders of the individual works
as follows:

EDGE OF FOREVER
Copyright © 1988 by Sherryl Woods

A NATURAL FATHER
Copyright © 2009 by Small Cow Productions PTY Ltd.

This edition published by arrangement with Harlequin Books S.A.

For questions and comments about the quality of this book
please contact us at Customer_eCare@Harlequin.ca.

www.Harlequin.com

Printed in U.S.A.

CONTENTS

Dear Friends,

Over the course of what now has become an amazingly long career, I've chosen most often to write about women who are survivors. That is certainly true of Dana Brantley, the heroine of *Edge of Forever*, one of my earliest books for Silhouette Special Edition. I'm absolutely delighted that her story is available again.

What do I mean by survivors? These are women who have faced almost insurmountable odds, a crisis so life-altering that many people would have given up. But not Dana Brantley, who has chosen to rebuild her life in a small riverfront community, hoping for anonymity while the wounds from her tragic past heal. Then along comes Nick Verone, whose attention threatens her hard-won serenity and whose love is almost sure to steal her heart. It's the story of a woman who's found the strength and courage to go on, and the man who's determined to stand beside her, no matter what.

I hope you'll find Dana's story both touching and inspiring, for the message I always want to communicate to you is that just beyond every dark corner, there is always hope.

All best,

Sherryl

Chapter 1

The lilac bush seemed as if it was about to swallow up
the front steps. Its untamed boughs drooping heavily
with fragile, dew-laden lavender blossoms, it filled the
cool Saturday morning air with a glorious, sweet scent.

Dana Brantley, a lethal-looking pair of hedge clippers
in her gloved hands, regarded the overgrown branches
with dismay. Somewhere behind that bush was a small
screened-in porch. With some strategic pruning, she
could sit on that porch and watch storm clouds play
tag down the Potomac River. She could watch silvery
streaks of dawn shimmer on the smooth water. Those
possibilities had been among the primary attractions
of the house when she'd first seen it a few weeks earlier. Goodness knows, the place hadn't had many other
obvious assets.

True, that enticing screened-in porch sagged; its weathered wooden planks had already been worn down by hundreds of sandy, bare feet. The yard was overgrown with weeds that reached as high as the few remaining upright boards in the picket fence. The cottage's dulled yellow paint was peeling, and the shutters tilted precariously. The air inside the four cluttered rooms was musty from years of disuse. The stove was an unreliable relic from another era, the refrigerator door hung loosely on one rusty hinge and the plumbing sputtered and groaned like an aging malcontent.

Despite all that, Dana had loved it on sight, with the same unreasoning affection that made one choose the sad-eyed runt in a litter of playful puppies. She especially liked the creaking wicker furniture with cushions covered in a fading flower print, the brass bed, even with its lumpy mattress, and the high-backed rocking chair on the front porch. After years of glass and chrome sterility, they were comfortable-looking in a delightfully shabby, well-used sort of way.

The real estate agent had apologized profusely for the condition of the place, had even suggested that they move on to other, more modern alternatives, but Dana had been too absorbed by the endless possibilities to heed the woman's urgings. Not only was the price right for her meager savings, but this was an abandoned house that could be slowly, lovingly restored and filled with light and sound. It would be a symbol of the life she was trying to put back together in a style far removed from that of her previous twenty-nine years. She knew it was a ridiculously sentimental attitude and she'd forced herself to act sensibly by making an absurdly low, very businesslike offer. To her amazement and deep-down delight it had been accepted with alacrity.

Dana turned now, cast a lingering look at the white-capped waves on the gray-green river and lifted the hedge clippers. She took a determined step toward the lilac bush, then made the mistake of inhaling deeply. She closed her eyes and sighed blissfully, then shrugged in resignation. She couldn't do it. She could not cut back one single branch. The pruning would simply have to wait until later, after the blooms faded.

In the meantime, she'd continue using the back door. At least she could get onto the porch from inside the house and her view wasn't entirely blocked. If she pulled the rocker to the far corner, she might be able to see a tiny sliver of the water and a glimpse of the Maryland shore on the opposite side. She'd probably catch a better breeze on the corner anyway, she thought optimistically. It was just one of the many small pleasures she had since leaving Manhattan and settling in Virginia.

River Glen was a quiet, sleepy town of seven thousand nestled along the Potomac. She'd visited a lot of places during her search for a job, but this one had drawn her in some indefinable way. With its endless stretches of green lawns and its mix of unpretentious, pastel-painted summer cottages, impressive old brick Colonial homes and modern ranch-style architecture, it was the antithesis of New York's intimidating mass of skyscrapers. It had a pace that soothed rather than grated and an atmosphere of unrelenting calm and continuity. The town, as much as the job offer, had convinced her this was exactly what she needed.

Four weeks earlier Dana had moved into her ramshackle cottage and the next day she'd started her job as River Glen's first librarian in five years. All in all, it had been a satisfying month with no regrets and no time for lingering memories.

Already she'd painted the cottage a sparkling white, scrubbed the layers of grime from the windows, matched wits with the stove and the plumbing and replaced the mattress. When she tired of being confined to the house, she had cut the overgrown lawn, weeded the flower gardens and discovered beds of tulips and daffodils ready to burst forth with blossoms. She'd even put in a small tomato patch in the backyard.

To her surprise, after a lifetime surrounded by concrete, she found that the scent of newly-turned earth, even the feel of the rich dirt clinging damply to her skin, had acted like a balm. Now, more than ever, she was glad she'd chosen springtime to settle here. All these growing things reminded her in a very graphic way of new beginnings.

"Better be careful," a low, distinctly sexy voice, laced with humor, warned from out of nowhere, startling Dana just as she reached out to pluck a lilac from the bush. She hadn't heard footsteps. She certainly hadn't heard a car drive up. On guard, she whirled around, the clippers held out protectively in front of her, and discovered a blue pickup at the edge of the lawn, its owner grinning at her from behind the wheel.

"I heard that lilac bush ate the last owner," he added very seriously.

Her brown eyes narrowed watchfully. She instinctively backed up a step, then another as the stranger climbed out of his truck and started toward her with long, easy strides.

Dana had met a number of townspeople since her arrival, but not this man. She would have remembered the overpowering masculinity of the rugged, tanned face with its stubborn, square jaw and the laugh lines that spread like delicate webs from the corners of his eyes. She would have remembered the trembling nervousness he set off inside her.

"Who are you?" she asked, trying to hide her uneasiness but clinging defensively to the hedge clippers nonetheless. It was one thing to know the adage that in a small town there were no strangers, but quite another to be confronted unexpectedly with a virile, powerful specimen like this in your own front yard. She figured the hedge clippers made them an almost even match, which was both a reassuring and a daunting thought.

The man, tall and whipcord lean, paused halfway up the walk and shoved his hands into the pockets of his jeans. If he was taken aback by her unfriendliness, there was no sign of it on his face. His smile never wavered and his voice lowered to an even more soothing timbre, as if to prove he was no threat to her.

"Nicholas...Nick Verone." When that drew no response, he added, "Tony's father."

Dana drew in a sharp breath. The name, of course, had registered at once. It was plastered on the side of just about every construction trailer in the county. It was also the signature on her paycheck. She was a town employee. Nicholas Verone was the elected treasurer, a man reputed to have political aspirations on a far grander scale, perhaps the state legislature, perhaps even Washington.

He was admired for his integrity, respected for his success and, since the death of his wife three years earlier, targeted by every matchmaker in town. She'd been hearing about him since her first day on the job. Down at town hall, the kindly clerk, a gleam in her periwinkle-blue eyes, had taken one good look at Dana and begun scheming to arrange a meeting. To Betsy Markham's very evident maternal frustration, Dana had repeatedly declined.

The connection to Tony, however, was what mattered this morning. Turning her wary frown into a faint tentative smile of welcome, she saw the resemblance now, the same hazel eyes that were bright and inquisitive and filled with warmth and humor, the same unruly brown hair that no brush would ever tame. While at ten years old Tony was an impish charmer, his father had a quiet, far more dangerous allure. The sigh of relief she'd felt on learning his identity caught somewhere in her throat and set off a different reaction entirely.

Ingrained caution and natural curiosity warred, making her tone abrupt as she asked, "What are you doing here?"

Nick Verone still didn't seem the least bit offended by her inhospitable attitude. In fact, he seemed amused by it. "Tony mentioned your roof was leaking. I had some time today and I thought maybe I could check it out for you."

Dana grimaced. She was going to have to remember to watch her tongue around Tony. She'd been alert to Betsy Markham's straightforward matchmaking tactics, but she'd never once suspected that Tony might decide to get in on the conspiracy to find his father a mate. Then again, maybe Tony had only been trying to repay her for helping him with his history lesson on the Civil War. At her urging, he'd finally decided not to try to persuade the teacher that the South had actually won.

"Well, we should have," he'd grumbled, his jaw set every bit as stubbornly as she imagined his father's could be. In the end, though, Tony had stuck to the facts and returned proudly a week later to show her the B minus on his test paper, the highest history grade he'd ever received.

At the moment, though, with Nick Verone waiting patiently in front of her, it hardly seemed to matter what Tony's motivation had been. She had to send the man on his way. His presence was making her palms sweat.

"Thanks, anyway," she said, giving him a smile she hoped seemed suitably appreciative. "But I've already made arrangements for a contractor to come by next week."

Instead of daunting him, her announcement drew a scowl. "I hope you didn't call Billy Watson."

Dana swallowed guiltily and said with a touch of defiance, "What if I did?"

"He'll charge you an arm and a leg and he won't get the job done."

"Haven't you heard that it's bad business to knock the competition?"

"Billy's not my competition. For that matter, calling him a contractor is a stretch of the imagination. He's a scoundrel out to make a quick buck so he can finance his next binge. Everybody around here knows that and I can't imagine anyone recommending him. Why did you call him in the first place?"

She'd called Billy Watson because he was the only *other* contractor—or handyman, for that matter— she'd been able to find when water had started dripping through her roof in five different places during the first of April's pounding spring showers. All of Betsy's unsolicited praise for Nick Verone had set off warning bells inside her head. She'd known intuitively that asking him to take a look at her roof would be asking for trouble. His presence now and its impact on her heartbeat were proof enough that she'd been right. To any woman determinedly seeking solitude, this aggressive, incredibly sexy man was a threat.

She stared into Nick's eyes, noted the expectant gleam and decided that wasn't an explanation she should offer. He was the kind of man who'd make entirely too much out of such a candid response.

"You're a very busy man, Mr. Verone," she said instead. "I assumed Billy Watson could get here sooner."

Nick's grin widened, dipping slightly on the left side to make it beguilingly crooked. A less determined woman might fall for that smile, but Dana tried very hard to ignore it.

"I'm here now," he pointed out, rocking back and forth on the balls of his feet, his fingers still jammed into the pockets of his jeans in a way that called attention to their fit across his flat stomach and lean hips.

"Mr. Watson promised to be here Monday morning first thing. That's plenty soon enough."

"And if it rains between now and then?"

"I'll put out the pots and pans again."

Nick only barely resisted the urge to chuckle. He'd heard the dismissal in Dana's New York-accented voice and read the wariness in her eyes. It was the look a lot of people had when first confronted with small-town friendliness after a lifetime in big cities. They assumed every neighborly act would come with a price tag. It took time to convince them otherwise. Oddly enough, he found that in Dana's case he wanted to see to her enlightenment personally. There was something about this slender, overly-cautious woman that touched a responsive chord deep inside him.

Besides, he loved River Glen. He'd grown up here and he'd witnessed—in fact, he'd been a part of—its slow evolution from a slightly shabby summer resort past its prime into a year-round community with a future. The more people like Dana Brantley who settled here, the faster changes would come.

He'd read her résumé and knew that one year ago, at age twenty-eight, she'd gone back to school to finish her master's degree in library science. He was still a little puzzled why a native New Yorker would want to come to a quiet place like River Glen, but he was glad of it. She'd bring new ideas, maybe some big-city ways. He didn't want his town to lose its charm, but he wanted it to be progressive, rather than becoming mired down in the sea of complacency that had destroyed other communities and made their young people move on in search of more excitement.

He figured it was up to people in his position to see that Dana felt welcome. Small towns had a way of being friendly and clannish at the same time. Sometimes it took a while for superficial warmth to become genuine acceptance.

He gazed directly into Dana's eyes and shook his head. "Sorry, ma'am, it just wouldn't be right. I can't let you do that." He saw to it that his southern drawl increased perceptibly.

"Do what?" A puzzled frown tugged at her lips.

"Stay up all night, running from room to room with those pots and pans. What if you slipped and fell? I'd feel responsible."

The remark earned him a reluctant chuckle and he watched in awe at the transformation. Dana smiled provocatively, banishing the tiny, surprisingly stern lines in her lovely, heart-shaped face. She pulled off her work gloves and brushed back a curling strand of mink-brown hair that had escaped from her shoulder-length pony-tail. Every movie cliché about staid librarians suddenly whipping off their glasses and letting down their hair rushed through Nick's mind and warmed his blood. Under all that starch and caution, under the streak of dirt that emphasized the curve of her cheek, Dana Brantley was a fragile, beautiful woman. The realization took his breath away. All Tony's talk hadn't done the new librarian justice.

"I swear to you that I won't sue you if I trip over a pot in the middle of a storm," she said. Her smile grew and, for the first time since his arrival, seemed sincere. Finally, she completely put aside the hedge clippers she'd been absentmindedly brandishing at him.

"I'll even put it in writing," she offered.

"Nope," he said determinedly. "That's not good enough. There's Tony to consider, too."

"What does he have to do with it?"

"Don't think I don't know that you're the one behind his history grade. I can't have him failing again just because the librarian is laid up with a twisted ankle or worse."

"Tony is a bright boy. All he needs is a little guidance." She regarded him pointedly. "And someone to remind him that when it comes to history, facts are facts. Like it or not, the Yankees did win the Civil War."

Nick hid a smile. "Yes, well, with Robert E. Lee having been born just down the road, some of us do like to cling to our illusions about that particular war. But for a battle here and there, things might have been different."

"But they weren't. However, if you're determined to ignore historical reality, perhaps you should stick to helping Tony with his math or maybe his English and encourage him to read his history textbooks. In the long run, he'll have a better time of it in school."

Nick accepted the criticism gracefully, but there was a twinkle in his eyes. "I'll keep that in mind," he said, careful not to chuckle. "Now about your roof…"

"Mr. Verone—"

"Nick."

"That roof has been up there for years. It may have a few leaks, but it's in no danger of caving in. Surely it can wait until Monday. I appreciate your offering to help, but I did make a deal with Mr. Watson."

Nick was already moving toward his truck. "He won't show up," he muttered over his shoulder.

"What's that?"

"I said he won't show up, not unless he's out of liquor." He pulled an extension ladder from the back of the pickup and returned purposefully up the walk, past an increasingly indignant Dana.

"Mr. Verone," Dana snapped in frustration as Nick marched around to the side of the house. She had to run to keep up with him, leaving her out of breath but just as furious. The familiar, unpleasant feeling of losing control of a situation swept over her. "Mr. Verone, I do not want you on my roof."

It seemed rather a wasted comment since he was

already more than halfway up the ladder. *Damn,* she thought. *The man is impossible.* "Don't you ever listen?" she grumbled.

He climbed the rest of the way, then leaned down and winked at her. "Nope. Give me my toolbox, would you?"

She was tempted to throw it at him, but she handed it up very politely, then sat down on the back step muttering curses. She picked a blade of grass and chewed on it absentmindedly. With Nick Verone on her roof and a knot forming in her stomach, she was beginning to regret that she'd ever helped Tony Verone with his history project. In fact, she was beginning to wonder if coming to River Glen was going to be the peaceful escape she'd hoped it would be. Sensations best forgotten were sweeping over her this morning.

While she tried to put her feelings in perspective, Nick shouted at her from some spot on the roof she couldn't see.

"Do you have a garden hose?"

"Of course."

"How about getting it and squirting some water up here?"

Dana wanted to refuse but realized that being difficult probably wouldn't get Nick out of her life any faster. He'd just climb down and find the hose himself. He seemed like a very resourceful man. She stomped off after the hose and turned it on.

"Aim it a little higher," he instructed a few minutes later. "Over here."

Dana scowled up at him and fought the temptation to move the spray about three feet to the right and douse the outrageous, arrogant man. Maybe then he would go away, even if only to get into some dry clothes, but at least he'd leave her in peace for a while. She still wasn't exactly sure how he'd talked her into letting him stay on the roof, much less gotten her to help him with his inspection. For a total stranger he took an awful lot for granted. He certainly didn't know how to take no for an answer. And she was tired of fighting, tired of confrontations and still, despite the past year of relative calm, terrified of anger. A raised voice made her hands tremble and her head pound with seemingly irrational anxiety.

So, if it made him happy, Nick Verone could inspect her roof, fix her leaks, and then, with any luck, he'd disappear and she'd be alone again. Blissfully alone with her books and her herb tea and her flowers, like some maiden aunt in an English novel.

Suddenly a tanned face appeared at the edge of the roof. "I hate to tell you this, but you ought to replace the whole thing. It's probably been up here thirty years without a single repair. I can patch it for you, but with one good storm, you'll just have more leaks."

Dana sighed. "Somehow I knew you were going to say that."

"Didn't you have the roof inspected before you bought the place?"

"Not exactly."

He grinned at her. "What does that mean?"

"It means we all agreed it was probably in terrible condition and knocked another couple of thousand dollars off the price of the house." She shot him a challenging glance. "I thought it was a good deal."

"I see." His eyes twinkled in that superior I-should-have-known male way and her hackles rose. If he said one word about being penny-wise and pound-foolish, she'd snatch the ladder away and leave him stranded.

Perhaps he sensed her intention, because he scrambled for the ladder and made his way down. When he reached the ground, he faced her, hands on hips, one foot propped on the ladder's lower rung in a pose that emphasized his masculinity.

"How about a deal?" he suggested.

Dana was shaking her head before the words were out of his mouth. "I don't think so."

"You haven't even heard the offer yet."

"I appreciate your interest and your time, Mr. Verone…"

"Nick."

She scowled at him. "But as I told you, I do have another contractor coming."

"Billy Watson will tell you the same thing, assuming he doesn't poke his clumsy feet through some of the weak spots and sue you first."

"Don't you think you're exaggerating slightly?"

"Not by much," he insisted ominously. Then he smiled again, one of those crooked, impish smiles that were so like Tony's when he knew he'd written something really terrific and was awaiting praise. Like father, like son—unfortunately, in this case.

"Why don't we go inside and have something cold to drink and discuss this?" Nick suggested, taking over again in a way that set Dana's teeth on edge. Her patience and self-control were deteriorating rapidly.

He was already heading around the side of the house before she even had a chance to say no. Once more, she was left to scamper along behind him or be left cursing to herself. At the back door she hesitated, not at all sure she wanted to be alone with this stranger and out of sight of the neighbors.

He's Tony's father, for heaven's sakes.

With that thought in mind, she stepped into the kitchen, but she lingered near the door. Nick hadn't waited for an invitation. He'd already opened the refrigerator and was scanning the contents with unabashed interest. He pulled out a pitcher of iced tea and poured two glasses without so much as a glance in her direction. To his credit, though, he didn't mention the fact that the door was missing a hinge. She'd ordered it on Thursday.

Nick studied Dana over the rim of his glass and tried to make sense of her skittishness. She was no youngster, though she had the trim, lithe figure of one. The weariness around her eyes was what gave her age away, not the long, slender legs shown off by her paint-splattered shorts or the luxuriant tumble of rich brown hair hanging down her back. Allowing for gaps in her résumé, she was no more than twenty-nine, maybe thirty, about five years younger than he was. Yet in some ways she looked as though she'd seen the troubles of a woman twice that age. There was something about her eyes, something sad and lost and vulnerable. Still, he didn't doubt for an instant that she had a core of steel. He'd felt the chill when her voice turned cold, when those intriguing brown eyes of hers glinted with anger. He'd pushed her this morning and she'd bent, but she hadn't broken. She was still fighting mad. Right now, she was watching him with an uneasy alertness, like a doe standing at the edge of a clearing and sensing danger.

"Now about that deal," he said when he'd taken a long swallow of the sweetened tea.

"Mr. Verone, please."

"Nick," he automatically corrected again. "Now what I have in mind is charging you just for the roofing materials. I'll handle the work in my spare time, if you'll continue to help Tony out with his homework."

Dana sighed, plainly exasperated with him. "I'm more than willing to help Tony anytime he asks for help. That's part of my job as librarian."

"Is it part of your job to stay overtime? I've seen the lights burning in there past closing more than once. We don't pay for the extra hours."

"I'm not asking you to. I enjoy what I do. I'm not interested in punching a time clock. If staying late will give someone extra time to get the books they want or to finish a school project, it gives me satisfaction."

"Okay, so helping Tony is part of your job. Then we'll just consider this my way of welcoming you to town."

"I can't let you do that," she insisted, her annoyance showing again.

"Why not? Don't tell me you're from that old-fashioned school that says women can't accept gifts from men unless they're engaged."

"I don't think fixing my roof is in the same league as accepting a fur coat or jewelry."

"Then I rest my case."

"But I will feel obligated to you and I don't like obligations."

"You won't owe me a thing. It's an even trade."

Dana groaned. "Is there any way I can win this argument?"

"None that I can think of," he admitted cheerfully.

"Okay, fine. Fix the roof," she said, but she didn't sound pleased about it. She sounded like a woman who'd been cornered. For some reason, Nick felt like a heel instead of a good neighbor, though he couldn't find any logical explanation for her behavior or his uncomfortable reaction.

Changing tactics, he finally asked, "How come I haven't seen much of you around town?"

"I've been pretty busy getting settled in. This place was a mess and I had the library to organize."

He tilted his chair back on two legs and glanced around approvingly. "You've done a lot here. I remember the way it was. I used to play here as a boy when old Miss Francis was alive. It didn't look much better then. We thought it was haunted."

He was rewarded with another grin from Dana. "I

haven't encountered any ghosts so far. If they're here, they certainly haven't done much of the cleaning. The library wasn't any improvement. It took me the better part of a week just to sweep away the cobwebs and organize the shelves properly. There are still boxes of donated books in the back I haven't had a chance to look at yet."

"Then it's time you took a break. There's bingo tonight at the fire station. Why don't you come with Tony and me?"

He watched as the wall around her went right back up, brick by brick. "I don't think so."

"Can't you spell?" he teased.

Her eyes flashed dangerous sparks. "Of course."

"How about counting? Any good at that?"

"Yes."

"Then what's the problem?"

The problem, Dana thought, was not bingo. It was Nicholas Verone. He represented more than a mere complication, more than a man who wanted to fix her roof and share a glass of tea now and then. He was the type of man she'd sworn to avoid for the rest of her life. Powerful. Domineering. Charming. And from the glint in his devilish eyes to the strength in his work-roughened hands he was thoroughly, unquestionably male. Just looking at those hands, imagining their strength, set off a violent trembling inside her.

"Thank you for asking," she said stiffly, "but I really have too much to do. Maybe another time."

To her astonishment, Nick's eyes sparked with satisfaction. "Next week, then," he said as he rinsed his glass and set it in the dish drainer. He didn't once meet her startled gaze.

"But—" The protest might as well never have been uttered for all the good it did. He didn't even allow her to finish it.

"We'll pick you up at six and we'll go out for barbecue first," he added confidently as he walked to the door, then bestowed a dazzling smile on her. "Gracie's has the best you've ever tasted this side of Texas. Guaranteed."

The screen door shut behind him with an emphatic bang.

Dana watched him go and fought the confusing, contradictory feelings he'd roused in her. If there was one thing she knew all too well, it was that there were no guarantees in life, especially when it came to men like Nick Verone.

Chapter 2

After a perfectly infuriating Monday morning spent waiting futilely for Billy Watson, Dana opened the library at noon. She'd found Betsy Markham already pacing on the front steps. Instead of heading for the fiction shelves to look over her favorite mysteries, Betsy followed Dana straight to her cluttered desk, where she was trying to update the chaotic card file so she could eventually get it all on the computer. The last librarian, a retired cashier from the old five-and-ten-cent store, obviously hadn't put much stock in the need for alphabetical order or modern equipment. When a new book came in, she apparently just popped the card in the back of whichever drawer seemed to have room.

"So," Betsy said, pulling up a chair and propping

her plump elbows on the corner of the desk. "Tell me everything."

Dana glanced up from the card file and stared at her blankly. "About what?"

"You and Nick Verone, of course." She wagged a finger. "You're a sly little thing, Dana Brantley. Here I've been trying to introduce you to the man for weeks and you kept turning me down. The next thing I know the two of you are thick as thieves and being talked about all over town."

Thick brown brows rose over startled eyes. "We're what?"

"Yes, indeed," Betsy said, nodding so hard that not even the thick coating of hair spray could contain the bounce of her upswept gray hair.

Betsy's eyes flashed conspiratorially and she lowered her voice, though there wasn't another soul in the place. "Word is that he was at your house very early Saturday morning and stayed for quite a while. One version has it he was there till practically lunchtime. Inside the house!"

When she noticed the horrified expression on Dana's face, she added, "Though what difference that makes, I for one can't see. It's not as if you'd be doing anything in broad daylight."

Dana was torn between indignation and astonishment. "He didn't stop by for some sort of secret assignation, for heaven's sakes. He came to look at my roof."

Betsy appeared taken aback. "But I thought you'd called Billy Watson to do that, even though I tried to make it perfectly clear to you that Billy's a bit of a ne'er-do-well."

"I had called him, and don't get me started on that. The man never showed up this morning. He said he'd be there by eight. I waited until 11:30." Dana wasn't sure what incensed her more: Billy Watson's failure to appear or having to admit that Nick Verone was right.

"Then I still don't understand what Nick has to do with your roof."

"Mr. Verone apparently heard about the leaks from Tony and stopped by on his own. He wasn't invited." Darn! Why was she explaining herself to Betsy Markham and, no doubt, half the town by sunset? Nick's visit had been entirely innocent. On top of that, it was no one's business.

Except in River Glen.

She'd have to start remembering that this wasn't New York, where all sorts of mayhem could take place right under your neighbors' noses without a sign of acknowledgment. Here folks obviously took their gossip seriously. She decided that Crime Watch organizers could take lessons from the citizens of this town. Very little got by them. Perhaps she should be grateful they hadn't prayed for her soul in the Baptist church on Sunday or put an announcement in the weekly paper.

Betsy was staring at her, disappointment etched all over her round face. "You mean there's nothing personal going on between the two of you?"

Dana thought about the invitation to bingo. That was friendly, not personal, but she doubted Betsy and the others would see it that way. She might as well bring it up now, rather than wait for Saturday night, when half the town was bound to see her with Nick and Tony and the rest would hear about it before church the next day. "Not exactly," she said finally.

Betsy's blue eyes brightened. "I knew it," she gloated. "I just knew the two of you would hit it off. When are you seeing him again?"

"Saturday," Dana admitted reluctantly, then threw in what she suspected would be a wasted disclaimer, "but it's not really a date."

Betsy regarded her skeptically, just as Dana had known she would. Dana forged on anyway. "He and Tony and I are going out to eat at some place called Gracie's and then to bingo."

She thought that certainly ought to seem innocuous enough. Betsy reacted, though, as if Dana had uttered a blasphemy. She was incredulous.

"Barbecue and bingo? Land sakes, girl, Nick Verone's nigh on to the richest man in these parts. He ought to be taking you to someplace fancy in Richmond at the very least."

"I think the idea is for me to get to know more people around here. I don't think he's trying to woo me with gourmet food and candlelight."

"Then he's a fool."

Dana doubted if many people called Nick Verone a fool to his face. But Betsy had taken a proprietary interest in Dana's social life. She might do it out of some misguided sense of duty.

"Don't you say one single word to him, Betsy Markham," she warned. "Barbecue and bingo are fine. I'm not looking for a man in my life—rich or poor. To tell the truth, I'd rather stay home and read a good book."

"You read books all day long. You're young. You ought to be out enjoying yourself, living life, not just reading about it in some novel."

"I do enjoy myself."

Betsy sniffed indignantly. "I declare, I don't know what's wrong with young people today. When my Harry and I were courting, you can bet we didn't spent Saturday night at the fire station with a bunch of nosy neighbors looking on. It's bad enough we do that now. Back then, why, we'd be parked out along the beach someplace, watching the moon come up and making plans."

She picked up a flyer from Dana's desk and fanned herself absentmindedly. There was a faint smile on her lips. "Oh, my, yes. That was quite a time. You young folks don't care a thing about romance. Everybody's too busy trying to get ahead."

Dana restrained the urge to grin. Being River Glen's librarian was hardly a sign of raging ambition, but if thinking it kept Betsy from interfering in her personal life, she'd do everything she could to promote the notion.

Dana reached over and patted the woman's hand. "Thanks for caring about me, Betsy, but I'm doing just fine. I love it here. All I want in my life right now is a little peace and quiet. Romance can wait."

Betsy sighed dramatically. "Okay, honey, if that's what you want, but don't put up too much of a fight. Nick Verone's the best catch around these parts. You'd be crazy to let him get away."

Dana spent the rest of the afternoon thinking about Betsy's admonition. She also spent entirely too much time thinking about Nick Verone. Even if her mind hadn't betrayed her by dredging up provocative images, there was Tony to remind her.

He bounded into the library right after school, wearing a huge grin. "Hey, Ms. Brantley, I hear you and me and Dad are going out on Saturday."

Dana winced as several other kids turned to listen. "Your dad invited me to come along to bingo. Are you sure you don't mind?"

"Mind? Heck, no. You're the greatest. All the kids think so. Right, guys?" There were enthusiastic nods from the trio gathered behind him. Tony studied her with an expression that was entirely too wise for a ten-year-old and lowered his voice to what he obviously considered to be a discreet whisper. It echoed through every nook and cranny in the library.

"Say, do you want me to get lost on Saturday night?" He blushed furiously as his friends moved in closer so they wouldn't miss a word. "I mean so you and Dad can be alone and all. I could spend the night over at Bobby's. His mom wouldn't mind." Bobby nodded enthusiastically.

If Dana had been the type, she might have blushed right along with Tony. Instead, she said with heartfelt conviction, "I most certainly do not want you to get lost. Your father planned for all of us to spend the evening together and that's just the way I want it."

"But I know about grown-ups and stuff. I don't want to get in the way. I think it'd be great, if you and Dad—"

"Tony!"

"Well, you know."

"What I know," she said briskly, "is that you guys have an English assignment due this week. Have you picked out your books yet?"

All of them except Tony said yes and drifted off. Tony's round hazel eyes stared at her hopefully. "I thought maybe you'd help me."

Dana sighed. She knew now where Tony had gotten his manipulative skills. He was every bit as persuasive as his daddy. She pulled *Robinson Crusoe*, *Huckleberry Finn* and *Treasure Island* from the shelves. "Take a look at these."

She left him skimming through the books and went to help several other students who'd come in with assignments. The rest of the afternoon and evening flew by. At nine o'clock, when she was ready to lock up for the day, she discovered that Tony was in a back corner still hunched over *Treasure Island*.

"Tony, you should have been home hours ago," she said in dismay. "Your father must be worried sick."

He barely glanced up at her. "I called him and told him where I was. He said it was okay."

"When did you call him?"

"After school."

Dana groaned. "Do you have any idea how late it is now?"

He shook his head. "Nope. I got to reading this. It's pretty good."

"Then why don't you check it out and take it home with you?"

He regarded her sheepishly. "I'd rather read it here with you."

An unexpected warm feeling stole into her heart. She could understand how Tony felt. He'd probably gone home all too often to an empty house. He'd clearly been starved for mothering since his own mother had died, despite the attentions of a maternal grandmother he mentioned frequently and affectionately. Whatever women there were in Nick Verone's life, they weren't meeting Tony's needs. A disturbing glimmer of satisfaction rippled through her at that thought, and she mentally stomped it right back into oblivion, where it belonged. The Verones' lifestyle was none of her concern.

Knowing that and acting on it, however, were two very different things. Subconsciously she'd felt herself slipping into a nurturing role with Tony from the day they'd met. Despite his boundless energy, there had been something a little lost and lonely about him. He reminded her of the way she'd felt for far too long, and instinctively she'd wanted to banish the sad expression from his eyes.

For Dana, Tony had filled an aching emptiness that increasingly seemed to haunt her now that she knew it was never likely to go away. From the time she'd been a little girl, her room cluttered with dolls in every shape and size, she'd wanted children of her own. She'd had a golden life in which all her dreams seemed to be granted, and she'd expected that to be the easiest wish of all to fulfill.

When she and Sam had married, they'd had their lives planned out: a year together to settle in, then a baby and two years after that another one. But too many things had changed in that first year, and ironically, she'd been the one to postpone getting pregnant, even though the decision had torn her apart.

Now her marriage was over and she wasn't counting on another one. She didn't even want one. And it was getting late. She was nearing the age when a woman began to realize it was now or never for a baby. She'd forced herself to accept the fact that for her it would be never, but there were still days when she longed for that child to hold in her empty arms. Tony, so hungry for attention, had seemed to be a godsend, but she knew now that her instinctive nurturing had to stop. It wasn't healthy for Tony and it assuredly wasn't wise for her— not with Nick beginning to hint around that it might be a package deal.

"Get your stuff together," she said abruptly to Tony. "I'll drive you home."

Hurt sprang up in his eyes at her sharp tone.

"I can walk," he protested with the automatic cockiness of a young boy anxious to prove himself grown up. Then his eyes lit up. "But if you drive me home," he said slyly, "maybe you can come in and have some ice cream with dad and me."

"Ice cream is not a proper dinner," Dana replied automatically, and then could have bitten her outspoken tongue.

"Yeah, but Dad's a pretty lousy cook. We go to Gracie's a lot. When we don't go there, we usually eat some yucky frozen dinners. I'd rather have ice cream."

Dana felt a stirring of something that felt disturbingly like sympathy as she pictured Nick and Tony existing on tasteless dinners that came in little metal trays. If these images kept up, she was going to have to buy army boots to stomp them out. The Verones' diet was of absolutely no concern to her. Tony looked sturdy enough and Nick was certainly not suffering from a lack of vitamins. She'd seen his muscle tone for herself, when he'd been stretching around up on her roof.

"So, how about it?" Tony said, interrupting her before she got lost in those intriguing images again. "Will you come in for ice cream?"

"Not tonight." Not in this lifetime, if she had a grain of sense in her head. She tried to ignore the disappointment that shadowed Tony's face as he gave her directions to his house.

It took less than ten minutes to drive across town to an area where the homes were separated by wide sweeps of lawn shaded by ancient oak trees tipped with new green leaves. The Verones' two-story white frame house, with its black shutters, wraparound porch and upstairs widow's walk, stood atop a low rise and faced out to sea. The place appeared to have been built in fits and starts, with additions jutting out haphazardly, yet looking very much a part of the whole. Lights blinked in the downstairs windows and an old-fashioned lamp-post lit the driveway that wound along the side of the house. More than three times as large as Dana's two-bedroom cottage, the place still had a warm, cozily inviting appeal.

She was still absorbing that satisfying first impression when the side door opened and Nick appeared. Tony threw open the car door and jumped out. "Hey, Dad, Ms. Brantley brought me home. I asked her to come in for ice cream, but she won't. You try."

Dana wondered if she could disappear under the dashboard. Before she could attempt that feat, Nick was beside the car, an all-too-beguiling grin on his face. He leaned down and poked his head in the window. His hair was still damp from a recent shower and he smelled of soap. Dana tried not to sigh. She avoided his gaze altogether.

"How about it, Ms. Brantley?" he said quietly, drawing her attention. "Will I have any better luck than Tony?"

She caught the challenge glinting in his hazel eyes and looked away. "It's late. I really should be getting home and Tony ought to have some dinner."

"You both ought to have dinner," Nick corrected. "I'll bet you haven't eaten, either."

"I'll grab something at home. Thanks, anyway."

She risked glancing up. Nick tried for a woebegone

expression and failed miserably. The man would look self-confident trying to hold back an avalanche single-handedly. "You wouldn't sentence Tony to another one of my disastrous meals, would you?"

Despite her best intentions, Dana found herself returning his mischievous grin. "Surely you're not suggesting that I stay for dinner and that I fix it."

His eyes widened innocently. On Tony it would have been the look of an angel. On Nick it was pure seduction. "Of course not," he denied. "I'll just pop another TV dinner in the oven. We have plenty."

Suddenly she knew the battle was over before it had even begun. If Nick had been by himself, she would have refused; her defenses would have held. He would have been eating some prepackaged dinner, while she went home to canned vegetable soup and a grilled cheese sandwich. The idea of being alone with him made her heart race in a disconcerting way that would have made it easy to say no, even when the alternative wasn't especially appealing.

But with Tony around, she began to waver. He needed a nourishing meal. And while a ten-year-old, especially one who already had matchmaking skills, was hardly a qualified chaperon, he was better than nothing. She wouldn't have to be there more than an hour or so. How much could happen between them in a single hour?

"Do you have any real food in there?" she asked at last.

"Frozen dinners are real food."

"I was thinking more along the lines of chicken or beef or fish. This town has a river full of perch and crabs. Surely you occasionally go out and catch some of them."

"Of course I do. Then we eat them. I think there might be some chicken in the freezer, though."

"And vegetables?"

"Sure." Then as an afterthought, he added, "Frozen."

Dana shook her head. "Men!"

Telling herself it might be nice to have a friend in town, then telling herself she was an idiot for thinking that's all it would be with a man like Nick, she reluctantly turned off the ignition and climbed out of the car. "Guide me to your refrigerator. We'll consider this payment for your first day's labor on my roof."

"So Billy didn't show up?" he said, jamming his hands in his pockets.

She scowled at him. "No."

"I told—"

"Don't you dare finish that sentence."

"Right," he said agreeably, but his grin was very smug as he turned away to lead her up the driveway.

If she'd thought for one minute that she'd be able to relax in Nick's presence, she was wrong. Her nerves were stretched taut simply by walking beside him to the house. He didn't put a hand on her, not even a casual touch at her elbow to guide her. But every inch of her was vibrantly aware of him just the same and every inch screamed that this attempt at casual friendship was a mistake. At the threshold, she had to fight against a momentary panic, a desire to turn and flee, but then Tony was calling out to her and curiosity won out over fear. She told herself she simply wanted to see if this graceful old house was as charming on the inside as it was outside.

In some ways the house itself had surprised her. She would have expected a builder to want something modern, something that would make a statement about his professional capabilities. Instead, Nick had chosen tradition and history. It raised him a notch in her estimation.

They went through the kitchen, which was as modern and large as anyone could possibly want. She regarded it enviously and thought of her own cantankerous appliances. A built-in breakfast nook was surrounded by panes of beveled glass and situated to catch the morning sun. This room was made for more than cooking and eating. It was a place for sharing the day's events, for making plans and shaping dreams, for watching the change of seasons. It was exactly the sort of kitchen she would have designed if she and Sam had ever gotten around to building a house.

Enough of that, she told herself sharply. She dropped her purse on the gleaming countertop and headed straight for the refrigerator. Nick stepped in front of her so quickly she almost stumbled straight into his arms. She pulled back abruptly to avoid the contact.

"Hey, don't you want the grand tour first?" Nick said. "I really didn't invite you in just to feed us. Relax for a while and let me show you around."

Once more, with her heart thumping crazily in her chest, Dana prayed for a quick return of her common sense. She knew she was feeling pressure where there was none, but suddenly she didn't want to see the rest of the house. She didn't want to find that the living room was as perfect as the one she'd dreamed about for years or that the bedrooms were bright and airy like something straight out of a decorating magazine. She didn't want to be here at all. Nick was too overwhelming, too charming, and there was an appreciative spark in his eyes that terrified her more with every instant she spent in his company.

She took a deep, slow breath and reminded herself that leaving now was impossible without seeming both foolish and ungracious. She took another calming breath and tried to remind herself that she was in control, that nothing would happen unless she wanted it to, certainly not with Tony in the house. Unfortunately, Tony seemed to have vanished the minute they came through the door. If only he'd join them, she might feel more at ease.

"Let me see what treasures are locked in your freezer first," she finally said. "Then while dinner cooks, you can show me around."

It was a logical suggestion, one that didn't hint of her absurd nervousness, and Nick gave in easily. "How about a drink, then?"

Once again, Dana felt a familiar knot form in her stomach. "Nothing for me, thanks." Her voice was tight.

"Not even iced tea or a soda?"

Illogical relief, exaggerated far beyond the offer's significance, washed over her. "Iced tea would be great."

They reached the refrigerator at the same instant and Dana was trapped between Nick and the door. The intimate, yet innocent press of his solid, very male body against hers set off a wild trembling. His heat and that alluring scent of soap and man surrounded her. The surge of her blood roared in her ears. She clenched her fists and fought to remain absolutely still, to not let the unwarranted panic show in her eyes. Nick allowed the contact to last no more than a few seconds, though it seemed an eternity. Then he stepped aside with an easy grin.

"Sorry," he said.

Dana shrugged. "No problem."

But there was a problem. Nick had seen it in Dana's eyes, though she'd looked away to avoid his penetrating gaze. He'd felt the shiver that rippled through her, noted her startled gasp and the way she protectively lifted her arms before she dropped them back to her sides with conscious deliberation. He was experienced enough to know that this was not the reaction of a woman who desired a man but who was startled by the unexpectedness of the feeling. Dana had actually seemed afraid of him, just as she had on Saturday, when she'd been brandishing those hedge clippers. The possibility that he frightened her astonished and worried him. He was not used to being considered a threat, not to his employees, not to his son and certainly not to a woman.

He'd been raised to treat everyone with respect and

dignity, but women were in a class by themselves. His mother, God rest her, had been a gentle soul with a core of iron and more love and compassion than any human being he'd ever met. She'd expected to be treated like a lady by both her husband and her sons and thought there was no reason other women shouldn't deserve the same.

"Women aren't playthings," she'd told Nick sternly the first time she'd caught him kissing a girl down by the river. He'd been fourteen at the time and very much interested in experimentation. Nancy Ann had the reputation of being more than willing. He never knew for sure if his mother had heard the gossip about Nancy Ann, but she'd looked him straight in the eye at the dinner table that night and said, "I don't care who they are or how experienced they claim to be, you show them the same respect you'd expect for yourself. Nobody deserves to be used."

Though his brothers had grinned, he'd squirmed uncomfortably under her disapproving gaze. He'd never once forgotten that lesson, not even in the past three years since Ginny had died and more than a few women had indicated their willingness to share his bed and his life. Dana's nervous response bothered him all the more, because he knew it was so thoroughly unjustified.

But *she* didn't know that, he reminded himself. Experience had apparently taught her another lesson about men, a bitter, lasting lesson. He felt an unreasoning surge of anger against the person who had hurt her.

Dana was already poking around in the freezer as if the incident had never taken place. Since she'd apparently decided to let the matter rest, he figured he should, as well. For now. In time, his actions would teach her she had nothing to fear from him.

Delighted to have such attractive company for a change, he leaned back against the counter, crossed his legs at the ankles and watched her as she picked up packages, wrinkled her nose and tossed them back. Finally she emerged triumphant, her cheeks flushed from the chilly air in the freezer.

"I'm almost afraid to ask, but do you have any idea how long this chicken has been in there?"

Nick reached out, took the package and brushed at the frost. "Looks to me like it's dated February something."

"Of what year?"

"It's frozen. Does it matter?"

"Probably not to the chicken, but it could make a difference in whether we survive this meal."

"We can always go back to the frozen dinners. I bought most of them last week." He paused thoughtfully. "Except for those Salisbury steak things. They've probably been there longer. Tony said if I ever made him eat another one he'd report me to his grandmother for feeding him sawdust."

The comment earned a full-blown, dazzling smile and Nick felt as though he'd been granted an award. Whatever nervousness Dana had been feeling seemed to be disappearing now that she had familiar tasks to do. She moved around the kitchen efficiently, asking for pans and utensils as she needed them. In less than half an hour, there were delicious aromas wafting from the stove.

"What are you making?"

"Coq au vin. Now," she said, "if you'll point out the dishes and silverware, I'll set the table."

"No, you won't. That's Tony's job. We'll take our tour now and send him in."

Nick anxiously watched the play of expressions on Dana's face as he led her through the downstairs of the house. For a man who'd never given a hang what anyone thought, he desperately wanted her approval. The realization surprised him. He held his breath until she exclaimed over the gleaming wide-plank wooden floors, the antiques that he and Ginny had chosen with such care, the huge fireplace that was cold now but had warmed many a winter night. The beveled mirror in a huge oak cabinet caught the sparkle in Dana's huge brown eyes as she ran her fingers lovingly over the intricate carving.

As they wandered, Missy, a haughty Siamese cat that belonged to no one but deigned to live with Nick, regarded them cautiously from her perch on the windowsill. Finally, she stood up and stretched lazily. To Nick's astonishment, the cat then jumped down and rubbed her head on Dana's ankle. Dana knelt down and scratched the cat under her chin, setting off a loud purring.

"That's amazing," Nick said. "Missy is not fond of people. She loved Ginny, but she barely tolerates me and Tony. Usually she ignores strangers."

"Perhaps she's just very selective," Dana retorted

with a lift of one brow. "A wise woman is always discriminating."

"Is there a message in there for me?"

"Possibly." There was a surprising twinkle in her eyes when she said it.

"You wouldn't be trying to warn me away, would you?" he inquired lightly. "Because if you are, let me tell you something: I don't give up easily on the things I value."

Dana swallowed nervously, but it was the only hint she gave of her nervousness. She met his gaze steadily as she gracefully stood up after giving Missy a final pat.

Tension filled the air with an unending silence that strummed across Nick's nerves. Flames curled inside and sent heat surging through him. Desire swept over him with a power that was virtually irresistible. For the first time in years he recalled the intensity of unfulfilled passion, the need that could drive all other thoughts from your mind. He gazed at Dana and felt that aching need. Dana, so determinedly prim and proper in her severely tailored brown skirt and plain beige silk blouse, was every inch a classy lady, but she stirred a restless, wild yearning inside him.

It was Dana who broke the nerve-racking silence.

"You can't lose what you don't have," she said very, very quietly before moving on to the next room. Left off balance by the comment, Nick stayed behind for several minutes trying to gather his wits and calm his racing pulse.

By the time they found Tony, it was time to serve

dinner. There was no time for a complete tour of the bedrooms. It was probably just as well, Nick told himself. The sight of Dana standing anywhere near his bed might have driven him to madness.

What caused this odd, insistent pull he felt toward her? Certainly it was more than her luxuriant hair and wide eyes, more than her long-limbed grace. Was it the vulnerability that lurked beneath the surface? Or was it as elusive as the sense that, for whatever reason, she was forbidden, out of reach? He'd been with her twice now, but he knew little more about her than the facts she'd put on her résumé. She talked, even joked, but revealed nothing. He wanted much more. He wanted to know what went on in her head, what made her laugh and why she cried. He wanted to discover everything there was to know about Dana Brantley.

Most infuriating of all to a man of his methodical, cautious ways, he didn't know why.

During dinner, Tony chattered away, basking in Dana's quiet attention, and Nick tried to puzzle out the attraction. Soon though, the talk and laughter drew him in and he left the answers for another day.

Saturday. Only five days and he would have another chance to discover the mysterious allure she held for him. Five days that, in his sudden impatience, yawned before him like an eternity.

Chapter 3

Dana spent the rest of the week thinking up excuses to get her out of Saturday night's date. None was as ir-refutable—or as factual—as simply telling Nick quite firmly: *I don't want to go.* Unfortunately, each time she looked into Tony's excited eyes, she couldn't get those harsh words past her lips.

She searched for a word to describe the tumult she'd felt after her visit to Nick's place. Disquieting. That was it. Nick had been a gentleman, the perfect host. On the surface their conversational banter had been light, but there had been sensual undercurrents so swift that at times she had felt she'd be caught up and swept away. Nick's brand of gentle attentiveness spun a dangerous web that could hold the most unwilling woman captive until the seduction was complete.

Yet he'd never touched her, except for that one elec-
trifying instant when she'd been accidentally trapped
between him and the refrigerator. She'd anticipated
something more when he walked her to her car, and
her heart had thundered in her chest. But he'd simply
held open the car door, then closed it gently behind her.
Only his lazy, lingering gaze had seared her and made
her blood run hot.

That heated examination was enough to get the message across with provocative clarity. Nick had more in
mind for the two of them. He was only biding his time.
The thought scared the daylights out of her. She'd been
so sure she had built an impenetrable wall around her
emotions, but in Nick's presence that wall was tum-
bling down. She didn't know quite how she'd ever build
it up again.

On Friday she sat on her front porch rocking until
long past midnight. Usually listening to the silence and
counting the stars scattered across the velvet blanket
of darkness soothed her. Every night since she'd come
to River Glen, the flower-scented breeze had caressed
her so gently that her muscles relaxed and she felt tension ease away. But tonight there was no magic. Cars
filled with rowdy teenagers split the silence and clouds
covered the stars. The humid night air was as still as
death and, in her distraught, churning state of mind,
just as ominous.

As a result, she was as nervous and tense when she
went in to bed as she had been when she'd first settled
into the rocker seeking comfort and an escape from her

troubling thoughts. She tried reading, but the words swam before her exhausted eyes. When she turned out the light, she lay in the darkness, staring at the ceiling, first counting sheep, then going over the titles of her favorite books, then counting sheep again.

Although she waged an intense battle to keep the prospect of tomorrow's date out of her mind, it was always there, lurking about the fringes of her thoughts.

It's only one evening, she reminded herself. *Tony will be there. So will half the town, for that matter.*

But even one evening in the company of a man with a surprising power to unnerve her was too much. It loomed before her as an endless ordeal to be gotten through, even though it would drain whatever supreme courage she could still muster from her worn-down defenses. Nick was constantly at the center of her thoughts, and in these thoughts his casual touches branded her in a way that awed and frightened her at the same time.

In reality, he was doing nothing but flirting with her. But how long would it be before those touches became intense, demanding? How long before the pressure would start and the torment would curl inside her like a vicious serpent waiting to strike?

Finally exhaustion claimed her and she fell into a restless, uneasy slumber. Considering her state of mind, it wasn't surprising that she awoke in the middle of the night screaming, her throat hoarse, her whole body trembling and covered with sweat. She sat up in bed shaking, clutching the covers around her, staring blindly into the darkness for the threat that had seemed so real, so familiar. At last, still shivering but convinced it had been only a dream, she reached for the light by her bed to banish the last of the shadows. Her hand was shaking and tears streamed down her face unchecked.

Oh, God, please, when will it end? When will I be free of the memories?

Tonight was the first time in months the nightmare had returned. In her relief, she had even deluded herself that her bad dreams were a thing of the past, that they'd been left behind in a Manhattan skyscraper. She should have known that horror didn't die so easily. Perhaps it was simply because for the first time in months, she had failed to leave a night-light burning, something to keep away the ghosts that haunted her. She vowed never to make that mistake again.

It was hours before she slept again and noon before she woke. Six hours before Nick and Tony were due. Six hours to be gotten through with nerves stretched taut, her mind restless. More than once she reached for the phone to call Nick and cancel, but each time she hung it back up, labeling herself a coward.

It was her first date since Sam, and first times were always the hardest. After tonight, she hoped the jitters would go away, although with Nick Verone, it was quite possible—likely, in fact—that they'd only become worse.

"I can't do it," she muttered at last. "I can't go, if I'm going to jump like a frightened, inexperienced schoolgirl every time the man gets within an inch of me."

This time when she picked up the phone, her hand

was steady, her determination intact. The resonant sound of Nick's voice seemed to set off distantly re-membered echoes along her spine, but she managed to sound calm and relatively sure of herself when she greeted him.

"Nick, there's a problem." She hesitated, then hur-ried on. "I really don't think I'll be able to go with you tonight after all."

"Why?"

"I'm not feeling very well." That, at least, was no lie, but she discovered she was holding her breath as she awaited his reply.

"I'm sorry," he said, and she could hear the genuine regret, the stirring of compassion. He didn't for a sin-gle instant suspect her of lying. "Is it the flu? Do you need something from the pharmacy? I could run by the grocery store and pick up some soup or something if you need it."

His unquestioning concern immediately filled her with shame. She swallowed the guilty lump in her throat. "No, it's not the flu," she admitted, closing her eyes so she wouldn't have to look at herself in the mirror over the phone table. "I just had a bad night last night. I didn't get much sleep."

"Is that all?" Nick's relief was evident. "Then take a quick nap. It's only five o'clock now. I'll give you an extra half hour. We won't pick you up until six-thirty. We'll still have plenty of time."

"No, really." She rushed through the words. "I won't

be very good company. I appreciate your asking. Maybe another time."

"Now you listen to me," he said, his voice dropping to its sexiest pitch, sliding over her persuasively. "This won't be a late night. I promise. Getting out will probably make you feel better. You'll forget whatever was on your mind, meet some new people, and tonight you'll catch up on your sleep."

Dana could almost envision him nodding his head decisively as he added, "No doubt about it. This is exactly what you need. I'm not taking no for an answer."

"But, Nick—"

"No buts. You're coming with us. If you're not ready when we get there, we'll wait. And what about Tony?" he continued. "You don't want to disappoint him, do you?"

Dana felt the pressure build, but oddly she was almost relieved that Nick wasn't listening to her ridiculous excuses. She had blown this single date out of proportion. Nick was right about her getting out and meeting new people. Maybe it would be the best thing for her to do. Besides, he wasn't about to let up now that he had her on the ropes. She sighed and conceded defeat. "You really don't care what kind of sneaky, rotten tactics you use, do you?"

Nick merely chuckled at her grumbling. "Well, he would be disappointed, wouldn't he? That's the unvarnished truth. I was just trying to point that out to you before you made a dreadful mistake that would make you feel guilty for the rest of your life."

"Precisely. You knew it would work, unless I was on my deathbed, right?"

She could practically visualize Nick's satisfied grin. "It was worth a shot," he agreed. "Did it work?"

"It worked. Make it six-thirty. The idea of a nap sounds wonderful."

"See you then," he said cheerfully. "Sleep well."

"Sleep well," she mimicked when she'd replaced the receiver. Blast the man! The only way she'd sleep now would be to get this evening over with. So instead of lying down, she went to the tomato garden and furiously uprooted every weed she could spot. If she was going to have a temper tantrum, it might as well serve a useful purpose. The tantrum felt good, even if it was misdirected. She could just imagine what the townsfolk would say if she pulled the hairs from Nick Verone's overconfident head just as enthusiastically.

An hour later, after a soothing bubble bath, she dressed with unusual care, wanting to find exactly the right look for her first social appearance in River Glen. The fact that she was making it on the arm of the town's most eligible bachelor should have given her self-confidence. Instead, it made her quake.

Barbecue and bingo hardly called for a silk dress, but jeans were much too casual. She finally settled for a pale blue sleeveless cotton dress that bared the slightly golden tan of her arms but not much else. Its full skirt swirled about her legs. She wore low-heeled sandals, though she had a feeling three-inch heels might improve her confidence. Then she thought of all the times she'd dressed regally in New York and realized the clothes had made no difference at all.

This time she heard Nick's car drive up before she saw him. She'd been pacing from room to room, refusing to sit out on the porch, where it might seem she was waiting for him. Nick called through the screen door in back, rather than knocking, and the sound of his low drawl sent a shiver down her spine. Did she feel dread? Anticipation? Did she even know anymore?

When she came to the door his gaze swept over her appreciatively, then returned to linger on her face. A slow smile lit his rugged features, making him even more handsome.

"Yet another personality," he muttered cryptically.

Dana gave him a puzzled glance. "What does that mean?"

"Last Saturday you could have been a farmer, all covered with dirt and sweat."

She wrinkled her nose. "Sounds attractive. I'm surprised you asked me out."

A teasing glint appeared in his tawny eyes. "I knew you'd clean up good. Monday proved it. You could have been working on Wall Street instead of our library in that outfit. The only thing missing was the briefcase."

"And now?"

"I'm not sure. I only wish we were going square dancing, so that skirt could fly up and—"

"Never mind," she interrupted quickly. "I get the idea."

"I hope so," he said so softly it raised goose bumps

on her arms. Unfortunately, her reaction was all too visible and Nick was rogue enough to take pleasure in it. He shot a very confident grin her way.

It was going to be a very long evening.

Despite his compliments and light flirting, Nick had noticed something else when Dana greeted him, something he politely didn't mention. The woman was exhausted. That story she'd spun on the phone to try to get out of their date hadn't been as manufactured as it had sounded. Underneath the skillful makeup, her complexion was ashen and there were deep, dark smudges under her eyes. Something was clearly troubling her, but he doubted if she'd bring it up and he had a feeling she wouldn't appreciate it if he did.

At Gracie's, where the tablecloths were plastic and the saltshakers were clogged because of the humidity, huge fans whirred overhead to stir the unseasonably sultry air. As they entered, every head in the place turned curiously to study the three of them with unabashed interest. Dana flinched imperceptibly under the scrutiny, but Nick caught her discomfort and they hurried straight to a table, rather than lingering to exchange greetings. He told himself there would be time enough for introductions at the fire station.

"So, what's it gonna be, Nick?" Carla Redding asked, stepping up to the table and leaning down just enough to display her ample cleavage.

Nick grinned at her and never once let his gaze wander lower than her round, rosy-cheeked face. "Are you trying to hustle us out of here in a hurry tonight, so you can pick up more tips? We haven't even seen the menu."

Carla straightened up and tugged a pencil out from behind her ear. "Menu hasn't changed in ten years, as you know perfectly well, since you eat here at least twice a week."

"But we have a newcomer with us tonight. This is Dana Brantley, the new librarian. Dana, meet Carla Redding. She owns this place."

"But I thought this was Gracie's," she said, as Nick chuckled at Dana's obvious confusion.

Carla grinned. "It was Gracie's when I bought it ten years ago. Saw no need to change it. Just mixes people up. You need to see a menu, honey?"

"Nick claims you have the best barbecue around, so I suppose I ought to have that."

"Good choice," Nick said. "We'll have four barbecue sandwiches." He glanced at Tony, who seemed to be growing at the rate of an inch a day lately. "Nope. Better make that five. Some coleslaw, french fries and how about some apple pie? Did you do any baking today?"

"I've got one hidden in the back just for you," she said with a wink as she ruffled Tony's hair. Nick glanced over to check Dana's reaction to Carla's determinedly provocative display of affection. He and Carla had gone through school together. There was nothing between them—not now, not ever. But from the look on Dana's face, he doubted she'd believe it.

As soon as Carla had gone back to the kitchen, Dana commented, "Interesting woman."

"She and Dad are old friends," Tony offered innocently.

"I'll bet."

Nick chuckled. "Her husband's a friend of mine, too. Jack has the size and temperament of a tanker. Carla just loves to flirt outrageously with all her male customers. She says it keeps Jack on his toes."

She grinned back. "I don't doubt it for a minute. She's very convincing."

Nick feigned astonishment and leaned over to whisper in her ear, "Don't tell me you were jealous?"

"Of course not," she denied heatedly.

But from that moment on, to Nick's dismay the evening went from bad to worse. Rather than the natural, somewhat aggrieved banter he'd come to expect, Dana was making an effort to be polite and pleasant. Her laughter was strained and all too often her attention seemed to wander to a place where Nick couldn't follow. Only with Tony was she completely at ease. A lesser man's ego might have been shattered, but Dana's behavior merely perplexed Nick.

Even in the small, friendly crowd at bingo, Dana seemed alienated and nervous, as though torn between wanting to make a good impression and a desire to retreat. Somehow he knew she suffered from more than shyness, but he couldn't imagine what the problem was.

When he could stand the awkwardness no longer, he suggested they take a walk. Dana glanced up from her bingo card in surprise. They were in the middle of a game and she had four of five spaces for a diagonal win.

"Now?" she said.

"Sure. I need some air." He saw her gaze go immediately to Tony, so he said, "You'll be okay here for a few minutes, won't you, son?"

"Sure, Dad. I'll play your cards for you." He looked as though he could hardly wait to get a shot at Dana's.

With obvious reluctance Dana got to her feet and followed him outside. There was the clean scent of rain in the air. Thunder rumbled ominously in the distance.

"Seems like there's a storm brewing," he said, as they strolled side by side until the sounds from the fire station became a distant murmur.

"It is April, after all," she replied.

The inconsequential conversation suddenly grated across his nerves. Nick was a direct man. Too direct for politics, some said. He had a feeling that's what they'd be saying if they could see him now, but he couldn't keep his thoughts to himself another second.

"What's troubling you, Dana? You've been jumpy as a cat on a hot tin roof all night."

"Sorry."

He felt an unfamiliar urge to shake her until the truth rattled loose. In fact, he reached for her shoulders but restrained himself at the last instant, stunned by what he'd been about to do. No woman had ever driven him to such conflicting feelings of helplessness and rage before. "Dammit, I don't want you to apologize. I want to help. Did I do something to upset you?"

Astonishment registered in her brown eyes before she could conceal it. "Why would you think that?"

"I don't know. Maybe it's just the way you went all silent after I teased you about being jealous back at Gracie's. You haven't said more than two words at a time since then except to Tony."

"Jealousy is a very negative emotion," she responded slowly, her expression distant again. "It's not something I like to joke about."

"I take it you've had some experience."

She nodded, but it was clear no personal confidences would be forthcoming. She had that closed look in her eyes, and it tore at him to see anyone hurting and seemingly so alone. The depth of his protectiveness startled him. It hinted of the sweet and abiding passion he'd felt only once before, with Ginny, whom he'd known all his life and who had hidden a gentle heart behind a determinedly tough tomboy facade. She'd accepted his protection only at the end, when cancer had riddled her body with pain.

Somehow he knew that Dana would be just as unwilling to permit him to take up her battles. Despite her vulnerability she had a resilience that he admired. He had been intrigued by her even before they'd met, because of her kindness to Tony. It had been uncalculated giving, unlike so many attempts he'd seen by single women to reach him through his son. Tony had sung her praises for days before Nick decided to meet her for himself. Her leaky roof had been no more than an excuse at first. Now he wondered if it might be the only link she would permit.

Suddenly Nick realized that Dana was shivering. He

hadn't noticed that the wind had picked up and that the air had cooled considerably as the storm blew in. He also hadn't realized just how far they'd walked while he tried to sort out his thoughts.

"You're cold," he said. "Let's go back."

"Would you mind terribly if we just got Tony and left?"

Nick sighed. "I hope it's not because I've stuck my foot in my mouth again."

"No. It's just that it's getting late and I really am tired."

Nick studied her face closely. He wanted to trace the shadows under her eyes, run his fingers along the delicate curve of her jaw, but he held back from that as cautiously as he'd kept himself from that more violent urge.

"Fine," he said eventually. "I'll get Tony."

The storm began with a lashing fury as he walked Dana back to the car. Nick took her hand and they broke into a run, hurrying to the relative safety of a darkened doorway. Both of them were soaked through, and as they huddled side by side, Nick's gaze fell on the way Dana's dress clung to her breasts. The peaks had hardened in the chilly air and jutted against the damp fabric. Tension coiled inside him. Dana shivered again and before he had a chance to consider what he was doing, he drew her into his arms.

She went absolutely rigid in his embrace. "Nick." His name came out as a choked entreaty.

"Shh. It's okay," he murmured, wondering how anything that felt so right to him could possibly scare her so. And he didn't doubt that she was afraid. He felt it in her frozen stance, saw the startled nervousness that had leaped into her eyes at his touch. "I just want to keep you warm until we can make a break for the car."

"I—I'll b-b-be fine."

"Your teeth are chattering."

"N-n-no, they're n-not," she said, defiant to the end. She struggled against him.

"Dana." This time his voice was thick with emotion and an unspoken plea.

Her gaze shot up and clashed with his. Then she held herself perfectly still, and he felt her slowly begin to relax in his arms.

The rain pounded down harder than ever, creating a gray, wet sheet that secluded them from the rest of the world. Nick could have stayed like that forever. Holding Dana in his arms felt exactly as he'd imagined it would. Her body fit his perfectly, the soft contours molding themselves to the hard planes of his own overheated flesh. He felt the sharp stirring in his loins again and wondered if he could fight it by concentrating on the distant sounds of laughter and shouts of victory drifting from the fire station down the block.

"Nick?" Her tentative voice whispered down his spine like the fingers of an expert masseuse.

"Yes."

"I have to get home." The words held an odd urgency. At his puzzled expression, she added, "The roof."

"The roof," he repeated blankly, still lost in the sensations that were rippling through him.

"I put the pots and pans away. The whole place will be flooded if this keeps up."

"Right. The roof." Reluctantly, he released her. He looked into the velvet brown of her eyes and saw that miraculously the panic had fled, but he wasn't sure how to describe the complexity of the emotion that had replaced it. Surprise, dismay, acceptance. Any of those or maybe all of them. Relief and hope flooded through him.

"You wait here. I'll go back for Tony and the car."

"I'm already drenched. I can come with you."

With her words, his eyes were drawn back to the swell of her breast, unmistakably detailed by her clinging dress. He held out his hand, and after an instant's hesitation, she took it.

"Let's run for it," he said, and they took off, her long-legged strides keeping up with his intentionally shortened paces. Rain pelted them with the force of hailstones, but they splashed through the puddles with all the abandon of a couple of kids. For the first time all night Dana seemed totally at ease.

When they reached the car, she moaned softly. "Your upholstery."

"Will survive," he said. "Now get in there. I think I have a blanket in the trunk. I'll get it for you."

He found an old sandy beach blanket and shook it out before draping it around her shaking shoulders.

"Is that better?"

"Much, thanks." She smiled up at him with the first unguarded expression he'd seen on her face all night.

It had been worth the wait and he was tempted to stay and bask in its warmth.

Instead, he nodded. "Good. I'll be back in a minute with Tony."

He walked into the fire station and scanned the room for his son. Water ran down his face in rivulets and squished from his shoes. Puddles formed where he stood.

Betsy Markham sashayed up and gave him a sweet, innocent smile. "Been for a walk?"

"Something like that."

"And here I always thought you have sense enough to come in out of the rain, Nicholas. Must be a pretty girl involved."

"Could be, Betsy."

Suddenly her expression turned serious and she wagged a finger under his nose. "You see to it that gal doesn't get pneumonia, Nick Verone, or I'll have your hide."

A chuckle rumbled up through his chest. He grabbed Betsy by the shoulders and planted a kiss on her cheek. She smelled of talcum powder and lily of the valley, just as his mother always had. His hands left wet marks on her shoulders, but she gave him a wink as she went back to her place beside her husband. Nick watched as the intent expression on Harry's face changed to delight when he looked up and saw Betsy. He saw Harry's arm slip affectionately around her waist for a quick squeeze before his attention went back to the game.

"Hey, Dad, what happened to you?" Tony regarded

his father with astonishment. "You're dripping all over everything."

"In case you haven't noticed, it's raining outside. Dana and I got caught in it. We've got to get her home."

"Aw, Dad, come on. It's early. Why don't I wait here? You can come back for me." He cast an all-too-knowing look up at his father. "You and Ms. Brantley probably want to be alone, anyway, right? I mean that's how you got wet in the first place, trying to be alone with her."

Nick managed a stern expression, though he was fighting laughter. Ignoring Tony's incredibly accurate assessment of his desires with regard to Dana, he said firmly, "You'll come with us now."

Tony knew that no-nonsense tone of voice. He shrugged and headed for the door without another protest. Nick stared after his son and wondered what perversity of his own nature had made him insist that Tony come with him.

"It's for the best," he muttered under his breath and he knew it was true. He wanted Dana Brantley, and without Tony along he might very well ruin things by showing her that. Whatever trust had just been born was still too fragile to be tested by any aggressive moves.

The rain let up as they drove to Dana's place. When he pulled up in front and shut off the engine, she turned to him. "You don't have to walk me in."

"Yes, I do. You could have a foot of water inside."

"I can take care of it."

"I'm sure you can, but why should you, when Tony and I can help?" He was out of the car before she could utter another protest. "Son, you wait here a minute until I check things out. If we need you, I'll yell."

"Right, Dad," Tony said agreeably, though there was a smirk on his face.

Dana was already up the walk and around the side of the house. He caught up with her as she tried to put the key in the door. It was pitch-dark and her hands were shaking. She kept missing the lock. Nick nudged her aside. "Let me."

"I forgot to leave the light on."

"No problem." The door swung open. He reached in and flipped on the kitchen and outdoor lights. "Let's check the damage."

There were pools of water on the floor in at least half a dozen places. "Where's your mop?"

"I'll do it," she insisted obstinately, a scowl on her face. "It's not that bad."

He planted his feet more firmly and glowered down at her. "You are without a doubt the stubbornest woman I have ever met."

Dana glared back at him. "And you're the stubbornest man I've ever met, so where does that leave us?"

"With a wet floor, unless you'll get the mop."

She whirled around and stomped away, returning with the sponge mop and a bucket. He grinned at her. "Thank you."

She perched on the edge of a chair and watched him work, a puzzled expression in her eyes. "I've been perfectly rotten to you all night and you're still hanging around. I don't understand it. Are you afflicted with some sort of damsel-in-distress syndrome?"

"Not that I know of."

"Then it must be a straightforward, macho mentality."

"Maybe I'm just a nice guy. You don't have to be macho to wield a mop."

"Exactly my point. I could have done this."

"Do you have some sort of independence syndrome?" he countered.

"As a matter of fact, I do," she said so softly that his head snapped up and he stared at her. Suddenly he realized that whatever was wrong went far beyond who mopped the floor.

"What happened to you that makes you want to close out people who care about you?"

She appeared disconcerted by the directness of the question. "That's none of your business."

"It is if I'm going to get to know you better."

"Like I said, it's none of your business." She got up and walked back into the kitchen, leaving Nick to mop alone and mull over the conversation. He'd just been granted an important clue to Dana's personality. Now he had only to figure out what it meant.

When he finished, he found Dana sitting at the kitchen table, her chin propped in her hand. She was staring out the door, a faraway expression in her eyes. Nick wanted to pull up a chair right then and finish their talk, but with Tony in the car, he couldn't. He'd already left him out there alone too long.

"I'll come over tomorrow and work on the roof," he announced quietly. Dana looked up at him, and for an instant, a challenge flared in her eyes. Then it died. She nodded, and for some reason Nick considered her acquiescence a major victory. He had the strangest sensation that she'd been unconsciously testing him all evening and that without knowing exactly how, he'd passed.

She stood up and walked him to the door, standing on the top step so that her eyes were even with his.

"Thank you," she said in a low whisper, pitched to match the night's quiet serenity now that the storm had gone.

"Did you have a good time, really?"

"Of course. It was my first chance to meet so many people. I enjoyed it."

The words were polite, the tone flat. Nick pressed a finger to her lips, wanting to silence the lies. He smiled. "Then maybe next time you'll look a little happier."

Dana flushed in embarrassment. "I'm sorry. I didn't realize…" She sighed. "I didn't mean to be rude."

"No, I'm the one who's sorry. I shouldn't have made such a big deal of it. Maybe sometime you'll tell me what really went wrong tonight."

"Nick—"

"Shh." He rubbed his finger across the soft flesh of her lips. "Don't deny it. Please."

Her eyes brimmed with tears, and she swiped at them with the same angry motion as a child who shows weakness when he craves bravery. She would have turned away to hide the raw emotion in her eyes, but Nick caught her chin and held her face steady before him.

"You're so beautiful, Dana Brantley. Inside and out. How could any woman as lovely as you have so much to be sad about?"

He caught a tiny flicker of something in her eyes—surprise, perhaps, that he'd guessed at the sadness that hid under her cool demeanor and quiet laughter. She licked her lips nervously and he couldn't take his eyes from the ripe moistness.

But when he leaned forward to kiss her, his heart pounding and his pulse racing, she pulled away, turning her face aside. Intuitively he knew it wasn't a coy reaction. There had been a real panic in her eyes. Again. He felt a hurt, one he imagined was every bit as great as hers, building up inside. God, he'd give anything to make things better for her, to make those smiles come more frequently, to hear the laughter without the restraint.

But Nick hadn't made a success of himself in business without knowing when to back away, when to let a deal simmer until the other person was just as hungry for a resolution. In time Dana would acknowledge that her hunger for him ran just as deep, was just as powerful as his was for her.

He brushed away a lone tear as it glistened on her cheek. "Good night, pretty lady. I'll see you in the morning."

He had nearly turned the corner of the house before he heard her faint response carried by the breeze.

"Goodbye, Nick."

There was a finality in her voice that sent a shiver down his spine. It also fueled his determination. This would not be an ending for them. It was just the beginning.

Chapter 4

"Don't you like my dad?" Tony asked Dana with all the disconcerting candor of an irrepressible ten-year-old. She came very close to choking on the glazed doughnut they'd just shared as they sat on her back step.

At least he'd waited until they were alone to start his cross-examination. Nick was on the roof, stripping off the old shingles. It was Sunday morning, and Tony and Nick had been on her doorstep practically at dawn, a bag of fresh doughnuts and a huge, intimidating toolbox in hand. Her eyes had met Nick's, then darted away as an unexpected thrill had coursed through her. She tried to recapture that sensation, so she could assess it rationally, but Tony was staring at her, waiting for her answer.

"He's very nice," Dana equivocated. Tony looked disappointed by the lukewarm praise.

Damn it all, the man was more than nice, she acknowledged to herself, even though she absolutely refused to acknowledge it aloud. Last night she had been rude and withdrawn without fully understanding why, but Nick had shown only compassion in return. She had sensed his struggle to understand behavior that must have seemed decidedly odd to him.

No doubt most women were eager for an involvement with one of the most powerful, eligible men in River Glen. At some other time in her life, she might have been one of them, but now that was impossible. She had nothing but trouble to bring to a relationship. And she knew as well as anyone that involvement always began with something as sweet and innocent as a kiss.

She'd given marriage a chance. Sam Brantley had been handsome, charming and brilliant—a real catch, as Betsy would say. There had been a classic explosion of chemistry the night they met, followed by a storybook courtship, then a lavish wedding and an idyllic honeymoon.

Dana had been twenty-three, only months away from receiving her master's degree, but she had given up school willingly to help Sam meet the social obligations of a young lawyer on the rise in a prestigious New York firm. They were the perfect couple, living in the best East Side condo, spending much of their spare time with the right friends at gala events for the most socially acceptable charities.

It had been slightly less than a year before the reality set in, before the pressures of keeping up began to take their toll. By their first anniversary, their marriage was already in trouble. It took much longer to end it.

She closed her eyes against the rest of the memories, the months of torment that had turned into years. It was over now. The past couldn't hurt her anymore unless she allowed it. And she wouldn't. She had put it behind her with a vow it would stay locked away forever.

"Are you okay?" Tony's brow was furrowed by a worried frown. "You look all funny."

"I'm just fine," she said as cheerfully as she could manage.

Tony looked doubtful but then plunged on with determination. "Then explain about my dad. If you think he's nice, how come you didn't kiss him last night? I know he wanted you to."

Dana was torn between indignation and laughter. "Tony Verone, were you spying on us?"

"I wasn't spying," he denied, his cheeks reddening with embarrassment. "Not the way you mean. Dad was gone a long time. I got tired of waiting in the car by myself. I decided to come check on him. That's all. That's not really spying."

"Your father would tan your hide if he knew what you'd done."

"No, he wouldn't," Tony said with absolute confidence. "He never spanks me. He says people should be able to talk out their differences, even kids and parents."

It sounded as though he were quoting an oft-repeated

conversation. The significance of Nick's philosophy of discipline registered in a corner of Dana's mind and she stored it away. She regarded Tony closely. "In that case, you'd be getting quite a lecture, wouldn't you?"

Tony met her gaze with a defiant challenge in his eyes, then hung his head guiltily. "Probably."

"Then I've made my point."

"Yeah. I guess."

"Now that that's settled, why don't you go inside and do your book report?"

"Okay," he said a little too agreeably, getting up from the step and heading inside. He opened the screen door, then gazed back at her inquisitively. "You're not really mad, are you?"

Dana smiled. "No, I'm not really mad."

Tony nodded in satisfaction. "So, are you going to kiss him next time?"

"Tony!"

"Yes, ma'am," he said politely, but there was an impertinent glint in his eyes that reminded her very much of his father.

Dana had to turn her face away to hide her smile until Tony had gone into the house. The kid was something else. Would she kiss his father next time? What a question!

Well, will you? a voice inside her head nagged.

"No, dammit," she said aloud, then glanced around quickly to make sure that no one had caught her talking to herself.

"Who are you talking to down there?" a voice inquired from above her head.

"I was just asking if you wanted something to drink," she improvised hurriedly.

"Oh, is *that* what you said?" Nick's voice was filled with amusement.

Maybe she should have a talk with him about eavesdropping. Then again, maybe there had been all too much talk around here this morning as it was.

She stepped out into the yard, then shielded her eyes from the sun as she scowled up at the roof. "Well, do you want something or not?"

He came to the edge, moving gingerly around the weak spots. Dana gazed at him and her breath caught in her throat. He'd stripped off his shirt as he worked and his tanned, well-muscled shoulders were glistening with sweat. Dark hairs swirled in a damp mass on his broad chest and narrowed provocatively down to the waistband of his jeans.

"I'd love some lemonade," he said.

"I don't think I have any," she murmured in a distracted tone, fighting the surprisingly strong urge to climb straight up to the roof so she could run her fingers over his bare flesh. She hadn't felt this powerful, aching need to touch and be touched in a very long time.

"I thought everybody had lemonade."

"What?" she said blankly, forcing her eyes back to his. That was a mistake, too, because there was a very knowing gleam in their hazel depths.

"I said I thought everybody had lemonade," he repeated tolerantly.

Dana clenched her fists, now fighting a desire not just to touch but to strangle the man. "Not me. Your choices are juice, iced tea, diet soda or water."

"But I have a yen for…" His eyes roamed over her boldly before he added with slow deliberation, "Lemonade."

"Nick," she snapped impatiently.

He chuckled at her obvious discomfort, apparently enjoying the heightened color in her cheeks. "Send Tony to the store. He can run up there and back in fifteen minutes."

"He's inside, doing his homework. If you can't live without lemonade, I'll go."

"Tony!" he called as though she'd never spoken.

The back door crashed open all too quickly and Dana got the oddest sensation that Tony had been waiting just inside. His refusal to meet her gaze as he stepped out to look up at his father virtually confirmed it.

"What do you need, Dad?"

"How about running to the store for me?" Nick climbed down the ladder, dug in his pocket and gave Tony some money and a list of provisions long enough to stock a refrigerator for a month.

When he'd gone, Dana glowered at Nick. "Why did you do that? I could have gone."

"But then we wouldn't have had a few minutes alone." He stepped toward her. Dana held her ground, but her pulse began to race.

"A few minutes? It'll take him the better part of an hour to get all those things. Are you planning to feed an entire army?"

"Just us. I'm very hungry," he retorted, drawing the words out to an insinuating suggestiveness. "And I want to know, just as much as Tony does, why you didn't kiss me."

Dana swallowed nervously. "I don't kiss men I don't know well." She sounded extraordinarily self-righteous and absurdly Victorian, even to her own ears.

"Who's fault is it we don't know each other better? I'm trying to change that." He took another step toward her. This time she backed up instinctively.

"Why did you do that?" he asked, and she could see he was more curious than angry.

"Do what?"

"Move away from me." A frown knit his brow. "Do I frighten you?"

"Of course not."

"Liar," he accused gently. "I do, don't I?"

"Don't be absurd."

He stood perfectly still, like a hunter waiting for his prey to be disarmed and drawn into his range. "Then let me kiss you, Dana."

His voice was a quiet plea that set off a violent trembling inside her. He wooed her with that voice.

"Dana, I'm not going to hurt you. Not ever."

There was so much tenderness in his voice. It touched a place deep inside her and filled her with unexpected warmth. Her eyes widened in anticipation, but he didn't move.

Finally, he sighed. "Someday, I hope you'll believe me."

His hand trembling, he brushed his knuckles gently along her cheek, then started back up the ladder. After he'd turned away, her hand went to her cheek and stayed there. With unwilling fascination, she watched the bunching of his muscles as Nick reached over his head to pull himself onto the roof. She heard the hammering begin again, and then, finally, she went inside, her knees as weak as if she'd just escaped from some terrible danger.

And she had. Nick Verone was getting to her. She could deny it all she liked. She could hold him at arm's length, but she knew perfectly well what was happening between them, and for the first time she began to sense the inevitability of it. She almost regretted not letting Nick kiss her now, not getting the agony of anticipation over with.

His backing off, however, both puzzled and pleased her. She had no doubt that Nick desired her. She'd seen the rise of heat in his eyes. But his willingness to wait told her quite a lot about his character and his patience. If they were ever to have a chance, he needed to have both.

To Dana it was soon apparent that Nick had more character than patience. Oblivious to her determination to avoid a relationship—or simply choosing to ignore her wishes, which was more likely—Nick Verone persisted in his pursuit throughout the following week. She had to give him credit. He was subtle and wily and he wasn't one bit above using Tony as his intermediary. He'd sensed that Tony was her weakness, that she would no more see the boy hurt than he would. It was Tony, as often as not, who suggested a drive in the country after the library doors were closed for the day. Or the fishing after Nick had spent an hour or two working on the roof. Or the twilight picnics on the beach.

With Tony along, she began to relax. By the end of the week she found that she was enjoying herself, smiling more frequently, laughing more freely, no longer frightened by shadows. She was actually disappointed when neither of them suggested an outing for the weekend.

On Saturday morning, feeling thoroughly disgruntled and furious because she felt that way, she pulled on her dirt-streaked gardening shorts and tied her sleeveless shirt just under her breasts. As soon as she'd finished her coffee, she went outside to tackle the thick tangle of weeds in the bed of tiger lilies. Sitting on the still damp grass, she yanked and grumbled.

"So, you don't have plans for the weekend. Big deal. You're the one who doesn't want to get involved."

The bright tiger lilies trembled in the stiff breeze coming off the river, but whatever opinion they might have had, they kept to themselves.

"Not talking, huh? That's okay. I can keep myself company." Had it been only a week ago that she'd craved being alone? Had it taken so little time for Nick to over-come her caution and become a welcome part of her life? "You made a humdinger of a mistake last time, Dana Brantley. Don't do it again."

"Talking to yourself again?" Nick inquired softly.

Dana's head snapped around so quickly she almost got whiplash. "Where do you have your car's engine tuned? Your mechanic must be a genius. I didn't even hear you drive up."

"No car," he said, pointing to the very obvious bike he was holding upright by its handlebars. His gaze traveled slowly over her, lingering on the expanse of golden skin between her blouse and shorts. "Nice outfit."

"You commented on it before. I believe you referred to it as my farmer look."

"I take it back. You're prettier than any farmer I ever saw, though I know a couple of farmers' wives who'd give you a run for your money."

"I'll just bet you do."

Nick pulled the bike onto the grass and laid it on its side, then headed for the house. Dana stared after him in exasperation. He was doing it again, just dropping in and taking over as though he belonged. One of these days they were going to have a very noisy confrontation about his behavior.

"Where are you going?" she inquired testily.

"To get some coffee. You have some made, don't you?"

"Of course, but…"

He was out of sight before she could finish her protest. "Back in a minute," he called over his shoulder.

Sparks flashed in her eyes, but just as she was about to stand up and go storming in the house after him, he shouted out, "Hey, do you want any?"

"Nice of you to ask," she grumbled under her breath. She peered in the direction of the kitchen and called back, "No."

She yanked a few more weeds out of the ground and tossed them aside with more force than was necessary. A colorful variety of names for the man now in her kitchen paraded through her mind. "Why don't you speak up and tell him he's driving you crazy?" she muttered aloud.

But she knew she wouldn't. She couldn't face the potential explosiveness of angry threats, the tension that made your heart pound, even the mild stomach-churning sensation of seeing control slip away.

"How long are you planning to be at that?" Nick suddenly inquired, hunkering down beside her.

Dana jumped a good three inches off the ground. "Dammit, Nick. Stop sneaking up on me."

"Sorry." He didn't look one bit sorry. "What's on your agenda for the day?"

"I don't have an agenda." She paused thoughtfully. "Do you know this is practically the first time in my life I can say that? First it was ballet lessons, then gymnastics, then piano. By the time I got to high school, it was cheerleading, half a dozen clubs and tennis lessons. College was more of the same and my marriage was a merry-go-round of luncheons and dinner parties and bridge. I don't think I ever had ten unscheduled minutes until I moved here."

"Good, then you can come with me."

Dana regarded him warily. "Where?"

"I thought we might go for a long bike ride."

"Don't you have things to do?"

"Nothing that appeals to me more than spending the day with you."

"Where's Tony?"

"He's at a friend's." He draped his arm casually over her shoulders and squeezed. "It's just you and me, kid."

The phrase reverberated through her head and set off warning signals, but that was nothing compared to the skyrockets set off by his touch. She started to look at Nick but realized he was much too close and turned away. She'd have been staring straight at his lips and she had a feeling she wouldn't be able to hide her fascination with them. Ever since she'd avoided his kiss after bingo and again on Sunday, she'd been wondering what his lips would have felt like, imagined them brushing lightly across her mouth or kissing the sensitive spot on her neck, just below her ear.

"I don't have a bike."

"No problem. You can borrow Tony's."

"I haven't ridden in years."

"It's something you never forget."

"But my legs are in terrible condition." Nick's dubious expression as his eyes traveled the length of said legs almost made her laugh, but she rushed on. "I wouldn't make it around the block."

"We'll only ride until you get tired."

"If we ride until I can't go any farther, how will we get back?"

"Hopefully you'll have the good sense to complain in front of some nice, air-conditioned restaurant so we can have lunch while you recuperate."

"We may need to have dinner and breakfast before that happens."

"I can live with that," he said with a dangerously wicked sparkle in his eyes. "Just be sure to collapse in front of an inn."

Dana laughed, suddenly feeling a carefree, what-the-hell sensation ripple pleasantly through her. It had been a long time since she'd done anything on the spur of the moment. "I give up. You have an answer for everything, don't you?"

"I am a very determined man," he replied so solemnly that her heart raced. She avoided his clear-eyed, direct gaze as she got to her feet.

"Let me take these weeds to the garbage and change. Then I'll be all set."

"I'll take the weeds. You go and get dressed."

A half hour later, after a wobbly start on Dana's part, they were on the road. Once she got the hang of riding again, it felt terrific. The spring sun was warm on her shoulders, the breeze cool on her face.

"This is wonderful," she called out to Nick, who was riding ahead of her past a huge brown field that was dotted with corn seedlings. He dropped back to ride beside her.

"Aren't you glad I didn't pay any attention to your excuses again?"

"Very."

"Can I ask you something?"

"Of course."

"Why do you need the excuses in the first place? Do you really want me to back off?"

Dana's heart thudded slowly in her chest. She met Nick's curious gaze and her pedaling faltered. She caught herself just before the bike went out of control. Staring straight ahead, she finally said, "It probably would be for the best."

"Best for whom? Not for me. I've enjoyed being with you the past few days. It's been a long time since I felt this way."

"What way?"

He seemed to be searching for words. The ones he found were eloquent. "As though my life was filled with possibilities again. When Ginny died, I didn't think I'd ever care for another woman. We'd had a lifetime together and that was important to me. We'd played together, tended to each other's cuts and bruises, gone to school together. We'd grown up together. There were no secrets, no surprises. We were blessed with love and understanding and we were blessed with Tony."

Dana heard the sorrow behind Nick's words, but she also heard the joy. For the first time in her life she was struck by an envy so sharp it rocked her. She wanted to share somehow in that enviable life Nick had led.

"Tell me about Ginny," she said, a catch in her voice.

Nick studied her closely. "Are you sure you want to hear about her?"

"Absolutely. I want to know what she was like, what you loved about her."

He nodded. "Okay, but let's get to a stopping place first."

A few hundred feet farther down the road, he pulled into the gravel parking lot in front of a small country store and gas station.

"I'll get us some soft drinks and a couple of sandwiches, okay?"

"Fine."

Dana propped her bike against the weathered side of the store and stared around her at the recently planted fields that were just beginning to turn green. She felt the same sense of peace and continuity she'd experienced when she'd discovered River Glen. She wanted to draw that feeling inside, to capture it and put her heart at rest. The air was heavy with the rich scent of the fields, the sun was hot on her skin, and she felt more contented than she had in years.

When Nick came out a few minutes later, she realized he was becoming a part of her contentment. There were no jarring notes with Nick, only an easygoing calm that fit well with the surroundings. If only that calm were real, she might dare to hope again.

"There's a place up ahead where we can sit under the trees for a while," he said, and led the way.

When they were settled on the cool grass, he opened the bag and handed her a drink, then held out the sandwiches. "Ham and cheese or tuna?"

"Ham and cheese," she said instantly.

Nick made a face. "I should have known."

"Is that what you wanted? Take it. I like tuna just as well."

"No you don't or you would have asked for it. Take the ham and cheese."

"We'll split them." She was proud of her ingenuity until she caught the expression in Nick's eyes. "What?"

"Why do you do that? Why do you go to such lengths to avoid an argument?"

Dana stared down at the ground. "I wasn't aware that's what I was doing. I just thought it would be nicer if we shared."

He shook his head. "It's more than that. There have been times in the past week when I know you've been furious with me…." He waved aside her instinctive denial. "No. It's true. But you've never once done more than snap a little. Sometimes I want to do outrageous things, just to see how you'll react."

"I don't see much point in arguing."

"Not even when you have a valid difference of opinion?"

"It depends on how important it is. If it's something that doesn't matter, like the sandwiches, it's easier to give in."

"And that's all it is?"

"What else could it be?" she said, retreating behind her shuttered expression again.

Nick felt like pounding the earth or snatching the damn tuna sandwich out of her hands. He wanted, just once, to see her reach her limits and say exactly what she thought, instead of tiptoeing around anything that wasn't pleasant.

It was Dana who broke the silence. "Do you realize how absurd we sound? We're sitting here fighting because I don't like to argue."

"I don't want to fight with you, Dana. I just want to be sure you're not afraid to say what you mean with me. You're entitled to your opinion, even when we disagree. That's what makes life interesting. If we agreed on every single thing, we'd be bored to tears in no time."

"You may be sorry you said that."

"Oh?"

"Once I get started, I might give you a very rough time."

"I'll survive."

Dana nodded. "Okay, Mr. Verone, from now on, you'll only hear the unvarnished truth from me. Now, you were going to tell me about Ginny."

"So I was."

Nick leaned back against the tree and let his mind drift back over the years of his marriage, over the entire lifetime he'd shared with Ginny. With three years of perspective, he could finally recall the good times, rather than dwell on those last painful months.

"She was someone very special," he said at last. A faint smile lit his face. "I remember once when we were maybe six or seven. My mom had bought strawberries to make strawberry shortcake for a big family dinner. Ginny was crazy about strawberries and she saw them sitting on the kitchen table and she couldn't resist. She climbed up on a chair and started eating. I kept begging her to get down, but she wouldn't. She just sat there with bright red juice all over her face and hands, stuffing them in.

"Then my mom came in. Oh, boy, was there hell to pay. Ginny just listened to her, then said, bold as you please, 'Nick dared me to.'"

Dana grinned. "I suppose you're the one who got punished."

"I spent the rest of the day in my room." He chuckled. "But it wasn't so bad. Ginny climbed a tree right outside the window and talked to me till suppertime."

"Did you always know you wanted to marry her?"

Nick grew thoughtful. "I think I did. I know there was never anyone else. I never met another woman who had her spirit, who reached out and grabbed the day and held on to it until she'd lived every single moment. Yet, for all that fire, she was also very gentle and caring."

He glanced up and met Dana's eyes, caught the tears shimmering in them. "In so many ways, you remind me of her."

Dana was shaking her head. "No, you're wrong. I'm not like that at all."

"I think you are. I see it in everything you do."

"But I don't take risks. You said it yourself. I just drift along, trying to keep things on an even keel."

He regarded her perceptively. "But I don't think you were always like that."

Dana closed her eyes as if to ward off some pain inflicted by his words. He reached over and touched her cheek, his callused thumb following the line of her jaw.

"Dana," he said softly.

Her eyes opened and a tear slid along her cheek.

"That is the woman I see when I look at you."

"You're wrong," she protested. "I wish I were like that, but I'm not."

"Then use my eyes as your mirror," he said gently. "See yourself as I do."

He knelt on the ground beside her, and this time when he lowered his head to kiss her she didn't pull away. Her lips trembled beneath his, then parted on a sigh. She tasted of sunshine and tears, a blend as intoxicating as champagne. He felt her restraint in the rigid way she held her body, in the stiffness of her shoulders, but her mouth was his, and for now, it was enough.

Chapter 5

Over the next few days, Nick thought about very little besides that kiss. It had brought him an incredible depth of satisfaction. He recalled in heart-stopping detail the velvet touch of Dana's lips against his, the moist fire of her tongue, the sweetness of her breath. The memory of each second stirred a joy and longing in him that went far beyond the physical implications of a single kiss.

Each time he replayed the scene in his mind it sent fire raging through his blood. He felt like an adolescent. His body responded to provocative images as easily as it had to the reality. Far more important, however, that kiss had told him that Dana was beginning to trust him. He was wise enough to see that earning Dana's trust in full would be no easy task.

As anxious as any lover—and astonished by the sudden return of the special and rare tug of deep emotion—he could hardly wait to see her when he returned from a four-day business trip. It was Thursday, one of the two nights the library stayed open until nine. He saw the lights burning in the windows when he drove into town. With Tony safely with Ginny's parents there was no reason he couldn't stop. No one expected him until tomorrow, but he'd been too impatient to see Dana to stay away another night.

He found her putting books back on the shelves. She didn't see him as he stood at the end of the aisle, watching as she lifted her arms and stood on tiptoe to reach the top shelf. Her hair had been swept up on top of her head in a knot, but curling tendrils had escaped and curved along her cheeks and down the nape of her neck. The little makeup she normally wore had worn away, leaving her lips a natural pink and her cheeks flushed from the effort of lifting the piles of returned books and carrying them back to the shelves. The stretching motion pulled her blouse taut over her breasts and he yearned to cup their fullness in his hands. His body throbbed with a need so swift and forceful he had to turn away to catch his breath.

"Nick!"

Taken by surprise, her voice was as excited as a child's on Christmas morning, and he turned to see that her brown eyes glowed with unexpected warmth. In an instant, though, she had tempered the display of honest emotion and he almost sighed aloud with disappointment.

"How was your trip?"

Endless, he wanted to say but instead said only, "Fine. Productive."

"Did you get the contract?"

"I won't know for sure until the final papers are in my hand, but it looks that way."

"Congratulations!" She reached out tentatively and touched his arm. "I'm proud of you."

Then, as if the impulsive gesture troubled her, she hurried back toward the desk and began sorting through another stack of books. Nick watched her for several minutes, wondering at the swift return of her nervousness. Finally he followed her and pulled up a chair, turning its back to her and straddling it, his arms propped across the back.

"So, what have you been doing while I've been gone?"

"I've done some more work on the house." Her eyes lit up with enthusiasm. "I found the perfect wallpaper for the bedroom and I'm going to tackle that project next, as soon as I can figure out how to hang the stuff. I'm terrified of getting tangled up in a sheet of paper and winding up glued up like some mummy."

"Want some help?"

Dana promptly looked chagrined. "Nick, I wasn't hinting. You spend all day working on houses. Why should you work on mine in your free time?"

"Because it makes me happy," he said simply. He

studied her closely, then promised quietly, "There are no strings attached."

His words, a recognition of what he perceived as her greatest fear, hung in the silence before she finally said, "I know that. You're not the kind of man who'd attach them."

"I'm glad you're finally able to see that."

Dana hesitated as she seemed to be searching for words. "Nick, my attitude toward you…well, it wasn't… it isn't personal."

"Meaning?"

"Just that."

"And you don't want to explain?"

She shook her head. "I'm sorry. I really am, but I can't."

He nodded, frustration sweeping through him until he reminded himself that they were making progress. Dana had as much as admitted that trust was growing between them. If he was any judge of her character, he would have to say that the admission had been a giant step for her.

"Shall we talk about your wallpaper instead?" he suggested, adopting a lighter tone. "We could work on it tonight."

She looked tempted but protested anyway. "You're just back from your trip. You must want to get home and see Tony."

"He's not expecting me back until morning and he loves staying with his grandparents. They spoil him, and he'll be furious if I turn up a day early. Now, come on. You can fix me a spectacular dinner while I hang that wallpaper."

Dana still seemed hesitant. Finally, as though she'd waged a mental battle and was satisfied at the outcome, she smiled. "If you'll settle for something slightly less than spectacular, you've got a deal."

"You've seen my refrigerator. You know I have very low standards. Anything you do would have to be an improvement. Now let's get out of here. I'm starved."

As soon as they arrived at her house, Dana threw potatoes in the oven to bake, tossed a salad and cooked steaks on the grill while Nick measured the wallpaper. He liked listening to the cheerful sounds from the kitchen as he worked. It reminded him of happier times in his past, of coming home to the smell of baking bread and to Ginny, waiting in the kitchen with a smile on her face, anxious to hear about his day. After being without those things for three years, he appreciated all the more Dana's ability to fill a house with welcoming sounds and scents.

He also approved of the simple wallpaper design Dana had chosen. Muted shades of palest mauve and gray intermingled with white in tiny variegated stripes that were both tasteful and easy on the eye. It wasn't frilly and feminine, although that would have suited her, too. It was sophisticated and classy, with just a touch of innocence. As he cut the strips, he chuckled at reading so much into a selection of wallpaper.

Dana already had a bedspread in similar tones on the brass bed, and matching curtains had billowed in the spring breeze. Nick pulled the furniture away from the walls and had taken down the curtains in readiness for hanging the first strip of paper. As he shifted the bed to the center of the room, he was struck by a powerful sense of intimacy. He felt as close to Dana as if they'd been in that bed together, clinging to each other in the heat of passion.

He could imagine lying there after a night with her in his arms, propped on one elbow, watching as Dana pulled a brush through her long hair. He envisioned all the thousand little things a husband learns about his wife by watching her dress in the morning. His gaze lingered on the pillow as if he could see the indentation from her head, before he finally blinked away the image just in time to hear her call his name from the kitchen.

"Well," she said when they were settled at the table, "are you regretting your impulsive offer?"

"Not a bit. I like to hang wallpaper. When Ginny was alive—" He stopped himself in midsentence. "Sorry. I shouldn't do that."

"Do what?" She seemed genuinely mystified.

"I shouldn't keep bringing up my wife."

"Don't be absurd. She was an important part of your life for a very long time. It's natural that you should want to talk about her."

"It doesn't bother you?"

There was a subtle shift in her mood, a hint of caution in her tone. "No. At least, not the way you mean."

He regarded her curiously, surprised to find her expression almost wistful. "I don't understand."

"I just mean that I wish everyone had a marriage as happy as yours was."

He recalled her comment once before about the social whirl her marriage had entailed and wondered again at the edge in her voice.

"How long were you married, Dana?"

"Five years."

The response was to the point. He sensed she had no desire to elaborate, but he asked anyway, "Do you want to talk about it?"

"No." The response was quick and very firm. "I'd rather leave the past where it belongs."

She retreated again to that place Nick couldn't follow, a place that separated them by both time and distance as effectively as if they still lived in separate worlds. She stared into space and placed her fork back on her plate. Nervously, she drummed her fingers on the table. When he couldn't bear witnessing her unacknowledged pain any longer, Nick put a hand over hers and rubbed his thumb across her knuckles.

"Sometimes that's not possible," he said softly.

Her gaze lifted to meet his, the mournful expression in her eyes painful to see. "It has to be," she said, an unmistakable edge of desperation etched on her face.

Then, as if she'd found some new source of inner strength, she pulled herself together and even managed a faltering smile. "Enough of all that. Surely we can find other things to talk about. Are you finished with your steak?"

"Dana…"

"No, Nick. Let it go." The words were part plea, part command. Her demeanor brightened with a determination that awed him a little, even as it worried him.

"I have strawberry shortcake for dessert," she tempted.

He gave in. "When did you have time to fix that?"

"Today. It was no trouble. I had the strawberries and it was easy enough to do the rest. I seemed to remember you like it."

"I love it."

"Would you like to eat on the porch? I think it's warm enough tonight."

"Sounds perfect."

Nick brought out a chair, and Dana settled into her creaking rocking chair. They sat for a long time in companionable silence, letting the night's calm steal over them as they ate.

"Would you like some more?" Dana asked when he'd finished.

"No, please. Another bite and I'll never get off this chair and back to your wallpaper."

"You don't have to do that."

"The matter is settled," he insisted, getting up. "Now come and help me." He held out his hand and pulled her to her feet. She stood gazing up at him, her wide brown eyes searching his face. She tried to withdraw her hand from his, but he held on tightly.

"Dana."

She waited, the only visible sign of her emotions the darkening of her eyes into nearly black pools of pure enchantment. He tried to interpret her expression, but anxiety made him wary of the message he thought he saw. Was it, in fact, a yearning desire or the now familiar trepidation? Never had he felt such uncertainty, such self-doubt. Would the kiss he wanted so badly be welcomed or would it drive her away?

Few things in life came without risks and fewer were more valued than emotional commitment between a man and a woman. True, his feelings for Dana were still too new to be called commitment, yet they tortured him for fulfillment. He stared into her upturned face and slowly, with great care not to frighten her, he lowered his mouth to hers.

It was like touching a match to dry timber. There was an explosion of light and heat. His arms slid around her and this time she accepted the intimacy of the embrace as willingly as she did the kiss. Her hands fluttered hesitantly in the air for no longer than a heartbeat, then settled on his shoulders as a sigh shuddered through her.

The flames burned brighter as memory became reality. His lips caressed her cheeks, sought the strong pulse in her neck and lingered where her perfumed scent rose to greet him. She was soft as silk beneath his plundering mouth, and though she was unresisting he sensed the hesitancy of a new bride. It was the only thing that kept him sane. If he were to let himself go, if he were to give in to the recklessness of his feelings, he knew he might very well lose her forever.

When he released her at last, his breathing was ragged, his pulse racing.

"I think I'd better go, after all. I'll come by the library tomorrow and pick up your keys. I can do the wallpaper while you're at work."

"What about your work?" She was suddenly stiff and distant again. He read regret in her eyes and wondered whether she regretted the kiss or regretted what might have been.

"This should only take a couple of hours and I'm not expected in the office until afternoon."

"Are you sure I'm not imposing?"

He grinned at the worried set to her lips. "You could never impose on me. I want to do this for you."

She nodded then, apparently satisfied, and offered no further protest.

With a second, much quicker kiss on the cheek, Nick left before he could change his mind, before temptation made him break his unspoken vow to move slowly with Dana, to set a pace that would coax her eventually into his arms.

Dana came home late on Friday, putting off her return to avoid another meeting with Nick in such a private setting. He'd come by the library early, as he'd promised, and even with people around, she'd felt the flaring of impatient desire. It was a sensation she had sworn to resist, but it was getting more and more difficult to do. Her traitorous body craved Nick's touch despite the warnings of her mind.

Now, as she walked through the cottage, it was almost as though she could sense Nick's presence, as though his male scent lingered in the air and his strength surrounded her. In recent days she'd come to trust that strength, rather than fear it, yet old habits were hard to break. Now that she was home, she almost wished that she'd arrived earlier so she could have thanked Nick in person for his efforts.

She found that her room was exactly as she'd envisioned it. The wallpaper was hung, the furniture back in place. Nick had even painted the woodwork. On the nightstand beside the bed, he had left a vase of white and lavender lilacs. The sweet fragrance filled the room. Dana picked them up and buried her face in the fragile blooms, filled with emotions she'd never expected to feel again.

When she put the vase back, she discovered a note.

Dana,
Hope you like the room. Tony and I will be by for you in the morning about eight-thirty. Bring your bathing suit. We're going to the beach.

Until then,
Nick

Her first reaction was annoyance. Once again he was making plans without consulting her, backing her into a corner. Then she reread the note and found that, despite herself, she was smiling, her heart beating a little faster. What woman could stay angry at a man who left flowers in a room he had prepared for her with such care?

That night she slept well for the first time in ages. The next morning she had barely turned over to peer at the clock when the impatient pounding started on the back door.

"Rise and shine, sleepyhead."

"Nick?" Her voice came out in a sleepy croak. She tumbled out of bed and pulled on a robe. She searched for her slippers but finally gave up and walked barefoot to the door.

"You're early," she accused as she opened the door to a grinning Tony and his very wide-awake father.

"See, Dad, I told you we should've called," Tony said.

From the expression in Nick's eyes, Dana could tell that he wasn't the least bit sorry he'd awakened her. In fact, he looked delighted to see her in her robe, with her hair disheveled and her bare toes curling against the cool floor. She belted the robe a little tighter and stood aside to let them in.

"I thought you said eight-thirty," she said, trying one more time for an explanation for the early arrival.

"I did, but it was such a beautiful day I thought we ought to get an early start." Nick nudged her in the direction of the bedroom. "Go, get dressed. I'll make some coffee. Do you want breakfast?"

"No, but if you want some, help yourselves."

"We've already eaten," Tony chimed in. "Dad fixed waffles. Sort of." He wrinkled his nose in disgust and Dana was immediately intrigued.

"Sort of?"

"Yeah. There's gunk all over the kitchen."

"Quiet," Nick ordered as Dana grinned. "Don't tell her all my bad traits. They tasted okay, didn't they?"

"Heck, yeah. I like charcoal," Tony retorted, ducking as his father took a playful swipe at him.

"Tony, if you want some cereal while you wait, it's in the cabinet by the stove," Dana offered, laughing.

"The waffles weren't that awful," Nick grumbled.

Impulsively, Dana patted him on the cheek. "I'm sure they weren't, but perhaps you should stick to building houses."

"Somebody in our house has to cook."

"I vote we eat here all the time," Tony said, his voice muffled as he poked his head into the cupboard. "Ms. Brantley's got lots of good stuff."

As Dana's eyes widened, Nick turned and grinned at her. "See, my dear, you have to be very careful what you say around him or he'll be moving in."

Before Dana could come up with a quick retort, Nick added in a seductive purr meant only for her ears, "And where my son goes, I go."

Dana's heart thudded crazily. "I'll keep that in mind," she said, hurrying from the kitchen.

She took her time dressing, trying to regain her composure. Nick always teased her when she least expected it and he had an astonishing ability to unnerve her. She knew he could do that only because she was beginning to lower her defenses. She might as well admit it; Nick was making her feel special. He also made her feel intelligent and desirable again. Their flirting was heady stuff, especially for a woman who'd felt none of those things in a very long time.

"Just don't let him get too close," she murmured as she slipped a pair of jeans on over her bathing suit.

As the day wore on, she found it was a warning that was getting exceptionally difficult to heed.

After riding along a winding road edged by towering pines and oaks they arrived at Westmoreland State Park. They spent the day swimming, walking along the trails, playing volleyball in the water and, finally, cooking hamburgers on a grill.

"Let Ms. Brantley do it, Dad."

"Oh, 'How sharper than a serpent's tooth it is to have a thankless child,'" Nick bemoaned dramatically.

"What?" Tony said.

"That's Shakespeare," Dana told him. "It's a line from *King Lear*."

"What's it mean?"

"It means, my boy," Nick said, "that a kid who is rotten to his old man may not get any birthday presents next week."

"That's a very loose translation," Dana noted dryly.

Tony grinned. "I get it, Dad. You want me to shape up or ship out. How about if I go swimming again?"

"Only if you stay where we can see you. No going out over your head, okay?"

"Promise," he said, taking off across the sand.

When he had gone, Dana and Nick were left alone, sitting side by side on a blanket.

"When is his birthday?" she asked, uncomfortably

aware that Nick's bare chest and long, muscular, bare legs were just inches away from her.

"Wednesday."

"Are you doing something special?"

"His grandparents are throwing a party for him." Nick trailed a sandy finger along Dana's bare back, moving back to linger at a tiny ridged scar on her shoulder. She could feel the sensation clear down to her toes. "Want to come with me?"

Dana tried to stay very still so Nick wouldn't see how his touch and his offhand invitation were affecting her. Then she drew her knees protectively up to her chest and folded her arms across them, resting her chin on her hands. She thought about Nick's invitation. It was one more link in the chain to tie her to him.

"I don't think so," she said finally.

"Because you don't want to go?"

She glanced over at him and shook her head. "No, it's not that."

"What, then?"

"I don't think I belong there."

"Why not? The party is for Tony's friends, and as you must know, he thinks you're one of his very best friends." His hand came to rest on her shoulder. "Dana, look at me. Is it because you think Ginny's parents might resent you?"

"That's certainly one reason," she said, struck anew by his perceptiveness and sensitivity.

"They won't. They've been asking for some time when they were going to get to meet you. I thought this might be a good time because there will be a lot of other people there. There won't be so much pressure on you."

"You're sure that's how they feel?"

"Absolutely. But you said that was *one* reason. Are there more?" Before she could reply, he said, "Of course there are, and I'll bet I can guess what they are. You think people will start making assumptions about us if we're seen together on a family occasion."

"That's part of it," she admitted. She hesitated, then took a deep breath. "It's more than that, though. To be honest, I'm also worried about what I'll feel."

"Trapped?"

She met his gaze and saw the guileless expression in his eyes. She nodded.

"You won't be. I'll never try to trap you into more than you're ready for, Dana. Never. This is just a birthday party for Tony."

She thought about what Nick was saying to her and realized that if she was ever to take another chance on letting a man get close to her, Nick was the right choice. She turned and smiled at him. "In that case, I'd love to come."

His gaze met hers and her breath caught in her throat. There was such a look of raw desire, of longing, in his eyes that it made her pulse dance wildly. His hand tangled in her wet hair and he drew her closer. Dana's heart thundered in anticipation, but before the longed-for kiss could happen, Tony's shout drove them apart. He was racing across the sand, tears in his eyes, holding his arm. Nick was on his feet in an instant, tension radiating from him.

"What is it, son?"

Tony looked disgusted. "Just a dumb jellyfish sting," he said, panting from his run across the sand.

"Are you okay?" Dana asked, noting the relief in Nick's eyes.

"Yeah, I'm used to 'em," Tony said bravely, surreptitiously swiping away the tears. "It just hurts a little."

Nick glanced at Dana with regret, then ruffled Tony's hair. "Come on, kiddo. We'd better go see the lifeguard and get something to put on that. Then we'd better think about getting home if you want to go to the early movie with your friends tonight."

When they got back to River Glen, Nick pulled up in front of Dana's house. "How about having dinner with me tonight? We'll go out for crabs."

"I'd like that."

Nick seemed startled by her quick acceptance. "Terrific. I thought I was going to have to twist your arm."

"Not for crabs. I've discovered an addiction to crabmeat since I moved here."

"Then we'll feed your habit tonight. I'll be by for you about seven."

Dana had butter dribbling down her chin and crab shells in her hair. Nick thought she'd never looked lovelier or more uninhibited. He reached across the table and wiped her chin with an edge of his napkin.

"You're really into this, aren't you?" he said with a

grin. "If I'd had any idea cracking crabs was the way to your heart, I'd have brought you here days ago."

Dana didn't even look up. She was concentrating instead on shattering a crab shell so she could get to the sweet meat inside. Newspapers were spread across the table, shells everywhere. Only one of the dozen crabs they'd ordered remained untouched. Nick sipped his beer and watched her pounding away on the next-to-last crab. The shell on the claw finally cracked and she lifted a chunk of tender white crabmeat as triumphantly as if it were a trophy.

"For me?" Nick teased.

She scowled at him. "You get your own. This is hard work."

"And you do it so neatly. If Tony could see this table now, he'd never again make sarcastic remarks about the messes I leave in the kitchen."

"I suppose you're any better at this."

"As a matter of fact, I am something of an expert," he retorted. "Which you would know if you'd been watching me, instead of smashing your food to bits."

He picked up the last crab and gently tapped it a couple of times. It yielded the crabmeat instantly. He picked up the biggest chunk on his fork, dipped it in butter and held it out for Dana. She hesitated.

"Don't you want it?"

"Oh, I want it. I'm just trying to decide if it's worth the price."

"What price?"

"You'll just sit around looking smug the rest of the night."

"No, I won't," he vowed. "Even though I'm certainly entitled to."

Dana wrapped her hand around his and held it steady while she took the crabmeat off the fork. As she bit down, her eyes clashed with his and held. Nick wondered if she could feel the tension that provocative look aroused. Every muscle in his body tightened.

"Dana," he murmured, his voice thick. She blinked and released his hand. "Dana, I want you."

She met his gaze, then glanced away, her expression revealing the agony of indecision. "I know." She sighed deeply and looked into his eyes again. "Nick, I can't get involved with you. I thought you understood that this afternoon."

"Why do you equate involvement with being trapped?"

"Experience."

"*Past* experience," he reminded her.

"It doesn't matter. I've made decisions about what I want for the rest of my life and involvement isn't included."

"How can you make a decision like that so easily?"

"It's not easy, believe me. Although I thought it would be before I met you."

She hesitated and Nick waited for the rest. "A part of me…a part of me wants what you want."

"But?"

"But I can't change the way I am. You have to accept me on my terms."

"Which are?"

"If you care about me, you'll accept that we'll never be any closer than this."

"I'll never accept that!" he exploded, feeling a fury fueled by frustration building inside him. He saw the flicker of fear in her eyes and tried to force himself to remain calm. "I'll give you space, Dana. I'll give you time, but I will never give up hope for us."

"You must." She touched his hand, then jerked away when he would have held hers.

"I can't," he said simply. "That would mean living a lie. I can't do that any more than you can."

"Nick, I don't want to talk about it anymore. My decision is final."

"Sweetheart, nothing in life is ever final," he said softly before calling for the check.

On the way home, Dana sat huddled close to the car door, as if afraid that by sitting any closer to Nick she would be tempting fate. When they got to her house, he walked her to the door, careful not to touch her.

"May I come in?"

She hesitated, then said, "Of course. Would you like some coffee or tea?"

"Tea."

She busied herself at the stove for a few minutes, her back to him. Nick tried to understand the stiff posture, the return of distance when they had seemed so close throughout the day. He knew Dana was afraid, but of what? He was certain it was more than commitment, but nothing he could think of explained her behavior.

"Would you like your tea in here or outside?"

"On the porch," he said, craving the darkness that might lower Dana's resistance, provide a cover for her wariness and make her open up to him.

They talked for hours, mostly about impersonal subjects, until Nick's nerves were stretched to the limit.

"It's getting late, Nick. Shouldn't you be getting home to Tony?"

"Tony's staying at his friend Bobby's tonight and I'm exactly where I want to be." He dared to reach across and clasp her hand. After an instant's hesitation, Dana folded her fingers around his. He heard her tiny sigh in the nighttime silence.

They sat that way until the pink streaks of dawn edged over the horizon, occasionally talking but more often quiet, absorbing the feel of each other. There was comfort just in being together, Nick thought, in seeing in the new day side by side.

And, despite Dana's protests to the contrary, there was hope.

Chapter 6

It was barely ten o'clock in the morning and the temperature in the library had to be over ninety degrees. Dana had clicked on the air-conditioning when she'd arrived at eight. It had promptly given a sickening shudder, huffed and puffed desperately, and died. She'd tried to open the windows, but most of them had long since become permanently stuck. She propped the front door open with a chair, then found an old floor fan in the closet, but it only stirred the humid air. With no cross ventilation, it didn't lower the temperature a single degree.

"Dana, what on earth's wrong in here?" Betsy Markham said, mopping her face with a lace-edged hankie as soon as she crossed the threshold. "It's hot as hades."

"The air conditioner broke this morning. Come on over and sit in front of the fan. It's not great, but it's better than nothing."

Betsy sank down on a chair by Dana's desk and fanned her face with a book. "What did we ever do before the invention of air-conditioning?"

"We sweltered," Dana replied glumly. Then she brightened. "Wait a minute. Betsy, you must know. Do we have a contract for repairs?"

"Never needed one. Nick's always done that sort of thing."

Dana groaned. "I should have known."

"What's that supposed to mean? I thought you two were getting close. Looked that way when I saw you together last week."

"That's the problem. I can't go running to Nick for help again. He's already done way too much for me, especially around the house. I feel like I'm taking advantage of our friendship."

"Land sakes, child, it isn't as if this is some personal favor. This is town property and Nick's always been real obliging about having his crew work on whatever needs fixing. He only charges for parts." Betsy regarded her closely. "You sure that's all it is? You didn't have a fight or something, did you?"

"No. You were right. We've been getting along really well. It scares me sometimes. Nick seems too good to be true."

"He's a fine man."

"I know that's what you think. I think so, too, but

can you ever really know a person well enough to be sure of what he's like underneath? What about all those women who wake up one day and discover they're living with a criminal? Or that their husband has three other wives in other cities?"

Betsy looked scandalized. "Goodness gracious, why on earth would you bring up a thing like that? Nick's never broken a law in his life, except maybe the speed limit."

"Do you really know that, though? You're not with him twenty-four hours a day."

Betsy seemed genuinely puzzled by Dana's reservations. "Honey, you're not making a bit of sense. With Nick, well, I've known him since he was just a little tyke. He's always been a little stubborn, maybe a wee bit too self-confident, but you'll never find a more decent, caring man."

The book's pages fluttered slowly, then stopped in midair as Betsy's thoughts wandered back. She shook her head sadly. "Why, the way that man suffered when Ginny was sick, it was pitiful to see. He couldn't do enough for her. Anybody with eyes could tell he was dying inside, but around Ginny he was as strong and brave as could be. He kept that house filled with laughter for her and Tony, and he made sure Ginny's friends felt like they could be there for her. Lots of times when someone's dying, folks don't want to be around 'cause they don't know what to say. Nick put everyone at ease for Ginny's sake. You can tell an awful lot about a man by the way he handles a rough time like that."

Dana felt that wistful, sad feeling steal over her again. "He obviously loved her very much."

Betsy seized on the remark. "Is that what's bothering you? Are you afraid he won't be able to love you as much?"

Dana sighed. "I wish it were that simple, Betsy."

"Then what is it, child? Something's sure worrying at you. Is it Nick who's got you so confused or something else?"

"I can't explain. It's something I have to work out on my own."

"An objective opinion might help."

"Maybe so, but I'm not ready to talk about it."

"Child, sometimes I think you and Nick were meant for each other," Betsy said in exasperation. "You're both just as stubborn as a pair of old mules and twice as independent."

"Betsy." There was a warning note in Dana's voice.

"Okay, I get the message. But if you ever feel the need to talk, just remember I'm willing to listen and I can keep my mouth shut." Betsy patted her friend's hand. "Now let me call Nick and get somebody over here to work on this air conditioner before you melt right in front of my eyes."

"Thanks, Betsy."

When Betsy had gone, Dana sat staring after her. Their talk had helped her to crystallize some of the uneasiness she'd been feeling lately. She and Nick really had become close. Sometimes it felt as if she'd known him all her life, as if he was a part of her. Occasionally, it seemed he knew what was going on in her mind before she did. That ability to communicate should have reassured her, but it didn't.

When she and Sam had met, they'd shared that same sort of intimacy. A glance was often enough to tell them what they needed to know about the other's thoughts. She had been awed by the closeness back then, but she'd learned from bitter experience not to trust it.

"What you really don't trust is your own judgment," she muttered, disgusted with herself. Nick had done nothing in the weeks she'd known him to betray her trust. People like Betsy, who'd known him since childhood, trusted him implicitly.

But everyone had trusted Sam, too, she reminded herself. He was a well-respected member of a highly prestigious law firm, a devoted son, a supportive brother, a sensitive and generous fiancé. He was all that, but he had been a terrible husband. For reasons she had never understood, he was incapable of dealing with his wife the way he dealt with the others in his life. She had learned that too late. The price for blinding herself to Sam's flaws had been a high one.

"Is the town paying you to sit here gathering wool?" Nick's hands rested on her unsuspecting shoulders. He leaned down to kiss her, but as his lips touched her cheek, Dana trembled.

Nick sat in the chair Betsy had vacated and studied her with troubled eyes. "Hey, I was just teasing. What's wrong?"

"Nothing a little cool air wouldn't cure."

"Coming up," he promised, getting to his feet. He hesitated. Hazel eyes swept over her as if by looking closely he could discover whatever it was she was hiding. "Is that all it is?"

"That's it. Mildew could grow on your brain in this humidity."

"A pleasant thought," he chided lightly as he went to the air-conditioning unit and began dismantling it. "I came over here thinking how lucky I was to get a chance to see my favorite lady in the middle of a workday and you want to discuss mildew."

"I don't want to discuss it. I want the damn air conditioner fixed!"

Nick spun around and stared at her in astonishment. The next minute, tears were streaming down her cheeks and he had her in his arms. "Dana, sweetheart, what is it?"

"I'm sorry," she mumbled against his shoulder.

"Don't be sorry. Just tell me what's wrong."

"Nothing. That's just it. There's nothing wrong."

"You're not making a lot of sense."

"Betsy said the same thing," she said, leaning back in his embrace and looking into his eyes. They were filled with concern and something more, a deeper emotion that she wanted desperately to respond to. She sighed and put her head back against his shoulder. His shirt was damp from her tears and the awful heat, but underneath his shoulder was solid, as if he could take on the weight of the world.

She wanted so badly to trust what she felt when he held her, but she wasn't sure she dared.

"Dana." He handed her a handkerchief.

"Thanks." She dried her tears and blew her nose. "I don't know what got into me."

"I think you do." Her eyes widened and she started to protest, but he put a finger against her lips. "I'm not going to try to make you tell me today, but someday you must."

She nodded. Maybe someday she would be able to tell him.

By the end of the day she was snapping at her own shadow. She was in no mood to be going to a birthday party at the home of Nick's former in-laws, but she knew a last-minute cancellation would puzzle Nick and hurt Tony.

Fortunately, Tony was so excited he kept up a constant stream of chatter most of the way to his grandparents' home outside of town. Nick kept casting worried looks in Dana's direction, but he maintained an awkward silence, speaking only when Tony asked him a direct question.

Finally, exasperated by the pall that had settled over the car, Tony sank back into his seat and grumbled, "You guys are acting really weird. Did you have a fight or something?"

"Of course not," they both said in a chorus, then looked at each other and grinned.

"Sorry," they said in unison, and chuckled.

Tony gazed from one to the other and shook his head. "Like I said…weird. I can hardly wait to get to Grandma's. Maybe there'll be some normal people there. You know, people who'll sing 'Happy Birthday' and stuff."

"You want 'Happy Birthday'?" Nick said, glancing at Dana. "We can give you 'Happy Birthday,' right, Dana?"

"Absolutely."

Nick's deep voice led off and Dana joined in. By the time they pulled into the Leahys' long, curving driveway, there was a crescendo of off-key singing and laughter. Nothing could have lightened Dana's mood more effectively. Whatever nervousness she'd been feeling about this meeting with Ginny's parents had diminished, if not vanished. Nick squeezed her hand reassuringly as she got out of the car, then draped his arm around her shoulders as they crossed the impeccably manicured lawn to meet the Leahys.

The older couple was waiting on the porch of an old farmhouse. Joshua Leahy's thick white hair framed a weathered face that seemed both wise and friendly. His ready smile deepened wrinkles that had been etched by sun and age. His work-roughened hands clasped Dana's firmly.

On the surface his wife's greeting was just as warm, but Dana sensed an undercurrent of tension.

"We're so glad you could come," Jessica Leahy said, her penetrating brown eyes scrutinizing Dana even as she welcomed her. Dana's own quick assessment told her that Mrs. Leahy had reservations about her but that she was holding them in check for the sake of her son-in-law and grandson.

"I'm glad you're here before the others," she said to Dana. "It'll give us some time to chat before they arrive. Nick, dear, why don't you and Tony help Joshua with the grill? He never can get the charcoal right. Dana, would you mind helping me in the kitchen?"

"Of course not," she said as Nick looked on and gave her a helpless shrug.

In the kitchen, Mrs. Leahy assigned tasks with the brisk efficiency of a drill sergeant. When she was satisfied that Dana was capable of following her directions to finish up the deviled eggs, she picked up a platter of ribs and began brushing them with barbecue sauce.

"So, Dana… Do you mind if I call you that?"

"Of course not."

"Well, then, Dana, why don't you tell me about yourself? Nick and Tony think the world of you, but I must admit they don't seem to know too much about your background."

"What exactly would you like to know, Mrs. Leahy?" Dana asked cautiously.

"Oh, where you're from, what your family is like. I find people absolutely fascinating, though sadly we don't get too many strangers settling around these parts."

She tried to make her questions seem innocuous, but Dana had a feeling they were anything but that. Mrs. Leahy had a sharp mind and she had every intention of using her wits to assure herself that her beloved family was not in any danger from the unknown.

"My background's no secret," Dana said as she spooned the egg mixture into the whites and sprinkled them with paprika for extra color. "I'm from New York. My family is still there. My father works for an international bank. My mother raises money for half a dozen charities. I have two sisters, both married and still living in Manhattan."

"You must miss them."

"I do."

"Why did you leave?"

"The pace of the city didn't suit me. I wanted a place to catch my breath, start over."

"Were you running away?"

Dana dropped the spoon with a clatter. "Sorry," she murmured as she bent to pick it up and clean up the egg that had splattered on the gleaming linoleum.

She stood up to find Mrs. Leahy staring at her astutely. "I'm sorry if my question upset you."

"Why should it upset me? I wasn't running away from anything." She met Mrs. Leahy's dubious gaze directly, challenging her. In the end, it was the older woman who backed down and just in time. Nick was opening the screen door and poking his head into the kitchen.

"Mind if I steal the lady for a minute, Jessica? There are some people here I want her to meet."

"Of course, dear. We're almost finished in here anyway." She gave Dana a measured glance. "It was nice talking to you. I'm sure we'll be getting to know each other better."

To Dana's ears, those words had an ominous ring, but then she told herself she was being foolish.

"Sorry about the inquisition," Nick murmured in her ear as they went into the yard. "Thwarting Jessica's plans is a little like trying to stop an army tank with a BB gun."

"No problem. She's bound to be curious about me."

"Did she unearth any deep, dark secrets I ought to know about?"

Dana frowned. "Why would you ask that?"

"I was only teasing." He studied her closely, an expression of concern in his eyes. "She must have been rough on you."

"Not really," she said, and put her hand on Nick's cheek. Suddenly she needed his strength, needed the reassurance of feeling his warm flesh under her touch. "Don't mind me. I'm just a very private person. It threw me a little to have someone I'd just met asking a lot of questions."

Nick wrapped his arms around her and linked his hands behind her waist. His chin rested on top of her head. Her body was locked against his, and the strength and heat she'd needed were there. Nick embodied vitality and caring, passion and sensitivity, and he was generously offering all of that to her.

With a final reassuring squeeze, Nick released her and took her hand. "Ready to face more people?"

"Do I have a choice?" she muttered. "Let's go."

The rest of the evening passed in a blur of children's laughing faces, introductions and reminiscences, all of which seemed to have Ginny prominently at the center. Dana felt slightly uncomfortable, but Nick appeared downright irritated by what seemed an obvious attempt to keep Dana firmly in place as an outsider.

After he'd dropped an exhausted Tony at home, he drove Dana to her house. "I'm really sorry for the way the evening turned out. I don't understand what got into Jessica tonight. She's not a petty woman."

"She's just trying to protect her family."

"From what?" he exploded. "You? That's absurd. The only thing you've done is bring happiness back into our lives."

"I'm sure that as she sees it, I'm taking her daughter's place."

Nick sighed and bent over the steering wheel, resting his forehead on hands that gripped the wheel so tightly his knuckles turned white. "Ginny is dead."

After a split-second hesitation, Dana reached over and put her hand on Nick's shoulder. "She knows that. That makes it even worse. Why should I be alive when her daughter isn't?"

"You're not to blame, for heaven's sakes."

"She knows that, too. I didn't say her feelings were rational. She may not even be aware of them. It just comes out subconsciously in her actions."

"I'm going to talk to her."

"No, Nick. Let it go. Give her time to adjust. This must be very hard for her. She doesn't understand that I'm not trying to replace her daughter."

Nick sat back and shook his head. "You're really something, you know that? How can you be so understanding after the rough time you've been through?"

"Don't go nominating me for sainthood," she cautioned with a grin. "There were a couple of times in the kitchen when I came very close to tossing a few deviled eggs at her."

Nick reached across and massaged Dana's neck. "I wish I didn't have to get home right now," he said softly, his eyes blazing with desire.

"But you do," she said, wishing in so many ways it were otherwise, while knowing at the same time that it was for the best. "There will be other nights."

When Dana made that vow, she meant it. She was sure she was prepared to risk taking the next step in her relationship with Nick. Like a wildflower that beat the odds to survive in a rocky crevice, love had bloomed in her heart. As impossible as it seemed, she was beginning to believe in a future with him.

Then the mail came on Thursday. In it was a letter from Sam's parents. When Dana saw the Omaha postmark and the familiar handwriting, her hands trembled so badly the letter fell to the floor. She stared disbelievingly at the envelope for what seemed an eternity before she dared to pick it up.

How in God's name had they found her? Surely her parents hadn't revealed her whereabouts.

What does it matter now? They know. They know.

It seemed like the beginning of the end of everything she'd worked so hard to achieve. Serenity vanished in the blink of an eye, replaced by pain. Hope for the future was buried under the weight of the past.

Reluctantly, she opened the envelope, daring for just an instant to envision words that would forgive, rather than condemn. Instead, she found the all-too-familiar hatred. The single page was filled with unrelenting bitterness and accusations. All of Sam's parents' pain had been vented in that letter. They promised to see her in hell for what she had done to their son.

What they didn't understand was that she was already there.

Badly shaken, Dana closed the library early and walked home. The arrival of that letter had convinced her that while the Brantleys might not make good on their threats to expose her today or even tomorrow, sooner or later the truth about her past would come out. When it did, it would destroy the fragile relationship she was beginning to build with Nick. She would rather die than see the look of betrayal that was bound to be in his eyes when he learned the truth.

Sitting on her front porch, idly rocking through dusk and on into the night, she decided it would be better to distance herself from Nick. She stayed up all night, and by dawn her eyes were dry and painful from the lack of sleep and the endless tears. She had vowed to end their relationship the next time she saw him. And if Nick wouldn't let her go, she was prepared to leave River Glen.

The next time she saw Nick began with a kiss so sweet and tender it made her heart ache with longing. Nick's lips were hungry and urgent against hers and Dana felt herself responding. Heat spread through her limbs until she was clinging to him. *The last time, the last time,* was like a refrain she couldn't get out of her head, even as her body trembled and begged for more.

At last she pushed him away. Turning her back on him so he wouldn't see the tears welling up in her eyes, she walked into the back room at the library and began unpacking the lunch she'd brought for the two of them.

"We have to talk," she announced.

Clearly puzzled, Nick studied her. "Why so serious?"

Dana took a deep breath and said, "We're spending too much time together."

He stared at her in astonishment. "Where did that come from?"

"It's something I've been thinking about since the other night."

"Since the birthday party."

She nodded.

"I see. Do I have anything to say about the decision or is it unilateral?"

"It's my decision and my mind is made up."

Nick watched her as he peeled a tart Granny Smith apple, then split it and gave her half. "The way I see it," he began slowly, never taking his eyes off her face, "we're not spending nearly enough time together. You and I are going to be together one day. It's as inevitable as the change in seasons. You know it, Dana."

She felt color rise in her cheeks, but she met his gaze straight on and made her tone cool. "I'm not denying the attraction, Nick. I'm just saying that's the end of it. Eventually you're going to want a wife. Tony needs a mother. We've talked about this before. I'm not about to be either of those."

She nearly choked on the words. The ache in her chest was something she would have to live with for the rest of her life.

"Why not?" Nick demanded. "You care for both of us." When she started to protest, he silenced her. "Don't deny it. I know you do and all that nonsense at the Leahys is just that: nonsense."

"That doesn't matter. How many times do we have to go through this? I've made choices for the rest of my life. You don't fit in. Leave it that way now, before we all get hurt."

"I can't do that, Dana. You're in my heart and there's no way to get you out. I said it the other night and I'll say it again and again until I make you understand: I'll give you time if that's what you need, but I won't leave you alone."

She grasped at straws. "People are already talking about us, Nick."

"Let them."

"That's easy for you. You've lived here your whole

life. People respect you. They don't even know me. I don't like being the subject of gossip. It hurts."

"If you're worried about your reputation, there's an easy way to resolve that. Marry me."

Dana's heart pounded and blood roared in her ears, but she forced herself to say, "You're missing the point. Didn't you hear what I said? There will be no marriage, Nicholas. Not for me."

"Was your last marriage such a disaster? Is that it?"

Dana felt something freeze inside her as her thoughts tumbled back in time. Sheer will brought them back to the present.

"I won't discuss my marriage with you," she said, her lips tightly compressed. "Not now. Not ever."

Sound seemed to roar in her head until she could stand it no more. The hurt look in Nick's eyes was equally impossible to bear.

She clamped her own eyes shut and held her hands over her ears, but she could still see, still hear. "Go, Nick. Please."

"Dana, this doesn't make any sense."

"It does, Nick. It's the only thing that does."

Nick stared at her, his eyes pleading with her to relent, but there was no going back. This was what she had to do. For Nick and Tony. For herself.

But, dear God, how she hated it.

Chapter 7

It was impossible to grow up in a small town without harboring a desire for privacy. The same things that made a community like River Glen so appealing were the very things that could set your teeth on edge. Friendly support could just as easily become outright nosiness. As a result, Nick was a man who understood the need for secrets, and until he had fallen in love with Dana he had been perfectly willing to let each man—or woman—keep his own.

But he sensed there was something different about Dana's secrets, something deeper and more ominous than an understandable need for privacy. Her reluctance to discuss even the most basic things about her marriage, her effort to maintain a distance, the tension-laden silences that fell in the midst of conversation, were all calculated to drive a wedge between them, to prevent him from asking questions about a past she didn't care to reveal.

Though he hated it, for days Nick tried playing by Dana's latest rules. He resumed eating his lunches at Gracie's and spent his evenings at home. He didn't even drive past her house, though there were times when he longed to do just that in the hope of casually bumping into her.

Foolishly, he thought time would make her give in or at the very least make it easier for him. Instead she held firm and it was getting more and more difficult for him to keep his distance. He was lonelier than he'd been since the awful weeks after Ginny's death.

With so many empty hours in which to brood, he even found himself jealous of his own son, who continued to spend his afternoons at the library and came home filled with talk of Dana. Nick listened avidly for some hint that she was as miserable as he was, but Tony's reports were disgustingly superficial and Nick was too proud to probe for more.

It wasn't until the following week when he stopped by town hall that Nick got any real insight into Dana's mood. He walked into Betsy's office and sank down in the chair beside her desk. He removed the hard hat he'd put on at one of his building sites and turned it nervously around and around in his hands.

Betsy glanced up from her typing, her fingers poised over the keys. She frowned at him.

"Nicholas." There was a note of censure just in the way she said his name.

"Morning, Betsy."

She took off her glasses. "You look like a man who could use a cup of coffee," she said more kindly, and went to pour him one. Then she sat back down, folded her hands on her desk and waited.

Nick scowled at her. "You're not going to make this easy for me, are you?"

"Should I?"

"I'm not the one at fault, Betsy, so you can just stop your frowning."

"Is that right?"

He finally swallowed his pride. "Okay, dammit, I'll ask. How is she?" Betsy opened her mouth, but it was Nick who spoke. "And don't you dare ask me who."

She chuckled. "I think I know who you're interested in, Nicholas. I'm not blind."

"Well?"

"Oh, I'd say she looks just about the way you do. Every time I've tried to get her to tell me what happened, she snaps my head off. Maybe you'd like to explain what's going on."

He crossed his legs, propped the hat on one knee and raked his fingers through his hair. "I wish to hell I knew. One minute everything was fine and the next she didn't want to see me anymore. I tried my darnedest to get her to tell me what was wrong, but she kept giving me all this gibberish about needing space."

"Maybe you pushed her back to the wall."

"Is that what she said?"

"She hasn't said a thing. She looked downright peaked when I saw her on Monday, so I went back to the library again yesterday and she was still moping around. I tried to get her to open up, but she just shook her head and said it was something she had to work out on her own. I invited her over to have dinner with Harry and me and she turned me down."

Betsy pursed her lips. "I don't like it, Nick. Dana's hurting about something and it's not good that she's closing out the only folks around here she knows well. She has to talk to someone or she'll explode one of these days. Can't you try to get through to her? Looks to me as though she needs a friend real bad."

"A friend," Nick repeated with a touch of irony.

Betsy reached over and patted his hand. "You always were an impatient man. Being a friend isn't such a bad place to start, Nicholas. Try to remember that."

Nick sipped his coffee to give himself more time before answering. At last he nodded. "You're right, Betsy. I'll talk to her tonight, if she'll see me."

"Maybe this is one time you shouldn't take no for an answer."

"Maybe so." He bent down and dropped a grateful kiss on her cheek before he left.

All afternoon he tried to plan his strategy. He vowed to unearth the real cause of Dana's sudden retreats, of her obvious fear of commitment. A woman as gentle and generous as Dana would make a wonderful wife and an incredible mother, but each time he stepped over

the boundaries she had set—both spoken and unspoken—something seemed to freeze inside her and the
chill crept through him, as well.

Nick had the resources to check into Dana's past,
but using them offended his innate sense of decency.
Confrontation would only send her farther away. The
only alternative was to push her gently, to create an atmosphere in which revelations would flow naturally.
Nick wondered if he possessed the subtlety necessary
for such a tricky task, especially when he felt like cracking bricks in two to vent his frustration.

It was dusk when he walked through town toward the
library. As he strolled, he was oblivious to the friendly
greetings called out by his neighbors, who stared after
him in consternation. All his attention was focused on
Dana and the intimidating realization that he was putting his happiness and Tony's at risk by forcing the
issue. He tried to remember Betsy's caution that what
Dana needed right now was a friend, not an impatient
lover.

As he waited for Dana to close the library, he leaned
against her car and listened to the calls of bobwhites and
whippoorwills as night began to fall. Fireflies flickered
and the first bright star appeared in the sky, followed
by another and then another, until the blue-black horizon was dusted with them. The air was scented by the
sweetness of honeysuckle and the tang of salt spray
from the river. It was a perfect night for romance and
his body throbbed with awareness.

"Nick!"

Dana's startled voice brought him out of his reverie. He looked up and grinned at her, hoping to get a smile in return. Instead, she wore a frown. She stayed away from him, her arms folded protectively across her chest. Her stance was every bit as defensive as it had been on the day they'd met, and the realization saddened him. How could two people spend so much time together and still be so distant?

"What are you doing here?" she asked warily.

"I thought we should do some more talking."

"Why didn't you come inside, instead of lingering out here in the shadows?"

"I wasn't sure I'd be welcome."

Her shoulders seemed to stiffen at the implied criticism. "The library is public property."

"That's hardly the point," he said gently. "The library is your domain and you made it very clear the other day that my coming there was a problem."

"I'm not sure I'm following your logic. You wouldn't come into the library because it might upset me, but it's okay to lurk around on the street."

"You didn't say anything about the street," he pointed out, hoping to earn even a brief grin from her. She didn't relent.

"It's not just your coming to the library, it's…oh, I don't know." She threw up her hands in frustration. "It wouldn't work for us. I was only trying to save both of us from being hurt somewhere down the line. Can't you see that?"

"I don't see how I could hurt much more than I do now. I've missed you."

For an instant he thought a similar cry might cross her trembling lips, but she only said, "Nick, it will pass. You'll meet someone new."

One brow arched skeptically. "In River Glen? I've known everyone here since I was born."

"You could drive to Richmond or Washington if you were all that interested in meeting new people."

He shook his head, dismayed by her cavalier attitude, her willingness to hand him over to some other woman. He felt an explosion building inside, but he fought to remain cool, controlled. "You just don't get it, do you? You're not some passing infatuation for me. I'm not chasing after you because you're the first attractive woman to move to town in years or the first one to tell me no. I…"

He stumbled over saying he loved her, afraid that such a declaration would be too intense for her to handle. Betsy had warned him of just that. "I care about you. You're a very special woman and I don't want to replace you."

"I have to have some space, Nick," she said at last, leaning up against the car beside him and staring into the darkness. "That's what I came here for."

"I've given you space."

Even in the shadows he could see her lips curve in a half smile. "No, you haven't. Until these last two weeks, you've been at the library every day for lunch. You've taken to dropping by my house whenever you like. Do you realize that in the two months I've known you, I haven't finished a single project around either the house or the library on my own?"

"We fixed the roof."

"You fixed the roof."

"What about the bedroom?"

"You did that, too."

"What about the garden? It's flourishing. When I helped you weed it…"

"You see? That's just my point. You're taking over. First the roof, then the bedroom, the garden. There's nothing left that I can point to with pride and say, 'That's mine.' I need that feeling of independence. I need to stand on my own two feet. I can't have you jumping in to do things before I even get a chance to try."

He tried not to show how much the comment hurt. "I thought I was helping."

"I know you did, and you were a help, Nick. There were a lot of things I couldn't possibly have done by myself, even if I'd wanted to, but you didn't even wait for me to ask."

"And that's a problem?"

"It is for me." She swallowed hard, then said quietly, "I don't want to begin to rely on you."

"I don't mind."

"I know you don't. You're a very generous man, but I feel pressured by that generosity."

"I don't mean to pressure you."

Dana sighed. "I know that. It's *me*. It's how I feel. I

won't allow myself ever to be trapped by a man again. I won't be dependent on someone else for my happiness."

The revelation took him by surprise, but it made sense. Everything she'd done pointed to a woman crying out for freedom and independence, a woman determined not to repeat some past mistake.

"Tell me about it," he pleaded, desperate for something that would make him understand. "Why did you feel trapped? Was it because of your marriage?"

"Yes," she admitted with obvious reluctance. "And that's all I'm going to say on the subject."

He reached out to touch her, then withdrew. "It's not enough. I need answers, Dana. More than that, I think you need to give them. You have to deal with whatever it is, then let it go."

"That's what I'm trying to to."

He felt the frustration begin to build again. "By keeping it all inside? You have friends who want to help. Me. Betsy. Let us."

"Can't you just accept the fact that this is the way it has to be and let it go?"

"No." The cornered expression in her eyes had almost made him relent, but he was determined to have this out with her. His vow not to confront her faltered in the face of her resistance. Confrontation now seemed to be the only way to open up a real line of communication. If she still wanted him out of her life, so be it, but he was going to know the reason why. The real reason.

Up to now that reason had been hidden behind her carefully erected facade. All this talk about feeling pressured and needing independence was part of it, but he sensed, as Betsy had, that there was more. Something had triggered those responses in her and apparently it had to do with her marriage.

"Dana, I'm not just being stubborn," he said at last. "Any fool can see that something is eating away at you. Can't you understand how important it is to me to be here for you? I think you and I could have something really special together, but it won't happen if you keep shutting me out. Talk to me. I can be a good friend, Dana, if that's what you need now. I'm on your side."

"This isn't a game where people have to choose sides, Nick." She sighed again. "Oh, what's the use? I knew I couldn't make you understand."

"Say something that makes sense," he retorted. "Then I'll understand."

"Nick, please. I don't want to hurt you. You have been a wonderful friend, but that's all it can be between us."

Dana watched as Nick fought to control his irritation.

"Isn't that what I just said?" he demanded, his voice rising. Dana flinched and felt the muscles in her stomach tense. Then she relaxed as he hesitated, swallowed and said in a more level tone, "Have I ever asked you for anything more?"

"You know you have."

Nick jammed his hands in his pockets in a gesture that had become familiar to her. "If I have, I'm sorry. When we make love, I want it to be what you want, too. I would never knowingly rush you into doing something you weren't ready for. If you want nothing more than friendship now, I'll give you that."

"But you'll go on wanting more. It's there in your eyes every time you look at me."

"It's in your eyes, too, Dana," he said softly.

Only a tiny muscle twitching in her jaw indicated that she'd heard him. She didn't dare linger to examine his meaning too closely. She didn't dare admit that he might be right. She couldn't cope with that explanation for the unending restlessness, for the inability to sleep after an exhausting day.

Ignoring the obvious, she went on determinedly without even taking a breath, "I'm flattered that you feel that way, but it won't work. I can't handle an involvement in my life. Not now. Maybe not ever. You're a virile, exciting man. You deserve more than I can offer."

She reached up, wanting to caress his cheek. Nick's breath caught in his throat, but in the end she drew back. She heard Nick's soft sigh of regret.

"Oh, Nick, please try to understand. You have big plans for the rest of your life," she said. "You can't put those on hold while you wait for me to see if I can deal with a relationship."

"You're at the center of my plans. Do you want to know what I see when I look at the future? I see you and me together forty years from now. We're sitting on the porch of that house of mine, looking at the river, talking, sharing, while a dozen grandchildren play in the yard. I see two people with no regrets, only happy memories."

Tears glistened in her eyes as she listened to his

dream, and her heart slammed against her ribs. She wanted that dream as much as he did. It cost her everything to resist the need to walk into his waiting arms, to kiss him until all of her doubts fled.

"It's a beautiful dream, Nick," she said gently. "I wish I could make it come true for you, but it's impossible."

"You keep saying that, but how can I accept it if you won't tell me why?"

"If you care about me as much as you say you do, couldn't you just accept it for my sake?"

Nick searched her eyes and Dana fought the desire to look away, to avoid the pain that shadowed those hazel depths. His shoulders slumped in defeat.

Finally, with obvious reluctance, he asked, "What do you want me to do?"

Hold me, her heart cried. *Fight me on this.*

Aloud all she could say was, "Let me go. Give me some space for now. We can still be friends. Stop by the library if you want, but no more, Nick."

"And Tony? Are you planning to cut him out of your life, too?"

"Of course not. I don't want to hurt him, Nick. I don't want to hurt anyone. This is the only way to do that. If we keep seeing each other, Tony will want more for the three of us, too."

He gave her a penetrating stare. "What are you afraid of, Dana? Aren't you really scared that you'll begin to feel as much for me as I do for you?"

She met his gaze evenly. "Maybe so," she admitted candidly.

She saw the brightening of his expression and was quick to add, "But that doesn't change anything."

Nick sighed heavily. "Okay, sweetheart, you win." He stood up and dropped a light kiss on her brow. "For now."

When he walked away, he didn't look back.

Dana watched him go, struck anew by his tenderness, by the gentleness that shone through even when he was frustrated and angry. If she'd ever doubted his love before, she did no longer. That love was strong enough to temper fury, resilient enough to withstand pain. It was a love some women never found, deep and true and lasting.

And because a love just as powerful was growing inside her, she had to let him go.

Once again, Nick tried giving Dana the space she claimed to need. In fact, just to prove a point, he gave her even more than she'd bargained for. It wasn't easy. His body tightened at the memory of her in his arms and he was filled with heated, restless yearnings. If the days were long without the excitement of those midday conversations at the library and the chance meetings around town, the nights were endless.

Irritated all the time, he'd just finished snapping at one of his employees when the private line in his office rang.

"Yes, hello," he barked.

"Nicholas, dear, I hate to bother you at work, but I need to see you," Jessica Leahy said, her voice taut. The tension in her greeting was enough to worry him and to temper his tone.

"Is there some problem, Jess? Is Joshua okay?"

"Joshua's fine, but we need to talk."

"It sounds urgent."

"I think it may be. Could you come by this afternoon?"

He didn't hesitate for an instant, despite his recent irritation with Jessica. He'd always loved his wife's family. They'd begun treating him like the son they'd never had long before he and Ginny had married. Since her death, they had remained close, growing even more so because of Tony. The only time he could ever remember growing impatient with Jessica was on the night of Tony's birthday party. Thanks to Dana's insights, he'd even come to understand her uncharacteristic behavior that night.

"I'll be there in a half hour."

When he arrived, his mother-in-law was sitting on the porch in her favorite rocker staring off into space, the rocker idle. Her figure as trim as a girl's, she was wearing jeans and a Western-style plaid cotton shirt. But despite the casual attire, every white hair was in place, her makeup flawless. There was a silver tray with a pitcher of iced tea with lemon and mint beside her. She was the picture of serenity, except for one jarring note—she was absentmindedly twisting a handkerchief into knots.

She watched him come up the walk with troubled eyes. When he'd perched on the porch railing beside her, she poured him a glass of tea and took her time adding the lemon and mint as if she wanted to postpone their talk as long as possible.

"I know how busy you are, Nicholas, so I'll get right to the point," she said finally. "How much do you know about this Brantley woman?"

Nick flinched at her phrasing. It implied that a judgment had been made, that Dana had been found wanting in some way. He took a slow, deliberate sip of the tea before he spoke. "All I need to know."

"I don't think so," she said, her tone curt to the point of rudeness. Her shrewd eyes assessed him. "Are you in love with her?"

"Yes."

As if his quick response pained her, she closed her eyes for an instant, then said softly, "I was afraid of that."

Nick exhaled sharply. So that was it. She was going to pursue this illogical campaign to discredit Dana in his eyes.

"She's a lovely young woman," he said gently. "I think if you gave her half a chance, you'd like her."

"I thought perhaps I could, too, but now I'm not so sure. There are some rumors going around." At his indignant expression, she held up her hand. "I know, Nicholas. I'm not one for gossip, either, but I think you'd better look into this. If it's true, then I think you should keep Tony away from her."

"What the devil are you talking about?" Nick said, getting to his feet and beginning to pace. The creaking boards under his feet only increased his agitation. He stared at Jessica incredulously. "There couldn't possibly be anything about Dana that would make me want to keep Tony away from her. She's absolutely wonderful with him. And he adores her."

"I'm very much aware of that. He talks about her all the time. That's why I'm so concerned. If she's to be a big influence on his life, I want to be sure she's a fit person. He's my only grandson, Nick. I want what's best for him."

"This is ridiculous. Of course she's fit. How can you even suggest something like that? Is it Ginny? Would you feel the same way about any woman?"

"Perhaps so, but I like to think not." Her expression softened and she caught his hand as he stood beside her. "Darling, I'm not just being jealous on my daughter's behalf. Honestly I'm not."

She waved aside his attempt to interrupt. "Wait a minute, please. I know that's the way it must have seemed the other night. Joshua read me the riot act over my behavior. I don't need you to do it, too. Ginny would be the first one to want you to be happy again. But if these things I've heard about Dana Brantley are true, I don't think this woman's the right one for you. If it were just you, perhaps I wouldn't be so concerned. You're a grown man. You can make your own choices, your own mistakes. But there's Tony to consider, too.

He's just an impressionable boy. I should think that would be important to you, as well."

"Dammit, you're being cryptic, and it's not at all like you to make judgments about people without giving them a chance. If you think you know something about Dana, tell me."

"I don't *know* anything. All I've heard is the gossip."

"Gossip that's usually nothing but half truths."

"An interesting choice of words, Nicholas. *Half truths.* Don't you deserve to know if there's any truth at all to the rumors? Find out about Dana Brantley's past. That's all I'm asking you to do. If she has nothing to hide, she'll tell you and that will be the end of it."

Suddenly the secrets and silences came back to haunt Nick. For the first time, he was genuinely afraid. If he probed too deeply, what would he find? Would it be the end for him and Dana?

Chapter 8

Thunder rumbled ominously as Nick drove away from his mother-in-law's house. Dark clouds rolled in, dumping a torrential rain in their wake. Troubled by his meeting with Jessica, Nick went to his favorite spot overlooking the river, parked under a giant weeping willow and sat staring at the water through the rain that lashed at the windshield. Usually the serenity of the Potomac soothed him, but today the storm-tossed water churned in a way that mirrored his emotions.

Why hadn't Jessica told him about the rumors and been done with it? But even as he asked himself the question, he knew the answer. She was not the type of woman to spread hurtful gossip. Whatever she'd heard about Dana must have been terribly convincing, and very damning, for her even to mention it. But for the life of him, he couldn't imagine Dana ever having done something for which she might be ashamed.

"We all make mistakes," he muttered aloud, thinking of Dana's silences. "We all do things we regret." As wonderful as he thought Dana was, she wouldn't be human if she hadn't made some mistakes in her life. Whatever hers might have been, he believed they could deal with them if they could only get them out in the open.

Dreading the task before him, Nick drove back to his office and called the library. It had been days since he and Dana had talked, and he had no idea what sort of reception she would give him. Dana answered on the fifth ring, her voice breathless and edgy.

Nick was immediately alert. "Hey, are you okay?" he asked. "Is something wrong?"

There was a long silence.

"Dana, what's going on over there?"

He heard her take a deep breath, as if she were drawing in the strength to speak.

"Nothing, Nick," she said finally. "I'm fine. I was up on a ladder in the back when the phone rang. It took me a minute to get here. That's all."

"I see."

This time he was the one who hesitated for so long that Dana eventually asked, "Did you want something, Nick?"

"Yes. Dana, could I see you tonight? There's something I think we should talk about."

More guarded silence greeted the suggestion. At

last, she said wearily, "Nick, we've been through everything."

"Not this."

"No. It's not a good idea."

"Dana, please. It's important. We could go to a movie."

"I thought you wanted to talk."

"I do. We can stop for coffee afterward." What he didn't say was that he wanted to prolong their time together, that sitting beside her in a movie would at least give him the temporary illusion of the togetherness he'd missed so much. It would also put off a conversation that was likely to have a profound impact on their future.

"How bad could it be spending a few hours together?" he coaxed. "It's even that George Clooney movie you've been wanting to see. Remember we talked about going?"

There was a heavy sigh of resignation. "Is this going to be like bingo? Are you just going to badger me until I give in?"

"Probably."

He thought he'd detected a glimmer of amusement in her voice, but it was gone when she answered. "Okay," she agreed with such obvious reluctance that it hurt as much as an outright rejection.

"I'll pick you up at six-thirty," he said. "We'll go to the early movie."

"Couldn't I just meet you there?"

Nick closed his eyes. "Why, Dana? Are you that afraid to be alone with me?"

There was a sharp intake of breath and this time there was real emotion in her voice. "Oh, Nick, I'm sorry if that's what it sounded like. Of course I'm not afraid to be with you."

"Fine. I'll pick you up at six-thirty, then."

Nick held the receiver for a long time after Dana had hung up, irrationally unwilling to break the connection. From that moment until six-fifteen, when he left his house after showering and shaving and sending Tony off with grandparents, he tortured himself over the questions he'd have to ask. He felt like a traitor for wanting to know about a past Dana clearly wanted to forget. He'd been expecting trust from her. Didn't he owe her as much?

When he arrived at her house, he was dismayed to see that the circles under her eyes were darker than ever. Her complexion had a gray cast to it despite the attempt to heighten her color with a touch of blusher. Her slacks hung loose, as if she'd lost weight just since he'd seen her last. Despite his worry, Nick's pulse raced with abandon. His body tightened and he had to resist the urge to draw her into a protective embrace.

As they drove through town, she said, "We could skip the movie and just get this over with."

He glanced at her, saw again the obvious signs of tension and exhaustion, then shook his head. "No. I think we both can use the relaxation."

She shrugged indifferently and settled back in the bucket seat. It took only a few minutes to reach the town's single theater, but the thick silence between them made it seem like hours. Tension seemed to have wrapped itself around Nick's neck, cutting off his voice. He was grateful they were a few minutes late and had no time to talk as they found seats in the already darkened theater.

The movie passed in a blur as his own reel played in his mind. He recalled Jessica's behavior on the night of Tony's party and again this afternoon. He had no doubt that her concern was genuine, but he was equally convinced it was unwarranted. Still, with Tony's welfare at stake, he had no choice but to explore her veiled charges about Dana.

He gazed at Dana, who sat stiffly next to him, and wondered how things had gone so terribly awry between them. Faced with the uncertainty of their situation, the tension inside him built. He felt as though he were out with a distant stranger, instead of the warm, giving woman with whom he'd fallen slowly but inevitably in love.

When the lights came up, Dana blinked and Nick realized she, too, had been lost in thought.

"Maybe we should stay for the next show," he suggested wryly. "I don't think either of us saw this one."

"I doubt it would help. I think we both have too much on our minds."

"Shall we go, then? Maybe we can unburden ourselves."

"Talking doesn't work miracles," she said with a note of regret.

"Maybe not, but it's a start."

He got to his feet and Dana followed. As they walked out into the deepening twilight, Nick saw two old friends. He'd known Ron Barlow and Hank Taylor since childhood, and though he had no desire to stop and chat with them now, he felt he couldn't ignore them.

"Do you mind, Dana?" he said, gesturing in their direction. "We should go over and say hello. Hank does a lot of subcontracting work for me. Ron is a vice president at the bank. The three of us used to bowl together with our wives when Ginny was alive."

"Maybe you should speak to them alone. I might make them uncomfortable."

"Don't be silly. Come on." He slid an arm around Dana's waist and steered her in their direction.

"Hey, Ron. Hank." He patted Ron on the back and shook hands with Hank. "Did you enjoy the show?"

"It wasn't bad," Ron mumbled awkwardly just as his wife, Lettie, came up and linked an arm through his. She didn't look at Nick at all, just whispered to Ron and hurried him away before Nick could even introduce Dana. Hank and his wife followed, though Hank shot a look of regret over his shoulder as they left.

"I don't understand," Nick apologized, staring after them in confusion. He gazed into Dana's eyes and saw the hurt she was trying so hard to cover. He searched for an explanation that made sense. "Maybe they're like Jessica. Maybe they're thinking about Ginny."

"Maybe so," Dana said tiredly.

The whole thing was a thoroughly disconcerting experience for a man who'd always made friends easily and usually commanded fierce loyalty from all who knew him. But tonight it was as though he and Dana were being intentionally shunned without knowing what they had done to deserve it.

No, he reminded himself. Dana might very well know why attitudes had changed so abruptly. Jessica certainly thought she did. That was what this evening was all about: putting an end to the secrets and evasions.

Even though she might know the cause, Dana seemed every bit as disturbed as he was by the whispers and covert examinations.

"Shall we stop by Gracie's for coffee and pie?" he suggested.

"No. We can talk just as well at my place," she said, staring after a woman who'd just ignored her greeting. It was evident to Nick that she didn't want to deal with another such rejection. By the time they got back to her house, she was badly shaken. He would have felt better if she'd simply been angry. Instead, she acted as though there was no fight left in her.

She poured them both a glass of iced tea, but her hand was trembling when she handed Nick his. Then she took up pacing around the kitchen. At last she asked, "Am I crazy or were people avoiding us tonight? Not just those two couples but everyone?"

"I'm sure it was just your imagination," he said, but his voice lacked conviction.

"What about your imagination? Was it getting the same impression?"

"There's probably some perfectly logical explanation. Maybe I just split the seat out of my pants and no one dared to tell me."

Dana glowered at him. "Don't try to make a joke out of this, Nick. Something's very wrong. Everyone's been very friendly to me since I arrived in town—until tonight. Have you heard any rumors going around?"

"What sort of rumors?" he hedged.

"I don't know. It seems around here buying a new dress is cause enough for gossip."

Nick's eyebrows arched at the sarcasm. "I've never heard you sound bitter before. Is it what happened tonight or is it something more? Have there been other incidents you haven't mentioned to me?"

Dana stopped her pacing to declare, "I'm just fed up with people digging around in my life. I came here to escape that. I should have known it would be worse than ever in a place like this." Angrily, she clenched her hands into tight fists. Nick reached out and caught one hand in his and rubbed his thumb across the knuckles until her grip relaxed.

"Come on," he urged. "Sit down. Let's talk this out. There has to be some reasonable explanation."

She yanked her hand away and began pacing again. "I can't sit down. Do you have any idea what it's like to feel people staring at you, making judgments about you, especially people you thought were your friends? It's awful," she said, her voice rising at first in outrage, then catching on a sob.

She stared at Nick and her mournful expression almost broke his heart. She sat down and put her head in her hands.

"I thought it was over," she said, her voice muffled. "I thought it couldn't follow me here, but it has."

Nick seized on the remark. "What has followed you? Dana, what are you talking about? What rumors could there be?"

She looked up and stared at him blankly, as if she'd been unaware of the full implications of what she'd said, then she shook her head. "Never mind."

"Dana, stop hiding things from me. I care about you. Please, can't you talk to me about what's worrying you? There's nothing you can't tell me. I promise you I won't make judgments."

Her lips quivered, but her voice held firm. "I can't, Nick."

"Why? Why can't you tell me, dammit? You know I'm not just being nosy."

Tears trickled down her cheeks and she bit her lips.

"Dana?"

When she still didn't respond, he slammed his fist down on the table and Dana's eyes widened in fear. "For God's sakes, Dana, talk to me. Fight back."

She shuddered, then squared her shoulders determinedly. "You can't help, Nick. I can't even help myself." Her eyes were empty, her voice expressionless. "Go on home. I just want to go to bed."

"Dammit, I am not leaving you alone when you're this upset. You're shaking, for heaven's sakes." All thoughts of his planned confrontation vanished now as he responded to her pain. "Dana, please, let me help you."

"I'll be fine," she insisted. "Go home to Tony."

"Tony's with his grandparents tonight. You're the one who needs me. I'm staying right here."

Dana apparently saw the implacable look in his eyes, because she finally shrugged and gave in. "Okay, fine. Stay if you like. You can sleep in the guest room."

With that she whirled around and left him alone at the kitchen table wishing he had some idea how to comfort her. But how could you offer comfort to a woman who refused to admit she needed it? Dana was all stiff-necked pride and angry determination. By hinting that he sensed a weakness, a vulnerability, he had forced a denial. She had virtually rejected him, as well.

He listened to the simple, routine sounds of Dana getting ready for bed: the water running, drawers opening and closing, then finally the rustle of sheets. Vivid images played across his mind, taunting him. When he could no longer see a light under the bedroom door, he tiptoed down the hall and stood outside her room, certain he could hear the choked sound of her muffled sobs.

"Dana."

Only silence answered him.

Dana bit her lip to keep from responding to Nick's call. Hot, salty tears slid down her cheeks and dampened the pillow. They were tears for a past she couldn't forget and a present she couldn't prevent from whirling out of control. Her arms ached from the effort it had cost her to keep from throwing them around Nick's waist and holding on for dear life. His strength could get her through this, but she didn't dare begin to count on it. Far more than pride had held her back. She loved him. No matter how she had angered him, how deeply she had hurt him, he had given her gentleness and understanding. She couldn't give him more heartache in return.

A fresh batch of tears spilled down her cheeks. Dear God, how she needed him, but she had to be strong enough to let him go. Tonight after the movies, feeling the stares burning into her, she had seen more clearly than ever that it was the only way. She couldn't embroil Nick in her problems, not when those problems seemed to be mounting every minute. She'd only be an albatross to a man who might one day want to run for office. She and Nick had never discussed his political aspirations, but she'd heard about them. He deserved the chance to make a fine legislator.

She swallowed another sob and clung to her pillow, pretending it was Nick she held. She tried to imagine his strength seeping into her. With him by her side, she could face almost anything. Without him, it was going to be hell all over again.

She heard the creak of the ancient bedsprings in the guest room and it sent a shiver down her spine. *You could be with him,* she told herself. *All you have to do is walk down the hall, go to him. He won't turn you away.*

But it wasn't nearly that simple and she knew it. In the morning she would find the strength to say goodbye again and convince Nick that this time she really meant it.

* * *

Nick woke before dawn, and after hesitating inde-
cisively in the hallway, he opened the bedroom door
and crept in to check on Dana. The dim light from the
hall cast the room into patches of golden brightness
and dim shadows.

Dana was in the middle of the bed in a tangle of
sheets, her nightgown of silk and lace twisted midway
up her thighs. She was sleeping soundly now, though
he had heard her restless tossing for most of the night.
He tiptoed closer and sat down carefully on the edge
of the bed.

She looked so peaceful and vulnerable lying there,
her hair flowing over her shoulders in rich brown waves,
her skin slightly damp and flushed from the summer
night's heat. He brushed the hair back from her face, then
lingered to caress her cheek. Even in sleep, a responsive
smile tilted the corners of her mouth. Unable to resist,
he leaned down to press a kiss on her lips. They were
like cool satin beneath his touch, smooth and resilient.

Dana sighed at the touch of his mouth on hers and
Nick deepened the kiss, lingering to savor the sensations it aroused, to delight in her sleepy responsiveness.
His hand drifted down to skim over her bare shoulder,
then slid the thin strap on her gown aside. His thumb
followed the curve of her jaw and his tongue tasted the
soft hollow of her throat. She stirred restlessly and he
tried to soothe her by gently stroking her arm.

Suddenly, as if trapped in the midst of a waking
nightmare, she sat straight up in bed. Her eyes snapped
open and stared around in unseeing terror. Her hands

were thrown protectively up in front of her. Her whole body shook violently.

"No, please. No."

The words were a desperate whimper that stunned Nick into silence as she frantically drew the sheet up like a protective shield, clutching it around her and huddling in a corner of the bed.

Finally, his thoughts whirling, he forced himself to speak. He had to break through this blind panic.

"Dana, love, it's me. Nick. It's okay. I'm not going to hurt you." His voice was low and soothing. He spoke steadily, despite the pounding of his heart and the fear unleashed inside him. "Shh, sweetheart, it's okay. Nobody's going to hurt you."

She blinked as his words began to register. "Nick." Her eyes seemed to focus. The fear seemed to slowly dissipate, but not the trembling.

"Darling, I didn't mean to frighten you. Can I hold you?" he asked softly, reluctant to make another move without her approval.

She sat rocking, wrapped in the sheet, her arms around her stomach, her gaze locked on some awful, distant memory.

"Dana?"

At last she nodded. "Please."

As Nick's arms went around her, one last shudder swept through her and she curved herself into his comforting warmth. Then her tears began. They flowed endlessly. She wept until he thought both their hearts would break.

Chapter 9

Dana clung to Nick, her whole body shuddering with deep, wrenching sobs brought on by the unexpected reawakening of old wounds. Nick's gentle kiss had plucked her from a lovely dream and cast her into a nightmare he couldn't possibly have anticipated. Yet despite the seemingly irrational violence of her reaction, he continued to soothe her, his hands gently massaging her back, brushing the hair from her face.

"It's okay, love. It's going to be okay," he promised, and because she needed to, she believed him.

His words soothed her like a balm until at last she was still, totally drained by the experience. She drew in a deep breath and tried to pull free, but Nick held her still. For once, she hadn't the strength to resist. She burrowed her face in the male-scented warmth of his shoulder, while his arms circled her, lending strength and comfort. His steady breathing and slow, constant heartbeat were like the rhythmic sounds of a train, lulling her.

For this brief moment in time Dana felt safe, as if no harm could ever come to her again. She knew all too well, though, how fragile and fleeting that feeling could be.

"Feel better?" he asked.

She nodded, unable to trust her voice. Deep inside lurked the fear that if she opened her mouth at all, it would be to scream with such agony that Nick would flee just when she was discovering she needed his steadiness and quiet calm the most. Already she'd shown him a side of her she'd hoped he would never encounter. She could only begin to imagine what he must think of her after her unintentional display of histrionics, yet he hadn't run.

"I'm sorry," she said finally.

"There's nothing to be sorry about," he said, giving her a reassuring squeeze. "I'm the one who should be apologizing. I obviously frightened you. I guess I wasn't thinking. You looked so peaceful while you slept, so beautiful, that I couldn't resist kissing you. When you kissed me back, I wanted more. I shouldn't have given in to the feeling. I should have realized you'd be startled."

Surprisingly, she felt her lips curve into a half smile. "I think that's a slight understatement. You must have thought I was demented."

"Hardly."

She felt his fingers thread through her hair. When he reached her nape he massaged her neck until the knots of tension there began to unwind, replaced by a slow-spreading warmth that settled finally in her abdomen. Desire, dormant for so long, flared at his touch. She felt alive again and, despite everything, hopeful. She relaxed into the sensations, allowing her enjoyment of Nick's seductive caresses to last far longer than was wise.

Just a few minutes, she said to herself. *Just let me have a few minutes of solace in the arms of a man I love. Let me feel again, just for a little while. Surely that's not asking too much.*

"Dana, talk to me about your marriage. What went wrong?"

The seemingly innocent request snapped her out of her quiet, drifting state. Her muscles tensed immediately and her heart thumped so loudly and so hard she was sure the sound must echo through the bedroom.

She shook her head. "I can't talk about it."

"You must. I finally realize that must be what has been standing between us from the beginning. It's the only thing it could be."

"Nick, please. Let the past stay buried."

"I wish that were possible, but it's obviously not. Just look at your reaction this morning."

She stiffened and her tone became defensive. "That's a pretty big leap in logic. What makes you think that has anything to do with my past? Any woman who normally lives alone would be startled to find herself being attacked while she's still half-asleep."

His brow lifted at her choice of words. "Is that what it was?" She heard the doubt in his tone, saw it in his eyes, and suddenly she couldn't bear to go on with the facade a minute longer. Nick truly cared about her, perhaps even loved her, though he'd never said the words aloud. She'd seen the emotion, coupled with desire, time and again in his eyes. At the very least he deserved the truth, no matter how difficult the telling of it might be for her.

Sighing in resignation, she met his gaze. "What do you want to know?"

"How did you meet your husband?"

"We were in college together. He was a few years older. He was already finishing law school just as I started undergraduate school. We met at a fraternity party."

"Did you marry right away?"

"No. We waited until he'd finished school and gone to work."

"Were you happy?"

"In the beginning, yes. We were very happy."

"But not always?"

"No."

"What happened? Did he start running around with other women? Spend too much time at work?"

"Why are you so sure that I'm not the one at fault?"

"Because it's very clear that commitment is not

something you take lightly. You'd fight for your marriage."

"Yes," she said very softly. "I suppose, in a way, I did."

A thousand images from those five long years flashed through her mind. The mental album began with Sam as he'd looked on their wedding day, his gray eyes watching her with pride, shining with love. She recalled vividly the nights of glorious passion, when his slightest touch fired her blood. Then there were the pictures of Sam at an endless series of parties, her arm tucked possessively through his, or Sam staring hard at her every second they were separated in a room as if in search of the slightest hint of betrayal. And then... She shut her eyes against the images of what happened next, but the visions stayed with her, burned indelibly in her memory.

Nick's arms tightened around her. "Tell me, love. Maybe talking it out will help." His breath whispered across her bare shoulder.

Dana had also once thought that talking was an answer. She had tried to talk to her family, but they'd turned a deaf ear. They'd been so impressed with her perfect marriage to a man they admired that they hadn't wanted to listen to the flaws. Her sisters had their own problems just trying to make ends meet. They couldn't understand how anyone with Sam's and Dana's financial resources could possibly be troubled.

The next time she'd dared to talk it had been to a psychiatrist, and by then it had been too late for anything to help. There was no reason to believe that opening up to Nick would bring her anything but more pain. She was so afraid of the expression she would see in his eyes when she'd finished. Pity, doubt or condemnation would be equally difficult to bear.

"Oh, Nick," she murmured in a tone that decried his innocence. Would he ever fully understand how truly fortunate he had been in his own marriage? How rare the unselfish joy he had found with Ginny was?

"You want to know what went wrong in my marriage, as if it were possible to pick out a single moment and say, 'Ah, yes, that's when it began falling apart. That's what all the arguments were about.' It doesn't work that way. The disintegration takes place in stages, so slowly that you don't always recognize it when it begins to happen and the cause may have very little to do with the symptoms."

Nick shook his head in denial. "I can't accept that. Maybe you can't see it at the time, but now, in retrospect, surely you can."

"Not really, and believe me, I've tried and tried. I kept hoping I could pinpoint the start of it so I could understand it myself. We had arguments at first, like any newly married couple trying to adjust. They were always over little things. I squeezed the toothpaste from the bottom, Sam squeezed it from the top. I left my pantyhose hanging in the shower. He dropped his socks on the bedroom floor. Was that when it began? Did it fall apart over toothpaste, pantyhose and socks?"

She looked to Nick for a comment, but he simply

waited. "Okay, maybe it was the first time he dumped an entire meal on the dining room floor because I'd fixed something for dinner he didn't like. Or maybe it was the first time he accused me of paying too much attention to one of his coworkers at an office party. Maybe, though, it wasn't until the night he slapped me for challenging his opinion in public."

Her tone took on an edge of belligerence. "Which time do I pick, Nick? Which time was just your normal, everyday marital squabble and which was the first sign that my husband was sick, that he was unable to cope with pressure and that I was likely to become the target for his anger?"

Nick swallowed hard as the implication of that sank in, but his gaze was unblinking, compassionate and unrelenting. "Go on."

Dana shivered in his arms and closed her eyes against the memories again, but as before, that only seemed to focus them more sharply.

She spoke in a voice barely above a whisper, fighting against the sickening tide of nausea that always accompanied her recollections.

"I remember the first time Sam hit me. I was so stunned." Even now her voice was laced with surprise. "I had known he was upset. His anger had been building for weeks. The pressures at work were getting worse and he was tense all the time. One night he just snapped. It was over what I'd considered a minor disagreement in public. When we got home, he started yelling at me about it. All of a sudden he was practically blind with rage. After he hit me, he cried. I sat on the bed with this red mark on my face and Sam kneeling on the floor beside me, crying, apologizing, promising it would never happen again, begging me to forgive him."

She looked up and saw tears shimmering in Nick's eyes. She had to turn away. His pity was unbearable.

"But it did happen again, didn't it?" he said softly.

She shrugged, trying to appear nonchalant. "That's the pattern, isn't it? The first time, the husband apologizes and the wife believes him and things do get better...for a while. Then it happens again." She pressed her hands to her face. "God, I was so ashamed. I kept thinking it must be my fault, that if only I were a better wife he wouldn't be doing this. I tried so hard not to do anything that might set him off, but it seemed as though the quieter and more amenable I became, the more outraged he was."

"Did he drink?"

"Sometimes. He knew he couldn't handle it, so usually he stayed away from liquor. It was always much worse when he'd been drinking. I used to turn down drinks, hoping that he wouldn't take one, either, but it didn't work. It just meant I was sober enough to watch while he got drunk, knowing that sooner or later he was going to take it out on me. Sometimes he would come home very late, after I had gone to bed, and he would wake me up...."

She choked back a sob and put her hands in front of her face. "He...he would wake me up and... Oh, God,

Nick, I felt so violated. It was like being raped by some horrible stranger."

Nick's breath caught in his throat. "Oh, my God." The words seemed to be wrenched from somewhere deep in his soul. "It was like that this morning for you, wasn't it? No wonder…"

"No, Nick. It wasn't like this morning," she said, reaching up to tentatively caress his cheek. She couldn't let him equate his tenderness with Sam's ugly violence. "You were gentle, not like Sam. It's just that when I first woke up I was disoriented. For a minute…"

"For a minute you thought it was happening all over again."

Dana nodded. She felt Nick's hand on her shoulder, warm and comforting as it tried to counter the chill that swept through her.

"I am so sorry, Dana. So very sorry."

"So am I," she said, her voice laced with bitterness. "But do you realize how many women go through exactly what I did? Some sources say around thirty percent. One out of every three women will be abused at some time by a man in her life, a husband, a boyfriend. Not just me. I couldn't believe it when the psychiatrist told me. I had been so sure I was all alone."

Nick drew her more snugly into his arms and held her. She felt his tears run down his cheek and mingle with hers. He rocked her back and forth, murmuring softly. She was hardly aware of what he was saying, just the soothing sound of his voice washing over her, trying to ease the pain.

Finally he loosened his embrace and brushed away her tears. She remembered being frightened of those hands, terrified of their strength, but now she felt only their gentleness.

"I want you to listen to me for a minute," he said. "I know that what you experienced was awful. I can't even begin to imagine how horrible it must have been for you, but that was Sam. Not me. It's over now. I can understand how you would be wary of men. In fact, a lot of things make sense to me now: your fear of getting close to me, your defensiveness, your need for independence. But, Dana, you can't build a wall around yourself and live the rest of your life in isolation."

"You're wrong," she replied wearily. "It's the only way I can live."

"Dana, I'm not like Sam Brantley. Don't you know I would die rather than harm you? What we have is special and good. We owe it to ourselves to give it a chance."

"I know that's what you want and on one level it's what I want. Intellectually I can tell myself that you and Sam are very different men, but emotionally I can't convince myself of that. There are too many scars." Nick flinched and she reassured him. "Not physical scars, psychological ones. They're just as long-lasting. I don't know if I'll ever feel totally comfortable around men again."

"Even after all these weeks, can't you see you can trust me?"

Dana heard the hurt in Nick's voice, but once started,

she had to tell him the truth. She touched his cheek with regret as she said, "No, I can't."

"But—"

"No, wait. This isn't something that's your fault, Nick. Without living through it, you can't possibly understand what abuse like that does to your ability to trust your own judgment," she countered.

She searched for words to make Nick understand the inexplicable. "My husband was attentive, kind and loving all during our courtship. He was an educated man with an excellent career. That's the man I fell in love with, but there was a dark side to him, a side I never saw before we were married. Maybe he hid it. Maybe I blinded myself to it. I'll never really know.

"You talk about the weeks we've shared. Remember, Sam and I had known each other for three years in college, and I still hadn't guessed that he was capable of violence. Sam would pick up an injured animal from the side of the road and take it to a vet. He was a soft touch for any sob story. How could a man like that possibly be abusive to another human being, especially his own wife?"

"I still don't understand why you didn't leave him once you did know, why you subjected yourself to more suffering."

"There are so many reasons a woman doesn't leave. For some it's the children."

"But you didn't have that problem."

"No, because I refused to get pregnant by a man with no control over his anger. We had some horrible fights over that. Sam wanted kids. We'd planned for them, but when the time came for me to stop using birth control, I couldn't go through with it. I even tried to use that as leverage to make him get help, but it was as if he had no idea why I thought he needed it."

"Then I'll ask you again. Why did you stay?"

Dana closed her eyes. "Oh, God, there were so many reasons. For a while I kept deluding myself that it would never happen again. There were good days, you know. Sometimes months passed, and then I could believe that Sam was still the wonderful man I'd married. I also didn't get much sympathy. The one time I tried talking to my parents, they sided with him. They were sure I must have deserved his anger or that I'd exaggerated it. After a while I began to believe that, too. Sometimes the psychological abuse is more devastating than the physical. Each day chips away at your self-confidence until no matter how bad it is, you're afraid to leave.

"Besides," she went on, "even if I had left, where would I have gone? I hadn't finished school. I had no marketable skills. I had no money of my own. Sam made sure I never forgot that. I halfheartedly tried hiding away some of the grocery money for a while, but he always found it. Finally I just stopped trying."

"There are shelters."

"I know that, but at the time I tried to convince myself I didn't need that. I wanted to believe that those shelters were for some other kind of woman, that if I tried hard enough I could handle Sam without anyone ever having to find out."

"What about your parents? Why didn't they listen to you?"

"They didn't want to hear. My parents were from the old school. They believed a wife made the best of whatever happened. Whither thou goest and all that. They wouldn't have taken me in."

Nick appeared shocked. "Surely they couldn't have realized how dangerous it was for you."

"No, they probably didn't. Maybe if I'd persisted, it would have been different. That's what they say now, anyway." She shrugged. "At the time, I was too embarrassed to tell them how bad it really was. They thought we were just having little spats. They never saw the bruises on my arms and legs or the gashes where his wedding ring cut into my flesh when he hit me. Ironic, isn't it, that the ring I'd given him in marriage was used as a weapon against me?"

A shudder swept through her. "Do you know once I actually went out to get a job? I thought if only I could be economically independent, I could get out. The only thing I could find was a job as a checkout clerk in a neighborhood grocery store. I took it. When Sam found out about it he accused me of trying to undermine his position in the law firm. He claimed my working in a demeaning position like that would make it seem as though he couldn't provide for me."

Her memory replayed the scene they'd had, and she drew her knees up to her chest and wrapped her arms around them as if to ward off the pain. "It was awful. He threatened to rip up all my clothes so I could never leave the apartment, and then he…" She swallowed a sob. "Then he saw to it that I had enough bruises to keep me from showing my face in public for a while. When I think back on the humiliation, I wonder how I lived through it."

"You made it because you're a survivor. You're stronger than you realize, Dana. After all that happened, you got out and you've pulled your life together. I wondered why you'd waited until last year to finish your master's degree. Now it makes sense. And I can see now why you would choose a place like River Glen."

He tilted her chin up until she was looking into his eyes. "Don't you see how far you've come? That's what's important. You took that experience and turned it around."

"I'm not so sure about that. Did you ever wonder why I would choose to be a librarian? I chose it because I was afraid, Nick. I was afraid of real people, of real emotions. I still am. I came here looking for a quiet, safe life. No bumps. No highs or lows, just a steady, predictable existence."

"Dammit, Dana, you deserve more than a mere existence. Let me make it up to you for all the years of happiness you missed. You got out of one kind of jail. Don't shut yourself up in another one."

"I wish I could accept what you're offering. With all my heart I wish that I could be the kind of woman you deserve."

"You are exactly the kind of woman I need in my life, Dana. You are gentle and giving, despite everything you've been through. Perhaps even more so because of it. Tony sensed that instinctively and so did I. Don't let bitterness and fear rule you. If you do, Sam Brantley will have won as surely as if you'd stayed with him. Are you willing to give a contemptible man like that so much power over the rest of your life?"

"Nick, I want to do as you ask, but it's too soon. The scars haven't healed yet."

"Then let's heal them together. Don't go through this alone when you don't have to. Let me in. Let Tony in. We love you. We can make it easier for you."

She heard more than Nick's words. She heard the pleading tone. His eyes were shining with love. He held out his hand.

"Please. Don't fight what you're feeling for me. Accept it, build on it."

Dana hesitated, tempted. She was filled with longing, but she was also tortured by fear. She gazed into Nick's eyes, then glanced at his outstretched hand. It was trembling as he waited for her decision. Her blood surged through her, hot and wild with the promise of a new chance.

"I'll try," she said at last, slipping her hand into his. "I can't promise any more than that, but I'll try."

Nick's fingers closed lightly around hers, enveloping her in warmth. Even the roughness of his skin felt right somehow, as if it was meant to show her that strength could still be tender.

"This is right, Dana," he said, as though he had read her thoughts. He drew her close until her back was resting against his chest, where she could hear the steady, reassuring thump of his heart. "I promise you."

And for now, with summer's brightest sunlight dappling the bed and Nick cradling her in his arms, she could almost believe in the future.

Chapter 10

The image of Dana's pale, silken flesh marred by bruises almost drove Nick insane. He swore if he ever ran into Sam Brantley, he'd make him pay dearly for what he'd done to Dana. The man—no, he was less than a man—deserved to suffer tenfold the same wretched humiliation his ex-wife had suffered.

For hours after Nick had left Dana's, he had seethed with both anger and a desire for retribution. Only the certainty that more violence would slow Dana's healing had kept him from traveling to Manhattan and going after Brantley.

Now Nick sat in his office, staring blankly at the walls. He vowed to concentrate on overcoming Dana's doubts. He would have to gentle her like a brand-new frightened filly and teach her that love could be tender and passionate, rather than filled with anger and pain. Now that he'd discovered the way it had been for her before, he would have to find new ways to prove that their love would be blessed with joy. Convinced more than ever that their relationship could be truly special, he pushed aside his mother-in-law's warnings. Surely now he knew everything.

With his goal firmly established, Nick picked up his phone and dialed the library, then tilted his chair back on two legs as he waited for Dana to answer. When she did, her voice bore no trace of the emotional turmoil she'd been through just a few hours earlier. If anything she sounded as though a tremendous weight had been lifted from her shoulders.

"I had an idea," Nick announced.

"That's your trouble," she retorted lightly. "You're always getting ideas."

"Not that kind of idea," he said, thoroughly enjoying her upbeat mood and the suggestive tone of her teasing. Perhaps on some subconscious level their talk had released her from some of the past.

"I think it's time we have some fun," he said.

"I thought that's what we'd been doing."

"Okay, more fun. Now will you be quiet a minute and let me tell you what I have in mind?"

"Certainly."

"Dancing. I think we should go dancing."

"In River Glen? Does Gracie's have a jukebox?"

"Very funny. No. I thought we'd go to Colonial Beach. There's a place there that has a band on weekends. It's lacking in decor, but it does sit out over the water. What do you think?"

She hesitated and Nick had a hunch he knew exactly what she was thinking. "Dana, you have to face people sooner or later. We really don't even know *what* they've heard. Maybe it had nothing whatsoever to do with you or your past. Whatever it is, the gossip will die down as soon as something more interesting comes along."

"When did you start reading my mind?"

"It's not all that difficult under the circumstances." He paused thoughtfully, considering something that had been bothering him. "Dana, do you have any idea how those rumors would have gotten started in River Glen in the first place? Could Sam have planted them somehow? Does he know where you are?"

Dead silence greeted his questions.

"Dana?"

"No," she said finally with absolute conviction.

"You're sure? He sounds like the kind of man who'd go to any lengths to hurt you."

"It wasn't Sam. I can't explain how I know that, but I do."

There was an odd note in Dana's voice, but Nick couldn't doubt her certainty. "Okay," he said at last, resolving to ask his mother-in-law where she'd heard the gossip. Perhaps he could trace it that way.

"Now," he said, "what about tonight?"

"If you want to endure my two left feet, it's fine with me."

"Terrific. I also thought maybe you and Tony and

I would have one of our backyard picnics tomorrow. I plan to challenge you to a championship-caliber badminton game afterward."

"In this steamy weather I think croquet is more my speed."

"Maybe it'll cool off by tomorrow. Anyway, are we on for all of it?"

"As long as I get to fix the food."

"Don't tell me you're casting aspersions on my cooking, too?"

"If the shoe fits, Mr. Verone," she teased, and her tone made him smile with delight.

"Oh, it fits," he retorted, "but it's damned uncomfortable. I'll pick you up at eight."

His pulse was racing and he was filled with anticipation as he hung up. He wasn't prepared to look up and find his mother-in-law in the doorway, a disapproving frown on her face.

"Jessica, what are you doing here?"

"I came to see you, obviously. Were you talking to that Brantley woman, Nicholas?"

His gaze hardened. He hated to be rude to her, but it was time she understood exactly where things stood. His relationship with Dana was not open for debate.

"Not that it's any of your business," he said curtly, "but yes."

"Then it's clear you haven't asked her about the rumors."

"Not directly, no, but I do have a question about them for you. Where did you hear the gossip?"

"It's not important."

"I think it is."

"Why? So you can rush out to her defense?"

"Dana doesn't need my defense. We've had a long talk and I think I have a pretty good idea what the rumors are about. I see no reason to hold Dana's past against her."

Jessica's eyes widened in shock. "You mean it *is* true! Then how can you say that?"

Nick lowered the front legs of his chair to the floor and stood up. He walked around his desk and put his hands on her shoulders. "Jessica, I am only going to say this once, so please listen very closely. I don't want to hurt you. You've always been a very important part of my life, but my relationship with Dana is none of your concern."

"It is when it involves my grandson."

"No, it isn't. If you really want to do what's best for Tony, you'll get to know Dana and welcome her into the family, because I have every intention of marrying her when she's ready."

His mother-in-law's lips tightened into a forbidding line and she shrugged off his touch. "Never, Nick. Obviously this woman has taken advantage of your good nature to lure you in, but I won't allow her to do the same with Tony. I'll fight you, Nick. In court, if necessary."

"That's an idle threat, Jessica. You have no case. I'm warning you, though, don't say one word to Tony about any of this." Nick's voice softened. "Don't you see you'll lose, Jess? Don't risk it. Don't risk losing your grandson's love."

"You've given me no choice," she said, whirling away and stalking from the office.

Nick stared after her, puzzled by her unforgiving attitude. How on earth could she hold Dana accountable for what had happened to her during her marriage? She had been the victim. Despite Jessica's attitude, though, he didn't for a moment believe she would make good on her threat. If she didn't drop the idea on her own, Joshua would see to it that she did. He was a fair man. He had already stood up for Dana once against his wife's unreasonable behavior. Nick had no doubt he would do it again, but in the meantime Jessica could make things damned uncomfortable. The only thing he could do would be to reassure Dana that she was not alone. They would face down whatever talk there was together.

With that thought, he put Jessica from his mind and began counting the hours until he would pick up Dana.

"Hey, Ms. Brantley," Tony said, pressing his thin body against her side as Dana sat at her desk. His eyes were cast down and he was chewing on his lower lip. She'd never seen him looking quite so troubled. "Can I ask you something?"

"Anything."

"How come my grandma doesn't like you? Did you have a fight or something?"

Dana felt a little frisson of fear curl along her spine

at Tony's guileless question. "Why would you think she doesn't like me?"

"She was acting real weird last night. Every time I said your name she'd change the subject and Grandpa kept making these funny faces at her. I think he was mad, 'cause after dinner they were arguing in the kitchen. Grandma broke one of her best plates, too. I heard it. And then she cried."

Dana felt like crying, too. How could Jessica put Tony in the middle this way? No matter what she thought of Dana, Tony's grandmother was wrong to let her feelings affect a ten-year-old who'd already suffered too much in his young life. "I'm very sorry about that, Tony. The last thing I'd ever want to do would be to come between you and your grandparents."

She took a deep breath and forced herself to say, "Maybe it would be better if you didn't spend quite so much time at the library for a little while, especially now that it's summer and school's out."

His eyes immediately clouded over and his shoulders stiffened at what he obviously considered a rejection. "Don't you want me here?"

She put a comforting arm around his waist and squeezed. "Oh, kiddo, don't ever think that. You're my best pal. But before I came to town, you used to go to your grandparents' place every day after school, didn't you? And I'll bet you'd been spending your summers out at the farm."

"Yeah, but I like it here better. There are other kids

around and you're here. Dad says it's okay with him if I come here instead. I told him I was helping you."

"And you are a big help. But did you ever think that maybe your grandparents are missing you? Grandparents are pretty special people. I never had a chance to know mine. They lived far away and they died before we could go to see them. I certainly don't want to keep you away from yours all the time."

Tony chewed on his lip as he considered what she'd said. "Maybe I could go there some days," he said grudgingly. "And I'm staying there again tonight. Dad said so when he picked me up this morning. He said he was gonna take you out."

"Oh, he did, did he?" Obviously she was going to have to stay on her toes or Nick would be railroading her into a relationship before she was ready. She had promised him a chance. She hadn't planned to let him dominate her life. Tonight she'd make that very clear.

But that night, Nick seemed determined that there would be no serious talk. Each time she tried to broach anything important, he took her back onto the virtually empty postage-stamp-size dance floor and whirled her around until she was too breathless to say anything.

"I'm too old for this," she said, gasping as she tried to return to the table.

"You're younger than I am. Get back over here."

"I have to have something to drink."

"No problem," Nick said, sweeping her into his arms. Two artfully executed and dramatic tango steps later, they reached their table and he picked up her glass of soda and offered it to her with a flourish.

"One sip," he cautioned. "The tango is my favorite dance. I don't intend to miss a second of it."

"Why couldn't you like to waltz?" she moaned, collapsing dramatically in his arms, an action that drew smiles and applause from the people at neighboring tables.

"Waltzing requires no energy."

"Do you consider this a form of exercise? I always thought dancing was supposed to be romantic."

"The tango is romantic."

"Two hours ago the tango was romantic. Now it's an endurance test."

"On your feet, Brantley. I didn't put this badminton net up for the fun of it," Nick said the following afternoon.

"I still haven't recovered from dancing," Dana said, lying on the chaise lounge waving a magazine to stir a breeze. She felt a little like the way Ginger Rogers must have felt after a particularly tiring movie date with Fred Astaire.

"Stop complaining, get up and serve."

She dragged herself to her feet, picked up the racket and shuttlecock. She took a halfhearted swing. The bird barely lifted over the net before taking a nosedive to Nick's well-tended lawn. He was caught standing flat-footed about ten yards back.

"What was that?" he demanded indignantly.

"A winning serve," she retorted modestly.

"Tony, get out here. Your father needs help. This woman is cheating."

"No, she's not," Tony called from the swing on the porch. "I saw her, Dad. She won the point fair and square."

"Thank you," Dana said. She glowered at Nick and said huffily, "If you're going to be a sore loser, we could switch to croquet."

"Just serve."

Dana won the game handily and turned the racket over to Tony. "Be kind to your father," she said in a stage whisper. "He's not as nimble as he once was."

"What's nimble?"

"It means his bones are getting old and creaky."

"Thanks a lot," Nick grumbled.

Dana waved cheerfully as she went inside to check on the potatoes for the German potato salad she'd promised to fix for Tony. As she plucked the steaming potatoes from the water and peeled them, she watched the badminton game through the kitchen window. Suddenly she realized she was humming and there was a smile on her face. She couldn't remember the last time she had ever felt this lighthearted. Her life felt right for the first time in years. This was what marriage was supposed to be like, relaxed and joyous with an edge of sexual tension. Yes, indeed, all the elements were there.

Lost in her thoughts, she didn't notice that the game had ended or that Nick had come into the kitchen.

"Why the smile?" he said, coming up behind her and

circling his arms around her waist. His breath whispered along her neck and sent shivers dancing down her spine.

"I was just thinking how good I feel. Complete, somehow. Does that make any sense?"

He turned her around in his arms and held her loosely. "I think it does, and you couldn't have said anything I would rather hear."

Nick's gaze caught hers and she swallowed hard at the look she saw in the hazel depths. "Nick…"

"Don't analyze it, Dana. Just feel." He hesitated. "Okay?"

Her heart raced, thundering in her chest. Never looking away from his eyes, she nodded and he slowly lowered his lips to hers. The quick brush of velvet was followed by the hungry claim of fire. Nick's hands rested lightly on her hips in a gesture meant to reassure her of her freedom to choose between the bright flame of passion and the gentle touch of caring.

She had thought the tenderness would be enough, that it would be all she could handle, but she found herself wanting more and she stepped toward the heat. Her arms slid around Nick's neck, lifting her breasts against his chest. The nipples hardened into sensitive buds. Her hands threaded through the coarse thickness of his hair. His tongue found hers and together they performed a mating dance as old as time.

She could feel the tension in the breadth of Nick's shoulders, could sense his struggle for restraint, and that, in the end, caused her to step away.

Nick watched her closely. "Are you okay?"

"It was just a kiss, Nick."

"It was more than a kiss and you know it. It was a beginning and we both know where it's going to lead."

Her pulse lurched unsteadily, but she couldn't tear her gaze away from Nick's intent examination. "I know," she finally said in a choked whisper.

"I won't rush you, Dana. It won't happen until you're ready."

"I'm not sure I'll know when that is."

"I will," he said, and his confidence made her blood sing with giddy anticipation.

"How could you possibly double with a bridge hand that looked like that?" Nick demanded of Dana a few nights later.

"I warned you I wasn't very good."

"But any idiot knows you don't double unless you have high points in your opponent's trump suit. Did you have a single diamond?"

"I had the two and five," Dana said meekly.

Nick's voice thundered through Betsy Markham's living room. "The two and five!" He came up out of his chair and leaned toward Dana. Instead of being frightened and backing away, she stood up, put her hands on the card table and glared right back at him. They stood there nose to nose, Nick glowering and Dana's eyes glinting with amusement.

"I warned you," she said again, relishing the new-found self-confidence that permitted her to bicker with Nick publicly without fear of repercussions.

Betsy chuckled. "Maybe I should get the peach pie now, before war erupts in my living room."

"Maybe you'd better," Nick agreed, still not taking his eyes away from Dana. When Betsy and Harry had made a discreet exit into the kitchen, Nick muttered, "Come here."

"Why should I get any closer if you're just going to yell at me?"

"I'm not going to yell."

"What are you going to do?"

"This." His mouth captured hers for a lingering kiss.

When he finally moved back, Dana caught her breath, then said, "I'll have to remember to foul up my bid in the next hand, too, if that's the punishment I'm going to get."

"That was no punishment. That was a warning. When you get to the library tomorrow, check out a book on bridge."

"Why don't you just play with Betsy as your partner? She knows what she's doing."

"Yeah, but she's not nearly as pretty." He punctuated his comment with another kiss. "Or as sexy." And another. "Or as much fun to tease."

The last kiss might have gone on forever, but Betsy and Harry came back with the pie and ice cream.

"We'll finish this lesson later," Nick promised, earning an embarrassed blush from Dana and a wide, approving smile from Betsy.

* * *

Dana found herself humming more and more frequently as the days sped by. She no longer froze up inside at Nick's caresses. She welcomed them. She even longed for them, when she was lying in her bed alone, an aching heaviness in her abdomen, the moisture of arousal forming unbidden at the apex of her thighs. The need to have him fill the emptiness inside her was growing, overwhelming her senses.

One morning she was wandering around the library daydreaming, humming under her breath, when the aging postman came by.

"Morning, Ms. Brantley."

"Hi, Davey. I hope that's not another batch of bills."

"Don't think so. Seems like there's a couple of new books today and a couple of letters."

"Thanks. Just put the whole batch on the desk. Help yourself to something cool to drink in the back if you want to. It's a real scorcher out there again today. I'm already looking forward to fall and it's not even the Fourth of July."

"I know exactly what you mean. Back when I was a kid around here we'd go to the icehouse on a day like this and get a bag of shavings and have a snowball fight. Cooled things down pretty well. Now I'd just welcome a soda, if you have any."

"They're in the refrigerator."

When Davey had gone into the back, Dana picked up the stack of mail and idly flipped through it. As Davey had said, it was mostly flyers from the publishers. The corner of a white envelope caught her attention. Suddenly her heart slammed against her ribs, then seemed to come to a halt.

Dear God, no. Not another one.

She gingerly pulled the letter from the pile as if it were dynamite. In a very real way it was. It threatened to explode everything she held dear.

With shaking hands, she ripped it open and found another hate-filled note from Sam's parents. Her eyes brimmed with tears as she read the cruel barbs, the vicious threats. They had seemed such wonderful people when she'd met them, kind and gentle and delighted about the marriage. They had adored Sam, however, and refused to see his faults, even after all the evidence was a matter of public record.

"Dammit, no," she muttered, shredding the letter with hands that shook so badly she could hardly grasp the paper. "I won't let them do this to me. I won't let them make me go through it again."

"Are you okay, ma'am?"

Dana blinked hard and looked up to find Davey staring at her, his rheumy old eyes filled with concern.

"I'm fine."

"Wasn't bad news or something, was it?"

"No, Davey," she said, trying to put a note of dismissal in her voice.

Davey took the hint, and after one last worried glance in her direction he shuffled out. "See you tomorrow, ma'am."

Dana didn't respond. She just sank down in her

chair and stared blindly at the shredded letter. Desperate to rid herself of the awful reminder, she jerked open the drawers of the desk one after another in search of matches. She knew she'd brought some in along with some candles, in case of a power outage during one of the frequent summer storms.

She finally found them in the back of the bottom drawer. She put the offensive letter in the trash can and set fire to an edge of one piece. She watched as the flame darkened the corner, then curled inward to consume the rest.

But even after the tiny fire had burned itself out, she sat there shaken, wondering how long she could live with this torment before she shattered like a fragile glass figurine thrown against a brick wall.

Chapter 11

Nick could hear the creaking of Dana's rocking chair as soon as he turned onto her street. He'd noticed for some time that the speed of her rocking increased in direct proportion to her level of agitation.

"She must be fit to be tied about something tonight," he muttered as he slowed his pickup to a stop. He tried to glimpse her through the thick green branches of the lilac bush, but his view was blocked. She never had gotten around to pruning it back.

He approached the corner of the porch and held a paper sack up high where she could see it.

"Hot apple pie from Gracie's. Interested?"

The rocking came to an abrupt halt, but she didn't answer.

"Dana?"

"Hi, Nick." There was absolutely no enthusiasm in her voice, and a knot formed in his stomach.

He parted a couple of branches so he could get a better look at her. "Hey, what's the story? Can't you do any better than that? Whatever happened to 'How thoughtful of you, Nick,' or maybe, 'You're wonderful'?"

He saw a faint smile steal across her lips, but it vanished just as quickly as it had come. She began rocking again and that, as much as the woebegone look on her face, sobered him.

Releasing the branches, which sprang back into place, he walked slowly around the house and entered through the back. He left the pie on the kitchen counter and went straight out to the porch. He caught hold of the back of the rocker and halted its motion long enough to drop a kiss on Dana's brow. He gazed into her eyes and found the all-too-familiar sadness was back.

"What you need," he prescribed, "is a long drive in the country."

She shook her head. "I don't feel much like going out."

"Which is exactly why you should go. It's a nice night. There's a breeze stirring. We can ride along the river, maybe stop for ice cream. If you play your cards right, I'll show you my favorite place to stop and neck. We can watch the moon come up."

"I don't think so."

Nick sat down next to her and put his hand on the arm of the rocker to stop the motion again. He struggled to curb a brief surge of impatience. "What's wrong?"

When she started to respond, he held up his hand. "If you tell me I can't help, I'm going to pick you up, rocker and all, and dump you in the river."

She blinked at the lightly spoken threat, and this time her smile was full-blown. Her eyes sparkled, albeit unwillingly.

"Oh, really?" she challenged. "You and who's army?"

"You don't think I can do it?" He got to his feet, put a hand on each armrest and lifted the chair. Dana crossed her legs and grinned at him.

"Now what?" she inquired demurely.

Nick tried to take a step, but the bulkiness of his burden made movement awkward, if not impossible.

"I thought so," she said. "All talk."

"Oh, yeah?" Nick lowered the chair, scooped Dana out of it and stalked across the porch and through the house.

"Nick Verone, put me down."

"And have you think I'm some hundred-and-seventy-pound weakling? Oh, no." The back door slammed open, rattling on its hinges.

"Nicholas, where are you taking me?" Her voice rose, but it was laced with laughter.

"I told you—to the river. It's a great night for a swim, don't you think?"

"Don't you dare."

"Who's going to stop me?"

"I am."

"Oh, really?"

"Yes, really," she murmured provocatively. Suddenly

Dana's lips found the sensitive spot at the nape of his neck. Nick gasped as her tongue drew a little circle on his flesh.

"Dana!" It came out as a husky growl.

"Umm?" She nibbled on his earlobe.

Blood surged through him in heated waves. His strength seemed to wane and he lowered her to her feet, letting her slide down his body as his mouth sought hers and captured it hungrily. Her arms slid around his neck and she pressed her body close to his until shudders swept through him. She smelled of lavender soap and feminine musk, and the scent drove his senses wild.

"Dana," he said softly, trying to tame the moment, but it was like trying to tame the wind.

"Hold me, Nick. Just hold me."

His arms tightened more securely around her waist and she fitted herself to the cradle of his hips, undaunted by the hard press of his arousal. Nick was caught between agony and ecstasy. Some unknown desperation had driven her into his embrace, but regret, he knew, would steal her away. He took a deep breath and stepped back.

Her eyes blinked open and she stared up at him in mute appeal. He ran a finger across her swollen lips. "Why, Dana?" he asked quietly. "Why tonight?"

A sigh whispered across her lips. "Why not?" she countered with a touch of defiance.

"Because when I walked onto your porch not ten minutes ago, you were barely speaking to me. Now you're ready to make love. It doesn't make sense."

She watched him, her expression turning grim. "Not much does these days." She regarded him wistfully. "Why couldn't you just feel, Nick? That's what you're always telling me to do."

"As long as it's honest. Can you tell me it would have been for you tonight? Or is there something you're trying to forget?"

"Maybe…maybe there's something I'm trying to remember." She gazed up at him, her eyes bright with unshed tears. "Can you remember what love felt like, Nick? I can't."

"Oh, babe." He swallowed hard and reached for her, but she shook her head sadly and held him off.

"No. You were right. It wouldn't have been honest. I'm not ready for a commitment and that's the only thing that would make it right."

Puzzled by her bleak expression, Nick brushed the hair back from her face and caressed her cheeks. "What happened today to put you in this mood?"

"Just a lot of old memories crowding in."

Nick held out his hand. "How about we go replace them with some new ones? That pie's still waiting."

She hesitated, but finally she took his hand and they walked slowly back to the house. They sat at the kitchen table, lingering over the pie and iced tea, talking about everything but what was really on Dana's mind.

By the time Nick left an hour later, her mood had lifted, but his was uneasy. He went home with an odd sense of dread in the pit of his stomach.

Over the next few days he saw that his fears were

justified. Dana began to withdraw from him again. She could pull back without saying a word. She'd stare at him blankly and let him see the emptiness. There was a perpetual frown on her lips, and dark smudges returned under her eyes. No matter how hard he tried to learn the cause, he kept bumping into silence. After days of feeling that happiness was within their reach, it suddenly seemed farther away than ever. It hurt all the more because he had no idea why this was happening. Dana evaded his questions with the deftness of a seasoned diplomat.

A few days after his visit Nick was sitting in his study supposedly going over the company books. Actually he was thinking more about Dana's odd mood. Tony crept in quietly and came to stand behind him, his elbows propped on the back of Nick's easy chair.

When Nick glanced around, Tony said, "Can we talk, Dad? You know, sort of man-of-man?"

Nick had to bite his lip to keep from smiling. Tony was far too serious to have his request taken lightly. He put down his pen and drew Tony to his side. "Sure, son. What did you want to talk about? Is there a problem at the day camp?"

"Nope. The camp's okay. I'm learning some neat stuff."

"That's terrific."

"It's okay." He shrugged dismissively. "But I wanted to ask you something about Ms. Brantley. Have you noticed how she's been acting kinda funny lately?"

Nick was instantly alert. If Tony had noticed, then

the problem was even more serious than he'd thought. No matter how distraught she'd been, she had always managed to hide it from Tony.

"What do you mean?"

"Well, like today. I went to the library right after camp and she wasn't in front like she usually is. The door to the back was closed, but I went in anyway and she was crying. I know I probably should have knocked, but I just forgot and she was real mad at me. She never used to get mad at me, Dad."

"Maybe she was just having a bad day. We all do sometimes. Did she say why she was crying?"

Tony shook his head. "But it's not the first time. I think somebody's making her afraid."

A frown knit Nick's brow. Tony was an unusual child in that he wasn't prone to flights of fancy. He'd never had an imaginary friend or exaggerated his exploits. If he thought Dana was afraid, then she probably was, but of what?

"Why would you think that?" Nick asked. "Has she said anything about being worried or afraid?"

"Not exactly, but you remember that day I had off from camp last week? Well, I went to the library earlier that day and Davey had just been there with the mail. When I went in, she was tearing up some letter."

"Maybe it was just junk mail."

"I don't think so, Dad, 'cause she burned it."

Nick was startled and more than a little unnerved. "She burned it?"

"Yeah, in the trash can, like you see sometimes on

TV. Do you think something's really wrong? I wouldn't want anybody to hurt Ms. Brantley."

Nick ruffled his son's hair, trying not to let him see the depth of his own concern. "We won't let that happen, Tony. I promise. Thanks for telling me."

Now more than ever Nick was determined to find out what was going on. That upsetting mail she was apparently getting would be a starting point. He wasn't about to give up on Dana without a fight. They'd come through too much already.

Nick made sure he was at the library day after day when the mail came. She usually left it in an untouched heap on her desk as they sat in her office sharing the sandwiches she once again automatically brought for them.

Fortunately, she didn't notice the way he surreptitiously sifted through the mail as he moved it aside, studying the return addresses, searching for something that might make an increasingly strong, always resilient woman cry. He had no doubt she'd be infuriated if she realized he was spying, no matter how well-intentioned his actions might be.

On the following Wednesday the stack was bigger than usual and Nick wasn't quite as quick. At first glance, it seemed as though there was nothing more than the familiar circulars for upcoming books, an assortment of magazines and end-of-the-month bills. Then he caught the panicked look in Dana's eyes as she spotted an envelope stuck between a farming journal and a women's magazine.

"I'll take all this," she said, grabbing for the mail. If it hadn't been for the edge of desperation in her voice, the offer might have seemed offhand and insignificant.

Nick let her take the stack, but he caught the edge of the letter and withdrew it.

"That, too," she said, reaching for it.

"What's so important about this?"

"Who said it was important? I just want to put it over here with the other stuff." Her feigned nonchalance was painfully transparent.

Nick held the letter away from her and studied the fearful look in her eyes. Tony was right. Whatever was in this envelope frightened her badly and she didn't want him to know about it.

"What is it about this letter that frightens you?"

"I'm not frightened."

"You are. I can see it in your eyes. You've had these letters before, haven't you?"

"Why would you say that?" The words were casual enough, but her tone was suddenly defensive. Nick knew he'd hit the mark.

"Because of the way you're acting. You're jumpy and irritable. It's not like you to snap, but you've been doing a lot of it lately."

Her eyes flashed at him. "If I'm snapping, it's because you seem to be intent on reading something that's personal. That letter is none of your business."

Nick ignored her anger. "You still haven't answered my question: have you had these before?"

"Yes, dammit! Now hand it over."

"So you can burn it?"

The mail fell to the floor as Dana shot him a startled glance. The color drained from her cheeks and her hands trembled, but she squared her shoulders and faced him defiantly. "How do you know about that?"

"Tony told me. He watched you do it. He's also seen you crying and it worried him. He finally came to me about it a few nights ago. Frankly, I'm glad he did. What's going on, Dana? Is Sam bothering you? If that's it, I'll take care of it. I'll go see him. We can get a court order, if that's what it takes."

She sank down in her chair and covered her face with her hands. Nick felt some of her fear steal into him, tying his stomach into knots.

"Dana?"

"It's not Sam."

"Then who? Is it some jilted lover who won't let go? Dana," he said softly. "Is that what it is? I can understand if there's some unresolved relationship in your past."

"If only it were that simple," she said with a rueful sigh. She glanced up at him. "After my marriage do you actually think I'd ever get seriously involved again?"

"You have with me."

"This is different. We're friends." The look she cast was pleading. It was clearly important to her that he accept that simplified definition of their increasingly complex relationship.

"Okay," he soothed. "If that's how you want to see it for the moment, I'll let it go. The important thing is these letters and what they're doing to you. Let me help. There's nothing we can't work out together."

"Not this," she said. "We can't solve this. Look what it's doing to us already. We're fighting about it."

"Sweetheart, I'm not fighting with you. I'm just trying to figure out why you're so afraid."

"Let it go."

"No. I've already done that too often. Let me see the letter."

She continued to hold it clutched tightly in her hand. Frustrated by her stubbornness and torn by her obvious distress, Nick risked infuriating her even more by snatching the letter away from her. To his surprise Dana accepted defeat stoically once he had it in his hands. Refusing to meet his gaze, she went to the window and stared out, her shoulders heaving with silent sobs.

Now that he had her tacit agreement, Nick held the cheap white envelope with its scrawled address and debated what to do. The honorable thing would be to give it back to Dana unopened, to let her deal with whatever crisis it represented in her own way. However, she wasn't dealing with it. Rather than asking for his help, she was allowing it to eat her alive. If the stress kept up much longer, she'd fall apart.

At the image of the deepening shadows under her eyes, he made his decision. He ripped open the envelope. At the sound of the paper tearing, he heard a muffled sob. It was almost his undoing, but in the end he knew he really had no choice if he was to help her.

"I'm sorry, Dana," he said finally, relentlessly taking the letter out of its envelope.

As he read the hastily penned lines, so filled with venom that they seemed to leap off the page, his complexion paled and his heart pounded slowly. He had no idea what he'd expected exactly, but it wasn't this. Dear God, in his wildest imaginings, he would never have considered something like this. He felt a surge of outrage on Dana's behalf even as bile rose in his throat.

At last, when he had won the fight for control over his churning emotions, his gaze lifted and met hers. Her eyes were filled with a heart-rending combination of anguish and dread.

"Is it true?" he asked, hating himself for even posing the question. His heart cried out that it had to be a lie. Yet on some instinctive level, he believed the words he'd read. They fit, like the last, crucial puzzle piece that made the picture complete.

"It's true," she said curtly.

Nick winced. He had to swallow hard to keep from barraging her with questions. She had to tell him the rest in her own time, but as he waited, he wondered if it was possible to go quietly mad in the space of a heartbeat.

He's so quiet, Dana thought miserably, watching Nick's struggle. *He must hate me now.* Then she wasn't thinking of Nick at all but of the horror of that night nearly eighteen months ago.

New Year's Eve, the beginning of a bright new year. What an incredible irony! Instead of bringing joy and anticipation, everything had ended on that night. There had been that split second of stunned disbelief, then a cold, jagged pain that tore at her insides and then, unbelievably, relief and a blessed emptiness. The guilt hadn't come until later. Much later.

And it had never gone away.

Now she looked directly into Nick's eyes and repeated quietly, "It is true. Every word of it."

She took a deep breath, then forced herself to say the words she'd never before spoken aloud.

"I killed my husband."

Chapter 12

The flat, unemotional declaration hung in the air between them. Dana had made her statement purposely harsh, wanting to shock Nick with the grim, unalterable truth. There was no point now in sparing him the ugliness.

As she had both feared and expected, his expression filled with stunned disbelief. He closed his eyes, and when he opened them it was as if he'd wrestled with some powerful, raging emotion. Finally, at immense cost, he brought it under control.

"How could you?" The words seemed to be torn from deep inside him.

Her lips twisted and she said bitterly, "Sometimes I only wonder how it took me so long."

Instinctively, he reached for her ice-cold hand and

caressed it, warming it. Then he released it, got up and walked away, prowling the room like an agitated tiger. Dana's breath caught in her throat as she waited nervously, watching the stark play of emotions on his face, praying for forgiveness or, at the very least, understanding.

When he finally turned back, to her amazement he apologized.

"I'm sorry. I didn't mean that accusingly, Dana. I meant that you're the gentlest person I've ever met. You couldn't even cut back that overgrown lilac bush, for heaven's sakes. I can't imagine you actually killing someone. God knows, from everything you've told me that husband of yours was sick and he probably deserved to die, but you…" His eyes were filled with pain and a tormented struggle for understanding.

Dana felt a new, raw anguish building up inside. She believed she was watching love wither and die right in front of her eyes. She deserved to lose his love. She'd been naive to dare to hope that with Nick things might be different, that eventually they could shape a future together without his ever learning the complete truth about her past. She'd wanted desperately to believe that he would never look at her the way he was staring at her now, his eyes filled with doubt and confusion and pain.

It had been a fool's dream. Secrets had a way of catching up with you, no matter how far you ran.

Just let him understand, she thought, then wondered if even that was asking too much. The real truth was that Nick was a compassionate, reasonable man. He saw honest, open dialogue as the solution to all problems. How could he possibly accept something as cold-blooded and final as murder? Never mind that the authorities had ruled it an accidental death. She was responsible just the same. Nick would have found some other way out of a situation as horrible as hers had been, but at the time, God help her, she'd felt trapped and defenseless and more alone than she'd ever imagined possible. Her troubles with Sam had escalated far beyond the reach of mere talk.

"Tell me about it," Nick said at last. "Please. I need to understand."

Dana sighed. She didn't want to relive that night. The events that had passed still came to her all too often in her dreams, tearing into middle-of-the-night serenity to shatter her all over again. During the day she was able to keep her thoughts at bay with hard work and endless, mind-numbing chores. Now a man she loved more than anything wanted her to explain that one moment in time, that single moment in her life that had changed things forever, and had made her an eternal captive of the past.

When she didn't speak, Nick pressured her, his words ripping into the silence. "Did you shoot him, stab him, what? For God's sakes, Dana, tell me. Nothing could be worse than what I'm imagining."

The demand for answers was raw and urgent. She couldn't possibly ignore it. Why keep it from him now, anyway? He already knew the worst, and if he was ever to fully comprehend the tragedy, he had to know everything.

"No, I didn't take out a gun and shoot him," she said, feeling numb and empty. Passiveness stole over her, distancing her from everything. She tried to blank out the horrifying images in her mind and envision only the words she had to say. "God knows, there were times when I wanted to, but I didn't have the courage."

She dared a glance at Nick and found there were tears of empathy that tore her in two.

"I know this is horrible for you. I can only imagine how horrible, but I have to know it all," he said with incredible gentleness. "If I'm going to help you, if we're going to put a stop to these letters and the threat they represent, I have to know exactly what happened."

Startled, she examined his expression and saw that he meant what he said. This wasn't the curiosity or pity she'd feared. There was no condemnation in his eyes. He needed to know not for himself but for her. Only time would tell if his feelings for her had really changed as a result of what he learned, but for now he was thinking only of protecting her from any more pain. He was viewing her as the victim, not the perpetrator. It was far more than she'd dared to hope, and a wave of incredible relief washed through her.

She took a deep breath and began again. Eyes closed, she spoke in a whisper, slowly, each hesitation an instant in which she relived the devastating horror of that last night with Sam.

"You know the background. This time it all started

at a party, I guess. Sam pulled me into the kitchen and accused me of flirting with some man. I don't really remember who, and it doesn't matter. It was always someone. His accusations were an excuse. When I denied everything, he pinned me against the wall and grabbed a butcher knife. He—"

She swallowed the lump in her throat. "He held it to my neck. I could feel the blade pressing against my skin."

She shuddered and clasped her arms around her middle. "Maybe it was because there were people nearby. Maybe it was just that I'd finally had too much and didn't care anymore. I don't know. Maybe I'd finally found my last shred of self-respect. Whatever it was, I screamed. I said if he ever came near me again, I'd kill him."

"And some people heard you say that."

"*Everyone* heard. They'd run toward the kitchen when they first heard me scream. Sam let me go, tried to make a joke of it. It was an awkward moment and everyone was obviously very relieved it was over. They were glad to take him at his word. But I knew that wasn't the end. I knew things would be worse than ever when we got home."

"Then why did you go? Why didn't you stay with a friend? Go to your parents? Anything, except go home with him."

Dana laughed, the sound echoing bitterly. "Would you believe that after all he'd done to me, I was still embarrassed? I still didn't want anyone to know. Everyone loved Sam. He was a real charmer. They only accepted me for his sake. My old school friends… I guess I'd cut myself off from them after the wedding. I'd tried so hard to fit in with his crowd."

When Nick attempted to protest, she stopped him. "No. It was true. In his circles I was an outsider. Because of that, I was at first afraid they wouldn't believe me. And then, after it had gone on for a while, I was too damned embarrassed to admit to anyone that I hadn't left him before."

"But just that one night, Dana. People knew you'd had a fight. No one would have questioned it if you'd just asked for a place to stay until your tempers cooled. They wouldn't have had to know about the rest."

"It all makes perfect sense when you say it, but you have to understand the syndrome. After a while you begin to feel utterly defeated and alone. You can't understand the true meaning of despair, Nick, until you've lived with it day after day, month after month. Not only that, Sam had repeatedly warned me that if I told anyone, if I tried to leave him, he'd come after me and make whoever took me in pay. I couldn't put anyone else at risk like that. And always, in the back of my mind, was that slim hope that this time would be different, that the wonderful man I'd fallen in love with would return, that he would be gentle and caring the way he was when we met. Some tiny part of me still loved that man."

She caught Nick's incredulous gaze, then glanced away. "I read something an abused woman in Maryland said not long ago. She said her marriage, her love for her husband in spite of all he'd done to her, was like an addiction. I think she's right. Making the decision to get out is no easier than kicking a drug habit or quitting smoking. All the well-meaning advice in the world won't make you leave, until you can admit to yourself that there *is* a problem."

"After all you'd been through, you couldn't admit even that much?"

"Not until that night. Until then, I had seen it as *my* failure."

Nick listened to the words and she could see that he was still tormented by the struggle to accept the twisted emotion behind them. Perhaps no one who hadn't experienced something like her situation could ever understand. She had made the only choices she could at the time, but she had learned from her mistakes. She would never again allow herself to be a victim.

"So you left together," Nick said, his tone dispassionate. It was as if he'd fought for objectivity and now clung to it desperately. "Did you fight on the way home?"

"No, the silence in the car was almost eerie. But by the time we got to our apartment, I thought maybe the worst of it was over after all."

Her lips curved in a wry grin. "'Hope springs eternal....' Isn't that what they say? As it turned out, that ride was simply the calm before an even more violent storm."

"What happened?"

"I went upstairs to the loft and began to get ready for bed. Sam stayed in the living room and had another drink. By the time he stumbled up the stairs, he was muttering jealous accusations again.

"I heard him and knew what was going to happen. I ran for the bathroom, planning to lock myself in, but he caught me. He grabbed my arm and whirled me around." Unconsciously she rubbed her arm where the bruises had marred her delicate skin for days afterward. She closed her eyes and the images flooded back.

"Sam was a handsome man, but that night his face was twisted with fury. He was somebody I couldn't even recognize. It was a frightening transformation, as if he'd finally gone over the edge. He was beyond thinking, beyond reasoning.

"When he pulled back his fist to hit me, something finally snapped inside me for the second time that night. I woke up to the reality. I knew then that things would never change, that if I didn't get myself out I was condemning myself to an eternal hell. I was the only one who could decide how I was going to spend the rest of my life."

"And so you fought back."

"This time I fought back with more strength than I imagined I had. I hit him first. The blow wasn't much, but it was enough to throw him off balance, and I ran toward the stairs. He lunged after me."

Her eyes clamped more tightly shut as tears began to roll down her cheeks. Even with her eyes closed, the visions came back, as vivid as the night it had happened. She shuddered.

"God, it was awful. Sam was very drunk, clumsy. I shoved him back, moved out of the way."

Suddenly she was choking, sobbing as the memories flooded back. "He...he threw...threw himself at me again."

She covered her face with hands that were shaking violently. "Then—I can't remember how—then he was falling, head over heels, down the stairs. Maybe I even pushed him. I don't know. There are a few missing seconds in my mind, a complete blank. The psychiatrist says I'll remember when I'm ready."

"Oh, babe." Nick reached out to her, but she shivered and pulled away.

The words came faster now, as if by getting them all out, by telling the whole story, it would somehow cleanse her at last.

"When I came to, I was standing at the top of the steps, shaking, staring down at him, his body all crumpled, his leg stuck out at an odd angle. I thought I heard him moan, but I was terrified to go down there. I couldn't bear the thought of touching him. It must have been ten minutes or more before I finally called the rescue squad, but it was too late. He was dead."

She sighed heavily and opened her eyes. "I'd already guessed as much. The police came and they called Sam's parents in Omaha. His mother was hysterical. She had to be hospitalized. Later they made a lot out of the fact that I was so calm. The doctor said it was due to shock, but Sam's mother and father didn't see it that way. Then a few people came forward and told about the threat I'd made at the party. The whole thing blew up into a pretty nasty scandal."

"But, Dana, it wasn't murder. It was an accident. That's all, and it's over now."

She shook her head. "That's what the court said, but it will never be over. His parents can't let it go. They've convicted me."

Her voice was flat and she stared at Nick with eyes that were empty. "And don't you see? That's not what really matters anyway, because of the way I felt."

"I don't understand."

"I was glad he was dead." Her tear-filled eyes gazed at Nick and her chin lifted defiantly. "I didn't mean to do it, I didn't mean for it to go that far, but I was glad that it was finally over. What kind of person does that make me?"

"A desperate one. A woman who had been hurt time and time again by a man she loved."

Nick's own eyes were damp and his whole body seemed to be shaking, but he took her in his arms and held her until both their trembling abated. Dana clung to him, drawing on his strength.

"Oh, babe, it's going to be okay," he promised. "It may take some time, but it will be okay."

Dana wanted desperately to believe Nick, but she'd lived through too much to believe in miracles. "You can't dismiss it that easily, Nick. Sam Brantley is dead because of me, and his parents will see to it that the story follows me wherever I go."

"There must be a way to stop them. We can see a lawyer this afternoon."

"It's too late. People here already know. I don't know how they found out, but they've obviously heard something. You've seen how I've been shunned the last few weeks. The word is spreading. It's bound to blow up pretty soon. The Brantleys won't rest until it does."

"Then that's all the more reason for us to fight back."

"For *me* to fight back, not us, Nick. It's my battle, one I'd hoped to avoid, but I'm going to stay here and fight it. I like River Glen. I'm happy with my new life. I won't let them take it away from me. I won't be victimized again."

She touched his lips with trembling fingers. "It's different for you, though. If you stay with me now, it will kill whatever chances you might have for a state or national political office."

"How can you even think about something like that? To hell with a political office, if the cost includes giving you up. Being a politician has never been my dream."

"But Betsy told me—"

"She told you that people around here think I should run for the General Assembly. That doesn't mean I've wanted to. I like what I do. Being a contractor, a father to Tony and maybe someday a husband to you—that's all I want. I have a good life, Dana. A rich, full life. I don't need to be running off to Richmond or Washington."

"If you gave that up for me, though, I could never

forgive myself. It's more than enough for me just to know you'd be willing to."

"I'm not giving up anything important. Maybe if we hadn't met, I would have run for office just because it would have filled the empty spaces in my life, given me something meaningful to do after Tony's grown. But there are no empty spaces now."

Dana watched in wonder as he opened his arms. She tried to read his expression, searching for doubts, but there were none. She found only unquestioning love that sent a wild thrill coursing through her.

"Are you sure?"

"Very sure."

After an endless hesitation, she nodded and stepped into his arms.

Chapter 13

The provocative sensation of Dana nestled in his arms, drawing comfort from his embrace, her body settled between his splayed legs, stirred far more than Nick's protective instincts. He wanted her with an untimely, unreasoning desire. For weeks now he had tempered his ardor, but he could no more. His blood roared through his veins, stirring a fierce, urgent passion. A low moan rumbled deep in his throat as he tightened his arms around her.

"I need you, Nick." The tentatively spoken appeal wrenched his heart.

"You have me, sweetheart. I'm not going anywhere."

Round eyes, shimmering with tears, stared back at him. "No. I mean I really need you. I need to be with you." Her voice broke. "Please. Make love to me, Nick. Help me prove to myself that I can still feel."

His heart hammered harder. He brushed her mussed hair back from her face and studied her expression. He was searching for a hint of the fear he'd seen so often in her eyes whenever he'd openly wanted her. He understood that fear now, knew its cause, and he wanted no part in resurrecting it. If he had to wait forever for Dana to feel right about the two of them as lovers, he would.

"Are you sure? You're very vulnerable right now. I don't want to take advantage of that."

"But you do want me, don't you?"

He drew in a ragged breath. "Oh, yes. Never doubt that, Dana. I want you so badly it frightens me. I've spent weeks lying awake at night wanting to hold you in my arms, wanting to explore every inch of your body with my kisses, wanting to bury myself in you. But now, Dana? Today? I don't know."

She bit her lower lip to still the trembling. "Because of what you found out about me? Does it bother you so much?"

He ached for her and cursed himself for raising new self-doubts in her. He should have realized instantly that this had been her greatest fear of all, that this was what had kept her silent.

"No, my love. It's not that. I swear it. I don't blame you for anything that happened in your past. I just don't want you to have regrets. If we make love now, with all that's gone on today, won't you wonder later why you did it?"

She shook her head, her brown eyes never leaving his face. They shone with surprising self-confidence.

"I know why, Nick. I love you. I was afraid to admit it before today. Even if you can't love me, I have to tell you how I feel."

She rubbed an unsteady finger across his lips and they burned in the wake of that fiery, gentle touch. "You've made me feel whole again. No matter what happens between us, you've given me that and no one will ever take that feeling from me again."

She said it solemnly, with absolute conviction, and Nick felt something tear loose inside him. Doubts fled and passion rampaged more violently than ever. He wouldn't make her ask again.

He nodded and took her hand. "Let's go home."

A sweet, sensual tension throbbed between them as Dana closed the library, turning off the lights in the back, making a sign for the door announcing that it would open again in the morning. It was nothing more than routine and yet there was nothing ordinary about it. The tasks took on a heightened significance. By the time she turned her key in the lock at last, Nick's nerves were stretched taut with anticipation.

"We'll take your car," he said, holding out his hand for the keys. She dropped them into his hand without comment.

During the brief drive to her house, he glanced at her often, still looking for some sign of reluctance, any indication that she was already regretting her impulsive declaration. He found none.

Dana met each glance with a faint smile that was almost shy in its pleasure. That look made Nick want to slay dragons for her. Perhaps, he thought once, perhaps that's what I'm doing.

When they reached the cottage, he turned off the ignition, then twisted around to read her expression again.

"Any second thoughts?"

"None," she said without hesitation. "This feels right for me, Nick."

"It feels right for me, too."

When she started to open the car door, he stopped her. "There's one more thing I want you to know now, before we go inside."

"What?"

"I love you, Dana. I don't ever want you thinking that we're here for any other reason." He touched her cheek and repeated quietly, "I love you."

A sigh shuddered through her. "Thank you for saying that. Thank you for everything."

The walk to the back door seemed endless. Nick's sharpened senses were overwhelmed by the heavy scent of an array of colorful blossoms, the summer sounds of birdsong and bees hovering over the flower beds and the subtly provocative sway of Dana's hips as she made her way through the ankle-high grass dotted with buttercups and dandelions.

On the way, Nick plucked a pale pink rose from a bush at the side of the house. He stripped it of its thorns and tucked it into Dana's dark hair, his fingers lingering to caress the sun-kissed warmth of her cheek.

"You are so beautiful," he murmured. "This setting suits you. There's a surprisingly earthy sensuality about you."

She smiled at him and reached up to touch the rose. "Why surprising?"

"Because for so long you only allowed me to see the cool indifference, the sophistication."

"I had no choice, Nick. I was too frightened to allow anyone to get too close, especially you."

"Why especially me?"

"Because I sensed from the beginning that this day would come. Even when I was fighting you the hardest, I trusted you and I wanted you. It terrified me, because the last time I felt that way about anyone—"

"I know. You were betrayed."

"No," she said sharply. "It was worse than a betrayal. It was a mockery of what love was supposed to be."

"That's all behind you now."

She shook her head. "No. It's still very much with me, but I can deal with it now. As long as I have you, I can face it."

"You have me," he whispered, his lips claiming hers in gentle confirmation of the promise.

From that moment on, things seemed to happen in slow motion, each sensation drawn out over time until it peaked at some impossible height of awareness. Dana moved through the house in a reversal of her routine at the library, opening windows, allowing the breeze to air the rooms. When she was finished she came back to the kitchen, where Nick was waiting, his heart in his throat.

"I couldn't find any champagne," he said, holding up two glasses of apple juice. "We'll have to toast with this."

Dana took a glass, her hand trembling. But when she met his eyes, her gaze was steady, sure.

"To beginnings," Nick whispered, touching his glass to hers.

"And to the endings that make them possible."

They sipped solemnly, their gazes clashing. It was Dana who took the glasses and set them aside. She reached for the buttons on his shirt, never taking her eyes from his. "Do you mind?"

"Be my guest."

His pulse raced as her fingers fumbled at their task. When his shirt was finally open, she touched the tips of her fingers to his heated flesh, at first tentatively and then with more confidence. Nick felt the wild pounding of his heart, the surge of his blood, and wondered just how much of the unbearable tension he could take. But it had to be this way. Dana had to be the aggressor. She had to see that with him she could be in control, not just of her own responses but of his. This first time had to have beauty and love and, perhaps most important of all, respect.

She ran her palms across his chest in a slow, sweeping gesture that set his skin on fire. When she left the matted hair on his chest and reached the curve of his shoulders, she caught the edges of his shirt and slipped it off, leaving him bare to the waist.

Her eyes lifted tentatively to meet his. "Okay?"

"Whatever you want," he said on a ragged sigh. "This is your show. You set the pace."

Her gaze swept over him lazily, and where it lingered, her touch followed so predictably that Nick could anticipate each one. The curve where neck met shoulder. The tensed muscles in his arms. The masculine nipples almost hidden beneath coarse, dark hair. The flat plane of his stomach.

But if Dana's touches were predictable, Nick's responses were another thing entirely. Never had he anticipated the sweet yearning that was building inside him. Never could he have predicted the urgent hunger, the demanding need that made his legs tremble and tightened his muscles until they ached for release. Never before had he known it was possible to feel so much at the simple brush of a finger, at the fleeting touch of lips. If Dana's thoughts were bold, her exploration was still shy and all the more exciting because of it.

She sighed softly. "I've wanted to do this for so long." She looked into his eyes. "Would you kiss me again?"

Nick touched one finger to her chin, tilted her face up and very slowly lowered his mouth to hers. The first kiss was sweet and gentle. The next was an urgent claiming. His body shook with the effort of restraint. When he would have pulled away, Dana slid her arms around his neck.

"No," she cried out softly, and this time it was her passion, her hunger, that showed him the way.

"Take me to bed, Nick," she said at last. "Make love to me."

Nick scooped her into his arms without comment, his mouth claiming hers again as he moved through the hall. Dana's shoes fell to the floor. Her arms circled his shoulders and she rained kisses on his cheeks, his nose, his neck and then, at last, his mouth, lingering there for a sensual dueling of tongues that left Nick gasping.

Before they even reached the bedroom, Nick had lowered her to her feet, allowing her to slide down his fully aroused body, wanting her to know in full measure what her touch had accomplished.

"I need you very badly," he said, tilting her hips hard against him. She held back for just an instant, then swayed toward him emitting a low whimper of pleasure. "Very badly."

Dana heard the urgency in his hoarse cry and felt at first a momentary fear, then a blessed sense of triumph. This was love as it should be, demand tempered with caring, need gentled by tenderness. She caught Nick's hands and drew them to the buttons on her blouse.

"Your turn."

His fingers were much more certain than hers had been, but still she felt the trembling as they grazed her skin. She watched his eyes and in their hazel depths she saw what she had never thought to see again. She saw love. So much love that it made her ache inside. She saw her beauty reflected in his eyes, and in that awed appreciation she found contentment, a serenity that would carry her through all time.

Her blouse fell away and then the lacy wisp of her bra. Nick cupped the fullness of her breasts in his hands, rubbing the nipples with his thumb until the peaks were sensitive coral buds more than ready for the soothing moistness of his tongue. The flick of his tongue magnified the sensitivity, sending waves of pleasure rippling through her.

When he reached for the clasp on her skirt, she drew in her breath, holding it as the skirt drifted down to her ankles. She stepped out of the circle of material, then waited, breathless, as he hooked his fingers in the edge of her slip and panties together and slid them off.

When she was standing before him completely nude and open to his touch, a shudder swept through him.

"You are so beautiful," he breathed softly. "So very beautiful."

"Only with you, Nick. I feel beautiful with you."

He scooped her into his arms again and at last they finished the journey to the bedroom. When Nick lowered her to the bed at last, Dana felt as if she had finally reached the edge of forever.

She watched through partially lowered lashes as Nick removed the rest of his clothes, then stood before her in unself-conscious splendor, his body as finely tuned and well muscled as an athlete's, tanned and proud. Her lips curved into a smile and she tilted her head thoughtfully.

"I think, perhaps, you're the one who's beautiful," she whispered huskily.

The mattress dipped as Nick stretched out beside her. A smile played about his lips and laughter danced in his eyes. "We could fight about which one of us is more beautiful."

Dana shook her head. "No fighting. Not now and certainly not about that. We have better things to do."

"We do?"

She rolled toward him, feeling the first thrilling shock of having the full length of his body against hers. "We most definitely do," she said as her mouth found his.

Nick's hands claimed her with a gentleness that she blessed at first, then came to curse. She wanted more than the light, skimming, feathery touches and she urged him on, gasping when he moved from the tender flesh of her thighs to the moist heat between her legs. He hesitated until she put her hand on his and encouraged more.

An unbearable tension coiled inside her until she was pleading for release, begging Nick to set her free. Unaccountably, his fingers stilled as he insisted that she drift back to earth and join him.

Her body glistened with perspiration, more sensitive than ever to his gliding touch.

"Why are you waiting?" she asked, confused and let down.

"This is your trip, Dana. I want to be very sure we take it when you're ready."

Suddenly she understood what he was doing and she felt a swell of love in her chest. "You told me once you'd know when I was ready."

"Oh, I think you are, but it's your decision, your move."

She knelt on the bed beside him. "Now, Nick. I'm ready now."

A faint smile touched his lips as he grasped her and lifted her into position straddling him. Slowly, with the utmost care, he settled her in place. As he filled her, Dana knew a glorious instant of possession and then she was beyond thought. She was only feeling as she rode him, taking her pleasure from him. The spiral of tension wound tight again and then, like a top, she was spinning free, exultant, taking Nick with her in a burst of joy that set them both free from the past and sent them whirling on, into the future.

Much later Dana awoke in Nick's arms, feeling secure and unafraid in the circle of his strength. The bedroom was in the shadows of twilight, and in the dim, gray light, she watched him sleeping and thought again how incredibly handsome he was and how utterly right their love was.

She must have sighed because Nick's arms tightened just a little and he murmured, "What is it? Are you okay?"

"I am—" she searched for the perfect word "—complete."

His fingers ran through her hair, combing the tangles free. "You're not sore? I didn't hurt you?"

"You could never hurt me."

"I hope not, Dana."

She was troubled by his too-somber tone. She propped herself up on his chest and ran her hand along the curve of his jaw, peering intently into his eyes. "Why do you say it like that?"

He caught the tension in her at once. "Oh, sweetheart, don't look so serious. I didn't mean anything by it. It's just that it's impossible to predict whether we'll ever hurt someone. I'm sure in the beginning Sam didn't realize he would hurt you."

Dana flung herself away from him and in a voice icy with anger she said, "I don't want Sam Brantley in this bed with us, Nick. Not ever. There's no comparison between the two of you."

Nick sat up and put his arms around her shaking shoulders, soothing her until he finally heard her sigh.

"I'm sorry," she said. "I shouldn't have exploded like that. It's just that I don't want to ruin what we have."

"No. I'm the one who's sorry. I shouldn't have brought up Sam. Do you suppose we can get back to us?"

"What about us?"

"Well, for instance, are you interested in getting out of this bed and getting some dinner?"

"Dinner's an interesting option," she conceded. "But I have a better alternative."

"What's that?"

"I'll show you."

And she did. Again and again, Dana tried to show Nick just how much he had freed her from her worst memories. She replaced old nightmares with new dreams. She was fire in his arms and he was more than willing to be consumed by her flame. She took what he offered and tried to give it back tenfold, proving without a doubt the depth of her love.

Then, sated at last, they slept again.

Chapter 14

When Dana awoke, pale streaks of dawn lit the room and Nick was gone, his place in her bed already cool. For an instant she panicked, her heart thumping wildly. Why hadn't she noticed this sooner? How had she slept through his leaving?

Then she saw the note propped on her bedside table.

It's very late. You were sleeping so peacefully I didn't want to wake you. I had to borrow your car to pick up Tony. I'll come by for you in the morning.

Love, Nick.

"Love, Nick." She repeated the words aloud, just to hear how they sounded. They sounded wonderful. Terrific. Great. She pulled his pillow into her arms and inhaled deeply, enjoying the lingering traces of his rich masculine scent, recalling in sensuous detail his possessive branding of her body. Her flesh still burned at the memory of his wicked touch. She was Nick's now in every way that counted.

She discovered with a sense of astonishment she was at peace at last. Her thoughts were decidedly pleasant, her heart incredibly light. The past was still very much with her, but it was where it properly belonged: behind her. Nick was her present, and if good fortune remained with her, he would be her future, as well.

She bounded out of bed and scurried into the shower, filled with plans for the day, beginning with a huge, sinfully caloric breakfast to make up for the dinner they'd never found time for. She sang lustily as the water flowed over her, soothing the unfamiliar aching in her thighs. She washed her hair with her favorite herbal shampoo and then toweled herself dry until her skin glowed with a healthy blush and her hair fell to her shoulders in a damp, shining cloud that would have to wait for the taming of brush and dryer.

She straightened the tangled sheets on the bed with a smile of remembrance on her lips and moved through the house in search of stray clothing that had been tossed aside haphazardly in the night's urgency. When the last traces of their passion had been removed from everything except her memory, she began to prepare their meal—bacon, waffles, eggs, fresh-squeezed orange juice and raspberry jam. She found a vase for the rose that Nick had picked for her and set it in the middle of the table.

With an uncanny sense of timing, Nick pulled up out front just as the waffle iron hissed its readiness when she sprinkled a few drops of water on its heated surface. She threw open the back door and waited for him to turn the corner of the house. For just an instant his expression was unguarded and troubled, but when he saw her waiting there, his eyes lit up and he smiled one of his beguilingly crooked grins.

"I hope you're hungry," she announced.

"I am," he said, stealing a kiss that rocked her senses. "For you."

"In that case, you should have been here at dawn. Now you'll have to settle for breakfast."

He seemed to bristle at her comment. "You know why I had to leave, don't you?"

Puzzled by his sharp tone, she said, "Of course. You had to get home to Tony. I wasn't criticizing."

He raked his fingers through his hair. "Sorry. I suppose I'm just a little out of sorts."

Dana studied his expression more closely and saw the tiny tension lines around his set mouth, the shadows in his eyes.

"Not enough sleep?" she asked, guessing at the cause.

Nick drew in a deep breath. "Not exactly."

His mood frightened her. "What is it, Nick? What's really bothering you? Are you regretting last night?"

"No. Of course not," he said quickly, but for some reason it didn't reassure her.

"Then what?"

"Let's go in and sit down."

She dug in her heels and put her hands on her hips defiantly. "Just tell me."

He sighed heavily. "Have you seen today's paper?"

"No, I get it at the library. Why?"

But before he could respond, she knew. As surely as if she'd read each word, she knew.

"Oh, no," she breathed softly. "Is it the Brantleys?"

Nick nodded. "They sent in a letter to the editor."

He reached out to circle her shoulders and draw her close. Dana trembled violently in the embrace. "How bad is it?" she asked, her voice muffled against the warm solidity of his chest.

"It's all there. Everything." She looked up in time to see a rueful grin. "Or almost everything. I've already called a lawyer and explained the situation. He seems to think there's not much we can do. They've been very careful with their accusations. There's nothing really libelous in there. They've stuck pretty close to the court records."

"But the court declared me innocent."

"Yes, well, that's the one little fact the Brantleys didn't mention."

"You know Cyrus Mason. Will he let me tell my side of it in tomorrow's paper?"

Nick frowned. "Are you sure that's what you want

to do? Do you really want to open up your past after you've tried so hard to forget it?"

"If I'm going to live in this town, I have to," she said with absolute certainty. "The Brantleys took the decision out of my hands."

"I see your point. But we'll go to the newspaper office together."

"No, Nick. I want to go alone. It's way past time I stood up for myself. Did you bring the paper?"

"It's in the car."

"Get it, Nick," she said. She felt her anger begin to build, fortifying her for the battle ahead. "I might as well see what I'm up against."

It was even worse than she'd imagined. There were innuendoes from her in-laws, unsubstantiated by police records, that she'd been drinking heavily the night of the accident. There was mention of the party, made out to seem far wilder than it was. There were suggestions that she had a history of instability, that she'd been hospitalized often for undisclosed reasons.

Facts had been taken and twisted to make a sensational story. The point? To attack her fitness as a public employee. It was the damning work of two people who had promised revenge and gotten it.

She looked up from the paper, her eyes blazing.

"They won't get away with it," she vowed. "I will not let them cost me my job, my new life."

"No," Nick said softly, his eyes shining with pride. He lifted her clenched fist to his lips and brushed a kiss across her knuckles. "This time I don't think they will."

Anxious to get on with things, she asked, "Do you still want breakfast?"

"No. I don't think either of us has the stomach for it."

"Then let me clean this up and we'll go."

She left the dishes on the table, dumped the waffle batter down the drain and slid the eggs and bacon into the garbage. Pots and pans were left stacked in the sink. Her resolve grew with every minute.

"Wish me luck," she said a half hour later as she dropped Nick off by the library so he could pick up his truck.

He grinned at her. "For some reason, I don't think you'll need it. I'll stop by the library later to see how it went."

He had started away from the car when she called him back. She touched the hand that rested on the car and gazed up at him. "Thank you."

"For what?"

"For giving me back my strength, for reminding me of who I was before Sam Brantley came along."

"I didn't do that, Dana. You did."

He leaned down and brushed his lips across hers. The kiss was greedy, but it was meant to reassure and it did. She drove away with fire in her veins and determination in her eyes.

She stalked into the *River Glen Chronicle*'s office a few minutes later and demanded to see the editor. No one dared to ask if she had an appointment. They just pointed her in the direction of a tiny, cluttered office that was littered with old newspapers and half-empty Styrofoam coffee cups.

She waited on her feet for the return of Cyrus Mason, the man listed on the masthead as editor and publisher. She paced the well-worn floor, fueling her anger and readying her arguments. By the time he came in, his shirtsleeves rolled up, his tie askew, Dana was prepared.

Apparently he was already well aware of her seething anger, because he treated her gingerly.

"Mrs. Brantley, won't you sit down?"

"You can. I don't want to." She threw the morning paper on his desk. "How dare you?"

He had no need to ask what she meant. "It was a legitimate letter," he said defensively.

"Legitimate? You call that pack of innuendoes legitimate? How carefully did you check it out, Mr. Mason? How far did you go to verify the facts? Not very far, I suspect."

"We—"

Dana didn't take note of his interruption. She never even took a breath. "If you had, you would know that I was acquitted of all charges in my husband's death on the grounds of self-defense. You would have learned that for five long years that paragon of virtue they described abused me."

Cyrus Mason turned pale. He ran his tongue over too-dry lips as Dana rushed on.

"I learned how to hide my bruises. Like a fool, I tried to protect my dignity and Sam Brantley's by keeping silent, but it all came out in court. Those hospital records they mentioned will show that I was admitted time and again to recover from the beatings their precious son gave me. Now, Mr. Mason, are you prepared to print that, as well?"

She was leaning across his desk, staring into his wide eyes, watching the beads of perspiration form on his brow. "Well, Mr. Mason?"

He swallowed nervously. "I had no idea."

"No, you didn't, did you? Isn't that your responsibility, though, Mr. Mason? Or were you afraid that the truth would ruin a sensational little tidbit for today's paper?"

"Mrs. Brantley, please, I'm very sorry."

"Sorry won't do it, Mr. Mason. This is a small town and my reputation is at stake. I want a complete and accurate report in tomorrow's paper or I will personally see to it that your lawyer spends every cent of your money defending a libel suit."

Dana knew she was bluffing at the end, but the quaking Mr. Mason did not. Perhaps he even had some sense of justice buried in his soft folds of flesh.

"I'll do whatever you like."

Dana nodded in satisfaction. "Send a reporter in. I'll do the rest."

She spent the better part of the morning with the reporter, detailing step by step the agony she had survived in her marriage. The reporter, a young girl barely out of college, had tears in her eyes when they finished talking.

"Why are you doing this?" she asked. "How can you bear to tell everyone what you suffered?"

Dana thought about the question. Until that moment, she hadn't been quite sure what her motivation was. Revenge? The salvaging of her own reputation? Or something more?

"I think maybe this is something I should have done a long time ago. Maybe by telling what I went through, it will help some other woman to avoid the tragedy of a wasted life. If just one woman reads this and finds the strength to ask for help, maybe it will give some meaning to those five years I spent in hell."

A rueful smile touched her lips as she continued. "Or perhaps I just needed to get it out of my system for my own sake, so I can move on. Maybe there's nothing honorable about my intentions at all."

The girl was shaking her head. "I don't think you can dismiss what you're doing so lightly. I think you're very brave."

"I wish I had been five or six years ago," Dana said with genuine regret. "Then perhaps Sam Brantley would still be alive."

Dana drove to the library feeling as though a tremendous burden had been lifted from her shoulders. Whatever happened now, she could deal with it. She could move on with her life. If she had a life left.

By midday she had already heard there were efforts to see that she was removed as librarian. Betsy was the bearer of the bad news.

"Dana, they've been swarming all over town hall

like bees. I tried to talk them out of it, but you know how quick some folks are to make judgments. They think you're going to corrupt the young people and turn the whole town into some sort of Peyton Place. You've never heard such ridiculous carrying on."

"I think I probably have," Dana retorted mildly. "Maybe when they see the whole story in the paper tomorrow, they'll stop and think about what they're doing."

"What if they don't? Tomorrow may be too late, anyway. Some folks don't give a hang about the truth. They'd just as soon run you out of town tonight."

"What about you, Betsy? You've already jumped to my defense and you don't even know what really happened."

"Good grief, girl, I don't have to ask. I know you about as well as I could ever know a daughter of my own. Whatever happened back then, you weren't to blame. Harry believes that, too."

Humbled by Betsy's trust, Dana had tears glistening in her eyes. "How can I ever thank you?"

"You just stick around here and fight back. Don't you go running anywhere."

"I'm not running this time, Betsy. I have something to stay and fight for."

"Nick?"

"Nick."

"Oh, child, I couldn't be happier."

"Neither could I."

But even that happiness was doomed to be short-lived. Betsy had no sooner left the ominously deserted library than Jessica Leahy came in. She circled Dana's desk like a wary fighter assessing his opponent.

"I saw the paper," she said at last.

"But you already knew, didn't you?"

Jessica nodded. "I had heard something about it. Mildred Tanner's son is a lawyer in New York. He told her, and she told me right after Tony's birthday party."

For a fraction of a second there was a look of regret in her eyes, then they were a cold, stormy gray again. "Despite what you think, I didn't want to believe it."

"I think perhaps you did."

"No, Dana. I asked Nick to talk to you. I wanted you to tell him it was all lies. I didn't want it to come to this. I didn't want to be forced into a showdown with Nick."

A twisting knot formed in Dana's stomach. "What kind of a showdown?"

"If Nick persists in this craziness of his, this idea of marrying you, then I'm going to court tomorrow to ask for custody of Tony. I think after he hears this, after he sees what kind of a woman Nick plans to bring into my grandson's life, I think the judge will grant my request."

"No!" The word echoed through the room. "You can't do that. It's so unfair."

"What you did was more than unfair. You took your husband's life."

"You're wrong, Jessica." Nick's voice was icy with rage. Neither of them had heard him enter and they turned to stare at him.

"We'll see who's wrong, Nicholas," Jessica said, undaunted by his fury and not waiting to hear more. "We'll see about that."

Then she turned and left, her back stiff, her chin held high.

In her wake, she left a terrible, gut-wrenching fear.

Chapter 15

Nick slammed his fist against the wall. "Damn her for this! I warned her to stay out of it."

"You knew she was considering this?" Dana said, horrified by what Jessica Leahy was threatening and equally astonished that Nick had apparently been aware of it. "You knew she was going to fight you for custody?"

"I thought she'd come to her senses."

"Nick, you have to go after her. You have to stop it."

Nick just stood there, obviously torn between offering support to her and going after his former mother-in-law.

"Go," Dana urged. "You can't let her go into court over this. You mustn't let Tony get caught in the middle because of me. Dear God, Nick, you could lose your son."

"It won't come to that," Nick said, his teeth clenched. "I won't allow it to come to that."

"The only way to stop it is to talk to her."

Troubled eyes surveyed her. "Will you be all right?"

"I'll be fine as soon as I know you've been able to resolve this with Jessica."

Nick nodded and left, leaving Dana's emotions whirling. What if he couldn't make Jessica back down? What if she insisted on going through with the custody battle?

Then she would have to leave River Glen after all. There would be no alternative. Dana wouldn't allow herself to come between Nick and his son.

It was one of the longest afternoons of Dana's life. Not one person came into the library. No one called. By six o'clock her nerves were stretched to the limit and her stomach was churning. On the short drive home, she almost ran her car off the road because she wasn't concentrating and missed a curve.

At home she was no better. She put the unused breakfast dishes away—in the refrigerator—and washed the pots and pans with laundry detergent. Then she scrubbed the kitchen floor, trying to work out her fears and anger with each swipe of the mop. She fixed a sandwich, then threw it in the trash after taking one bite.

When the phone rang, she knocked over her glass of tea in her haste to get to it, then skidded on the pool of liquid and nearly lost her balance.

"Yes. Hello," she said breathlessly.

"Dana, it's Betsy."

Disappointment flooded through her. "Oh."

"Were you expecting someone else?"

"I was hoping Nick would call."

Her comment was greeted with a silence that went on far too long. "Betsy, what is it? Is it about Nick?"

"Nick's at town hall. They called a special meeting to decide what to do about you and your job. It starts in a half hour."

Dana sank down in a kitchen chair and rubbed her hand across her eyes. The dull pounding in her head picked up in speed and intensity.

"Should I come down there?"

"Nick told me not to call. He said you'd already been through too much today, but I think perhaps you should be here. After all, it's your fate they're deciding. You should have a chance to speak up for yourself."

"Thanks, Betsy. I'll be there in a few minutes."

When Dana got to town hall, she could hardly find a place to park. She didn't consider it a good sign that most of the town had turned out for this impromptu meeting. It had all the characteristics of a lynch mob. The phone lines must have been buzzing all afternoon. She could hear the shouts through the building's opened windows.

Reluctantly she climbed the front steps and went down the hall to the auditorium, trying her best to ignore the occasional stares in her direction. The doors had been propped open to allow for the overflow of people who were milling around in the corridor before the meeting officially got under way. Most were so busy spreading their own versions of the gossip they took little note of Dana's arrival. She slipped inside the room and stood by the back wall.

Moments later the mayor gaveled the meeting to order. It took some time for everyone to calm down. Dana saw Nick and Betsy at the front, along with the council members. Jessica Leahy was only two rows from the front, her expression grim and very determined.

Suddenly Dana felt a tug on her arm and looked around to see Tony at her side, his eyes bright with unshed tears.

"Tony! What are you doing here?"

"I was supposed to be with Grandpa, but I snuck out. I heard they were going to try to get rid of you."

Dana was stumped over what to tell him other than the truth. "That's what some people would like to do."

"But why? You can't go away, Ms. Brantley. Dad and me need you." He wrapped his arms around her waist and buried his head against her side. She could feel the hot dampness of his tears through her blouse.

Dana tried to swallow the lump in her throat and blinked back her own tears. "Let's go outside."

"No," he said, clinging harder. "I want to stay."

"No. I think we'd better talk."

She took Tony's hand and led him outside. At the moment, as frightened as she was about her own future, nothing was more important than trying to explain to him what was happening.

"Let's sit over here," she said, drawing him toward the wide concrete railing alongside the steps. He sat as close to her as he could, his thin shoulders shaking. Dana put an arm around him and sighed. "How much do you know?"

"Only what Grandma said. She told Grandpa they were going to run you out of town on a rail."

"Did she say why?"

"I couldn't hear everything. Grandpa kept telling her to keep her voice down."

Dana took a deep breath. "Okay. Let me try to explain what's happening so you can understand it."

She paused, trying to figure out how on earth she was going to do that. How did you tell a ten-year-old boy that you were responsible for your husband's death? If adults found it inexplicable, what on earth would Tony think?

"You know that I was married before?" she began at last.

He nodded. "Dad told me. He said you weren't anymore, though."

"Well, that's true. When I was married, it wasn't like it was for your mother and father. They loved each other very much. Sam and I loved each other, but we weren't very happy. Sometimes we got really angry and we fought."

"Lots of grown-ups do that."

"That's right. One night Sam and I argued and he… he fell down some stairs."

"Was he hurt bad?"

"Yes, Tony. He was hurt very badly. He died."

Tony seemed more perplexed than ever. "And that's why they want you to go away? That doesn't make any sense."

"Some people don't understand what really happened that night. They think I made Sam fall on purpose. They don't think a person who did something like that should be around kids."

"But you didn't mean to do it."

Dana hugged him. A tear spilled over and ran down her cheek. "No. I didn't mean to do it."

"Then go tell them, so it'll be okay." He wrapped his arms tight around her. "I don't want you to leave."

"She won't have to, son."

Dana and Tony both looked up to find Nick towering over them. She tried to read his expression, afraid to hope that his words meant what she thought.

"It's over?" she whispered, suddenly very, very scared.

He sat down next to her and took her hand. "It's over."

"And?"

"They want you to stay on."

Relief and confusion warred for her emotions. "But how? What happened? Did you convince them of what really went on that last night with Sam?"

"I didn't have to. Cyrus Mason came and brought his reporter with him. She read the story she'd written for tomorrow's paper. It was an eloquent defense."

"And they believed me?"

"They believed you."

Nick's gaze caught hers and held, and time stood still for the two of them.

"Let's go home," he said at last, getting to his feet. He put an arm around each of them and steered them through the crowd.

When they reached Dana's car, Nick touched her cheek. "I have to take Tony home."

"I know."

"I'll see you in the morning. We have a lot to talk about."

Dana nodded and watched them walk away. They hadn't gone far when Tony turned around and ran back to throw his arms around her. "I'm glad you're staying, Ms. Brantley."

She smiled at him and ruffled his hair. "Me, too, kiddo."

It was only after he'd run back to his father that she noticed Jessica Leahy watching them from the shadows. Suddenly those fleeting moments of relief and happiness were spoiled by the memory of what Jessica had sworn to do. Even after what she'd heard tonight, would Jessica still condemn her? She took a step toward the older woman, hoping to make peace or, at the very least, get some answers, but Jessica turned away.

Dana was awake all night thinking about the expression she'd seen on the older woman's face and about the threat she'd never retracted. Last night's revelations should have paved the way for her to have a future with Nick in River Glen, but now that future seemed in doubt. If, despite all the evidence, Jessica still condemned her and went on with her custody fight, then her own life here would mean very little. She wouldn't be able to bear seeing Nick and Tony parted. Nor would she be able to stay if she was forced to give up Nick so that he could keep his son.

There was only one thing to do. She had to be the one to see Jessica. She had to make at least one last attempt to make peace between the two of them.

As soon as she'd eaten breakfast the next morning, she drove out to the farm. She found Joshua on his way to the barn. He walked over to greet her, his expression every bit as warm as it had been the first time they met.

"Congratulations, Dana. I'm glad things worked out for you last night."

"Thank you." She regarded him closely. "I suppose you know why I'm here."

He nodded. "She's inside. I think you'll find her in the kitchen. She's making bread. It's what she always does when she's got some thinking to do."

Dana could feel Joshua's eyes on her as she slowly crossed the lawn to the back door. The feeling that she had his blessing gave her the strength to go on. She hesitated on the threshold, watching as Jessica kneaded the dough, pounding it with her fists. Her anger was evident with each blow.

At last, Dana took a deep breath and rapped sharply. Jessica looked up and the two women stared at each other, tension radiating between them.

"Come in," she said at last.

Dana moved to the kitchen table and sat down, linking her hands in front of her. Now that she was here, she was unsure how to begin.

"Joshua says you bake bread when you have some thinking to do," she said finally.

"I do." The lump of dough hit the counter with a crash and flour rose like a fine mist.

"I hope you're thinking about the custody suit."

"I am." *Slam* went the dough again.

"Have you decided anything?"

"Not yet."

"Would it help for me to tell you that I love Nick and Tony very much? They are very special, thanks in large measure to the gift of love your daughter gave them. I envy the time they shared. I...my marriage wasn't like that. I wish to God it had been."

When she looked up, there were tears shining in Jessica's eyes. "Oh, my dear, can you ever forgive me? All I wanted to do was protect my family."

Dana got up and went over to Jessica. She put her hand on hers, oblivious to the flour and dough that covered it. She could feel the trembling and knew something of Jessica's fear.

"Don't you think I know that?" she said gently. "I can see how much you care about them, how much they love you. I just want to be a part of that, not take it away from you."

The room crackled with silent tension.

"I won't fight you," Jessica said finally.

"Thank you. That's all I can ask."

Dana was hardly aware of how long she'd spent at the farm or how late it was as she drove back to town. When she arrived at the library both Nick and Betsy were pacing the front steps, Betsy's strides only half as long as Nick's.

Betsy saw her first. "There she is," she cried, running down the steps, Nick hard on her heels.

"Where have you been?" he demanded. "We've been half out of our heads worrying about you."

"Why?"

Nick cast an incredulous look at Betsy, who shrugged. "The woman wants to know why. Good heavens, lady, after all that's gone on around here, do you even have to ask?"

"But it's all resolved now," she said cheerfully, getting out of the car. "I took care of the last detail this morning."

Nick's shoulders tensed. "What detail?"

"I went to see Jessica."

"You what!" Nick demanded.

"I went to see Jessica."

"Why?" Betsy asked. "Why on earth would you go to see her first thing in the morning?"

Nick and Dana exchanged a knowing look. She reached out and put a reassuring hand on his arm, rubbing until she felt the knotted muscle relax.

"Everything is okay."

"Everything?" he repeated as if he couldn't quite dare to believe her.

"Will someone tell me what you're talking about?" Betsy demanded indignantly.

Nick put his hands on Dana's waist and scanned her face, his expression softening. "I think we're talking about getting married, aren't we?"

"If someone asks me, we could be."

Betsy's sharp intake of breath was the only sound for the longest time. Finally Dana chuckled.

"If you don't ask me pretty soon, Betsy's going to do it for you."

"Oh, no," Nick said. "This is my proposal. Betsy can go find someone else."

"Then get down on your knee," Betsy prodded.

"Are you planning to stick around to coach me through this?" Nick inquired.

"If it'll get you moving any faster, I am."

Nick finally shrugged and sank to one knee. He glanced to Betsy for her approval. She was beaming.

"Now?" she urged.

"Dana Brantley, would you do me the honor of becoming Mrs. Nicholas Verone?"

"Can't you do any better than that?" Betsy huffed. "What did I tell you, Dana? You young folks today have no sense of romance."

Dana's heart was pounding against her ribs, and her eyes were shining as she met Nick's heated gaze.

"I think we have a very good idea of romance," she retorted softly, taking Nick's outstretched hand. "Do you think anyone would mind if I left the library closed for the day?"

"I don't think anyone would mind at all," Nick said, getting to his feet and slipping an arm around her.

As they walked away, he glanced back over his shoulder. "This part is private, Betsy."

"As long as you invite me to the wedding."

"You can be the matron of honor," Dana told her.

But when she and Nick were alone at last, she touched his cheek with trembling fingers. Her self-confidence faltered. "Are you very sure about this?" she asked, searching his eyes for signs of doubt. "My past…it can't be an easy thing to accept."

"Dana, you've already been much harder on yourself than I could ever be. What happened was a terrible tragedy. Not just Sam's death, but all the years of pain that led up to it. It's time now to let it go."

"I want to, Nick. God only knows, I want to." She struggled against the relentless claim of the past. "I don't know if I can."

Nick's arms encircled her with warmth and strength and love. "We can do it," he promised. "Together."

His lips met hers, gently at first, the touch of sunshine, rather than fire. It was a kiss meant to reassure. Then hunger replaced tenderness and trust surmounted doubts.

"Forever," Dana murmured, eyes blazing with life and her heart filled with the hope she'd never dared to feel before.

"Forever."

* * * * *

Dear Reader,

A Natural Father was my very first Harlequin Superromance, and as such it was a voyage of discovery for me. After writing over a dozen Blaze books, I was suddenly in the realm of pregnancy and family—and I loved it. One of the other things I most loved about writing *A Natural Father* was the chance to bring the Italian side of Melbourne, my home city, to life. I'm a sucker for a good Italian meal, but I'm an absolute walkover for a good Italian man. Turns out the same goes for my heroine, Lucy Basso!

Lucy is a woman on the verge of huge change— she's pregnant and staring down the barrel of single parenthood thanks to the breakup of her long-term relationship. The last thing she's looking for is romance. But Dominic Bianco has had a thing for Lucy ever since they were kids, and now that he's free, he's decided that life is too short to hang back and wait. I really loved telling Lucy and Dom's story, particularly the parts that involved their extended families. Helping these two people find their happy ever after was enormously satisfying for me—and I hope will be for you, too.

I love hearing from readers so please drop by my website, www.sarahmayberry.com, and drop me a line if you feel so inclined.

Happy reading,

Sarah

A NATURAL FATHER
Sarah Mayberry

Thanks to the team at *Neighbours* for inspiring this story, particularly you, Mr. Hannam, with your talk of delicious, barefoot Italian men making gnocchi.

As always, this book would not exist if Chris was not by my side, mopping my fevered brow and rubbing my shoulders and making me laugh.

And then there is Wanda, who always makes my writing better, always knows best and always makes me laugh even when I think I want to cry. You rock.

Chapter 1

"I don't feel so good." Lucy Basso pressed a hand to her stomach. "Maybe I should do this another time."

Her sister Rosetta rolled her eyes and passed the menu over.

"Stop being such a wuss," Rosie said, scanning the menu. "I'm going to have the pesto and goat's cheese focaccia. What about you?"

"How about a nervous breakdown?" Lucy said.

Around them, the staff and patrons of their favorite inner-city Melbourne café went about their business, laughing, talking, drinking and eating as though none of them had a care in the world.

Lucy stared at them with envy.

I bet none of you are unexpectedly pregnant. I bet none of you are so stupidly, childishly scared of telling your Catholic Italian mother that you decided to do it in a public place so she couldn't yell too loudly. I bet none of you are contemplating standing up right now and hightailing it out of here and moving to another country so you never have to look into her face and see how disappointed she is in you.

Her sister placed the menu flat on the table and gave Lucy one of her Lawyer Looks. Over the years, Rosie had perfected several, and Lucy kept a running tally of them. This was Lawyer Look Number Three—the my-client-is-an-idiot-but-I-will-endure-because-I'm-being-paid one.

"There's no point worrying about something you can't change. And it's not like you've robbed a bank or become a Buddhist, God forbid. You made a baby with the man you love. So what if you're not married to him? So what if he's just left you for another woman? None of that is your fault. Well, not technically."

Lucy narrowed her eyes, for a moment forgetting her nerves. "What's that supposed to mean? Which bit is *technically* not my fault? Us not being married or his leaving me? And please do not tell me that you think us being married would have made a difference to this situation, because that's so not true. I'd just be sitting here with a stupid ring on my finger and he'd still be having tantric sex with Belinda the Nimble."

Rosie smiled. "There, see? All you needed was to get a little temper going, and you're fine."

She looked so pleased with herself, Lucy had to laugh.

"You are the worst. Please tell me you have a trick like that up your sleeve for when Ma starts crossing herself and beating her chest."

"She hasn't beaten her chest for years. Not since we told her it was making her boobs sag prematurely," Rosie said. "And what's with the nimble thing, by the way? You always call Belinda that. Personally, I prefer 'that slut,' but I'm hard like that."

Lucy reached for the sugar bowl and dug the teaspoon deep into the tiny, shiny crystals.

"It's one of the things Marcus said when he told me he was leaving. That he'd met someone, and she was beautiful and captivating and *nimble*."

Even though two months had passed since that horrible, soul-destroying conversation, Lucy still felt the sting of humiliation and hurt. She'd been so secure in Marcus's love. So certain that no matter what else was going wrong in her life—and the list seemed to be growing longer by the day—he'd always be there for her.

Ha.

"Nimble. What the hell does that mean? That she can put her ankles behind her ears? Like that's going to see them through the hard times," Rosie said.

Lucy shrugged miserably, then caught herself. She was wallowing again. The moment she knew she was pregnant, she'd made a deal with herself that self-pity was out the window. The days of self-indulgent cannoli pig-outs were over. She had another person to consider now. A person who was going to be totally dependent on her for everything for so many years it was almost impossible to comprehend.

"Hello, my darlings, so sorry I'm late."

Lucy and Rosie started in their seats. When it came to sneaking up on people unawares, their mother was a world champion. It was a talent she'd mastered when they were children, and it never failed to unsettle them both.

"Why you had to choose this place when the parking is so bad and my cornetti are ten times better, I don't know," Sophia Basso said as she scanned the busy café, clearly unimpressed. "We could have had a nice quiet time at home with no interruptions."

"Ma, you've got to stop sneaking up on us like that. You're like the Ninja Mom," Lucy said.

"I can't help that I step lightly, Lucia," Sophia said.

Small and slim, she was dressed, as always, with elegance in a silk shirt in bright aquamarine, a neat black skirt and black shoes. Over it all she wore the black Italian wool coat her daughters had bought her for her birthday last year.

"I know it's hard to park here, but Brunetti's make the best hot chocolate in town," Rosie said.

Sophia sniffed her disagreement as she folded her coat carefully over the back of her chair. Then she held her arms wide and Rosie stood and stepped dutifully into her embrace, followed by Lucy a few seconds later.

"My girls. So beautiful," Sophia Basso said, her fond gaze cataloging their tall, slim bodies, dark shiny hair and deep-brown eyes with parental pride.

She sank into her chair and Lucy and Rosie followed suit.

Sometimes, Lucy reflected, meeting with her mother was like having an audience with the queen. Or maybe the pope was a better comparison, since there was usually so much guilt associated with the occasion, mixed in with the love and amusement and frustration.

"You've put on weight, Lucia," Sophia said as she spread a napkin over her lap. "It's good to see. You're always much too skinny."

Lucy tensed. She was twelve weeks pregnant and barely showing. If she lay on her back and squinted, she could just discern the concave bump that would soon grow into a big pregnancy belly. How could her mother possibly notice such a subtle change?

Lucy exchanged glances with her sister.

Just say it. Spit it out, get it over and done with.

Ever since she found out she was pregnant five weeks ago, she'd been coming up with excuses for why she couldn't tell her mother. First, she'd decided to wait to make sure the pregnancy was viable before saying anything. Why upset her mother for no reason, after all? But the weeks had passed and she'd realized she was going to start to show soon. The last thing she wanted was for her mother to find out from someone else. She could just imagine Mrs. Cilauro from the markets or old Mr. Magnifico, one of her customers, asking her mother when Lucia was due.

The thought was enough to make her feel lightheaded. For sure the chest-beating would make a reappearance. And she would never be able to forget causing her mother so much pain. Not that being single and pregnant wasn't going to score highly on that front. Her mother had struggled to raise her and Rosie single-handedly after their father died in a work-site accident when they were both just toddlers. Sophia's most fervent wish, often vocalized, was that her two daughters would never have to go through the uncertainty and fear of single motherhood.

Guess what, Ma? Surprise!

"I saw Peter DeSarro the other day. He asked me to say hello to you both," Sophia said, sliding her reading glasses onto the end of her nose. "He asked particularly after you, Rosetta. You broke his heart when you married Andrew, you know."

"Oh yeah, I was a real man killer," Rosie said dryly. "All those guys panting on my doorstep all the time."

Sophia glanced at her elder daughter over the top of her glasses.

"You were too busy with your studies to notice, but you could have had any boy in the neighborhood."

Rosie laughed outright at that.

"Ma, I was the size of a small country in high school. The only boys interested in me were the ones who figured I was good for a free feed at lunchtime."

"Rosetta! That is not true!" Sophia said.

Lucy squeezed her eyes tightly shut. Any second now, the conversation was going to degenerate into a typical Rosie-Sophia debate about history as they both saw it, and Lucy would lose her courage. She took a deep breath.

"Mom, I'm pregnant," she blurted, her voice sounding overloud in her own ears.

Was it just her, or did the world stop spinning for a second?

Her mother's eyes widened, then the color drained out of her face.

"Lucia!" she said. Her hand found Lucy's on the tabletop and clutched it.

"It's Marcus's. We think maybe a condom broke. I'm due in late October. Give or take," Lucy said in a rush.

Her mother's face got even paler. Lucy winced. She hadn't meant to share the part about the condom breaking. She'd never discussed contraception with her mother in her life, and she wasn't about to start now.

"You're three months already?" her mother asked, her voice barely a whisper.

Lucy nodded. She could see the stricken look in her mother's eyes, knew exactly what she was thinking.

"I didn't want to tell you until I was sure," she said. It was flimsy, and all three of them knew it. "I didn't want you to worry about me," she said more honestly.

Her mother exhaled loudly and sat back in her chair. Her hand slid from Lucy's.

"Now Marcus will have to step up and take care of his responsibilities," Sophia said. "You are angry with him, Lucia, I know, but for the sake of the baby you will take him back. You will buy a nice house, and he will get a real job to look after you and the baby."

Lucy blinked. Fatten her mother up, give her a sex change and stuff her mouth with cotton wool, and she'd be a dead spit for Marlon Brando in *The Godfather* right now, the way she was organizing Lucy's life like she was one of the capos in her army.

"Ma, he's with someone else now. He loves her," Lucy said flatly.

Sophia shook her head. "It doesn't matter anymore. He has responsibilities."

"Since when did that ever make a difference with Marcus?" Rosie said under her breath.

Lucy's chin came up as the familiar urge to defend Marcus gripped her. She frowned.

He's not yours to defend anymore, remember?

"This child needs a father," Sophia said, her fist thumping the table.

Lucy knew that her mother's words were fueled by all the years of scraping by, but they weren't what she needed to hear. She couldn't undo what had happened. She was stuck. She was going to have to do the best she could with what she had. And she was going to have to do it alone.

Rosie's hand found her knee under the table and gave it a squeeze.

"It's not like I planned any of this," Lucy said. "It was an accident. And I can't make Marcus love me again. I have to get on with things. I've got the business, and Rosie and I have been talking—"

"The business! I hadn't even thought about that! How on earth will you cope with it all on your own?" Her mother threw her hands in the air dramatically. "All those fruit deliveries, lifting all those boxes. And it's just you, Lucia, no one else. This is a disaster."

"Ma, you're not helping. You think Lucy hasn't gone over and over all of this stuff?" Rosie said.

"She hasn't gone over it with me," Sophia said, and Lucy could hear the hurt in her voice.

"I know this is the last thing you want for me," Lucy said. "I know you're disappointed. But it's happening. I'm going to have a baby. You're going to be a grandmother. Can't we concentrate on the good bits and worry about the bad bits when they happen?"

Suddenly she really needed to hear her mother say something reassuring. Something about how everything would be all right, how if she had managed, so would Lucy.

Tears filled Sophia Basso's eyes and she shook her head slowly.

"You have no idea," she said. "Everything becomes a battle. Just getting to the grocery store, or keeping the house clean. Every time one of you was sick, I used to pace the floor at night, worrying how I was going to pay for the medicine and who was going to look after you when I had to go into work the next day. All the times the utilities were cut off, and the times I couldn't find the money for school excursions… I would never wish that life on either of you."

"It won't be the same, because Lucy has us," Rosie said staunchly. "What Lucy was about to tell you is that she's moving into the granny flat at the back of our house. When the baby comes, Andrew and I can help out. Between all of us, we'll get by."

Lucy saw that her mother's hands were trembling. She hated upsetting her. Disappointing her. Deep down inside, in the part of her that was still a child, Lucy had hoped that her mother would react differently. That she'd be more pleased than concerned, that she'd wrap Lucy in her arms and tell her that no matter what happened she would be there for her.

The nervous nausea that had dogged her before her mother's arrival returned with a vengeance.

She was already scared of what the future might hold. Of having a baby growing inside her—a crazy enough concept all on its own—and then taking that tiny baby home and having to cope with whatever might happen next without Marcus standing beside her. She'd told herself over and over that hundreds of thousands of women across Australia—probably millions of women around the world—coped with having babies on their own. She would cope, too. She would. But she knew it would be the biggest challenge she'd ever faced in her life. And it would be a challenge that would never stop, ever. At seventy, she would still be worrying about her child and wanting the best for him or her. She only had to look at her mother's grief-stricken face to know that was true.

She stood, clutching her handbag.

"I can't do this," she said. "I'm sorry, Ma. But I can't do this right now."

It was too much, taking on her mother's trepidation and doubts as well as her own.

Her mother gaped and Rosie half rose from her chair as Lucy strode for the entrance, fighting her way through the line of people waiting for service at the front counter.

Outside, Lucy stuffed her hands into the pockets of her coat and sucked in big lungfuls of air. She stared up at the pale blue winter sky, willing herself to calm down.

It's going to be okay. I'm twenty-eight years old. Last year, I started my own business. I can do this. I'm a strong person.

She found her car keys in her bag and started to walk, chin up, jaw set.

After all, it wasn't as though she had a choice.

A month later

Dominic Bianco ran his hands through his hair and stifled a yawn. If anyone asked, he was going to blame the jetlag for his tiredness, but the truth was that he'd gotten out of the habit of early starts while he'd been visiting with family back in the old country. Six months of touring Italy, hopping from one relative's house to the next had made him lazy and soft. Just what he'd needed at the time, but now he was back and there was work to do. As always.

Around him, the Victoria Market buzzed with activity. Situated in the central business district, the markets were the heart of the fresh produce trade in Melbourne, supplying suburban retailers, restaurants and cafés across the city. Bianco Brothers had occupied the same corner for nearly thirty years, ever since new immigrants Tony and Vinnie Bianco started selling fruits and vegetables as eager young men. Today, the family stall sprawled down half the aisle and turned over millions of dollars annually.

Dom checked his watch. Five o'clock. One hour until customers started arriving.

He wondered if he would see her today. Then he shook his head. What was he, sixteen again?

"Grow up, idiot," he told himself as he turned toward the pallet of boxed tomatoes waiting to be unloaded.

She might not even come. For all he knew, she might not even be buying her produce from his father anymore.

He flexed his knees and kept his back straight as he hoisted the first box of tomatoes and lugged them over to the display table. His uncle Vinnie was fussing with the bananas, ensuring the oldest stock was at the front so they could offload it before the fruit became too ripe.

"Be careful with your back, Dom. You know what happened with your father," he said as Dom dumped the first box and went back for another.

Dom smiled to himself. For as long as he could remember, his uncle had said the same thing every time he saw anyone carrying a box. Dom figured the hernia his father had had while in his twenties must have really messed with his uncle's head.

By the time Dom had unloaded all the tomatoes, he'd worked up a sweat beneath the layers of sweatshirts and T-shirts he'd piled on that morning. He peeled off a couple of layers, enjoying the feeling of using his muscles again.

It was good to be back. He'd felt a little uneasy as the plane took off from Rome two days ago, but it was nice to be home. Even returning to the old house hadn't been that big a deal.

Danielle's stuff was gone. The only sign that she'd ever lived there was the pile of mail addressed to them both that his sister had left on the kitchen counter.

Mr. and Mrs. Bianco. He wondered if Dani was planning on reverting to her maiden name now that their divorce was final. It wasn't something they'd ever discussed. He frowned as he thought about it. It would be strange to learn she was calling herself Dani Bianco. As though the only part of him that she still wanted was his name.

"Dom, how many boxes iceburg lettuce we got?" his father called from the other end of the stand.

Dom shook his head when he saw that his father had his clipboard out and pencil at the ready. For thirty years Tony Bianco had kept track of his stock and sales in the same way—on paper in his illegible handwriting. Any notation he made would be indecipherable to anyone else.

Dom did a quick tally of the boxes stacked beneath the trestle tables.

"We got two-dozen boxes, Pa," he called. Enough to see them through the day.

Before he'd left for Italy, he'd spoken to his father about bringing the business into the twenty-first century. There were a bunch of user-friendly, highly efficient software systems available for running businesses like theirs. Knowing what stock they had on hand, what it was costing them, how much they were selling and who their best customers were at the touch of a button would be of huge benefit to Bianco Brothers. Currently, all that information was stored in his father's head and consequently Tony's business decisions were often based more on gut-feel and instinct than hard figures.

Predictably, his father had been resistant to the idea of change.

"I do it this way for thirty years," he'd said, then he'd gestured toward the long rows of produce and the customers lining up to make their purchases. "We do okay."

His father was being modest. They did more than okay. They did really, really well. But, in Dom's opinion, they could do better. He'd backed off last time because he'd been too messed up over Dani to concentrate on the business, but now that he was back it was time to start pushing harder. He was going to be running this business someday, since none of his cousins were even remotely interested. He didn't want to have to deal with boxes full of his father's scrawlings when he tried to work out where they stood.

He dusted his hands down the front of his jeans and glanced over the stand, checking to see that all was as it should be. Everything looked good, and he turned back to the stack of pallets piled behind their displays. Might as well get rid of those before the rush.

By the time he'd tracked down one of the market's forklift drivers and arranged for him to shift the pallets to the holding area, half an hour had passed. The bitter cold was starting to burn off as the sun made its presence felt, and Dom shed another layer as he made his way back to the stand.

He'd just finished pulling his sweatshirt over his head when he saw her.

She was wearing a long, cherry-red coat, the furry collar pulled up high around her face as she talked to his father. Her long, straight dark hair hung down her back, glossy in the overhead lights. She turned her head slightly and he watched her smile, noting the quick flash of her teeth, the way her eyes widened as she laughed at something his father said.

As always when he saw her, his gut tightened and his shoulders squared.

Lucy Basso.

Man, but she was gorgeous. Her sleek hair. The exotic sweep of her cheekbones. Her ready smile. The elegant strength of her body.

Gorgeous—and now he didn't have to feel guilty about noticing.

He stepped closer, automatically smoothing a hand over his hair to make sure he didn't have any goofy spikes sticking up from dragging off his sweatshirt. Just to be safe, he checked his fly as well. Never could tell when a clothing malfunction was loitering in the wings, waiting to bring a guy down.

All the while, he drank her in with his eyes. She looked even better than he remembered.

Lucy and her sister had grown up in Preston, just one suburb across from his own family's stomping ground in Brunswick. They'd gone to different schools but the same church, and he'd been aware of her from the moment he'd first started noticing girls. There was something about the way she held herself—tall and proud, as though she knew exactly what she was worth.

He hadn't been the only guy in the neighborhood who'd noticed. He'd never been put off by competition, but somehow the timing had never been right to make his move. Life kept intervening—other girlfriends for him, then, when he was free, she'd be with some other boy. Then they'd stopped running into each other altogether as they grew up and went out into the world. He'd only reconnected with her in the past year when she'd approached his father about the new door-to-door fresh produce delivery service she was starting up. After that, he'd seen her every day for six months before he bailed on his life for Italy. And he'd felt guilty every time he looked at her and felt the pull of desire. It wasn't like he'd needed the added hassle as he and Dani battled through the ugly death throes of their marriage, and often he'd resented the attraction he'd felt.

Bad timing—again.

But things were different now. He was a single man.

Divorced. Not exactly a shining badge of honor, not something he'd ever planned, but it was what it was.

And Lucy Basso was standing in front of him, looking amazing, daring him to reach out for something he'd always wanted.

She'd been one of the reasons for coming home. Not the main reason, not by a long shot. But he'd always wondered where she was concerned. What if…? And now there was nothing stopping him from finding out.

He was about to take the last step forward when a voice piped up in his head.

What are you doing, man? What happens if things get serious and she discovers you're an empty promise?

He pushed the thought away. He refused to live half a life, no matter what had happened with Dani. Especially when Lucy was standing within reach.

"Lucy Basso. Good to see you," he said.

She was already smiling as she turned to face him, her olive skin golden even under the harsh fluorescent lights.

"Dom! Hey, long time no see. I heard you'd taken off for Italy," she said.

She had an amazing voice. Low and husky.

"Decided it was time to take a look around the old country, see what all the fuss was about," he said. He tucked a hand into the front pocket of his jeans and rested his hip against the side of the stall.

"And?" She cocked an eyebrow at him, a small smile playing around her mouth.

"The Vatican is an okay little place. And they did

some nice work at the Coliseum. But, to be honest, it would have been much more impressive if they'd finished building it."

She laughed and pulled a face at him. "Bet you didn't make that joke when you were in Rome."

"As a matter of fact," he said, "I didn't."

She laughed again.

He shot a glance toward his father, aware that Tony was watching their exchange with a big smile on his face.

Go away, he urged his father silently. *There's no way I'm asking her out with you standing there. I'll never hear the end of it.*

"I bet you're glad to have him back, Mr. Bianco," Lucy said.

"I save work especially for him," Tony said, rubbing his apron-covered belly with his hands, his smile broadening. "To make up for long holiday."

His father was looking at Lucy with admiring eyes and Dom realized he wasn't going anywhere soon. He might be pushing sixty, but Tony knew a beautiful woman when he saw one and he wasn't above a little harmless flirtation in his old age.

"Six months in Italy. I can only imagine," Lucy said, closing her eyes for a beat. "Heaven. The way I'm going, I'll get over there when I'm ready to retire," she said.

"Make the time. It's worth it," Dom said. "Even if you only go for a few weeks."

She shrugged, her hair spilling over her shoulder.

"Nice idea, but it's not going to happen," she said ruefully.

Then she reached for her purse to pay for her order, and her coat fell open.

The words Dom had been about to say died in his throat as he registered the gentle bump that had been hidden by the long lines of her coat.

She was pregnant.

Lucy Basso was pregnant. Which meant she was married. Not free. Not available. And definitely not about to go out with him.

Bad timing again. The worst timing in the world, in fact.

Fifteen years of lust, blown away in a few seconds. *Damn.*

Chapter 2

Somehow Dom managed to make coherent conversation for the next few minutes, but his gaze kept dropping to the bump swelling Lucy's sweater. After a while, she placed a hand there and blushed.

"Starting to show now, I guess," she said.

"Uh, yeah. When are you due?" he asked.

"Just before Christmas."

"Wow. I guess your husband must be over the moon," he said, fishing unashamedly.

Who had she married? How come his mother hadn't mentioned it in one of her letters to him? He'd gotten updates on every other birth, death or marriage in the neighborhood. Why would she miss Lucy Basso's?

Lucy tugged her coat closed and slid a button home to keep it that way.

She shrugged casually, as if to say that her husband's happiness was a given.

"You know, I'd better get going with all of this." She gestured toward the trolley she'd filled with her supplies for the day.

Dom frowned as he noted several large boxes and bags of produce in her order.

"I'll give you a hand," he said, stepping forward.

"It's okay. I've got a hydraulic tailgate in the back of the van," she explained.

"Right." He rocked back on his heels.

She was nothing to him, a neighborhood acquaintance and now a customer, but he hated the idea of her lugging groceries around all day when she was four months pregnant.

She laughed, obviously interpreting the look on his face.

"Italian men," she said, shaking her head. "Honestly, I'm fine. I wouldn't do anything to put my baby in danger."

She curved her hand possessively over her bump, and he felt that tight feeling in his gut again.

Forget it, buddy. Forget her. It's over.

"Okay. If you're sure," he said.

"I'm sure. I'll see you tomorrow. You, too, Mr. Bianco."

She smiled once more before pushing her trolley up the aisle.

He wasn't aware that he was staring after her until his father came and stood next to him.

"Beautiful girl."

Dom forced a casual shrug. Beautiful, married and pregnant. Not exactly a winning combination.

"Yeah, she's nice," he said.

He turned back toward the stand. Ridiculous to feel as though he'd just lost something valuable. For all he knew, she was a ball-breaking shrew with bad breath and a worse temper. There was nothing for him to mourn, no loss had occurred. They barely even knew each other.

He was so absorbed in trying to look busy that he almost missed his father's next words.

"Such a shame. Her mother very worried, I hear."

"Worried? Why?" Dom asked. Then his mind jumped to the obvious. "Is there something wrong with the baby?"

He knew what it was like to hope each month for good news, only to learn that once again all the wonders of modern medicine could not make up for the failures of nature. For four years he and Dani had tried in vain to have a baby. He could only imagine how wrenching it would be to have all the joy of finding out you were pregnant, only to learn there was something wrong with your child.

"Something wrong with the baby? How would I know?" his father asked, giving him a look.

Dom returned it in full measure.

"You're the one who said her mother's worried. What's she worried about if it's not the baby?"

Tony rolled his eyes, then held up his left hand, pointing to his own well-worn wedding ring.

"No husband. Lousy no-good left Lucy for other woman," he said. He looked like he wanted to spit, the notion offended him so much. "Poor Lucy, she left with business and bambino all on her own."

Dom stared at his father.

"She's not married?" he asked, just in case his ears were deceiving him, feeding him what he wanted to hear.

"Didn't I just say that?" his father asked. Muttering to himself in Italian, he strode off to serve the customer hovering nearby.

Dom stared blankly into space for a few long seconds.

Not married.

Single, in fact.

A smile curved his lips. He even turned on his heel, ready to race after her and ask her out.

He stopped before he'd taken a step.

She was pregnant.

Four months pregnant with another man's child.

Not exactly your typical dating situation.

"Hey, Dom, those arms of yours painted on?" his uncle Vinnie called from the other end of the stall.

Dom blinked. A queue of customers had formed in front of him, waiting to be served.

Right. He was at work. There was stuff to do. He could think about Lucy Basso later.

It was a great theory, but he found it impossible to

stop himself from thinking about her as the morning progressed. The flash of a red coat glimpsed briefly through the crowd. The sight of a woman pushing a baby stroller. A young couple walking hand in hand, both glowing with obvious contentment over her big, swollen belly. Everything seemed to remind him of her. She'd rocketed from being a vague incentive to come home to the most important thing on his agenda in the space of a few minutes.

Why was that? Because of the profound disappointment he'd felt when he'd thought she was married, lost to him for good?

Man, she's pregnant, he reminded himself for the twentieth time that day.

But did that really matter? Really?

That night, Lucy sat with her laptop at her dining table and stared at the number at the bottom of her monthly spreadsheet. It wasn't abysmal. It was almost respectable, considering her business, Market Fresh, had been in operation just over twelve months. But would it be enough to impress the man at the bank tomorrow?

Market Fresh had seemed like such a great idea when she came up with it two years ago. She'd been working as hostess in a busy suburban restaurant and listening to the chef's constant complaints. He didn't have time to get into the city markets every day to pick produce for himself, and he was perpetually disappointed in what he could source locally. Because she lived close to the city, Lucy had offered to stop by the markets on the way into work each day and fill his shopping list. The restaurant paid her for her time, and she selected the best produce at the best prices, going straight to the wholesaler rather than allowing a retailer to act as the middleman.

The chef had been so impressed with what she'd brought back and how much money she'd saved him, he'd bragged about it to his chef friends. Before long, Lucy had two, then three, then four shopping lists to fill each day. After a while, she realized that she'd accidentally discovered a niche in the market, and Market Fresh was born.

She did her homework for a whole year before jumping in. She took some small-business courses, and she went through the sums over and over with her sister. Finally, she leased the van and pitched herself to her former employer and his friends. After a few ups and downs, the business was now holding its own.

Except she'd reached a difficult stage in her company's growth. She needed more clients, but she couldn't afford to put on an extra driver to service them until she had more money coming in. Also, she needed to up her game to ensure she retained her existing clients. The answer to all her problems was obvious but expensive: the Internet. Ever since she'd found out she was pregnant, Lucy had been exploring the idea of taking Market Fresh online. With a Web site, she could deliver a real-time list of available produce to her clients each day and receive and collate their orders automatically. She

already knew from discussions she'd had with several
of her key clients that they were attracted to the conve-
nience of the idea. She was confident that new clients
would be equally drawn.

She just had to find the money to get online. Hence
her appointment with the bank tomorrow.

Lucy rubbed her belly. She hated the thought of taking on more debt. She already made lease payments
on the van, and while she was keeping her head above
water, it would take the loss of only a few clients or a
hike in fuel costs to put her in the red again. She didn't
want to risk that, not with the baby on the way.

But she also wanted to ensure her child's future.
Build something that would keep them both safe and
warm for many years, without having to rely on the
generosity of Rosie and Andrew, or handouts from her
mother.

She closed her eyes at the very thought. Since the
meeting a month ago when she'd told her mother she
was pregnant, she'd been on the receiving end of all
the fussing a pregnant woman could endure. Home-
cooked meals appeared magically in her fridge, and
every time her mother visited she brought something
for the baby—stacks of disposable diapers, a baby bath,
receiving blankets, tiny baby clothes. The study nook
where she planned to put the baby's cradle was already
jammed to overflowing with her mother's gifts.

It was incredibly generous, and it also took a huge
burden off Lucy's shoulders in terms of her baby bud-
get. But every time her mother handed over an offering,

Lucy remembered the nights her mother had stayed up late ironing business shirts for fifty cents apiece. And the weekends she'd spent sewing wedding and bridesmaid dresses, and confirmation dresses for the girls in the neighborhood. And all the times Lucy had watched her mother carefully count her change into the rainy-day jar. Her mother was retired now, living off a small pension and her savings, and Lucy knew that every gift to her came at her mother's expense.

Her mother had sacrificed so much to give her and Rosie a good home, and now she was sacrificing again to support Lucy's unplanned pregnancy.

Lucy shoved her chair back so sharply it screeched across the timber floor.

She had to convince the people at the bank that she was a good risk. Somehow she had to push the business into the next phase, and she had to look after herself and her baby without leaning on her mother. It wasn't right. It wasn't the kind of daughter Lucy wanted to be. She remembered how proud she'd felt when she and Rosie had presented their mother with the lush, expensive Italian wool coat. Sophia's eyes had lit up then filled with tears when she'd understood that the beautiful garment was hers, a token of her daughters' esteem and affection.

That was the kind of daughter Lucy wanted to be— the kind of daughter who gave instead of took, the kind of daughter who could give her mother the retirement she deserved after all her hard years of work.

Lucy ran a hand through her hair and let her breath hiss out between her teeth, wishing she could release her tension as easily. She had her business papers in order and her best suit was hanging at the ready—even though she had to use a couple of safety pins and leave the zipper down to get the skirt on. As long as she didn't take her jacket off, no one would ever know.

"They'll listen," Lucy said out loud, trying to convince herself. "They'll see my vision. They have to."

"First sign of madness, you know," Rosie said from behind her, and Lucy started.

"For Pete's sake!" she said, one hand pressed to her chest. "Have you been taking lessons from Ma or something?"

"I knocked," Rosie said, gesturing toward the door that connected the flat to the kitchen of the main house. "You were too busy talking to yourself to hear me."

Lucy punched her sister on the arm. "That's for scaring the living daylights out of me."

Rosie rubbed her arm. "If you weren't knocked up, you'd be in so much trouble right now," she said. "But even a lawyer has to draw the line at taking on a pregnant woman."

"Very noble of you."

"I'm good like that. You coming in to watch a movie with us?" she asked.

Lucy shot a look toward her laptop. She had her accounts in order, but her nerves demanded she go over them one last time, just to be sure.

"I think I've got too much work to do," she said.

Rosie's face immediately creased with concern. "Everything okay? You're all good for the bank?"

"Sure. No problems," Lucy said, careful to keep her voice casual.

"I can still cancel my afternoon appointment and come with you," Rosie said.

While a part of Lucy wanted her support more than anything, she knew she had to do this alone. The whole point of getting the loan and growing the business was to become more independent and self-sufficient. Lucy didn't want to be a charity case for the rest of her life. She owed her baby a better start than that.

"It's all good. Really. I've already ironed my shirt and everything," she said.

Rosie looked like she wanted to argue some more, so Lucy said the first thing that popped into her head.

"Hey, guess who's back in town? Dominic Bianco. Saw him at the market this morning."

As she'd hoped, her sister stopped frowning and got a salacious, speculative look in her eye. Rosie had always had a thing for Dom Bianco.

"How long was he away? And is he as hot as ever?" Rosie asked.

"Six months. And he looks the same as always," Lucy said.

"Ow. Must have been some divorce that he needed six months time-out to recover," Rosie said with a wince. "Nice to know he hasn't lost his looks, though. Tell me, does he still wear those tight little jeans?"

"At this point I feel honor-bound to remind you that you're a married woman."

"I can still admire from a distance. And Dominic Bianco is worth admiring. Those cheekbones. And those black eyes of his. And that body." Rosie fanned herself theatrically.

"Careful or I'm going to have to hose you down."

"How can you look at that man and not have sweaty, carnal thoughts?"

"Um, because I'm four months pregnant," Lucy said, "and about to become a walking whale?"

"Irrelevant."

"Maybe he's not my type."

"You have twenty-twenty vision and a pulse, and you're pregnant so it proves you're heterosexual. He's your type. Next," Rosie said, wiggling her fingers in a gimme-more gesture.

Lucy frowned. She'd never seriously given the matter much thought before. In fact, she'd never really paid much attention to Dominic, truth be told. He'd been married until recently, and she'd been living with Marcus, and Rosie had always had a thing for him—he'd been out of bounds for a bunch of reasons, really. And Lucy wasn't the kind of person who got off on lusting after the forbidden.

"I don't know. Maybe I never let myself notice," she said finally.

"Ha!" Rosie said triumphantly. "I knew it!"

"You want to share what you know? 'Cause I'm still in the dark here."

"You have the hots for him. Only someone who really has the hots for someone would completely block out the other person's attractiveness like that. And The Bianco definitely qualifies as attractive. The man is a god. Sex on legs. H-O-T."

"Okay, I got it." Lucy shook her head at both her sister's convoluted logic and her use of her teen code name for Dom. "Is this the kind of argument you try on in court, by the way? Do judges buy this crap?"

"It's the only explanation," Rosie said, crossing her arms smugly over her chest.

"Really? How about this—you've been hot for Dom for so many years that you're trying to live vicariously through me?"

Rosie cocked her head. "Hmmm. That's not bad."

They both laughed.

"You're a dirty birdy," Lucy said, reaching out and tugging on her sister's shoulder-length hair.

"Thank you. I do try." Rosie turned toward the door. "Sure you're not up for ice cream and a movie?"

Lucy bit her lip, tempted now that she'd let go of some of her anxiety. It wasn't as though she hadn't already gone over and over her application. "What flavor have you got?"

"New York cheesecake *and* macadamia toffee," Rosie said.

Lucy slung an arm around her sister's neck. "Have I told you lately that I love you?" she said, planting a kiss on her sister's cheek.

"You, my dear, are an ice-cream hussy," Rosie said. Then she slung her arm around Lucy's fast-disappearing waist and kissed her back. "Love you, too."

* * *

Later that night, Rosie finished smoothing moisturizer into her face as she sat in bed. She dropped her hands into her lap, her thoughts on her sister. Lucy was so strong and bright and determined, but Rosie couldn't help worrying about her. It was part of the job description of elder sister, but it also came down to simple empathy. Her sister was in a tough situation and Rosie would feel for any woman faced with the same challenges. The difference was, Lucy *was* her sister, and Rosie had a lifetime of feeling responsible for her to add to her natural sympathy. It made her want to move mountains for her, even though she knew her sister was determined to stand on her own two feet.

If only Marcus wasn't such a loser. It wasn't the first time Rosie had had the thought, and it wouldn't be the last. From the moment she'd met him she'd spotted him for what he was—a moocher, content to pursue his "art" while someone else footed the bill for all the everyday things like food, water, shelter. That someone else had been Lucy for so many years that Rosie had almost gone crazy biting her tongue. And now Marcus had shown his true colors and bailed on her sister when she needed him the most.

What an asshole. Lucy deserved so much better.

"What time are the Johnsons coming in tomorrow?" Andrew asked as he exited the ensuite bathroom.

He had stripped down to his boxers, and as usual the sight of his solid, muscular body filled Rosie with a warm sense of comfort and proprietorial pride. He worked hard to stay fit, and she made a point of admiring the results as often as possible because she knew that, like her, he'd been an overweight teen and the ghosts of past shame still lurked in the corners of his mind.

"Looking fine, Mr. James. Looking fine," she said, giving him her best leer.

Andrew struck a few muscleman poses, each more ridiculous than the last. She was laughing her head off by the time he slid into bed beside her.

"Come here," he said, sliding an arm around her waist.

She went willingly, curling close to his big, warm body, her head resting on his shoulder. She wondered for perhaps the millionth time how she'd gotten so lucky. She'd had the hots for Andrew James since she walked into her first common-law lecture at Melbourne University. He'd been sitting in the third row, his long legs stretched out in front of him. He'd glanced up from his notebook, and her brown eyes had met his blue, and the deal had been sealed then and there. He hadn't even needed to smile, but when he did, she'd literally gone weak at the knees.

Rosie smiled as she remembered. She hadn't believed in love at first sight until that moment. Life sure showed her.

"What are you smiling about?" Andrew asked.

"Just thinking about the first time I saw you," she said.

"That old thing," he said. "What is it with women, always mythologizing the past?"

She dug an elbow into his ribs. "Don't ruin my sentimentality with your man-logic."

Her thoughts inevitably clicked to the subject she'd been worrying at before Andrew came through from the bathroom.

"I wish Lucy could have met someone like you instead of Marcus the moocher," she said.

"She'll be fine. Stop worrying."

"I can't help it. It's in my genes."

"It's not like she's in this alone. She's got Sophia and she's got us. We'll all pitch in."

"It's not the same."

"I know. But it's close, and it's more than a lot of people have. Lucy's a lot tougher than you give her credit for, you know."

"I know."

"Anyway, it'll be good practice for us, being Uncle Andrew and Aunty Rosie. By the time our own kids come along, I'll have mastered the whole diaper thing, no problems."

She tensed.

"Wow. I'll have to tell Lucy you're volunteering for pooper-scooper duty," she said.

She felt his chest rise as though he'd taken a breath to say something, but he didn't speak. For a moment there was a whole world of not-talked-about stuff hanging in the air between them.

"Oh, I forgot. The Johnsons. They rebooked for eleven," she said.

"Right. Yeah, I'd forgotten," he said.

He stretched to the side and clicked off the bed-side lamp.

"Good night," he said, kissing the top of her head.

She kissed his chest one last time and slid back to her side of the bed. As much as she'd love to fall asleep on him, she knew she'd just wake up in half an hour with a numb arm.

The sheets were cool on her side and she stared up at the ceiling, reliving that telltale little hitch in their conversation.

You have to pay the piper sometime.

There was a conversation coming, looming on the horizon. She knew that. And it filled her with fear. Because she knew how much Andrew wanted children—and she had no desire at all to be a mother.

Chapter 3

Rosie's words returned to haunt Lucy as she approached the Bianco Brothers stall at the market the next morning. Dom was at the front of the stand and she was about to call out a greeting when he stooped to lift a box of potatoes. He was wearing a pair of well-worn Levi's, and the soft denim molded his butt and thighs as he lifted the heavy load. His biceps bulged, visible against the tight cotton of a long-sleeved T-shirt, and Lucy found herself swallowing unexpectedly.

Then Dom turned and saw her, and his dark eyes lit up and his straight, white teeth flashed as he smiled. His black hair was curly and unruly around his face, and he was tanned from his months in Italy.

Okay. Maybe Rosie was on to something when she

said he was a god, Lucy admitted to herself as she stared at him. *Maybe he is attractive.*

"Lucy. Be with you in a minute," he said, dropping the potatoes onto another customer's trolley.

Then he grabbed the hem of his long-sleeved T-shirt and tugged it over his head. Lucy's eyes widened as she scored an eyeful of tanned, hard belly as whatever he was wearing underneath clung to the top he was removing.

Okay. Attractive is the wrong word. Sexy. Very, very sexy.

Lucy dragged her eyes away, frowning.

She was pregnant. Having a baby. With child. She had no business ogling hot guys at the market. She cursed her sister mentally. This was all Rosie's doing, planting stupid suggestions in her head. If she hadn't said all that stuff about Dom last night, there was no way Lucy would be standing here right now feeling like a pervert.

"How can we help you today?" Dom said, closing the distance between them.

Lucy smoothed her hands down the sides of her skirt and shook her head slightly to clear it.

"All the usual staples. Plus I need eggplants and a whole lot of fresh herbs," she said, consulting her list.

"May I?" Dom asked. He held out a hand for the list.

"Sure."

She'd given her list to Mr. Bianco a hundred times. So why did it feel different giving it to Dom?

Damn you, Rosie, and your stupid teen crush.

"Sorry, did you say something?" Dom asked.

"No! At least, I don't think I did," Lucy said.

"The eggplants are down here. You want to come check them out?" he asked after a small silence.

"Sure." She waited until his back was turned before she hit herself on the forehead with her open palm. Then, just in case her stupid brain hadn't gotten the message, she slid a hand over the baby bump beneath her suit coat.

The smooth, taut curve of her belly grounded her in an instant. She was pregnant and scheduled for an important meeting with the bank. Her days of getting goofy over guys were over.

One hand on her tummy, she followed Dom.

"Nice and shiny," Dom said as he showed her the eggplants. "Just the way we like them."

"Definitely," she said.

She kept her gaze focused on the dark purple vegetables in front of her.

"I'll take three boxes," she said.

"Not a problem."

She stood back as Dom hefted a box from beneath the trestle table, lifting it easily onto her trolley. When all three boxes were stacked neatly, he turned to face her.

"What next?" There was a smile in his eyes and it quickly spread to his mouth. For the first time she noticed that he had a single dimple in his left cheek.

Rosie hadn't mentioned that last night.

"Um, the herbs," she said.

They were about to move to the other end of the stall when Mr. Bianco found them, a clipboard in hand and a frown on his face.

"Dom, you remember how much onions we order last week? Oh, hello, Lucy. You looking lovely today."

For some reason, Dom's father's compliment made her blush. Which was stupid. Every morning he said something along the same lines to her. Why should today feel any different to any other time?

Because you were eyeing up his son like a side of beef five minutes ago? Because all of a sudden a part of you would like to really be looking lovely today?

She squashed the little voice with a mental boot heel. She really was going to have words with her sister for causing all this crazy, too-aware-of-Dom stuff.

"Hi, Mr. Bianco," she said. "How are you today?"

"No complaints," he said, patting his belly complacently. "But I interrupting. I wait."

"It's fine. No worries," she said, gesturing with her hand that they should go ahead and have their conversation.

Dom shot her an appreciative look. "Two seconds," he promised as he turned to talk with his father.

She moved away a few steps to inspect a pile of zucchini while they talked, but she was aware of lots of hand gesticulating and the frustrated tone of their conversation as father and son discussed something intently.

"Okay, sorry about that," Dom said a few minutes later as he rejoined her.

He was frowning and the smile had gone from his eyes.

"If there's a problem, I can wait for one of the other servers to be free," she said.

Dom shook his head. "No problem. Just stubborn pigheadedness."

"Right."

He sighed, and his frown eased a little.

"You see that clipboard he's holding? That's the complete record of our stock on hand for the week," he said.

Lucy's gaze took in the many feet of frontage the Bianco Brothers occupied, all of it filled to overflowing with fresh produce.

"You're kidding me."

She carried a tiny fraction of the inventory the Biancos did, and she kept it all neatly organized via a simple computer program. She couldn't even imagine how Mr. Bianco kept track of his stock with paper and pen.

"It gets worse. He's the only one who can read his own handwriting. So whenever Vinnie or I or one of the others needs to check on something, we have to find him and get him to interpret for us."

"Wow," Lucy said.

"Yeah," Dom said, a world of frustration in his voice.

"Driving you crazy?" she guessed.

"Just a little. There's so much stuff we could be doing. Even having an up-to-date list of what's available on a Web site would be a huge bonus. We get fifty phone calls a day from customers asking what we've got on hand. But Pa thinks that because his way has worked for thirty years, there's no reason to change."

He ran a hand through his hair, his gaze distant as he looked down the aisle. Then his eyes snapped back into focus and he gave her a rueful smile.

"Sorry. This isn't getting your order filled, is it?" he said, pulling her list from his pocket again.

"It's okay. I can barely have a conversation with my mother these days. I can't even imagine working with her," Lucy confessed.

Dom's gaze instantly flicked to her stomach. She felt heat rise into her face. Yesterday when she'd seen him, she'd deliberately been vague when he'd asked about her husband. But she could tell by the awkward silence that had fallen that he knew the truth. There were precious few secrets in the close-knit Italian community they'd grown up in, and she should have known he'd soon find out she was single. Why she'd even bothered to cover yesterday she had no idea. At the time, it had seemed…messy to try to explain about Marcus and the fact that she was all alone.

At least be honest with yourself if you can't be honest with anyone else, Lucia Basso.

The truth was that she'd been embarrassed. She stopped short of labeling the emotion she'd experienced shame. She wasn't ashamed of her baby. She refused to be. But there was no getting around the fact that she was a good Catholic girl who was having a baby on her own because her boyfriend had abandoned her for another woman.

She opened her mouth to try to explain her omission, then swallowed her words without speaking them. Dom wouldn't care. Her being pregnant or not or married or not meant nothing in his world. They had a business relationship, nothing more.

But still she felt uncomfortable. And the feeling seemed to be mutual. Dom shoved a hand into the back pocket of his jeans and shifted his feet.

"She'll come around. Once she sees that little baby, she'll be putty in your hands," he said.

It was too complicated a situation to explain over a trestle table of zucchinis. Lucy smiled and waved a hand.

"It's fine. We're fine. It's all good," she said.

Dom hesitated a beat before nodding. "Okay, let's get you those herbs."

They were both careful to keep things surface-level for the rest of the transaction, and Lucy left the stall feeling oddly depressed. Which was as stupid as blushing over Mr. Bianco's compliment. There was nothing in her relationship with Dominic Bianco that she had any reason to feel depressed about.

Still, she found herself going over their conversation again as she broke up her stock into separate orders in the back of the van prior to her first delivery of the day.

It was the fact that he'd confided about his father that had made her drop her guard, she decided. Dom had always been friendly, but in a professional way. Today was the first time that either of them had offered each other anything beyond polite small talk.

"Ow." Lucy looked to where she'd caught her knee against the corner of one of her crates.

Great. She'd been so distracted thinking about Dominic that she'd put a run in her panty hose. Now she'd have to find the time to buy a new pair and wriggle into them before her bank appointment that afternoon.

A surge of nerves raced through her as she thought about the bank and the loan and what it meant for her future.

Get your head together, girl, because you will not get a second chance to get this right.

It was a scary thought—more than scary enough to sweep any other thoughts away. She didn't have the luxury of being distracted right now.

Grimly determined, she finished breaking up her orders.

Later that afternoon, Dom stood in the refrigerated storeroom Bianco Brothers rented and broke the tape seal on the small box in front of him. Inside was a state-of-the-art handheld data unit, ideal for inputting stock information and orders for a wholesale company like his father's.

Dom had picked up the unit yesterday after work, and today he was determined to start phase one of his plan to modernize the business. His father was going to be resistant to change, he knew that. But Dom would show him how much easier and more efficient life could be. In essence, that was what phase one was all about—massaging his father into letting progress do its thing.

It wasn't like he was asking his father to take on the burden of learning the new software himself. Dom would do all that. At worst, Tony would have to learn how to pilot one of these handheld units, and the literature promised that they were as simple to use as a pocket calculator.

After studying the instructions for a few minutes, Dom powered up the unit and experimented with a couple of functions. Satisfied that he had the basics sorted, he turned to the stacks of crates towering around him. He'd catalog the stock in the storage space, then download the data into the new software program on his computer, then he'd show his father what they could do with the information. His father was stubborn, maybe even a little scared and intimidated by new technology, but Dom was confident that the old man would switch on to computerizing once he understood the benefits.

His thoughts drifted to Lucy as he began to punch in data. She'd looked good today, if a little pale. The bulge of her pregnancy was still in the burgeoning stage, cute and round rather than big and heavy. She'd always been beautiful, but being pregnant had added an extra dimension to her appeal.

He shook his head as he caught his own thoughts. He was not hitting on a pregnant woman. He'd already decided against it. She was vulnerable, for starters. Abandoned by her boyfriend, running a business on her own. She had too much at stake and inserting himself into the mix was only going to make things worse. Plus— pure selfishness here—he didn't want to have any doubt about why Lucy was attracted to him. If that miracle ever happened. Not that he figured her for the type of woman who would seek out a man to provide security for herself and her unborn child, but he didn't want there to be any confusion around the issue.

Once again they were the victims of bad timing. But maybe when she'd had the child, when her world was more settled... Maybe then he'd make his move, try his luck.

"Dom. We're starting to close up. You ready in here?"

Dom turned to find his father standing in the doorway, his body a dark silhouette against the pale winter sunlight. There was a small pause as his father's eyes adjusted to the difference in light, and Dom didn't need to see his father's face to know that he'd spotted the handheld unit.

"What you doing?" Tony asked. His voice was flat, absolutely expressionless.

Bad sign.

"I picked this up yesterday on the way home from work," Dom said, facing his father. "I wanted to show you what it can do."

"I told you, we not interested. Vinnie and me have discussed."

"But, Pa, we can do so much more with this software in place. Project sales, pick up on trends. Cut down on spoilage."

Dom hated that he sounded like a beseeching child trying to cajole a parent into taking him to an amusement park. This was a smart business decision and he should not have to cajole his father into anything. He was part of Bianco Brothers, too. It was time his father and uncle started respecting his opinion more.

"Take it back. I hope they give you money back," Tony said dismissively.

"Why don't you come over and take a look at what it can do? I've just entered this whole wall of stock in about five minutes," Dom said. "It's every bit as fast as writing it down on your clipboard, and everyone can have access to the data."

"Don't talk like I am little child," Tony said. His voice was sharp. "I not idiot. Your uncle not idiot. We know how to run business. You bide time, be good boy, and one day you will run. Until then, you do things our way."

Dom flinched from the tone and intent of his father's words.

"Speaking of talking to people like children. In case you hadn't noticed, I'm not a boy anymore," he said. "Also, just so you know, Luigi Verde and his son have installed a computer system. And the Kerrimuirs have had one for two years. We're going to be left behind if we don't step up now and start offering our clients more services."

He hadn't meant for things to get this heated so quickly, but he also hadn't expected his father to be so adamant on the issue. At the least, he'd expected his father to be curious, to explore the idea a little before rejecting it.

"It not matter. Our clients are loyal. They not forget us."

Dom couldn't help himself: he laughed.

"Pa, welcome to the twenty-first century. There's no such thing as loyalty anymore. As soon as our customers know they can get a better deal or more value for money from one of our competitors, they're gone. Don't believe for a second that they come to you and Uncle Vinnie for any other reason except that it lines their pockets."

His father waved a dismissive hand in the air and made a spitting noise.

"What you know? Your generation not understand. You not understand sticking to something, making work no matter what. You think if something hard, must be wrong. You walk away from commitments like mean nothing."

Dom went very still.

"You're talking about me and Dani, aren't you?"

If his father wanted to throw accusations around, Dom was going to be damn sure they both knew what they were talking about.

Tony shifted his bulk, then tucked his thumbs into the waistband of his apron and just stared back at Dom. His stillness was his answer: yes, he thought his son had given up on his marriage rather than do the hard yards to fix it.

Hot anger stiffened Dom's neck and squared his shoulders. He'd known that his father was unhappy about the divorce, but not this unhappy.

"I guess I should thank you for the honesty. At least we both know where we stand."

"You think your mother and I not have hard times? You think I never look at other women and wonder if they wouldn't be easier to love?"

Dom held his hand up. "Wait a minute. You think I *cheated* on Dani? Is that what you're saying?" he asked. His voice had slipped up an octave.

His parents had known he and Dani were trying for children, that there had been problems, but Dom had never discussed the finer points of the issue with them. He'd never quite known how to explain to his father that thanks to the case of mumps he'd had when he was twenty years old, he was sterile and would never be able to father children of his own. He'd figured he'd get around to it, eventually.

And now his father was suggesting that the reason his marriage had fallen apart was because he'd strayed. So. Not only was Dom a man who couldn't go the distance and honor his commitments, he was a cheat, too.

"Why else marriage break up? Dani was nice girl. She would never cheat," his father said.

Dom rocked back on his heels. "This is unbelievable. How long have you felt this way, Pa? How long have you thought your son was a no-good sleaze?"

It was his father's turn to rock back on his heels. "That not what I said. You never talk, you never say anything. You come to me and your mother and say marriage over. What we supposed to think?"

"Shit, I don't know. Maybe the best of me? Maybe

that there was a bloody good reason for my divorce and that I'd tell you once I could handle talking about it?"

"Talk now. Tell me now," Tony demanded, thumping his chest.

"Why would I bother?" Dom said. "You have your own ideas about me, and you obviously like them a lot more than the truth."

He grabbed his jacket and strode toward the doorway. He couldn't remember ever being more furious with his father—and they'd had some rip-roaring fights over the years.

His father held his ground until the last possible moment, then stepped to one side.

Dom thrust the handheld unit at him as he passed.

"Do what you like with it. You won't hear another word from me on the subject," he said.

Then he marched back toward the stand. There was work to do, after all. He'd hate for his father to think his no-good son was adding shirking to his list of crimes.

"I can't believe they said no."

Lucy forced a small smile. "Well, they did. Apparently I'm a bad risk. No assets, no security."

"But you're making a profit. And you'll make a bigger one once you get the site up and running and you attract more business," Rosie said.

"Said all that. They didn't care."

"Crap," Rosie said. Then she sat straighter. "We'll try another bank. There's got to be someone out there with a bit of vision."

"Rosie, I have my van lease with them, do all my banking through them. If they don't want to do business with me, no one else is going to step up to the plate."

"You don't know that. We have to try." Rosie pulled her cell phone from her bag. "What's the name of that new bank, the one advertising all the time?"

"I've already called the other three major banks, and two of the building societies," Lucy said.

"And?"

"Like I said. No one wants to take a risk on me. And that's before they've gotten an eyeful of this." She indicated her belly.

Rosie stared at her, clearly at a loss as the facts sank in. "Crap," she said again.

"Oh yeah," Lucy said.

A waiter appeared at their table and Rosie waved him away.

"No, wait. I need chocolate," Lucy said.

"Good idea," Rosie said.

They both ordered hot chocolates and cake before returning to the crisis at hand.

"There has to be some way around this," Rosie said.

Lucy pushed her hair behind her ear. She was tired, exhausted really, but she was hoping the chocolate would give her a much needed kick. Crawling into bed and sleeping for a day was not an option open to her right now.

"I've been doing some sums. If I save my ass off between now and when the baby is due, I can put aside enough to cover my bills for three months. Ma mentioned the other day that Cousin Mario is looking for work. I thought I could offer him the driver's job for three months. He can take my wage, I'll live off my savings. It might work."

Rosie was staring at her. "What if you need more than three months? What if Mario won't do it for what you pay yourself? Which, let's face it, is a joke."

Lucy felt the heat of threatening tears, and she clenched her jaw. "I guess I'll cross that bridge when I come to it."

"No. It's a make-do, Band-Aid plan, and it's not going to cut it. You need that twenty thousand."

"Really? Do you think?" Lucy said. She so didn't need her sister pointing out the obvious to her, not when she was trying to be stoic.

"We'll lend it to you," Rosie suddenly announced, slapping her hands onto the table so hard she made the sugar dispenser jump.

"What?"

"Andrew and I have got some money put aside for renovations at the office. We can put them off and lend it to you instead," Rosie said.

Lucy stared at her sister. "God, I love you, you idiot, but there's no way I'm taking money from you and Andrew. Forget about it. I'll talk to Cousin Mario tonight, get something else sorted. It'll be fine."

"Listen to me," Rosie said, leaning across the table until she was right in Lucy's face. "That money is just sitting there. We've been talking about hiring an architect for years and it hasn't happened. We'll draw it up like a loan, if that makes you feel any better. You can pay us interest, make regular payments. We'll be just like the bank, only nicer."

Lucy shook her head. "No. You've already taken me into your home. You won't let me pay more than a token rent. I can't keep taking your charity forever, Rosie. What kind of a mother am I going to be if I can't stand on my own two feet?"

"Exactly. And the fastest way for you to get there is to get that Internet site happening and grow your business. I know it hurts your pride, but taking a loan from your family is the best thing for you and the baby. And that's the truth." Rosie sat back in her chair, her case made.

Lucy stared at her, her mind whirling.

It was so tempting. Rosie and Andrew had the money. Lucy could stick to her original game plan. She'd already spoken to a Web site design company in anticipation of today's bank appointment. She could go full steam ahead with her schedule and be online within a month.

"Say yes. Be smart. For the baby," Rosie said.

"It's so much money," Lucy said. "And you guys have got plans for it."

"They'll wait."

"What about Andrew? It's his money, too."

"He loves you almost as much as I do, and he'll understand."

Lucy closed her eyes. So many big decisions lately. If only she had a crystal ball. She opened her eyes again.

"Yes. Okay. I can't believe I'm saying that, but thank you. Thank you so much. Where would I be without you?"

"Good girl!"

"I won't let you down," Lucy said. "I promise I'll pay back every cent."

"I know you will. I know where you live, remember?"

They were both blinking rapidly. Lucy shook her head.

"I feel like I just got off a roller-coaster. Talk about up and down."

"Welcome to parenthood, I guess," Rosie said. "From what I hear, this is just the beginning."

They both smiled, and Lucy reached across to grab her sister's hand, overwhelmed with gratitude and relief.

"Hey there. Long time no see," a familiar male voice said.

Lucy looked up to see Dominic Bianco standing next to the table. She felt her sister's fingers convulse around hers in reaction and had to fight the urge to giggle. Truly, Rosie's crush on The Bianco was a hoot.

"Dom. You're not just finishing work for the day, are you?" Lucy asked, noting he was still wearing his Bianco Brothers shirt.

"Something like that. Hey, Rosetta, how are things?"

Rosie was smiling at Dom with slightly glazed eyes. "G-good. Things are good. I'm married now, you know," she said.

Dom's eyebrows rose a bit at her sister's odd segue.

"Congratulations. When was the wedding?" he asked politely.

"Eight years ago," Lucy said.

"Right," Dom said. He looked confused, as well he might.

"Lucy tells me you've come back from six months in Italy," Rosie said.

Now it was Lucy's turn to be embarrassed. She didn't want Dom to think she spent her spare time talking about him.

"Yeah. Had a few months in Rome, Florence and Venice, checked out the countryside."

"Andrew and I were going to go for our honeymoon, but we wound up in Thailand instead," Rosie said. "I guess you got a bit of sun while you were there, huh? You're really tanned."

Rosie's eyes were on Dom's forearms as she spoke, and she looked as though she was about to lunge across the table and sink her teeth into him. Lucy drew back her knee in case she had to kick her sister.

"It was summer over there. What can I say?" he said.

He turned his attention to Lucy. "Your client happy with the herbs for his wedding dinner?"

"As happy as he can let himself be. He's French. He makes it a point to never smile too much."

Dom laughed, and Lucy felt a surge of satisfaction that she'd amused him.

"We've got a few French chefs as clients. They like to keep us on our toes, that's for sure."

"Pretty amazing, Lucy winding up as one of your

customers after all these years," Rosie said. "It's a small world."

"Even smaller when you're Italian," Dom said. "Lucy is one of our favorite clients. My father and I fight over who gets to serve her."

Even though she knew he was only joking, Lucy shifted in her chair.

"That's rubbish. You almost always serve me," she said, aware of her sister's speculative glance bouncing back and forth between them.

"That's because I cheat," Dom said with an unrepentant grin.

The waiter arrived with their hot chocolates and cake, and Dom checked his watch.

"I'll leave you to it—looks as though you've got your work cut out for you," he said, indicating the generous slices of cake.

"See you tomorrow," Lucy said.

Dom smiled and gave a small, casual wave before moving to the other side of the café, out of sight behind the central counter.

"Oh. My. God. Pass me the chocolate. I need emergency therapy," Rosie said, slumping in her chair and fanning herself. "He's better-looking than ever. What a hunk. I mean, wow."

"Oh, look, there's Andrew," Lucy fibbed.

Rosie immediately sat up straight. Then she realized her sister was yanking her chain.

"Good one. Very funny."

"Just a timely reminder."

"Hey, I love Andrew with everything I've got, don't you worry. I'm not going anywhere, with anyone. But I can still admire The Bianco. It's a sentimental thing."

"It's sad. And, can I say, just a little embarrassing. You almost got drool on your good shirt."

"Pshaw," Rosie said, flicking her fingers in the air. "I was in total control the whole time."

Lucy rolled her eyes and spoke to the ceiling. "Delusional. The woman's delusional."

"Anyway, he never even noticed me. He was too busy looking at you like he wanted to lick you all over."

Lucy stared at her sister.

"He was not!"

"Uh-huh. He was, and he was flirting with you, too."

"Get out of here. I look like I've got a beach ball stuck up my top. He was not flirting with me."

"Lucy is one of our most favorite clients ever. My father and I wrestle to the death over who gets to serve her. What do you call that?"

"Being polite. Or being funny. Maybe both. But not flirting."

Rosie gave her a get-real look. "Seriously? You seriously didn't think he was flirting with you?"

"Of course not. Duh," Lucy said, pointing to her belly.

"Man. We are going to have to do something about your dating skills, because if you're not picking up signals that strong, you are never going to find another man," Rosie said.

Lucy knew her sister was only joking, but her words still caught her on the raw.

"Hey, what's wrong?" Rosie asked as Lucy reached for her hot chocolate and concentrated on stirring it.

"Nothing. Nothing's wrong."

"Bad at flirting and bad at lying. What am I going to do with you?"

Lucy stopped stirring her drink and met her sister's eyes.

"I don't want another man. I want Marcus. I want the father of my baby," she said in a small voice.

Her sister stared at her, her face full of sympathy.

"Go on, say it. Tell me I'm pathetic for wanting someone who doesn't want me," Lucy said.

"I don't think that's pathetic. Marcus is the pathetic one. I just feel sad that I can't give you what you want."

Lucy sighed heavily and picked up a fork.

"I guess all this chocolate is still very necessary, after all," she said.

"Chocolate is always necessary, whether it be for celebration or commiseration," Rosie said.

Her sister waited until Lucy was swallowing a chunk of sinfully rich frosting before speaking again.

"And he was flirting with you. The Bianco was fully, blatantly, balls-out flirting with you."

Chapter 4

"Did you even consider discussing this with me first?" Andrew asked.

Rosie put down her knife and fork and gave her husband her full attention.

"I should have waited to talk to you, I know—"

"You think?"

Rosie blinked. Andrew didn't often lose his temper but when he did it was usually well-earned. Like tonight. As soon as she'd given it some thought, she'd known she should have spoken to him before offering the money to Lucy. But she couldn't undo what had already been done.

"I'm sorry. I got carried away. All I was thinking about was Lucy and how I could help. I hate that she's in such a difficult position."

"I hate it, too. But we've already given her a home. We can't afford to give her our savings, too."

"I hear what you're saying, but that money's just sitting in the bank, collecting interest. Why not use it to help Lucy? She'll pay us interest like the bank. It's a win-win situation."

Andrew pushed his chair back from the table and stood.

"What about our plans to renovate the practice? What about getting a junior partner? All that just goes by the wayside, does it?"

"No, of course not. But it's not like we were actually ready to do any of that. We haven't even decided on an architect yet."

"Because you keep putting it off."

Rosie stood, hating being at a disadvantage. "I haven't put anything off. Neither of us has pushed for the renovation. We've been too busy building the practice."

Andrew looked at her, his face tense.

"Rosie, every time I suggest we start talking to architects you come up with a reason for why we can't. First it was the Larson trial, then it was the Bigalows' divorce. The time after that you strained your Achilles' at the gym and you didn't want me doing all the legwork on my own." He stared at her, his jaw set. "If you're not ready to have children, tell me and stop stringing me along."

Rosie took a step backward. She hadn't been expecting such a direct confrontation, not after the way they'd both been sidestepping the issue for so long. It had become a game of sorts, the way they skirted around the all-consuming subject of when to start a family.

"I'm not not ready," Rosie said quickly, even though her stomach tensed with anxiety. "I'm not stringing you along. The time simply hasn't been right before."

Andrew sighed heavily. His blue eyes were intent as he looked into her face. "So when will the time be right if we give all our savings to Lucy? Five years? Ten years? You're thirty-one. How old do you plan on being when our kids are in college? You're the one who insisted we needed to add a junior partner to the firm before we even considered starting a family. And we both agreed we couldn't do that until we'd renovated the practice to create an extra office."

Again the tightness in her belly.

"Lucy probably only needs the money for a year or two," she said. "As soon as she's paid us back, we'll renovate and start trying."

"Rosie. Be serious. It will take longer than two years for Lucy to pay out a loan. She'll be working part-time, she'll have expenses for the baby. It could take her years to get on top of things. We've dealt with enough bankruptcies to know that most small businesses don't survive the first few years."

"Lucy is not going to go bankrupt!"

"I didn't say she was. But she's also not going to suddenly become Martha Stewart, either."

He watched her, waiting for her to acknowledge that he was speaking the truth.

Finally she nodded. "Okay. You're right. It probably won't be two years."

He returned to the dining table and sat. His meal was only half-eaten, but he pushed it away.

"So we need to make a decision. Do we invest in our dream or your sister's?" he asked quietly.

She sat, too. Suddenly she felt very heavy.

"We could remortgage," she suggested.

"We're already leveraged because of buying the office. And once you have a baby and we put a partner on, our income will be reduced. That was the whole point of socking away extra money to pay for the renovations rather than taking on more debt. You know I would have been happy if we were pregnant years ago. But I know financial security is important to you, so we did things your way. Now you're telling me you want to put things off again while we lend our renovation fund to your sister?"

Rosie picked up her fork and pushed it into the pile of cold peas on her plate.

"Do we put off having a family or not, Rosie?" he asked.

She raised her gaze to him. She knew exactly how much he wanted children. It was one of the first things they'd discussed when they got together all those years ago. He wanted at least three children, wanted to build a family that would make up for the lack in his own shitty childhood. Even though the thought had scared her even back then, she'd invested in his dream, built castles in the air with him. And for the past eight years she'd been burying her head in the sand, pretending this day would never come.

"I shouldn't have offered the money to Lucy," she said quietly. "I'm sorry."

Andrew waited patiently for her to answer properly.

"We're not putting off starting a family," she confirmed. "I'll tell Lucy that we can't lend her the money after all."

Andrew's shoulders relaxed. She saw for the first time that there was a sheen of tears in his eyes. This meant so much to him.

"I'll come with you. We'll explain together," he said.

Rosie shook her head.

"No. It was my mistake. I'll do it."

She stood. She hated to think of how disappointed Lucy would be. Her sister had been so excited this afternoon.

If only she hadn't acted so impetuously. If only she'd stopped to think, waited to talk to Andrew tonight. But she hadn't, and now she had to go break her sister's heart to avoid breaking her husband's. And then, somehow, she had to overcome this terror that struck her every time she thought about becoming a mother.

Lucy dragged herself to the market the next morning. Never had she wanted to stay in bed so badly, not even the morning after Marcus left.

She felt defeated, and it scared her that she couldn't see a way out. She had no choice but to keep on working for as long as she could and hope that her cousin was prepared to drive for her at minimum wage and that she had a problem-free pregnancy before giving birth to the world's most perfect baby.

She didn't blame her sister for reneging on the loan. Rosie's offer had been generous and impulsive, and Lucy totally understood why she and Andrew had decided they had to retract it once cooler heads had prevailed.

She just wished she had an Option C to fall back on now that Option B had gone up in flames.

"Lucy. Managed to brave the cold, I see," Dom said as she stopped her trolley in front of the Bianco Brothers stall.

"Yeah," she said. Today even Dom's smile and charm couldn't nudge her out of her funk. All she wanted to do was to go home, curl into a ball and sleep until the world had righted itself. She fished in her bag for her shopping list, growing increasingly frustrated when she couldn't put her hand on it.

"Sorry. Give me a minute," she said. She pulled handfuls of paper from her bag, angrily riffling through them for the one she needed. She was such a train wreck—couldn't even get one little thing right today.

She could feel Dom watching her as she went back and forth through the papers. The list had to be in here somewhere. And if it wasn't, it meant a trip home to collect it from her flat. She felt dangerously close to bursting into tears and she blinked rapidly.

"Here."

She looked up to find a takeout coffee cup under her nose. She automatically shook her head.

"I can't drink coffee."

"It's hot chocolate. And you look like you need it more than I do."

As he spoke, the smell of warm chocolate hit her nose and her mouth watered.

"Come on, take it," he said, waving the cup invitingly.

"Thanks." She took the cup with a small smile. The first mouthful was hot and full of sugar. Just what she needed.

"Better?" Dom asked.

"Thanks."

He smiled, the dimple in his cheek popping. She glanced down at her papers and realized her shopping list was right on top of the pile.

"Typical," she muttered as she handed it over.

Dom scanned it quickly. "No problems here. Why don't you kick back and I'll get this sorted?"

He was already moving off. She knew she should object, at least pretend to inspect the produce on offer. But she trusted him. And today—just today—she needed a break. Tomorrow she would take on all comers again.

She rested her elbows on the push bar of her trolley, watching Dom sort through produce for her as she sipped his hot chocolate.

He was a nice man. Sexy, too. Although she still wasn't sure that she was grateful to her sister for pointing that fact out. She wondered what had gone wrong with his marriage. Then she realized what she was doing and dragged her attention away from his broad shoulders and flat belly.

"Okay. I think that's everything. I threw in some extra leeks for you. We overordered, and I'm sure you can find a customer to give them to," Dom said when he'd finished loading her trolley.

Lucy looked at him steadily for a moment before speaking.

"Thank you," she said. She hoped he understood that she meant for everything—the produce, the hot chocolate, giving her a helping hand when she was bottoming out on self-pity.

He shrugged. "It's nothing. You look after yourself."

She opened her mouth to say more, but he was already greeting another customer. She'd taken up far too much of his time. Her stomach warm, she headed to her van and a full day of deliveries.

Dom found the paperwork sitting among the boxes of broccoli in front of the stall. Four pages, stapled together with a brochure for a Web site design company. They looked important, and he put them aside in case a customer came looking for them. It was only when they were packing up the stall for the day that he noticed the papers again.

The sheets obviously couldn't have been too vital, since no one had claimed them. He was on the verge of throwing them out when something about the loopy handwriting on the front page jogged his memory. He flicked through, and Lucy Basso's signature jumped out at him from the last page. He remembered her agitation this morning, the way she'd fumbled in her bag. She had to have lost this when she was looking for her shopping list.

Dom stared at her signature for a long beat. He could wait till tomorrow and hand them back to her.

Or he could take them to her.

He folded the papers in two, sliding them into his back pocket. Lucy Basso was not in the market for romance. He knew that, absolutely. And yet he was still going to take advantage of the opportunity these papers represented.

Later that night, he balanced a takeout pastry box in one hand while knocking on Lucy's front door with the other. Music filtered out into the night, Coldplay's "Everything's Not Lost." He glanced over his shoulder at the backyard of the house her flat was piggybacked onto. He'd had to decipher his father's handwriting on the much-thumbed index cards that constituted the Bianco Brothers' customer database to find her address. He eyed the flattened moving boxes stacked against the house and wondered how long she'd been living here.

Footsteps sounded on the other side of the door, and he blinked as it opened and light suddenly flooded him.

"Dom! Hi," Lucy said. She sounded utterly thrown, and her hands moved to tighten the sash on her pale-blue dressing gown.

She was ready for bed. He gave himself a mental slap on the head. Of course she was ready for bed—

she was pregnant, and like himself she had to be up at the crack of dawn.

"Hi. Sorry to barge in like this. You left some papers at the stall today and I thought they might be important," he said.

"Oh. Wow. Thanks."

She smiled uncertainly and pushed a strand of thick dark hair off her face. For the first time he noticed her eyes were puffy and a little red.

She'd been crying.

That quickly his self-consciousness went out the window. The thought of Lucy crying on her own made him want to hurt something.

He lifted the pastry box.

"And I brought dessert, in case you hadn't had any yet."

She frowned as though she didn't quite understand what he was saying.

"Dessert?" she repeated.

"You know, the stuff everyone tells us is bad for us but that we keep eating anyway."

She laughed. "Right. Sorry. I wasn't expecting… Come in," she said.

She stood aside and he stepped past her into the flat. He took in her small combined living and dining room, noting her rustic dining table and her earthy brown couch with beige and grass-green cushions. A number of black-and-white photographs graced the walls—the desert at sunset, an empty beach, an extreme close-up of a glistening spiderweb.

"You really didn't have to do this," Lucy said as she moved past him to the kitchenette that filled one corner of the small flat.

"It was no big deal. It's on my way home," he said.

Technically, it was kind of true. If he was taking the really, really scenic route.

Lucy placed two plates on the counter.

"Would you like coffee or something else with… I don't even know what you brought," she said. She sounded bemused again but he refused to feel bad about ambushing her.

"Tiramisu. Like a good Italian boy," he said.

"I love tiramisu."

"It's in the blood. We've been trained from birth to love it."

He handed over the pastry box and she peeled away the paper.

"Good lord, this thing is monstrous. There's no way we can eat all of this," she said.

He made a show of peering into the box.

"Speak for yourself."

She smiled and gave him a challenging look as she divided the huge portion into two uneven servings, sliding the much larger piece onto a plate and pushing it toward him.

"I dare you."

"You should know I never back out on a dare," he warned her.

She handed him a fork, a smile playing about her lips. He followed her to the dining table where she sat at the end and he took the chair to her left. She'd barely sat before she was standing again.

"Coffee! I forgot your coffee. These bloody pregnancy hormones have turned my brain into Swiss cheese," she said.

He grabbed her arm before she could move back to the kitchen.

"Relax. I don't need coffee," he said.

Her arm felt slim but strong beneath his hand. He forced himself to let her go, and she sank into the chair.

For a moment there was nothing but the sound of forks clinking against plates as they each took a mouthful.

"Before I forget," Dom said.

He leaned forward to pull her papers from his back pocket, then slid them across the table.

Lucy's face clouded as she looked at them.

"Thanks."

"Why do I feel like I just handed you an execution order?"

Her gaze flicked to his face, then away again.

"It's nothing. Less than nothing. I'm sorry you wasted your time on them."

She pushed the papers away as though she never wanted to see them again.

He took a mouthful of his dessert and studied her. She looked tired. Maybe even a little beaten. The same vibe he'd sensed from her this morning.

"You want to talk about it?" he asked quietly.

She looked surprised. Then she shook her head. "You

don't want to hear all my problems," she said after a long moment.

"Come on, you have to talk to me. You made me come all this way for papers that mean nothing, you're eating my tiramisu. What's in this for me?" he said.

She huffed out a laugh at his outrageous twisting of the truth. "When you put it that way…" She gave him a searching look then shrugged. "Just yawn or fall face-first into your food when you've heard enough."

"Don't worry. I have plenty of cunning strategies to escape boring conversations. I have three aunts and four uncles."

Briefly she outlined her plans for Market Fresh—her goal to go online to grow the business, her plans to lease a second delivery van. She sat a little straighter as she talked and color came into her cheeks. She loved what she was doing, what she was building. And he was quietly impressed with her strategy. Apart from the all-too-apparent hiccup curving the front of her dressing gown, she sounded perfectly situated to take the next step.

"Absolutely," she agreed with him. "Except for one tiny little thing—the bank doesn't agree with me. They won't lend me the money I need to get my Web site built. Without the site, I can't generate more business, and without more business I can't afford to put on a second van."

Lucy looked down and seemed surprised that she'd polished off her dessert.

"So, basically, I'm screwed," she said.

"Lucia Basso. If your mother could hear you now,"

he said, mostly because he hated the despairing look that had crept into her eyes.

"It's okay. She already thinks I'm screwed. It won't be news to her."

She met his gaze across the table, and they both burst into laughter. She laughed so hard she had to lean back in her chair and hold her stomach. By the time she'd gained a modicum of control, tears were rolling down her face.

"God, I needed that," she said. Then her eyes went wide and she straightened in her chair as though someone had goosed her. "Oh!"

Both hands clutched her belly and she stared at Dom.

"What? Is something wrong?" he asked, already half out of his chair.

"The baby just moved!"

"Right." He felt like an idiot for being on the verge of calling the paramedics.

"It's the first time," she explained excitedly. "All the pregnancy books say I should start feeling something about now, and I've been waiting and waiting but there's been nothing—"

Her eyes went wide again and she smiled.

"There he goes again!" she said. "This is incredible! Dom, you have to feel this."

Before he knew what she was doing she'd pushed aside her dressing gown to reveal the thin T-shirt she was wearing underneath, grabbed his hand and pressed his palm to her belly. He could feel the warmth of her skin through the fabric, the rise and fall of her body as she breathed.

"Can you feel it?" she asked, her voice hushed as though the baby might overhear her and stop performing.

He shook his head, acutely self-conscious. He didn't know what to do with his fingers, whether to relax them into her body or keep his hand stiff. He could smell her perfume and feel the swell of her breast pressing against his forearm.

"Relax your hand more," she instructed, frowning in concentration. He let his hand soften and she slid it over her belly, pressing it against herself with both hands.

Still he could feel nothing. She bit her lip.

"Maybe he's tired," she said.

Beneath his palm, he felt a faint surge, the smallest of disturbances beneath her skin.

He laughed and she grinned at him.

"Tell me you felt that?"

"I felt it."

They smiled at each other like idiots, his hand curved against her belly. He knew the exact moment the wonder of the moment wore off and she became self-aware again. He pulled his hand free at the same time that she released her grip on him. They both sat back in their chairs, an awkwardness between them that hadn't been there a few minutes ago.

"I should go," he said. "You've got an early start tomorrow."

"Yours is earlier," she said.

They both stood.

"About the business…something will come up," he said.

She shrugged. "Or it won't. I'll muddle through, I'm sure."

Her hand found her stomach, holding it protectively. He followed her to the door.

"Thanks for the tiramisu," she said with a small smile. "And for bringing my Web site stuff back."

"Like I said, it was on the way home. And I would have eaten all the tiramisu on my own if I'd had the chance. You saved me from myself."

He patted his stomach and she laughed, as he'd known she would. He hovered on the doorstep, unwilling to leave her just yet.

"What does it feel like?" he asked suddenly. "When the baby moves inside you?"

Her expression grew distant, and she cocked her head to one side. He had to resist the urge to reach out and touch her cheek to see if her skin really was as soft and smooth as it appeared.

"The books say it's like butterflies fluttering," she said after a moment. "Some women say it's like gas."

"Butterflies or gas. Right."

She smiled. "The closest thing I can come up with is that it's like when a goldfish brushes up against your hand. Only on the inside, if that makes sense."

She was so beautiful, standing there with her uncertain eyes and her smiling mouth and her rounded stomach. He wanted to kiss her. He took a step backward.

"Good night, Lucy Basso," he said.

"Good night, Dom."

He told himself he was being smart and fair as he walked down the darkened driveway to the street. She was pregnant. He had no business chasing her.

And yet he felt like he was letting yet another opportunity slip through his fingers.

He flexed his hand as he remembered the flutter of movement he'd felt beneath his palm. A smile curved his mouth as he started his car. She'd been so delighted, so amazed. He was stupidly happy that he'd been there to share the moment with her.

He sobered as he registered where his thoughts were going. This wasn't his baby. Lucy wasn't his wife or partner. He wouldn't be sharing any more moments of discovery with her—or with any other woman, for that matter.

There was a message from his father on his answering machine when he arrived home, asking him to call back. His father sounded sleepy when he answered the phone.

"You are late. Where have you been?"

Dom raised his eyebrows at his father's nosiness. "Out. What's up?"

"Out where? Out with girl?"

The joys of working with his family—they felt they owned his life.

"Pa."

He heard his father sigh.

"I need you to make run to Lilydale tomorrow to

collect more zucchini from Giametti's. We short and I promise dozen boxes to Vue De Monde," his father explained.

Dom rubbed his eyes and stifled a yawn. What his father was suggesting would mean he had to get up an extra two hours early in order to have the stock on hand for their customers.

"You know, if you'd let me manage the stock on the computer, we wouldn't have these kinds of problems," he said lightly.

To his surprise, his father blew up, sending a string of expletives and curses down the phone.

"I sick of hearing about computers. You said you not talk about them again. I expect you to honor this even if you honor nothing else!"

Dom let his breath out between his teeth. He loved his father, but he wasn't a little boy anymore, and he certainly didn't have to take crap from him—especially when it was out-of-line, unearned crap.

"Am I part of Bianco Brothers or not?" he asked.

"You are my son. This is stupid question."

"Answer the question, Pa."

"You are part of business. You there every day. You can't work out for yourself?"

"So I'm an employee. Like Steve and Michael and Anna?"

"You are my son."

Dom didn't say a word, waiting for his father to stop hedging. The silence stretched tensely for long seconds before his father spoke again.

"What you want from me? You my right-arm man," his father said, messing up his Anglo phrasing the way he often did. "I not manage without you. There. Happy now?"

"If that's true, if I'm your second in command, I want a say. I want a vote. And I want a bit of respect while you're at it," Dom said.

"Respect! You talk respect when you speak to your own father like he is idiot who doesn't know anything about anything. You have place in my business, good job. You should be grateful, counting your lucky stars, instead of whining and complaining."

Dom held the phone away from his ear and swore long and loud. Why did he bother? Hadn't he banged his head against this brick wall just the other day? His father didn't want to change. He was old. And the truth was, Bianco Brothers was so successful that his father wouldn't notice the business they would lose over the coming years as their competitors got leaner and meaner and more efficient. By the time his father was ready to retire—or he dropped dead on the job, which was just as likely—Dom would be left with the task of picking up the pieces and trying to claw back market share.

If he chose to take it.

"Good night, Pa," he said. Then he ended the call.

"My business," his father had said. Not "our business."

Dom leaned against the kitchen counter. He had some decisions to make. If his father wasn't going to allow him to grow, to have a say… Well, maybe Dom needed to forge his own way.

Lucy felt ridiculously shy as she arrived at the market the following morning. Last night she'd pressed Dom's hand against her belly, practically strong-arming him into sharing her baby's first movements.

What had she been thinking? As if he cared what was going on in her belly. He was her wholesale supplier, for Pete's sake. The guy who used to sit two pews forward of her own family in church when they were kids. He didn't want to know what her baby felt like when it kicked. Every time she remembered how she'd pressed his hand against herself her toes curled in her shoes.

It wasn't until after he'd gone that she'd looked in the mirror and seen how puffy and red her eyes were. There was no way he wouldn't have guessed she'd been crying. She could only imagine what he thought of her: poor, lonely Lucy, desperate for company.

She was relieved when she approached the stall and saw Dom was busy with another customer and his father was free. Mr. Bianco could help her with her order, and she wouldn't have to talk to Dom today. One small thing going her way for a change.

"Lucy. You look beautiful," Mr. Bianco greeted her, his chubby arms spread wide.

Dom glanced up from where he was standing nearby. His dark gaze was unreadable as he noted her.

"I'll look after Lucy, Pa," he said.

"You are busy," Mr. Bianco said dismissively.

"I'll just be a minute," Dom said, addressing Lucy and not his father.

There was a definite tension between the two men, and Lucy shrugged uncomfortably.

"Sure. Whatever suits you guys," she said.

Mr. Bianco opened his mouth to protest, but Dom nailed him with a look that had Mr. Bianco muttering under his breath as he moved off to serve someone else.

Lucy fiddled with the strap on her bag, nervous all over again now that she was going to have to face Dom after all. Maybe she should apologize for last night, for thrusting her baby bump at him. Just get the awkwardness out of the way and move on.

"Okay. Sorry about that," Dom said.

She looked up, words of apology on the tip of her tongue.

"Listen, have you got time for a coffee? Sorry, a hot chocolate? Twenty minutes?" Dom asked.

She opened her mouth but no sound came out. Why did this man keep taking her by surprise?

"Sure," she finally managed to croak.

Dom called out to his father that he was taking a break. Lucy left her trolley next to the stall and followed him to a café in the group of permanent shops that ran along Victoria Street beside the market. The woman behind the counter greeted him with a smile.

"We'll have two hot chocolates, Polly," he called as they sat.

Lucy clasped her hands nervously in front of her as Dom gave her his full attention. She had no idea what he was going to say to her, and she found his intense gaze unnerving. Suddenly all she could think about was how hot and heavy his hand had felt against her body last night.

Talk about inappropriate.

"I've been giving some thought to what we talked about last night," he said. "About your business and your plans for the future."

Lucy nodded. Right. He was going to offer her some advice, probably suggest she talk to one of the second-tier banks like everyone else had. She schooled herself to be patient. He was being kind, after all. And she'd shown herself to be in need of kindness last night.

"How would you feel about taking on a business partner?" Dom asked.

She blinked. "Excuse me?" she asked stupidly.

He smiled. "Bit out of the blue, huh? I think you've got some great ideas for your business, and I think you've tapped into a strong niche market. Market Fresh has a lot of potential. There's no reason why you couldn't be operating across the city, even expanding into other states."

He smoothed some papers out on the table between them.

"What I'm proposing is a fifty-fifty business part-nership. I'll put up the capital to expand the business and build the Web site. You'll bring the existing business and your expertise to the table." He paused to look at her, his eyebrows raised in question.

She was too busy grappling for a mental foothold to

say anything. Dom wanted to buy into her business? Become her partner? Give her the money she needed to make her business a success?

"But you already have a business," she said, blurting out the first thought that popped into her mind.

"No. My father has a business. I just work for him," he said. There was a tightness around his mouth that hadn't been there yesterday. A determination.

"You don't know anything about my business. You haven't seen the books. You have no idea what my turn-over is," she said, frowning.

"Of course I'd want my accountant to take a look at things before we signed anything. I guess what I'm asking at this stage is if this sounds like something you might consider?" Dom asked.

Their hot chocolates arrived, and Lucy bought some time by fiddling with her cup and saucer.

Did she want a business partner? Being her own boss had been part of the appeal of starting Market Fresh, but taking on a partner wouldn't necessarily mean she wouldn't still have her independence. It would mean compromises though, having to listen to other ideas and incorporate them into her plans.

She eyed Dom assessingly. She hardly knew him really. Didn't know if he was hot tempered or easygoing, impulsive or rational. All she knew was what she'd observed of him over the year she'd been a customer at Bianco Brothers. He was good with customers. He was smart. He knew his product. He knew the industry.

"I've never thought about taking on a partner. Mostly

because it's never come up before." She studied his face. She didn't quite know how to ask her next question, so she decided to just go for it.

"Why me? Why Market Fresh?"

He took a sip of his hot chocolate before answering.

"I'm thirty-one and I've been working for my father all my adult life. I've always thought I'd take over when he retired. But I'm beginning to realize that that might be a long way off. And that maybe I don't want to be Tony Bianco's boy anymore. I have ideas, things I want to try, and he's not open to them."

"Okay. I get that part. But you could do anything."

"Sure. I could start my own business. Go through all the pain of establishing myself, learn a new industry. Or I could find someone like you who has done all that hard stuff already."

He eyed her over the rim of his cup.

"And you need help," he added. "Which, speaking from a purely selfish point of view, means I've got a certain amount of leverage."

Lucy dipped her head in acknowledgment of his brutal honesty. "Well. I asked," she said ruefully.

"Yep."

He sat back in his chair, his hands toying with his cup, spinning it on the saucer. His eyes never left hers as he waited for her to think things over some more.

What did she have to lose, after all? Her business, was the answer. And she was very afraid that she would do just that if she *didn't* take him up on his offer. She needed capital to grow. That was the bottom line.

"Okay. I'm interested," she said.

He smiled slowly. Suddenly she wished that her sister had never made her take a second look at him. Two weeks ago, he was a man, a human being like any other. Today, thanks to Rosie's teen obsession, Lucy felt a distinct frisson race up her spine as she registered how very, very good-looking he was.

Again, so not appropriate. Especially given her situation and the offer he'd just put on the table.

"Great. Why don't we meet on Sunday? That will give me time to get a preliminary offer drawn up. Rosetta will probably want to take a look at it, right?"

"Oh yeah. She'll probably want to pat you down and ransack your house and run an FBI check on you," Lucy said.

He smiled again. "I've got nothing to hide."

He leaned across the table and held out his hand. She hesitated a second before taking it. His hand was warm and firm.

"To new beginnings," he said.

She nodded, unable to speak for some reason while he held her with his dark gaze.

"We'd better get you on the road," he said.

She followed him to the stall, feeling more than a little dazed. After what had happened with her sister's offer of a loan, she knew it would be stupid to get too excited. So many things could go wrong. Dom could change his mind after he'd looked at the books. His lawyer or accountant might have objections. Anything could go wrong.

And yet a slow excitement was bubbling through her blood. If this came off, her problems were solved. She'd have the capital she needed to grow. She'd have a fighting chance to secure her and her baby's future.

She closed her eyes for a minute.

Please, please, please let this happen.

She wasn't quite sure who she talking to, but she hoped like hell they were listening. It was about time she scored a break.

Chapter 5

"You're not wearing that," Rosie said as Lucy loaded paperwork into her tote bag.

After two weeks of negotiations and discussions, she and Dom had signed a partnership contract the previous day. Lucy still couldn't quite believe that her money problems were over. Well, not over, but at least in a holding pattern for a while. She had a chance now to do what she needed to grow her business. Which was what today's lunch meeting with Dom was all about—planning for the future.

"Lovely. Thank you for the confidence boost," Lucy said.

"I didn't mean you look bad. You just look…ordinary," Rosie said.

Lucy looked down at the plain black pants, black

turtleneck and black boots she was wearing. The pants were new, the first of her true pregnancy wardrobe. The turtleneck was old and would probably never look the same again after being stretched over her belly.

"I *am* ordinary," she said dismissively.

"Why don't you wear that red stretchy shirt? That always looks great with black."

"It makes my boobs look huge."

"Exactly," Rosie said with a grin.

Lucy rolled her eyes. "You are seriously turning into a pimp. You need help." She was only half joking—her sister's continual comments about Dom were starting to wear her down.

"He asked you to lunch," Rosie said.

"It's a work meeting, not a date."

"He likes you, Lucy. He flirts with you every time we see him. Yesterday, when we signed the contract, he even ordered you food from the bar without asking because he knows you get hungry all the time. How many more signs do you want that this man has the hots for you?"

"None. I just signed a partnership contract with him. I don't want him to have the hots for me." Lucy shook her head. "Why are we even having this conversation? He does not have the hots for me. He's a nice guy. He's considerate. He's like that with all his customers. He's like that with you."

"He doesn't look at me the way he looks at you," Rosie said.

"And how does he look at me?" Lucy asked, hands on hips.

"Like he wants to take a bite out of you," Rosie said. "Like a starving man looks at a feast."

Lucy hooted with laughter.

"You are so deluded. Starving man, my ass. He's newly divorced, he's just spent six months traveling through Italy. He's probably got women lined up around the block to throw themselves at him. There's no way he's interested in a five months pregnant woman. No. Way."

"You're nineteen weeks," Rosie said a little sulkily. "Not quite five months."

"Which means I'm only cow-like instead of elephant-like. You need to stop trying to live out your teen obsession through me."

"It wasn't an obsession," Rosie said.

Lucy gave her a look.

"Okay, it was slightly obsessive. But that's not why I want you to wear the red shirt. He's a nice guy. I think he'd make a great father."

Lucy stilled, the smile fading from her lips.

"I'm not looking for a father for my baby," she said.

"Marcus isn't going to help you carry the load, Lucy," Rosie said.

Lucy eyed her sister steadily. She needed Rosie to understand that she couldn't buy into the romantic fantasy she was spinning. She didn't have the luxury to indulge those kinds of dreams anymore.

"I know you're trying to help, but please can we stop

it with the whole Dom-likes-me thing? He's my business partner. All I want from him is hard graft and a cash injection. I don't want him to like me. And I don't want to like him. We're business partners, and I need one of those much more than I need a man in my life. Even if that was an option that was on the table. Which it isn't."

For a moment Rosie looked as though she was going to object, then she sighed and shrugged a shoulder.

"Fine. Bury your head in the sand."

Lucy palmed her car keys. "Thank you. You know how much I like it there."

Dom had given her directions to his house in Carlton and she found it easily. A double-fronted terrace house, it was a pale cream color, the trim painted heritage green and red. Someone had placed terra-cotta planter boxes along the front edge of the front porch, but they were full of dirt and nothing else. She wondered if Dom's ex-wife had been the gardener and felt sad for him. No one got married expecting it to end in divorce.

Warm air rushed out at her when he opened the door to her knock.

"Lucy. Come on in. I'm just finishing up the gnocchi dough," he said.

She managed a greeting of some description, but she had no idea what she'd actually said. She was too busy reeling from the impact of Dominic Bianco in bare feet, well-worn jeans and a tight, dark gray T-shirt. His hair was ruffled and casual, his eyes warm.

He was so earthily, rawly sexy it took her breath away.

She barely noticed the polished hardwood floor beneath her feet or the ornate plasterwork on the cornices and ceiling as she followed him down the hall.

She gave herself a mental slap. She had no business being so aware of Dom as a man. It was ridiculous and counter-productive and she needed to get a serious grip. Right now. Dom was her business partner. End of story.

"I'm making my mama's secret gnocchi," Dom said over his shoulder. "If you notice any of the ingredients, you have to take the information to your grave with you."

They entered a wide, spacious living area with a vaulted ceiling. Immediately in front of them was a sleek, dark stained table. To the left was a modern white kitchen with dark marble countertops. Beyond she could see comfortable-looking brown leather couches and French windows that opened onto a deck.

"I promise not to look," Lucy said.

She noted the two place settings at the table. Everything looked perfect, from the red roses in a sleek vase to the snowy white linen napkins folded neatly across each side plate. She frowned.

Dom moved behind the island counter and reached for a handful of flour. She watched as he dusted the counter prior to rolling out the dough.

She smiled uncertainly when he glanced up at her.

"You want to take your coat off? I should have asked before I got flour on my hands again. Just throw it on the couch."

She took advantage of his suggestion to try to pull

herself together, but nothing could stop the way her brain was suddenly whirring away.

He'd gone to a lot of trouble for a simple business meeting. The flowers, the beautifully set table. Unless she was hugely mistaken, he'd even ironed the napkins. And he was making pasta by hand for her.

Was it just her, or was Dom pulling out all the stops for what was supposed to be a simple working lunch, their first as business partners?

She studied him carefully as she crossed to the kitchen. His hair was slightly damp, as though he'd just had a shower. But that could mean anything. Maybe he'd slept in, maybe he'd been to the gym. Maybe he'd even had someone stay the night and they'd whiled away a weekend morning in bed together before he'd had to get ready for this meeting.

She frowned as she registered her distinct unease at the thought of Dom with another woman.

"You want to open the sparkling grape juice?" he asked as he began to roll out thin ropes of dough with his fingertips.

"Um, sure."

She collected the glasses from the table and poured the juice, then placed his within reach on the counter.

"Thanks." The smile he gave her was warm. Then his gaze dropped below her face.

He did not just do an eye-drop on me, she told herself sternly, even though it had looked distinctly like he was checking out her breasts. *He's probably worried that my turtleneck won't withstand the pressure of being stretched over my bump and that the whole thing will suddenly rip in two like the Hindenburg.*

She took a healthy sip of the juice and welcomed the distracting taste as it slid down her throat. When she dared look at Dom again he was cutting the dough into one-inch sections.

See? He's not interested in your boobs. You've been spending too much time with your delusional sister.

"Do you cook often?" she asked.

She did a mental eye roll at the question. She might as well have asked about the weather. She'd had several meetings with him since he'd proposed their partnership and yet each time she seemed to feel less comfortable, not more so. Now she was trotting out the kind of polite, stiff chitchat she usually saved for new acquaintances.

"When I can. I try to make some meals on the weekend for during the week. It's easy to get lazy when I'm home late from the market," he said.

He began marking the gnocchi with a fork, expertly rolling each piece off the tines and onto a floured plate.

"You've done this before," Lucy noted. "Don't tell anyone, but I buy mine from the supermarket."

He tsk-tsked and shook his head.

"Lucia, Lucia. Don't you know that food is the way to a man's heart?" he said in a flawless impersonation of any number of elderly Italian women she knew.

"Damn. That was where I went wrong," she said, snapping her fingers in mock chagrin.

Dom winced.

"Sorry," he said. His gaze dropped to her belly. "I didn't think."

She shrugged. "It's okay. It wasn't my store-bought gnocchi that scared Marcus away. He fell for his yoga instructor."

"Yoga instructor. That's a new one. I thought it was usually the secretary."

"Marcus is a photographer, so he had to improvise. But he's making out just fine. Apparently what she lacks in the dictation department she makes up for in flexibility," Lucy said. Then she flushed as she realized how jealous and bitchy she sounded.

The corners of Dom's eyes crinkled as he grinned at her.

"Saucer of milk, table two," he said.

She pulled a face. "Sorry. I didn't mean to say that."

"Yeah, you did. It's okay. You're supposed to be pissed off. The only people who are cool with being betrayed are people I don't want to know."

He took the gnocchi over to the stove and slid them into a pan of boiling water. His arms flexed as he brushed the last pieces from the plate. He hadn't shaved today, she noted, and his jaw was dark with stubble, enhancing his rumpled, casual appeal.

Bare feet and stubble ought to be banned, she thought. *I'd have to turn the hose on Rosie if she was here.*

Dom turned his head and caught her staring. A slow smile spread across his mouth. She tore her gaze away and frowned down into her drink. Her heart was suddenly pounding, and she didn't know what to do with her hands.

"So, um, what did your father say about us becoming partners?" she asked abruptly, desperate for distraction.

"I haven't told him. It's none of his business what I do with my investments," Dom said.

"Wow. You guys must have had one hell of an argument."

His mouth quirked wryly. "You could say that."

He didn't offer any more information, and she wasn't about to push. They were business colleagues, not friends. On the personal front, they owed each other nothing.

"So, Lucy, the big question—do you like it hot?" he asked.

She blinked. "Um, sorry?"

He laughed. "Maybe I should rephrase that. Can you eat chilies without getting heartburn?"

"Oh. So far, so good. But I'm definitely more on the coward's side of the chili divide than the courageous."

"Okay, why don't you come over here and try the sauce, let me know if I've gone too crazy with anything." He gestured for her to join him at the stove.

She came to a halt a few feet away, and he dipped a wooden spoon into a saucepan.

"Come a little closer so I don't spill."

She stepped forward, feeling acutely self-conscious. She was standing so close now that if she inhaled deeply her baby bump would jostle him. He lifted the spoon to her mouth.

"Blow on it a little, it's hot," he said.

She pursed her lips and blew gently. She could feel him watching her and heat stole into her cheeks. She told herself it was because she was standing near the stove and she was wearing a turtleneck, but she knew it had more to do with how broad his shoulders were up close and how good he smelled and how acutely aware she was of all of the above.

Desperate to get the moment over and done with, she leaned forward to taste the sauce. Tough luck if she burned her mouth. It would be worth it to gain some distance and some perspective.

The flavors of rich tomato, fresh basil, subtle garlic and the perfect amount of chili chased each other across her palate.

"Oh, that's good!" she said, closing her eyes to savour the flavors.

When she opened her eyes again Dom was staring at her, his eyes very dark and very intent. Her breath got caught somewhere between her lungs and her throat and her gaze dropped to his mouth. He had great lips, the bottom one much fuller and softer-looking than the top. She wondered what it would feel like to kiss him.

Dear God.

She took a step backward.

"You know, I might go powder my nose before we eat," she said in a high voice she barely recognized as her own.

"Second door on your right," he said easily.

She nodded her thanks and scooped up her handbag

on the way. She heaved a sigh of relief when she was safely behind the closed bathroom door. Then she dived into her bag and found her cell phone. Rosie answered on the second ring.

"Aren't you supposed to be in a meeting with The Bianco?" her sister asked, not bothering with a greeting.

"I need advice. He's cooking for me," Lucy whispered into the phone.

"What? Why are you whispering? Of course he's cooking for you—he invited you to lunch," Rosie said.

"I'm whispering because I'm in the bathroom, and I'm in here because he's set the table with flowers and linen napkins and he's made gnocchi from scratch and he just fed me sauce and looked at me as though maybe he really does want to take a bite out of me," Lucy explained in a rush.

"Oh boy. I need to sit down."

"Me, too," Lucy said. She put down the lid on the toilet and sat.

"I'm freaking out here, Rosie. I have no idea if I'm reading things into the situation that aren't there or I don't know what," she whispered, glancing toward the door.

"Calm down. Let's assess the situation logically. You said there were flowers. What kind?"

"Roses."

"And linen napkins. And he's making pasta for you?"

"Yep. And there's sparkling grape juice. And I think I saw some kind of cake sitting on the counter for later."

"He *baked* for you? Maybe I need to lie down," Rosie

said. "I can't believe The Bianco is making a move on you."

Lucy sucked in an outraged breath. "What do you mean you can't believe it? You're the one who told me he wanted me. You're the one who told me to wear the red shirt and that this was a date, not a business lunch."

"Yeah, but this is *really happening!*" Rosie said excitedly.

Lucy closed her eyes. She felt dizzy, scared, even a little sweaty. She couldn't handle this. She didn't want Dom to look at her with bedroom eyes. She didn't want to be aware of him as a woman. She was pregnant. A tiny little person was growing inside her body. Soon, she'd be looking after that little person night and day.

"I think I should leave," she told her sister. "I'll tell him I don't feel well and come home."

"Are you kidding me? Stay. Stay and see what happens."

Lucy clutched the phone.

"Rosie. Be serious. This is not a game. This is my life. Isn't it complicated enough already? I just signed a contract to share my business with Dom. If anything happened between us—" She broke off, shaking her head. She couldn't even allow herself to go there. It was so absurd, so crazy. She still couldn't believe that she'd seen what she'd thought she'd seen in his eyes.

"But he likes you," Rosie said, as though that resolved everything.

"I don't like him," Lucy fired back.

"Liar. If you didn't like him, you wouldn't be hiding out in the bathroom calling me because he looked at you."

"Rosie. Be serious. I just gave half my business to this man."

Rosie sighed. "Fine, be sensible then. Tell him you're not interested. Get it out of the way now, off the agenda. That way you both know where you stand."

Lucy realized that every muscle in her body was tense and made a conscious effort to relax.

"Okay, good. That's what I'll do, nip it in the bud," she said, nodding her agreement. "Thanks, Rosie. I needed to hear that."

"Did you?"

"Stop trying to be Dr. Freud. You don't have the beard for it."

She ended the phone call after promising to call Rosie the moment the meeting was over. Then she flushed the toilet and washed her hands and eyed herself sternly in the mirror.

The very next time Dom smiled at her in that special way or looked at her as though she were chocolate-coated, she'd call him on it. They'd lay their cards on the table, establish some ground rules and move on. Problem solved.

Dom was dressing a salad when she returned to the living room.

"We're about two minutes away. Would you mind taking our glasses over to the table?" he asked.

"Sure."

She placed the glasses on the coasters he'd provided and hovered awkwardly beside one of the chairs.

"Does it matter where I sit?" she asked.

"Help yourself."

He brought the salad to the table, then served the pasta. Aromatic flavors wafted up from her meal as he placed it in front of her.

"This looks wonderful," she said.

"I take no credit. My ma perfected this recipe over twenty years. All I did was follow instructions," he said.

He smiled and she searched his face for any of the heated intent she'd registered earlier. But for the life of her she could find nothing apart from friendly warmth and welcome.

"You want Parmesan?" he asked, offering her a small bowl of freshly grated cheese.

She sprinkled Parmesan on her gnocchi and took her first mouthful. It really was fantastic—the tomatoes tangy, the chili providing the exact right amount of background burn. The gnocchi was light and fluffy, with the hint of something elusive in the mix.

"This is great," she said, gesturing toward her plate with her fork.

"Yeah? Glad you like it. I made so much, you can take some home with you, save you cooking dinner."

There was a solicitous note in his voice. She darted a look at him, ready to deliver her clear-the-air speech at the first sign of anything remotely unbusinesslike. But again he simply looked friendly and interested. The perfect business partner, in fact: cooperative, person-able, intelligent.

She was on tenterhooks throughout the entire meal, waiting for a repeat of the moment by the stove. It never happened. After they cleared the table, he brought out his paperwork and notepad and got down to business in earnest. Not once over the subsequent hours did he so much as hint that he saw her as anything other than his business partner.

No hot looks. No lingering glances. No intimate smiles. Nothing except sensible, incisive business dis-cussion.

After two hours of intense strategizing, Lucy re-treated to the bathroom again.

She was confused. She'd been so sure…. The but-terflies in her stomach, the pounding of her heart, the steamy intent in his eyes—was it really possible that she was so out of practice with all things male-female that she'd misread his signals? Could she have simply imagined that moment of connection? Was that really possible?

She checked her reflection in the bathroom mirror and groaned as she realized she'd spilled sauce on her-self, her baby bump having obligingly caught it. She stared at the red splodge, bright against the dark of her turtleneck, like a beacon drawing attention to her belly.

"You're an idiot," she told her reflection.

The tension she'd been carrying with her all after-noon dissipated as she sponged her top clean, shaking her head all the while.

Call it hormones, call it nerves, call it whatever—she'd clearly misinterpreted Dom's behavior. Of course she had. She was pregnant. Hardly an object of desire. She had to have been temporarily deranged to even entertain the idea in the first place.

Feeling calm and centered for the first time all afternoon, she returned to their meeting.

Thank God she hadn't delivered her little speech.

Chapter 6

Dom couldn't stop thinking about Lucy. While he cleaned up after their lunch, he thought about how she didn't take herself too seriously, how she liked to laugh. How smart she was in a school-of-hard-knocks kind of way.

During his run afterward, he thought about how gutsy and brave she was.

He liked her. He liked her a lot. The admiration and curiosity and attraction he'd felt for her previously had been based on what little he knew of her via their brief daily encounters at his father's stall. Now, however, he'd seen Lucy at home, watched her interact with her sister, had numerous meetings with her, and he was beginning to understand just how special she was.

As he paused at a traffic light, he registered that he'd

spent the past hour thinking about Lucy Basso. And not in a business kind of way.

Sweat ran down his back and the smile faded from his lips as he remembered the moment by the stove. He'd almost kissed her. She'd been standing so close and he'd been staring into her face and the need to taste her lips, to touch her to see if she was as smooth and warm and soft as he imagined had almost overwhelmed him.

He was a bastard. The light changed and he took off across the intersection.

The moment he'd decided to offer her a partnership, he'd known it meant the end of his chances with her. Lucy did not need her new business partner lusting after her. She needed help, support, money. Anything beyond that was simply not on the agenda. And he was a selfish prick for even letting himself go there. He lengthened his stride, angry with himself. He needed to get a grip on his attraction to her.

Ten minutes later, he slowed his pace, switched off his iPod and opened the gate to his parents' house. His mother looked up from the kitchen table when he entered via the back door.

"Dominic! At last you come. I was beginning to forget what my boy looks like," she said, pushing herself to her feet with an effort.

Like his father, his mother had turned into a round little barrel as she aged, her love of pasta and rich meats catching up with her. Her long gray hair was pinned on the back of her head, and she wore a voluminous apron over her dress. Her hands were dusted with flour, and she held them out from her sides as he kissed her.

"You all sweaty," his mother said, eyeing him with concern. "You should get out of those damp clothes. Have a shower. Put on something of your father's."

"I'm fine. I just dropped in for a quick hello," he said.

His mother's lips immediately thinned.

"I never see you anymore. First you go away for six months, then you come home and still you are stranger."

Guilt stabbed him. He *had* been avoiding home— or, more accurately, he'd been avoiding his father. At the market, work acted as a buffer between them, but at home there was no place to hide the fact that he and his father were barely on speaking terms.

"I've been busy. Work and some other things."

His mother sat back at the table and resumed rolling out the mixture for her biscotti.

"Your father is in the front room. You should go say hello to him," she said.

He hesitated a fraction of a second before nodding. "Sure."

He could feel her watching him as he walked up the hallway.

His father was in his favorite chair, the seat reclined as far as it could go, the Italian-language newspaper, *Il Globo,* spread across his belly. Dom watched him sleep for a moment, noting how old his father looked without his larger-than-life personality to distract from the new wrinkles in his face and the sag of his jaw. Age spots had appeared on his hands in the past few years and the gray in his hair was turning white. He was fifty-nine and still he woke every day at 5:00 a.m. to tend the stall at the market, despite the fact that they could easily afford to hire staff to cover the early shift.

Stubborn bastard.

"Pa," he said quietly.

Tony started, the newspaper rustling. He frowned, jerking the chair into the upright position.

"Was reading newspaper," he said.

Dom gestured back toward the kitchen.

"I dropped in to see Mama for a bit," he said.

Tony nodded. "Good, good. She worries when she not see you."

Conversation dried up between them. Dom felt the silence acutely. He and his father had had their moments over the years, but he'd never felt as distant as he had recently.

He cleared his throat. "There's something I've been meaning to tell you. Lucy Basso was looking for an investor in Market Fresh, so I've bought in. We're partners."

"What is this? Partners? How can you be partners with another business when you have Bianco Brothers?"

"It's not a full-time gig. At the moment, at least. When things pick up, I might have to rethink. But in the meantime nothing has to change."

His father's face reddened. "You work for me! You always work for me."

"I'm not resigning, Pa. I'm just exploring other opportunities."

His father glared at him for a long moment.

"This is because of computers."

"I want to make my own business successes," Dom said, sidestepping the issue.

"After everything I give you, everything I do for you. You tell me this, no discussion, nothing."

Dom refused to feel guilty. He had a life to live, too.

"I'm not a kid, I don't need to ask your permission." He felt like he'd been saying that a lot lately. "I just thought you'd like to know what was going on."

He headed for the kitchen. His mother looked up from spooning biscotti mixture onto a tray when he entered.

"Listen, I have to go. But maybe I could come around for dinner during the week?"

His mother frowned, then her gaze slid over his shoulder.

"Bianco Brothers is for you. For all my children. And you throw back in my face," Tony said from the doorway.

Dom saw his father's hands were shaking and his eyes were shiny with tears. Dom rubbed the bridge of his nose and reached for patience.

"What am I supposed to do, Pa? I have a business degree, I have ideas, but you won't listen to any of them. So either I sit around and suck it up and stew in my own juices, or I do something for myself. I chose Option B. You still have Vinnie and the rest of the staff. There's nothing I do that they can't."

"What is going on? What is happening here?" his mother asked.

"Dominic is leaving business," Tony said, his chin stuck out half a mile.

Dom raised his eyebrows. "That's not what I said."

"What do you call when you buy another business?"

"I'm a partner. Lucy will still run it. I'm just helping out. I promise this won't be a problem, okay?" he said. "Look, we can talk about this more tomorrow at work."

When you've had a chance to cool down and think instead of react.

He turned to his mother.

"Save some biscotti for me," he said. She nodded absently and kissed him good-bye.

Out in the street, Dom took a deep breath, then let it out again. He'd done it. It hadn't been pleasant, but it was over.

The look on his father's face flashed across his mind. He'd looked betrayed. Hurt. Baffled.

Dom started to run, lengthening his stride with each step. Soon he was breathing heavily, sweat running down his chest and spine.

He refused to look back, and he couldn't stand still forever. His father was going to have to come to terms with his decision. And if he didn't…well, they would cross that bridge when they came to it.

Later that evening, Rosie stood in the kitchen making spaghetti with meatballs with her husband. As usual, he was cutting the onions because they made her howl like a baby and she was mashing the canned tomatoes in the saucepan.

"Do you think it would be wrong for me to invite Dominic Bianco to the Women's Institute fund-raiser next week without telling Lucy first?" she asked during a lull in their conversation.

"Why would you do that?" Andrew asked.

"Because if I tell Lucy, she'll tell me not to invite him."

"Okaaaay," Andrew said, frowning. "Why do I feel like I'm missing a vital part of this conversation?"

"I think Dom likes Lucy."

His eyebrows rose toward his hairline.

"She's pregnant," he said.

"So?"

He clanked a frypan onto the stove.

"You're serious? You need me to explain?"

"It's happened before in the history of the world." Rosie was aware she sounded defensive. Was she the only one who saw the potential here? "Lucy is still gorgeous and fantastic. Would it be any different if she was a single mom and she met a guy?"

Andrew looked confused for a minute as he thought it over.

"Yes. And I don't know why, it just is. Pregnant women are for protecting and admiring, not lusting after," he said unequivocally.

She grunted.

"Hey, I can't help the way the male mind works. This

stuff is hardwired in, along with the ability to kill spiders and take out the garbage."

She rolled her eyes but couldn't help smiling.

"I'm still going to invite him," she said.

"I'd be disappointed if you didn't."

She threw the tea towel at him.

"I almost forgot. I picked up that new George Clooney movie for you on the way home," Andrew said as he measured olive oil into the frypan and added the onions.

"Have I told you lately that you're the man of my dreams?" she said.

"Yeah? Prove it," he said. He pulled her close for a kiss, and only the hiss of the olive oil forced them to call a halt.

"Phew. Someone's looking for some action tonight," she said, fanning herself with a hand.

"You know it, babe."

She smiled at him, anticipating the night ahead. A couple of hours with George on the TV and her husband beside her on the couch—the perfect man sandwich. Then bed, with sleep not on the immediate agenda. Sounded pretty damn fine to her.

"You know, I've been thinking," he said as she began to form the meatballs. "This whole thing with Lucy—the baby, the renovation fund."

She tensed, forewarned by the odd stiffness to his speech. Almost as though he'd rehearsed what he wanted to say.

"I'm thinking we should start the office renovation now," he said.

She let out a silent sigh of relief.

"Okay. Good. That sounds good," she said.

"And that maybe we should start trying for a baby at the same time."

She suddenly had trouble swallowing.

This is it, the moment of truth. Speak now or forever hold your peace.

"I thought we were going to wait until we had a junior partner on board," she said slowly.

"Sure. But the odds are good we won't get pregnant straight away. Even if we do, there's a whole nine months to find someone and train them. I was talking to Lincoln Sturt during the week, and he thinks the renovation would only take a month or two to finish. He even suggested his draftsman for the design work."

Rosie stared at him. Lincoln Sturt was one of their clients, a builder. That Andrew had consulted him without talking with her first was unsettling.

"You never mentioned this before," she said.

Andrew shrugged, but he darted her a quick, assessing look. The rehearsed speech, his obvious tension, the homework he'd put in—this was important to him. But she'd always known that. And crunch time had to come sometime, right? This was what she'd signed up for when she married him.

He wanted to be a father. He wanted to have children with her.

She licked her lips. Took a deep breath.

"Okay. All right. Let's do it," she said.

For a long moment there was only the sound of the

onions cooking. Andrew stared at her. Then a smile lifted the corners of his mouth.

"Really?" he asked. He looked slightly dazed and she realized he'd anticipated more resistance from her.

"Sure. Let's go for it," she said.

Andrew gave a whoop of joy then swept her into his arms. She found herself laughing along with him, her head whirling as he spun them both around.

"No more sleep-ins. No more weekends away. No more dinners for two," Andrew said.

"Nope. Not for at least twenty years. And even then we'll have to pry them out of the house with a crowbar."

Andrew laughed and kissed her soundly. Then, to her surprise, he dropped her back on her feet and headed for the door.

"Hey! Where are you going?"

He merely waved a forefinger in the air to tell her she'd have to wait. He was back in seconds with something shiny in his hand.

It took her a moment to realize it was the blister pack for her contraceptive pills.

"I've been wanting to do this for ages," he said, pulling a pair of scissors from a drawer.

Rosie lifted a hand in protest, but the scissors were already slicing through the shiny foil. The pack fell into the rubbish, slice by slice.

Andrew threw her a triumphant smile.

"There. Done," he said.

"Yep," she said dryly.

He looked so happy. Alive in a way that she hadn't seen him in a long time.

"I love you," she told him. "You know that, don't you?"

He kissed her. "I love you, too, babe."

Rosie closed her eyes and held him tight. She could do this. Thousands of women took the plunge into motherhood every day. She was smart, resourceful, kind. She would be a good mom. Of course she would.

A week later, Lucy smoothed on lip gloss and stepped back from the mirror to check the effect. She'd decided to wear her hair up for the Women's Institute fundraiser, a fashion show where all the clothing would be auctioned off at the end of the night, the money going toward the local women's shelter. She'd added another element to her pregnancy wardrobe for the event, a sleeveless black stretch dress that promised to give as she grew. Paired with a bolero cardigan with intricate beading on the front, she figured she looked about as good as she was going to. Her lips were shiny, her hair loosely gathered on her head in big, loopy curls, and if nothing else the dress underlined the fact that she'd gone up a whole cup size since becoming pregnant.

A rap sounded on the connecting door. Before she could call out that it was okay to come through, it opened to reveal her mother and Rosie, both also done up to the nines.

"My goodness, Lucia!" her mother said, stopping in her tracks. "You are so big all of a sudden!"

Sophia's eyes were glued to Lucy's belly.

Lucy looked down at herself. "No, I'm not. The doctor said the baby is normal size, and that I'm normal size."

Her mother tilted her head to one side and did a slow walk around Lucy as she stood in the center of the living area.

"It is this dress—it is too tight. I think maybe you should wear something different," Sophia said. "Something less revealing. What about that long coat you have?"

Lucy felt her hard-won confidence seeping out the soles of her shoes.

"I think you look stunning," Rosie said. "If I had boobs like that, I'd show them off, too."

Lucy glanced down at her chest then. Great. Huge belly, enormous breasts. Probably there was something wrong with her hair and makeup, too.

"I think it's too late to hide that I'm pregnant," Lucy told her mother.

"What about a brooch? Do you have a thing for me to pin this shut with?" her mother asked, holding the two sides of Lucy's bolero top shut over her cleavage.

Rosie laughed.

"It's too late to preserve Lucy's virtue now, Ma. She's been got at, good and proper."

"You're hilarious," Lucy told her sister.

Rosie blew her a kiss.

"Are we ready, ladies?" Andrew asked from the doorway. He was wearing a dark navy pinstripe suit and a white shirt with no tie. With his midbrown hair freshly cut, he was looking very sharp.

"Hey, you look great," Lucy told him.

Andrew shrugged a shoulder.

"Thanks."

He shot Rosie a long, warm look. Lucy watched as her sister blushed, then got busy picking a piece of lint off the hem of her dress as though nothing had happened.

That sealed it. Something was going on. Her sister and Andrew had been acting weird all week, but until now Lucy had been half-convinced she was imagining it.

Not the only time she'd imagined something lately, of course, so her track record wasn't exactly spotless. She still squirmed with self-consciousness every time she remembered that panicked phone call to her sister from Dom's bathroom. She had to have been temporarily insane. Not once since that afternoon had he been anything less than professional and friendly with her. Scrupulously so. No lingering looks, no checking out her breasts, nothing.

Andrew jingled his car keys.

"Let's hit the road."

Lucy turned back to check herself in the living-room mirror one last time. She could only see her top half but what she saw looked pretty good, her family's comments aside.

For just a second, she wondered what Dom would think if he saw her like this. He'd only ever seen her bundled up for work in the mornings or dressed for comfort for their meetings. Or—worse still—in her pyjamas, ready for bed. Would he even notice the difference?

Lucy shook off the thought with a frown. It didn't matter what Dom thought of how she looked, for Pete's sake. It was irrelevant.

Her mother chattered all the way to the community center, discussing carpet colors and window furnishings for the office renovation. Lucy smiled to herself as she heard the rising frustration in her sister's voice as Rosie tried to put forward her own opinions. For once, it was nice not to be the center of her mother's attention.

The center had been professionally decorated for the fashion parade with lots of draped black fabric on the walls, small nightclub tables with candles and big, arty tangles of fairy lights. A T-shaped runway bisected the room, and a bar had been set up immediately to the left of the entrance.

Andrew slipped off to grab drinks for them all as Lucy craned her neck to see if she recognized anyone. She started when a warm hand landed on the small of her back and a deep voice sounded near her ear.

"I was wondering when you guys were going to show up."

Lucy's heart did a strange shimmy in her chest as she breathed in Dom's spicy, woody scent. She turned to face him, not registering how close he was standing until her breasts brushed his arm. She took a hasty step backward, alarmed by the rush of heat that raced through her body.

"Dom. I didn't know you were coming," she said.

"Didn't you? Rosie invited me," Dom said.

He threw a curious look her sister's way. Rosie just did her impersonation of the sphinx. Clearly she had done this on purpose.

"You look great," Dom said, drawing Lucy's attention back to him. He did a slow scan of her body, taking in every curl on her head and every curve on her body. "Beautiful."

For some reason she was having trouble finding her voice. She told herself it was because he'd surprised her, but she suspected it had more to do with how good he looked in a finely cut leather coat, crisp charcoal shirt and charcoal trousers with a fine red pinstripe. He looked like he should be up on the runway, not down here with the plebs.

"Um, thanks. You look nice, too."

Immediately she felt like a dork. Dom smiled, the corners of his eyes creasing attractively.

"I even ironed, so it must be a special occasion," he said.

Lucy felt a pronounced dip in the region of her stomach as he held her gaze.

Okay, there's that look again. And this time I am definitely not imagining it.

His gaze dropped below her chin and into her cleavage. She forgot to breathe. She could feel his attention like a touch, skimming across her skin.

That *is definitely an eye-drop. Dear lord. Is it hot in here or is it just me?*

"Good to see you, Dom," Rosie said pointedly from somewhere behind them.

Dom grinned as he transferred his attention to her sister.

"Rosie," he said. "You look lovely, too."

"Sure I do," Rosie said dryly. "You remember our mother, Sophia Basso? Ma, this is Tony Bianco's son, Dominic."

Lucy started for the second time that night. She'd been so busy staring at Dom, being mesmerized by his intense regard, she'd completely forgotten her mother was with them.

"Dominic. Yes, I remember you from church," Sophia said slowly. "I hear you and Lucia are in business together now."

Dom leaned forward to shake her hand.

"Yes, that's right. It's nice to see you again, Mrs. Basso."

Lucy darted a look at her mother. Sure enough, her mother was watching her like a hawk, waiting to swoop in and demand what was going on between her daughter and Tony Bianco's son. Lucy groaned mentally. Now she was in for it.

"I reserved us a table," Dom said.

He led them across the room to a table with a good view of the runway. Andrew joined them with a carafe of wine and a cluster of wineglasses.

"There's juice for you, Lucy, but I only had two hands," Andrew said as he set his load down.

"I'll get it," Dom said.

He headed for the bar. Lucy found herself following his progress compulsively, unable to take her eyes off his broad shoulders and dark head.

"I thought he was your business partner," her mother said sharply.

Lucy dragged her attention back to the table.

"He is."

"I am not an idiot, Lucia."

"I didn't say you were."

"That is not the way a man looks at a woman when they are in business together. Not the kind of business I am used to, anyway."

Lucy straightened the skirt of her dress. "You're as bad as Rosie."

"Hey, I didn't say a word. I told you I wouldn't and I haven't," Rosie said, holding both hands in the air as if to proclaim her innocence.

Lucy glanced toward the bar and saw Dom was already on his way back to them.

"Nothing's going on," she said firmly. "Can we just drop it, please?"

The thought of Dom overhearing the women of her family discussing his purported attraction to her made her want to cut a hole in the floor and jump through.

Sophia sat back in her chair and crossed her arms over her chest, her posture announcing more clearly than any words that this discussion was far from over.

Dom placed the carafe of orange juice on the table and took the empty seat next to Lucy. She looked at him, searching for confirmation of what she'd seen. But, once again, she could find nothing in his face or demeanor that even hinted at the desire she'd read in him moments before. One minute it was there, the next it was gone.

He caught her staring and smiled slightly, cocking an eyebrow.

"Everything okay?"

You tell me.

"Of course," she said.

She looked away, a frown on her face.

"So, Mrs. Basso, Lucy tells me you're retired now," Dom said politely.

For the next twenty minutes, conversation ebbed and flowed around Lucy as she sipped her orange juice, her mind racing. To quote her sister, Dominic Bianco had looked at her as though he wanted to lick her all over. Slowly. She had not imagined it—even though he was sitting next to her now looking as though butter wouldn't melt in his mouth. As shocking and impossible and scary at it seemed, he saw her as a woman and not just a business partner or a life-support system for a baby. And he wanted her the way a man wanted a woman.

The thought alone was enough to make her heart slam against her rib cage. She shifted in her chair, recrossing her legs.

She felt fifteen again, unable to look a boy in the eye. He was her business partner and, she hoped, her friend. She didn't need this added complication to their relationship.

For a moment she felt a rush of frustrated anger toward him. Why did he have to make things harder? Having him on board was supposed to make things easier, not more difficult. Now he'd messed everything up by noticing she was a woman.

You hypocrite, a voice whispered in her ear. *Like you never noticed he was a man.*

Again she shifted, crossing her legs the other way. No matter what she wanted to tell herself, there was no denying the thump of awareness she'd felt when his hand landed on the small of her back, or the heat she'd experienced when his arm brushed against her breasts when she'd turned.

She wasn't immune to Dominic Bianco.

There, she'd admitted it, if only to herself. Despite what she'd told her sister, she was powerfully aware of Dom.

For example, right now, without looking at him, she knew how he was sitting, who he was talking to, whether he was smiling or not. She could feel the warmth coming off him although he was surely too far away for her to really register his body heat.

I don't need this.

The thought stood out among the chaos in her mind. It was too much. She had been swimming against the tide since Marcus left and she'd found out she was pregnant. She didn't need or want this added complication in her life. Nausea swirled in her stomach, and she put her hand to her mouth.

"Are you okay?" It was Dom—of course—leaning solicitously toward her as the lights lowered and the music came up for the start of the fashion show.

"I need the bathroom," she said.

He nodded and stood, helping her to her feet. Rosie and her mother glanced across but Dom leaned toward them, murmuring something. Then he was leading her to the restrooms at the back of the hall.

Her stomach had settled by the time she was alone in a cubicle. She sat on the closed lid and reflected that she'd spent more time hiding in bathrooms since she'd become Dom's business partner than she had in her entire life previously. Closing her eyes, she took a handful of deep breaths. Slowly her heart rate calmed. She exited the cubicle and ran cold water over her wrists.

Dom was waiting for her when she emerged from the ladies' room.

"Better?" he asked. She could read concern in every line of his body, and she was terrified by how much she wanted to drop her head onto his shoulder and let him comfort her.

"I think I should go home," she said.

Behind them, the first of the models were strutting down the runway. The music was loud and spotlights roamed and flashed. It was all too hectic when she was feeling so confused and confronted.

"Let me tell the others where we're going and I'll take you," he said.

"No! I'll get a taxi. I don't want to ruin it for everyone. I think I just need an early night."

"No one is going to let you get a taxi home on your own, Lucy."

His expression dared her to argue, and she knew he was right—one of the many crosses a pregnant woman had to bear was communal concern about her welfare. Rosie and her mother would be all over her if they thought she was unwell.

"Okay. But I'll come with you to tell them. They'll freak otherwise."

It took her five minutes to assure her mother and Rosie and Andrew that she really was fine, merely tired and a bit overwhelmed by all the noise. She insisted that they stay and enjoy the show—Dom was going to drop her home and come right back again. Finally they let her go.

She heaved a sigh of relief when they stepped out into the cool night air.

"Thank God."

Dom threw her an unreadable look. "My car's over here."

He led her to a sleek black two-door Mercedes and opened the door for her. She looked around with dismay as she sank into soft leather. The car was intimate and luxurious, with burled wood inserts on the dash and deep seats. She felt as though she'd just agreed to step into a closet with him, and the feeling only intensified as he settled into the driver's seat and shut the door.

Out of the corner of her eye she could see his long

legs stretching out in front of him and his hand selecting a gear. She swallowed and clenched her hands around the sash of her seatbelt.

Chill out, she told herself. *We're only five minutes from home. This will all be over in a minute or two.*

Then she'd have the time and space she needed to come to terms with the ridiculous nervousness and awareness that had dogged her since she'd looked into Dom's eyes and realized he wanted her.

"You sure you're okay?" Dom asked as he pulled away from the curb.

"Yes," she said.

He didn't say anything more. She only loosened her grip on the seat belt as they turned into her street.

"Thanks for this, I really appreciate it," she babbled as she slid out of the car, barely waiting for it to stop rolling. "I'll, um, see you at the market on Monday, okay?"

Dom didn't say anything, simply turned off the ignition and exited the car.

"I'll see you to the door."

"There's no need," she said.

He looked very tall standing next to her. The street-light made his hair shine, but his eyes were masked by shadow.

"My mother would skin me alive if she knew I'd left you out on the street. Then your mother would step in to finish me off."

She made an impatient noise.

"Fine," she said. She was being ungracious, but

couldn't the man take a hint? She wanted—needed—to be alone.

Her one-inch heels tapped briskly on the driveway as they walked past the main house to the door to her flat. She searched in her handbag for her house keys, fumbling them awkwardly as she pulled them free. They hit the ground with a metallic clink.

"Damn it."

"I'll get them," Dom said.

She was already sinking to her knees.

"It's all right."

"Lucy. For God's sake," Dom said.

He knelt, too, and they groped around in the dark together. She found the ring of keys at the same time he did. She snatched her hand back when she felt the warmth of his fingers beneath hers.

There was a long, tense pause. Then Dom stood and held out his hand. Wordlessly she took it and let him help her to her feet.

"What's going on, Lucy?" he asked quietly.

She pulled her hand from his grasp, but she could still feel his warmth on her skin.

Before she could think, the words were out her mouth.

"Do you want to kiss me?"

Her armpits and the back of her neck prickled with embarrassed heat, and she rushed into speech again, trying to explain her impulsive words.

"I mean, the other day at your place, when you asked me to taste the sauce. I got the feeling… It seemed to me that something…" She shook her head, unable to articulate her thoughts now that she'd blurted her stupidest suspicions.

She wished for a minor earthquake or some plummeting space station debris or even an escaped animal from the zoo—anything, to distract him and give her the opportunity to bolt inside her flat and barricade herself behind the door and never come out again.

"Yes," he said after what felt like a long time.

She blinked.

"Yes?"

"Yes," he said. "I wanted to kiss you the other day at lunch. And yes, I want to kiss you right now."

For a moment the world was very, very quiet. She wanted to pinch herself to make sure she wasn't dreaming. She wanted to pinch *him* to make sure he was fully *compus mentis*. Did he have any idea what he'd just said? How big a can of worms he'd just opened?

"Why?" she asked.

He laughed, the sound deep and low.

"For all the usual reasons. You want me to draw a picture?"

"This can't be happening."

"Why not?"

Because I'm carrying another man's baby. Because I am so far from being available it's not funny. Because this is nuts, absolutely insane and I can't believe we're even having this conversation.

"Because," she said.

She wasn't about to lay all her defects and liabilities

out in front of him. Surely it was obvious why his admission was so shocking to her?

"Look, I know this is a difficult time for you," he said. "That's why I wasn't going to say anything. But since you brought it up... I've always been attracted to you."

"Really?" Her voice came out as a squeak of incredulity.

"Since we were kids. I used to watch you walk to church in that little blue skirt you used to wear.... Let's just say I have fond memories. When I got back from Italy and learned you were single, I thought about asking you out. But I figured it wasn't great timing."

He didn't need to gesture toward her stomach for her to understand what he meant.

"That blue skirt wasn't that little," she said vaguely, too overwhelmed by his words to make sense.

"My imagination was plenty big enough to compensate, believe me."

She didn't know what to think, how to feel. She hadn't expected him to say yes. In her heart of hearts, she'd still believed she'd imagined his interest. And yet he was standing in front of her, telling her she hadn't.

"I don't know what to say."

"Maybe we should go inside," he said.

"No."

For some reason, going inside with him felt too scary right now.

"Okay. What do you want to do, then?" he asked.

"We're business partners," she said. "This is a really bad idea."

"Having a conversation?"

"You liking me. You wanting to kiss me."

"It doesn't change anything."

"Yeah, it does."

He was silent for a beat. "I'm not putting any pressure on you, Lucy. Just being honest. I don't expect anything from you."

"How am I supposed to pretend it's business as usual when every time I look at you I'm going to be thinking about this?" she asked. She could hear the panic in her own voice.

"I shouldn't have said anything."

She stared at him, frustration welling inside her.

"I don't want this," she whispered. She blinked rapidly, feeling overwhelmed on every level.

"Hey," Dom said. He stepped closer and rested a hand on her shoulder.

"It's okay, Lucy," he said. "The last thing I want to do is make things tougher for you. Forget I said anything. We'll pretend the last five minutes never happened."

A single tear slipped down her cheek. He swore quietly.

"Don't cry."

His hand moved from her shoulder to cup her face. His thumb swept across her cheekbone, catching her tear. He felt so warm and strong. She could smell his aftershave intensely. She turned her head slightly, instinctively seeking more of the woody spiciness. Her lips grazed his palm. She froze and so did he.

For a long moment there was nothing but the heavy beat-beat of her blood in her ears.

"Lucy," he said, his voice very deep. It was part warning, part declaration of intent.

She saw him lower his head. Knew she should step back or at least turn her head away, especially since she'd just told him she didn't want this. But she didn't do either of those two things. Instead, she lifted her face and closed her eyes and waited.

If she was honest with herself, she'd been waiting for this ever since he'd smiled at her that morning at the market after Rosie had awakened her to how attractive he was and she'd caught that flash of his hard belly. All these weeks she'd been waiting and wondering....

His lips were warm and firm yet gentle. He kissed her lightly, teasing first one corner of her mouth, then the other. His hand slid to the back of her neck, palming her nape and drawing her closer. His tongue traced the fullness of her lower lip and she shuddered. She opened to him and his tongue slid inside her mouth. He tasted of wine and coffee. Deep inside her, desire roared to life. Her hands curled around his arms. He felt so good, so real and strong.

It had been so long since anyone had kissed her, wanted her, needed her, and she'd wanted and needed in return. Not since Marcus left, nearly six months ago—

She stiffened and jerked her head back. What was she *doing*?

"Lucy," he said as she took a step away from him.

"I can't believe—"

A sudden, searing pain stabbed through her abdomen. She clutched her belly, her mouth open in a silent cry. Between her thighs, she felt a flooding warmth.

"No," she whispered. "Please, no."

She pressed her hand between her legs, dreading the worst. When she lifted her hand, something dark and wet shone in the dim light.

"You're bleeding!" Dom said.

Pain gripped her again and she hunched forward, wrapping her arms around herself.

"Oh God," she groaned.

Lost in a world of pain, she could hear Dom on the phone, speaking urgently.

"I need an ambulance for 56 Parkside Street, Northcote. She's twenty weeks pregnant and she's bleeding."

"My baby," she said, her eyes closed tight. "My baby."

Strong arms closed around her, bracing her.

"Hang in there, Lucy. They're on their way."

She leaned forward, pressing her face into the cool cotton of his shirt. She was too afraid to move, too afraid to breathe lest anything she did made things worse.

My baby.

"It's going to be all right," he said.

She knew he couldn't possibly know that for sure, but she was endlessly grateful for the confidence and determination in his voice. In the distance, she head the wail of a siren.

"Ambulance," she said unnecessarily.

Thank God. Thank God.

"They said they weren't far away."

Another cramp hit her and she gasped into Dom's chest. His arms tightened around her.

She wasn't supposed to be cramping or bleeding. Her baby was tiny, nowhere near close to being able to survive in the outside world.

This was wrong. All wrong.

Chapter 7

Dom turned his phone over and over in his hands as he sat in the waiting area of the emergency department, his thoughts on Lucy and what might be happening up the corridor in the curtained cubicle they'd whisked her into the moment they'd arrived. As far as he knew, she'd had a problem-free pregnancy. She was fit, young, healthy. Surely that had to count for something?

"Damn."

He stood and shoved his phone into his pocket. One minute she'd been warm and willing in his arms, then she'd pushed him away. Seconds after that she'd doubled up with pain. It was all inextricably bound together in his memory—the kiss, her rejection, her pain.

And now they were in hospital, and he could do nothing to help her.

"Mr. Bianco? Dominic Bianco?"

He spun toward the doorway. It was a middle-aged nurse with short steel-gray hair.

"Ms. Basso is asking for you," she said.

His long stride ate up the corridor as he followed her to Lucy's cubicle.

"Dom," Lucy said when she saw him, reaching out a hand.

He took it and tried not to show how shocked he was at its icy coldness. She was terrified, he told himself. It was nothing more sinister than that.

They'd put her in a hospital gown, and it was folded back to expose her belly. Two black belts spanned her bump, and an electronic display beside the bed recorded the rapid beats of her baby's heart.

"How are you doing?" he asked.

"They've given me something to stop the cramping," she said. "The doctor wants to do an ultrasound to find out what's going on."

"Okay, fair enough."

She squeezed his hand tightly and closed her eyes.

"I'm so scared," she whispered. "Would you mind staying with me?"

He couldn't help himself. For the second time that night he reached out to cup her face. She opened her eyes and stared at him.

"I'm not going anywhere," he said.

"I want this baby," she said. "I know it's been tough and I've been scared, but I want this baby so much."

"I know you do." He cleared his throat. "I called Rosie. She's on her way."

"Oh. Good. Thank you. I didn't even think…" She frowned. "God. Marcus. I should tell him what's going on. He'd want to know."

"Give me the number, I'll take care of it for you."

He punched the number into his phone and walked back to the waiting area to make the call, since cell phones were not allowed in the emergency department. The phone rang out and went to a machine. He left a brief message explaining where Lucy was and what was wrong, then ended the call.

She was being prepped for a portable ultrasound when he returned. She reached for his hand again as a guy in his late thirties wearing a white coat smoothed gel onto her belly.

"This is Dr. Mason," Lucy explained.

Dom exchanged nods with the other man.

"You've had one of these before, right, Lucy?" Dr. Mason asked.

"Yes. At twelve weeks and then again a few weeks ago," she said.

"Then you know how this works."

"Yes."

Dom held his breath as Dr. Mason pressed the wand firmly against her belly and began moving it back and forth. Beside the bed, a portable monitor threw up grainy black-and-white images from inside Lucy's womb: a rounded shape, then something that looked like a leg, then a whirling, pumping round thing.

"Do you know the sex of your baby, Lucy?" Dr. Mason asked, his gaze fixed on the monitor.

"No. Is that important?" she asked earnestly.

The doctor smiled. "Not at all. I just don't want to give anything away if you decided to wait."

Lucy huffed out a little relieved laugh.

"Sorry. I thought you meant…" Her eyes widened as the import of what he'd said hit home. "My baby's going to be all right?"

"From what I can see, everything looks normal with the fetus. And it's pretty clear what's causing the bleeding."

The doctor moved the wand lower on Lucy's belly. They all stared at the blurry images appearing on the monitor.

"What you're looking at is your placenta. It's very low in your womb, close to your cervix. That's what caused your bleed tonight. It's called a marginal placenta previa, and it's not that uncommon a complication of pregnancy."

Lucy's hand tightened around Dom's.

"But doesn't the baby have to come out through the cervix?"

"In a natural birth, yes. If things don't change, you'll be looking at a caesarean delivery."

"Oh. That means I won't be able to do much for about eight weeks after the birth, right?"

Dom knew what she was worried about.

"Forget the business. I'll cover everything," he said.

Her gaze shifted to his face and her frown cleared.

"Right. I'm so used to worrying about everything on my own, I keep forgetting I don't have to anymore," she said.

"Well, get used to it. Whatever happens, we'll work it out."

Lucy bit her lip and nodded, and he squeezed her hand.

If she was his, he would never let her get that hunted look in her eyes again. He would ban it from their lives, no matter what it took.

"You may not necessarily need a caesarean. In many cases of previa, the placenta shifts farther up as the womb enlarges to accommodate the growing baby. If that happens, there's no reason why you can't have a natural birth," the doctor explained.

"When will we know if that's happened?" Lucy asked hopefully.

"We'll get you in for more regular scans from now on. We should have some indication of how we're going in about four weeks. The good news is, with marginal previa like yours, the placenta almost always shifts."

"What about the bleeding? Does that mean tonight was a one-off and it won't happen again?" Lucy asked.

Dr. Mason shook his head.

"We can't guarantee that. Because of the precarious position of the placenta, previa mothers are more prone to bleeds than other women. We'll keep you in overnight to make sure things have settled, and then you can go home. But you'll have to be careful. No heavy lifting. Nothing too vigorous. No sex."

He gave Dom a significant look.

"Oh, we're not… Dom is my business partner," Lucy explained.

Her cheeks were pink with embarrassment.

"Right. Well, important for you to know, just the same," Dr. Mason said.

Dom avoided looking at Lucy, giving her a moment to compose herself. Hell, maybe he was giving himself a moment, too. Not many guys in their thirties were warned off sex before they'd even gotten to second base.

The doctor reached for a tissue to wipe the gel off Lucy's belly.

She bit her lip again. Dom could feel her indecision.

"What?" he asked.

"Did you have another question, Lucy?" Dr. Mason prompted.

"When I had my last scan, they said they couldn't tell whether it was a boy or a girl because of the position the baby was in. I decided it was a sign that it was supposed to be a surprise."

"But now you've changed your mind?" Dr. Mason asked.

"Maybe." Lucy looked up at Dom. "What do you think? If it was your baby, would you want to know?"

The question hit him like a blow to the solar plexus.

If it was his baby…

The world would be a very different place indeed if that were the case.

For a moment he felt a tight, fierce ache in his chest.

He would never stand beside his wife and have this discussion. Ever.

But Lucy didn't know that.

"I'd want to know," he said. His voice was low and thick with emotion. He cleared his throat. "I'd definitely want to know."

She nodded. "I think I do, too."

She turned back to the doctor with an expectant look. Dr. Mason smiled.

"You're having a girl," he said simply.

Lucy's eyes filled with tears.

"A little girl!" she said.

"Get ready for the joys of the teen years," the doctor said dryly as a nurse began to pack away the ultrasound machine. "I'll check in with you later, Lucy."

"Thank you," Lucy said, distracted by the news.

Dr. Mason and the nurse left the cubicle and Lucy spread her hands over her stomach. Her eyes were liquid with unshed tears as she looked up at Dom.

"I'm going to have a daughter," she said.

He couldn't speak. He looked into her face, filled with hope and excitement, and the pain was back in his chest.

If you were mine…

If this baby were mine…

He forced a smile.

"Yep. Hope you like pink," he said.

She laughed. "I hate pink! But I'll get used to it."

A nurse stepped through the curtain.

"Excuse me. We need a moment with Ms. Basso,"

she said. She was holding a washcloth and a bowl of water.

"I'll wait outside," he said.

He sank into a chair in the waiting room and tried to pull himself together. He wasn't the kind of man who relished being helpless, especially when someone he cared about was in pain.

He scrubbed his face with his hands.

She was okay. And the baby was okay. Those were the two most important facts. Anything else was unimportant, including how he felt about her and how much he wanted to right the world for her.

It was amazing how exhausting it was reassuring people that you were okay—especially when one of those people happened to be your theatrically inclined mother. Lucy had been transferred to a ward by the time Rosie, Andrew and Sophia arrived, and Lucy spent their entire visit telling them over and over what the doctor had told her. Eventually Andrew suggested they leave her to get some rest. Lucy threw him a grateful smile as he herded her sister and mother from the room. She was exhausted, but there was one thing she needed to do before she could even thinking of sleeping.

She leaned out of the bed, trying to hook her hand bag off the floor.

"I'll get it," Dom said from the doorway.

She sank back on the pillows as he handed over her bag. She hadn't seen him since her family had arrived. He'd faded discreetly into the background when they bustled in and clustered around the bed, and the next time she'd looked up he'd been gone.

"Thanks. I thought you might have gone home by now," she said.

"No."

He didn't say anything else and for some reason she couldn't hold his eye. Now that she knew her baby was safe, fear had receded and the memory of their kiss was like a third presence in the room.

Craziness, all of it. What had she been thinking? What had *he* been thinking?

Flustered, she indicated her bag.

"I wanted to check to see if Marcus had called. It occurred to me he might have tried my cell phone."

"Right."

Dom's face and voice were neutral, but she found herself feeling defensive on Marcus's behalf.

"He's probably out doing something and has left his cell at home," she said.

She checked her phone quickly, but there were no messages.

"He mustn't have got the message yet," she said.

"Can I get you anything?" Dom asked.

"No, thank you. I'm going to try to sleep, I think."

"Good. You look tired," he said.

"I feel tired."

He stepped closer to the bed and leaned toward her. She held her breath as his lips brushed her cheek.

"Sleep well. I'll see you tomorrow."

"You don't need to bother," she said. "Rosie and Andrew will take me home in the morning once I've been cleared for discharge, and then I'll probably rest."

"I'll see you tomorrow," he repeated.

She stared at the empty doorway for a long moment after he'd gone, his words from earlier in the evening echoing in her mind.

I've always been attracted to you.

She had no idea what to think or feel about his declaration. She certainly didn't know what to think or feel about his kiss—apart from the fact that it had been the hottest damn thing she'd experienced in a long time.

Craziness.

She reached for the switch beside her bed and turned off the overhead light. Then she rolled onto her side, one arm cradling her belly.

Lying in the dark, the depth and breadth of what had almost happened tonight hit her. She shuddered as she relived the horrible moment when she'd lifted her hand from between her legs and seen blood. She was so lucky. For the long, tense minutes of the ambulance ride and the first hurried moments in the emergency department she'd been so sure she was losing her baby. But her daughter was still alive inside her. It felt like a miracle.

Not that a previa diagnosis was to be taken lightly. She was going to have to be very careful from now on. But her baby was alive.

She closed her eyes as she smoothed circles on her belly and whispered quietly to her little girl.

"You gave Mommy a scare, didn't you, little one? Let's never do that again, okay?"

She was so tired. She wanted to sleep very badly, but her body remained tense. It wasn't until she heard the distant ring of a phone at the nurses' station and realized she was straining her ears, waiting for the footfall of a nurse coming to tell her she had a call that she understood what she was doing: waiting for Marcus to call.

There were a million explanations for why he hadn't shown up at the hospital or at the very least called to check on her and the baby. He could have gone away for the weekend and forgotten his phone. He might have forgotten to charge it. Or he might be at the movies or someplace else where he couldn't have his phone on.

She closed her eyes again. Her baby needed her to sleep. She could worry about Marcus in the morning.

In the end, Marcus didn't call until 11:00 a.m. the following day when she was about to leave the hospital with Rosie and Andrew.

"Lucy, what's going on? Are you okay?" he asked when she took the call.

"I'm fine. I have to be careful, but the baby is well and so am I," she said.

Her sister collected Lucy's things and stepped out into the corridor to give her privacy.

"That's a relief. I wasn't sure if I should call the hospital first, but then I figured if you answered your cell things couldn't be too bad," he said.

"I was very lucky. My placenta is low in my womb, but the doctor told me that there's every chance it will shift as the baby gets bigger."

"Well, good to know it was just a false alarm," Marcus said.

He sounded distracted. She could hear noise in the background, as though he had the television on.

"It was more a warning than a false alarm," she said, frowning. "I'm going to have to be very careful the next few weeks."

"Right."

Her hand tightened on the phone.

"I'll be home this afternoon if you wanted to hear more about what the doctor said," she prompted when he didn't ask any more questions.

"I know the important stuff already. You're going to be okay."

"And the baby," she said.

"Right."

Rosie returned to the doorway. Lucy glanced up and met her sister's watchful, sympathetic eyes. She dropped her gaze to her feet.

"I found out the baby's sex," she said.

Marcus was silent for a moment before exhaling loudly.

"Listen, Luce, all that stuff is great, but I don't know if it's the sort of thing I need to know."

"Sorry?"

"This is your baby, not mine. I don't want to get too attached. I've got my own life now. I don't think it's helpful for either of us to get things too confused."

"You don't even want to know if I'm having a boy or a girl?"

He sighed heavily again. "Sure. Why not, if you want to tell me."

Lucy hunched forward as though she could somehow protect her baby from his disinterest.

"On second thought, I've changed my mind," she said in a rush. Then she ended the call and let the phone drop to the bed.

Rosie sat beside her.

"He doesn't want to know anything about the baby," Lucy reported.

"No."

Her sister didn't sound surprised.

"I know he's been absorbed with Belinda the Nimble, but I figured that something like this…"

"He's a selfish little boy, Lucy. Always has been, always will be."

Lucy stared at her sister.

"I'm so stupid."

"No, you're not."

"I am. I expected him to rush to the hospital. I expected him to care."

"That doesn't make you stupid."

Lucy stared down at her hands. "I want to go home now."

"Okay."

She stared out the window all the way from the city to Northcote.

She felt as though the rug had been jerked from beneath her feet. Which was irrational, because Marcus had been gone for months. He was in love with another woman; he'd abandoned her utterly. Yet somehow, despite all of that, she'd still expected him to be there for her and the baby if she needed him. She'd still expected him to care. To want to know. To participate. To want to be a father, even if he didn't want to be her partner anymore. The baby she was carrying was half his—surely that was an ironclad guarantee that he was as invested as she was?

Apparently not. Apparently he had no interest in his daughter at all.

She stared blindly at the cars and trees and houses flashing past.

It's just me. Rosie and Andrew and Ma are there, but when it all boils down to it, it's just me and no one else.

For a moment, fear gripped her. Could she really be everything to her baby, both mother and father? Was she up to it? Strong enough? Brave enough?

She took a deep breath. She thought about the tiny person she'd seen on the ultrasound last night. She straightened as resolve hardened inside her.

She could handle this alone. She *would* handle this alone. And from this moment on, she wouldn't allow herself the indulgence, the luxury of ever imagining that she didn't have to. No more secret, hidden beliefs that Marcus would come through for her. No more thinking of Dominic Bianco and letting herself wonder what if.

It was tempting to buy in to the fantasy that Dom represented—a new romance with a hot, desirable man who just happened to have no problems whatsoever with the fact that she was about to give birth to another man's child. A man apparently willing to share the load, wake to feed the baby, change diapers, cook dinner, rub her aching back. In short, a man who would slot ready-made into her life and fill the roles of husband, partner, father and lover all in one.

But she would have to be very foolish and very reckless to believe in that fantasy. And she was neither of those things—she couldn't afford to be.

She was almost glad Marcus had been so blunt, so direct in his rejection of her and her child. She'd needed the wake-up call. The time for dreams and fantasies was over.

It was nearly midday Monday and Dom had just finished his last Market Fresh delivery for the day when his cell rang. He smiled to himself when he saw it was Lucy. He knew she'd be unable to resist checking up on him.

He'd seen her the previous day to collect the van and her customer orders, but he hadn't stayed very long. Her family had circled the wagons to fuss over her. He'd felt like he was intruding.

"Are your feet up?" he asked as he took the call.

"I beg your pardon?"

"Are you lying down?" he repeated.

He wondered if she was frowning or smiling at his interference. Maybe a bit of both.

"I'm sitting on the couch."

"Okay, then I can tell you the deliveries are all done for the day and I'm about to head back to the market."

"Already? You were fast." She sounded surprised.

"I thought you were usually done by midday."

"I am. But you're the new guy. You're supposed to be slower."

Definitely she was smiling. He leaned against the side of the van. Even over a cell phone call, her voice had the slight husk in it that always grabbed at the pit of his stomach.

"I want you to know, I really appreciate this, Dom," she said. "I know this wasn't part of our deal and that I was supposed to be the one who was hands-on with the business, at least until we got the Web site up and running and a second van on the road."

"You're right, it wasn't part of our deal. So I guess you owe me."

There was a small silence, then she laughed.

"Okay. Sure. When this is over, I owe you two weeks of hard labor. Fair deal," she said.

The sun came out from behind a cloud, and he lifted his face to the warmth.

"Do I get to choose the labor?" he asked.

For a moment the only thing coming from the other end of the line was silence. When she spoke again her tone was brisk.

"I don't think so. But you can trust me to ante up," she said.

He straightened and opened the door to the van.

"I've been thinking, since you're off the road for the next couple of weeks, this is a perfect time to kick-start the Web site development," he said.

"That was what I was going to suggest, too." She sounded surprised.

"Great minds think alike."

"I guess so. I've been going over my plans, but I wanted to talk to you before I brief the development company."

"Why don't I drop in after work tonight and take a look at them?"

"Okay." There was a short pause. "Do you want to stay for dinner? Ma has made me about fifty casseroles. I can barely get a slice of cheese into the fridge."

He hadn't expected to see her until the end of the week. Tonight was much better.

"Sounds good," he said. "I'll see you later."

He was smiling as he ended the call. Then he remembered the little hiccup in their conversation.

Neither of them had mentioned the kiss. Other things had kind of gotten in the way. But he hadn't forgotten. And neither had she, clearly. He stared out the windshield.

She hadn't liked it when he got personal. And he'd promised her that he wouldn't pressure her.

But she'd kissed him on Saturday night. She'd opened her mouth to him and pressed herself against him and held on to his arms as though she wanted to be as close to him as much as he wanted to be close to her. He hadn't imagined that moment.

He started the van. He was seeing her tonight. That would have to be enough for now.

* * *

Lucy was a ball of nerves by the time Dom was due at her place that evening. She could feel her heart beating against her ribs, her palms were sweaty and she kept needing to go to the bathroom.

Grow up, she told herself sternly. *You need to do this, and then it's done and you won't need to worry about it ever again.*

She nearly jumped out of her skin when he knocked on the door.

"Hey. I brought dessert," he said when she let him in. "I figured your mother's catering might not run to three courses."

"It doesn't," she said.

He brought the smell of rain with him, and his dark hair sparkled with droplets.

"I hadn't even noticed it was raining," she said.

"Oh yeah. Cats and dogs and even a couple of cows."

She glanced away as he shrugged his broad shoulders out of a navy peacoat.

"Smells good," he said, sniffing appreciatively.

"Well, I can't take any credit for that. It's all Ma," she said.

She fidgeted with the oven mitts she'd left on the kitchen counter. Then she took a deep breath and met his eyes.

"Dom, we need to talk."

"Okay," he said easily. He propped a hip against the counter and raised his eyebrows expectantly.

"What happened the other night was a mistake," she

said stiffly. "I just wanted to establish that so we could both put it behind us and move on."

His expression became wary.

"You mean our kiss?"

"Your kiss," she corrected him.

He smiled a little.

"I know a gentleman never brags, but you kissed me back, Lucy," he said.

When she'd rehearsed this in her mind last night, it hadn't been nearly as difficult. But then Dom hadn't been standing there in a snug knit top, dark cords hugging his thighs, his eyes warm on her.

"Fine. Have it your way. The important thing is that it can't happen again."

"Okay," he said slowly. "That's your call. I promised you I wouldn't pressure you, and I meant it."

She blinked.

Wow. That was easy. She'd been nervous all day, thinking about having this conversation, but he'd folded like a cheap deck chair.

She wasn't sure if she was pleased or slightly disappointed.

Which is exactly why this conversation had to happen, her better self reminded her sternly.

"Can I ask one question?" Dom asked as her shoulders began to relax.

"What?" Her shoulders tensed again.

He tilted his head to one side, studying her.

"Was it because you didn't like it?"

She picked up the oven mitt and began to twist it

in her hands. "Whether I liked it or not has nothing to do with it."

"I just thought that if you didn't like it, if you're not attracted to me, that was one thing. But if it was something else…?"

"It's irrelevant. This whole flirting thing has to stop."

"Flirting. Is that what you think I'm doing?" he asked. He looked and sounded surprised.

She put down the oven mitt.

"I don't know what you're doing, I only know it needs to stop."

"Because you don't like it," he said.

"No." She realized what she'd inadvertently admitted but plowed on anyway. "Because I'm pregnant, in case you hadn't noticed."

His gaze dipped to her belly.

"I noticed," he finally said.

"It's kind of hard to miss." She crossed her arms over her chest.

"But it doesn't change how I feel about you."

He looked deep into her eyes when he said it and her heart pumped out a couple of double-time beats.

She pointed a finger at him.

"That's exactly the kind of thing I'm talking about. You can't keep saying stuff like that and looking at me like that."

"Lucy, I like you. I already told you that," he said.

She hated how calm he sounded, how in control, while she felt like a can of soda that had taken a spin in the clothes dryer. She stared at him, frustrated that she couldn't articulate her feelings more clearly.

"Don't you understand? I can't do this kind of stuff anymore. I can't look at a man and feel weak in the knees and look at his mouth and want to kiss him. I'm going to have a baby. I can't afford to fool around like that."

"This man you're going weak at the knees over and thinking about kissing—can I assume that's me?" he said.

She ran her hands through her hair, then spread them wide. Her Italian blood coming to the fore, she growled low in her throat, an expression of absolute frustration with her inability to explain.

Dom moved closer and took both her hands in his.

"You like me," he said. "That's what you're trying to tell me. We can both feel this thing that's between us."

She looked into his beautiful eyes. At any other time, she would be ready to throw caution to the wind to be with a man who moved her as easily, as readily as he did. But he was an impossible dream.

"I can't afford to like you, Dom," she said quietly.

He frowned. Then, abruptly, his expression cleared. "You don't think I'm serious."

She closed her eyes. At last, they were on the same page. "Yes."

"I'm not a kid, Lucy. I'm thirty-one years old. I know what I want."

"You hardly know me."

"I know enough."

"No," she said, shaking her head. "Not for the kind of journey I'm about to go on."

"But isn't that what this is about?" he said, gesturing back and forth between the two of them. "Getting to know and understand each other, exploring the attraction?"

She shook her head slowly. She thought back to the terrifying sense of loneliness she'd experienced when she'd realized that Marcus wanted nothing to do with his daughter.

"I can't afford to explore. I'm about to become a single mother. I don't have time for dead ends and experiments."

"This is because of Marcus. Because he didn't show up."

She wasn't sure how he knew about that—Rosie?— but it didn't matter. He took a step closer and lifted a hand to her face. She closed her eyes for a long moment as his fingers slid into her hair and his thumb caressed her cheekbone.

God, it felt good when he touched her. Made her feel like a teenager again, as though everything was hot and new and untried.

"This is real," he said. "This isn't a game, or me killing time or you indulging in a flirtation. This is real, Lucy."

He lowered his head toward her. Her gaze fixed on his lips. She wanted his kiss so much—too much.

"You don't know that," she whispered, as much to

herself as to him. "You can't know how real this is, how long it will last. A week, two weeks, a month."

He shook his head, denying her words.

"You. Don't. Know," she said again.

He hesitated, his mouth so close she could feel the heat of him.

Very deliberately, she turned her head to disengage from his hand and took a step backward.

"I'm incredibly flattered," she said, "but this isn't going to happen."

He didn't say anything for a long moment, then he nodded.

"Okay. I told you the other night that I wouldn't put any pressure on you, and I won't. You know how I feel, the ball's in your court."

She eyed him uneasily. "There is no ball," she said. "No court, for that matter, either."

"I'm not going anywhere, Lucy. And my feelings aren't going to change. What you do with that information is up to you."

She frowned.

"And in the meantime, it's strictly business. Okay?" he added.

He held his hand out to seal the deal. She stared at it for a long moment before taking it.

"Nothing's going to change," she warned him.

"I know."

She looked away from the certainty in his eyes.

The important thing was that she'd done it. Cleared the air, created some boundaries.

There would be no more kissing, no more hot looks. From now on, they were about nothing but business.

Chapter 8

Two weeks later, Lucy sat in the van and watched as Dom exited the rear of The Lobster Cove restaurant, their last delivery for the day. His jeans rode low on his hips, and his face was dark with the beginnings of five-o'clock shadow. His hair was pushed back from his forehead, and he looked big and strong and beautiful as he strode toward her. She didn't realize she was staring until he caught her gaze and held it.

She broke the contact well before he reached the van.

Today had been her first day back at work since the doctor had given her the all-clear to resume duties. To say it had been awkward driving around with Dom beside her all day was an exercise in gross understatement.

Things had been weird between them since her clear-the-air conversation. Nothing she could put a finger on, but they were both being too polite, too careful with what they said and where they put their bodies, as though any false word or move might upset the status quo.

It was exhausting, and she wished she knew how to fix things but she didn't. She'd been protecting herself and her baby, but she'd made things weird between her and Dom.

"Okay, that's us for the day," Dom said as he slid into the passenger seat. They'd had a very civilized, bloodless battle this morning about who would drive. She'd won, and she planned to continue to win until she couldn't squeeze behind the wheel and reach the brake pedal at the same time. He was already doing so much; she needed to know she was pulling at least some of her weight.

"What did John say when you explained about the tomatoes?" she asked.

"He was fine. More than happy to take the romas over the beefsteaks."

"Good," she said.

She started the van and pulled out into traffic. As it had all day, the silence stretched between them. She racked her brain for something—anything—to say but all she could think about were the long legs in her peripheral vision. She wished like hell she was less aware of him, but she wasn't.

She punched the radio on out of desperation. An old Guns 'n' Roses song was playing and she tapped her hand on the steering wheel in time to the beat, doing her best impersonation of a woman at ease.

She pulled up at the lights and caught Dom eyeing her curiously.

"What?"

"Nothing. Just never pegged you as a Guns 'n' Roses fan," he said.

"Well, maybe you don't know me very well."

"Hmmm."

She gave him a challenging look.

"What kind of music are you into?" she asked.

"A bit of everything. Coldplay, Nina Simone, Fat Freddy's Drop—"

"Fat Freddy's who?"

"They're a New Zealand band. Kind of a new take on reggae. Very cool," he said.

"I'll take your word for it."

He shrugged.

"I'll bring them along tomorrow."

"Okay."

"You should bring something, too," he said. "It'll be like a cultural exchange."

"My heavy metal for your reggae?" she said as she stopped at a light.

"Why not?"

She smiled and glanced at him and caught him looking at her. Their gazes locked for a heartbeat too long before both of them looked away. Successfully killing the only decent conversation they'd had all day.

It has to get better. We're both mature adults. Once this stupid physical awareness fades, it will all be good.

Still, she was exhausted by the time she parked the van in front of Rosie and Andrew's place later that evening.

She let herself in and decided she couldn't face cooking. She wondered if Andrew and Rosie were up for pizza and wandered through to the house to find out. She tracked her sister down in her study and found her frowning over a chunky legal text.

"Hey. Feel like pizza for dinner and listening to me moan about Dom?" she asked, propping her hip against the door frame.

Rosie looked up from her book, her reading glasses balanced on the end of her nose. She looked deeply troubled, maybe on the verge of tears.

"Rosie! What's wrong?"

She could count on the fingers of one hand the number of times she'd seen her sister cry. Lucy was the sook, not Rosie.

"Nothing."

"Bullshit."

Lucy shut the door and hooked the leg of the guest chair with her foot and pulled it toward herself. Then she sat and crossed her arms over her chest.

Rosie took off her glasses and rubbed her eyes. She sighed and let her hands drop heavily onto her thighs.

"Andrew and I have been trying to get pregnant for the past few weeks, but I got my period this morning and we were both disappointed. No biggie, really. It's just the first month. Stupid to think it might happen so quickly. It'll happen soon, I'm sure."

"Oh my God! That's fantastic," Lucy said. "If you get pregnant soon, our kids can grow up together."

"Yep. It's all good." Rosie smiled with her mouth but not her eyes.

Lucy frowned. Her sister had always been a hopeless liar.

"Okay. What's really going on?" she asked.

"Nothing. Like I said, it's just a bit disappointing."

Lucy simply stared her sister down. After a few seconds, Rosie sighed and rubbed her eyes again.

"You know Andrew has always wanted to have kids. He's been talking about it ever since we got together. It's not like this is out of the blue."

"But?"

Rosie's eyes brimmed with tears. "I'm scared."

Lucy shifted her chair closer to her sister's.

"Having a baby *is* scary. But it can't be that hard, right? There are billions of people in the world. I figure if other women do it every day, I can probably pull it off."

Rosie stared at her, her face pale with misery.

"I don't mean I'm scared of *childbirth.* Although I'm not exactly thrilled about it. I'm scared about *everything.*"

"Everything. Could you narrow that down for me?"

Rosie held up a hand and started counting things off on her fingers.

"Okay, first, what if I can't get pregnant? All these

years I've been sitting around thinking it's my choice, but it might not be. Maybe my body isn't even capable of getting pregnant. Then there's actually *being* pregnant, having something growing inside you. Is it just me, or is that supremely weird? I know there are all these pictures of glowing women with their big bellies and you make it look so easy, but I've seen *Alien* and that's all I can think about when I think about having a baby growing inside me. Which is not natural, right?

"Then there's childbirth itself. You probably don't need me to explain that one. Watermelon, garden hose—we've all heard the jokes. Then there's afterward. The no sleep and the learning to breast-feed and the being tired all the time. You know how cranky I get without my eight hours. And what if there's something wrong with the baby? What if it needs special help or treatment? What if it gets sick? What if we have a child that will never really grow up and will always need us our entire lives?"

Lucy blinked and opened her mouth to respond, but her sister was just getting started.

"Then there's my body. I know I'm no supermodel, but I like my boobs and I know once I've breast-fed they're going to be hanging down around my knees. It's horribly vain, I know, but I don't want to lose my one good feature. And what if I put on weight during the pregnancy and can't take it off again? I don't ever want to be big again, Lucy. I've had my fat years and I won't go there again.

"And sex. It's supposed to be different afterward,

right? Again, watermelon, garden hose. How can it not be different after that kind of wear and tear? What if it's not good anymore? What if I'm so tired from all the breast-feeding and sterilizing bottles and pureeing fruit that I never want to have sex again, anyway? Then Andrew will get resentful and frustrated and we'll turn into one of those horrible married couples who are always sniping at each other. I'll be angry with him because he's always at work, and he'll dread coming home because I've been stuck with the baby all day and the moment he walks in the door I'll start nagging him. Pretty soon we'll forget why we ever liked each other in the first place and the only reason we'll still talk to each other at all is because of the fact that our genes are joined together in another human being."

Lucy waited to make sure her sister was really finished this time. When Rosie just stared at her expectantly, she figured she had the floor.

"You've thought about this *a lot*," she said.

"Yes. All the time." Again Rosie's eyes brimmed with tears.

"Everyone worries about all that stuff, Rosie. I worry about it all the time. Having children is a huge leap of faith," Lucy said. "It's like falling in love. You just have to plunge in and hope for the best."

"But what if the best doesn't happen?"

"Then you deal with it. Like you've dealt with every other challenge that has come your way."

Rosie stared at her hands where they were twisted around each other in her lap. Her lips were pressed together so firmly they'd turned white, and Lucy realized there was something else, something her sister couldn't bring herself to say.

"Rosie," she said. "Talk to me."

Tears finally spilled down Rosie's cheeks as she began to talk, the words coming with more difficulty now.

"I had this client a few years ago. She was successful, midthirties, owned her own business. She was a great person, smart, funny, sharp. She got pregnant unexpectedly. Anyway, she had the baby. And it was a disaster. She couldn't bond with it. She had no maternal feelings or instincts at all, Luce. She just felt…nothing. None of that amazing love women talk about. Nothing. She struggled for two years before she realized that the baby would be better off with someone else. So she gave him up for adoption."

Rosie's face was twisted with fear as she stared at Lucy.

"What if that happens for me? What if I have a baby and it turns out I'm a bad mom?"

Lucy didn't know what to say. She groped for the right words.

"That woman is the exception, not the rule. That's not going to happen for you."

Rosie shook her head, wiping tears from her cheeks with shaking hands.

"You don't understand because you've always wanted kids. Until I met Andrew, I didn't think I'd ever have a husband, let alone a family. It never entered my head.

Even when we were kids I never played mamas and bambinos. Remember?"

Lucy dredged up a memory. "You always wanted to play shopkeeper," she said slowly.

Rosie nodded. "That's right." She paused and took a deep breath before looking Lucy in the eye. "I've been thinking about this so much lately. Maybe I'm like my client, Luce. Maybe I'm not meant to be a mom."

Every instinct Lucy had wanted to reject her sister's words because they struck so close to the heart of things she'd always held dear—family, children, the need to nurture and create. To her, they were the stuff life was made of, as essential as breathing. But Rosie had been brave enough to bare her soul and clearly she was deeply concerned about this issue. Lucy owed it to her to consider her words as objectively as she could.

It was possible, of course, that her sister was right, that she was missing the maternal instinct—if such a thing even existed.

"Not every woman in the world has to have children," she said after a short, tense silence. In the back of her mind there was a queue of ifs, buts and maybes lining up, ready to insert themselves into the argument. She'd always imagined her and Rosie's children growing up together, a true extended family. But that was her dream, not Rosie's, and she refused to force her own values on her sister when she was already so distressed over the choices before her.

"Andrew wants children," Rosie said flatly.

"I know. Have you guys spoken about this?"

Rosie shook her head.

"It's kind of important stuff, don't you think?" Lucy said gently. "Something only the two of you can work through, at the end of the day."

Rosie squared her shoulders. "I always knew he wanted children. I married him knowing that."

"But if you don't feel the same way—"

"I'll get over it," Rosie said.

Lucy stared at her sister. Rosie had just cried and wrung her hands and literally trembled with fear and doubt over the huge life change that potentially lay ahead of her. Lifting the rug and sweeping all that emotion neatly out of sight hardly felt like an option.

"Rosie. Talk to Andrew."

"I can't. I've stalled and held him off for too long. I love him. I want him to have the family he's always wanted."

"What about you? What if it's not what you want?"

Rosie bit her lip, then her chin came out in a gesture Lucy knew only too well.

"I'll be okay. It's like you say, everyone worries about this stuff. Once I'm pregnant, it will all fall into place."

Rosie turned back to her book then, picking it up in a clear signal that their conversation was over. Lucy remained where she was, deeply troubled by her sister's confession.

She worried about being a good mom. She worried about the future. But not to the degree her sister obviously did. The set of Rosie's jaw, the squaring of her shoulders—she was like a novice skydiver, bracing herself for her first jump even though she'd much prefer to be safely on solid ground.

"Thanks for listening, Luce. I appreciate it," Rosie said.

There was a firm, no-nonsense note to her sister's voice. The time for heart-to-hearts was definitely over.

Lucy stood. "Please come and talk to me if you need to. I hate the idea of all that stuff just percolating inside you all the time."

"I will. I promise," Rosie said with a quick smile.

Lucy let herself out of the study and returned to her own flat.

Rosie and Andrew's marriage had always seemed rock solid, an absolute certainty in a world full of uncertainty. Now, for the first time, Lucy could imagine a future where that wasn't necessarily true. If they weren't talking to each other about such a big issue…

She considered what would happen if they *did* talk. Andrew wanted children. Rosie, it seemed, did not. At the very least she had some serious doubts. Many a marriage had foundered on smaller differences, Lucy knew.

Feeling every ounce of the extra weight she was carrying, she sat on her couch and tucked her legs beneath herself.

As she'd told her sister, sometimes you simply had to have faith that things would work out. And that if they didn't, that you could handle the consequences.

She hoped her sister found more comfort in the concept than she did right now.

* * *

Two weeks later, Dom approached the Bianco Brothers' stand with a box full of sealed invitations under his arm. It was early, but the first pallets had already been moved across from the cold storage. Dom slid the box under the nearest trestle table and got to work. Half an hour later, his father arrived, his breath misting in the cold morning air. Even though they were well into August, spring seemed a long way off. Even longer when his father scowled at him by way of greeting.

It had been like that between them since he'd told his father about his investment in Lucy's business. His father was hurt, jealous, offended and probably a bunch of other things that Dom chose not to explore. He was not his father's property or a household pet. His father had had the chutzpah to start his own business when he was still a very new immigrant to Australia. If he couldn't understand Dom's need to be involved and stimulated and challenged, then they were doomed to be this distant and cool toward each other for a very long time.

"You have not given me the time sheets for last week," Tony said hard on the heels of his scowl.

Dom pulled the forms from his back pocket. His father never used to review this kind of paperwork, but he'd started asking for it four weeks ago—ever since Dom began doing Market Fresh's deliveries each morning. That the business had not been affected by Dom's absence for three hours every morning mattered not one iota to his father—with him, it was always the principle.

"I was five hours down last week," Dom reported. "You'll see I've deducted it from my wages."

He'd been working extra hours at the beginning and end of each day to ensure Bianco Brothers' wasn't adversely affected by his involvement with Market Fresh, but it was impossible to make up all the time. He'd told his father when he'd first started doing the deliveries that he'd deduct any hours he lost, and he'd stuck to his word.

His father squinted at the page briefly, then grunted. Dom hid a smile. Stubborn old bastard. Then he remembered something Lucy had told him while they were on deliveries last week—that it took two to tango and he was just as stubborn as his old man.

Probably it was true. But acknowledging it didn't mean he was going to do anything about it.

At least things had eased between him and Lucy at last. It had been awkward at first, there was no doubt about it. They'd both been on their best behavior, wary of putting a foot wrong. But it was impossible to remain stiff when you were trapped in a small tin can with someone every day. By the end of the first week, they'd relaxed enough to squabble over where they stopped for lunch and whose music they'd listen to during deliveries. By the end of the second week, they'd been swapping childhood stories and family anecdotes.

The fact that there might have been something else between them was almost forgotten. Almost.

Dom was pulled out of his thoughts as his father

kicked the box of envelopes he'd stored beneath the table earlier.

"What is this?" his father asked.

"Invitations. The Web site is ready to go, and Lucy and I are having a launch party at my place to showcase it to our clients," he said.

He stooped to pull the front envelope from the box. It was addressed to his parents. He offered it to his father.

"We'd like you to come. It'll be good for people to meet the man who supplies most of their produce."

His father stared at the envelope as though it was contaminated.

"Why would I want to go?" he said with a dismissive wave of his hand. "I not know anyone there. Is nothing to do with me."

Dom kept the invitation hanging in the air between them.

"Then come for me, to see what we've been doing. You never know, you might get something out of it."

It was the wrong thing to say. His father's heavy eyebrows came together and his jaw clenched.

"There is nothing for me to get," he said, then he walked away.

Dom gritted his teeth and slid the invitation back into the box. So much for that great idea.

"Yo! Bianco!"

He glanced up just as a scarf hit him in the face. Lucy grinned at him from behind her trolley.

"You left it in the van yesterday," she said.

"Thank you for returning it so promptly."

"Always my pleasure to be of assistance," she said.

Just as he did every day, he had to fight not to let his gaze drop to her body. She'd grown noticeably rounder in the past few weeks, but she was still beautiful and he still wanted her.

Who was he kidding? He'd passed *wanting* a long time ago. He longed for her, and not just in a physical sense. The smell of her hair. The way she tilted her head when she smiled at him. The way her hands got busy when she was nervous, pleating her clothing or fiddling with paperwork. The sound of her laughter. The thoughtful look in her eyes when she was listening to him. The occasional spark of wickedness in her.

She was…extraordinary.

And he was wholeheartedly, tragically, hopelessly in love with her.

Which just went to show what a masochist he was. She'd warned him off, told him she wasn't prepared to risk exploring the attraction between them. And in response he'd fallen the rest of the way in love with her.

As if he'd had a choice. She was irresistible. Adorable. Sexy. Funny. Warm. And out of his reach thanks to the bump that no longer allowed her to button her coat.

And he was doomed to travel the streets of Melbourne with her until that bump became a baby and she wouldn't need him anymore. He wasn't sure if he was looking forward to that moment or not, sad case that he was.

"Did you get your invitations done?" she asked.

They'd divided their guest list to split the labor, although he'd done his level best to ensure he got the li-on's share.

"Sealed and ready to go," he said, stooping to collect his box.

He rounded the table to dump it on the trolley.

"Should have known. Do you ever let anyone down?" she asked lightly.

Briefly his thoughts flashed to Dani, to the bitter disappointment he'd visited on her.

"I've had my moments," he said.

Lucy frowned, but his father arrived to draw her curiosity away. Despite the fact that Dom had been in the doghouse since investing in Market Fresh, his father still doted on Lucy. Go figure. Not that Dom would want her to be subjected to the same moody disapproval. That would only have made a difficult situation more impossible. But still…

"Lucia. You are looking well. So wonderful," Tony said, holding his arms wide. "Every day you look wonderful."

She laughed. "Does Mrs. Bianco know what a ladies' man you are?"

His father's chest swelled. Dom was sure his father had never seriously looked at another woman in his life, but the idea of being a lady-killer clearly appealed to his vanity.

"Mrs. Bianco knows she is on to good thing," he said roguishly.

Lucy laughed, her hand absently going to her belly to smooth a reassuring circle on her bump. The baby had to be kicking—she always did that when the baby was active.

"I have something for you, Mr. Bianco," she said.

She avoided Dom's eye as she reached into her coat pocket. He tensed as he saw what she held—a second invitation to their Web site launch. She'd obviously decided to do her bit to heal the rift between father and son.

Dom crossed his arms over his chest. Good luck to her. He just hoped his father was more polite in his refusal second time around.

"This is for the party Dom and I are having to celebrate our new Web site," she said, offering the envelope to his father. "We'd love you and Mrs. Bianco to come. We're going to have catering, all prepared from your produce, and I would really like my customers to meet the person who handpicks all their supplies."

Dom waited for his father to scowl or wave his hand dismissively, as he had moments ago when Dom issued his invitation.

"I not very good at parties," his father said.

"I refuse to believe that," Lucy said. "I've seen the way you talk to your customers. It will be just like that, with food and vino."

She leaned forward and tucked the invitation into the pocket on his father's apron.

"If you don't come, I'll be very disappointed. I ordered the caterers to make some Sicilian cannoli for you because I know how much you love them."

"Hmmph. I will show Mrs. Bianco, see what she

says," Tony said. Then he gave Lucy a wave and moved off to serve another customer.

Immediately Lucy turned to him and pointed a finger at his chest.

"Not a word. I refuse to be the reason you and your father aren't on good terms," she said.

He simply looked at her until her cheeks turned pink.

"What? Did I forget to brush my hair or something?" she asked, reaching up a self-conscious hand.

"I already gave my father an invitation to the launch party."

"Oh." Her color deepened. "I'm sorry. No wonder he looked so surprised. He must think I'm an idiot."

"He refused to accept it. Wouldn't even take the envelope out of my hand."

Lucy frowned, then a small smile appeared on her mouth.

"Huh. Well, I guess you just have to know how to handle Italian men," she said.

"And you do, do you?" he asked.

She breathed on her fingernails and pretended to buff them on her coat collar. "I've got a few tricks up my sleeve."

"Such as?"

He couldn't help it, he'd moved closer to her. She was too beautiful, too funny.

"Well…it helps if you have one of these," she said, pointing to her belly. "The bigger it gets, the more power I have."

"Is that so?"

"Definitely. Any good Italian boy is helpless in my hands. Want me to demonstrate?" she asked, her brown eyes shining with laughter.

"You don't need to," he said.

She glanced up at him, then seemed to suddenly realize how close they were standing. Her mouth parted. He stared at her lips for a long moment, then he took a deep breath and a step backward.

Man, but honoring the deal they'd made got harder every day.

"You got today's shopping list?" he asked.

She handed it over and they both concentrated on filling the order. When the trolley was stacked high, he shifted the boxes into the back of the van. Lucy took over from there, allocating orders with a speed and efficiency that always amazed him. She seemed to have a photographic memory for each customer's requirements and only ever consulted their lists once or twice. She also made sure that at least once a week there was a surprise in their package—maybe some fruit that had just come into season, or an order of herbs they hadn't requested. She understood the importance of making people feel valued.

As she had every day that they'd driven together, she slid into the driver's seat once the orders were allocated. She knew he liked to drive, too, but he'd yet to win that battle.

"Stop giving me that look," she said as he slid into the passenger seat.

"Soon you won't be able to reach the wheel," he said smugly.

"Soon we'll have two vans and you won't have to covet mine," she said.

She smiled, and as he did every day, he wondered how any man could walk away from her. He couldn't, and he'd never even had her.

On the way back to the city after their deliveries, Lucy kept checking the time on the dash, her gaze darting between it and the congested roads ahead of them. When she started biting her lower lip, he decided it was time to speak up.

"What are we late for?" he asked.

"Not we, me. I've got a checkup with the doctor." She flashed him an uncertain look. "It's been four weeks."

Right. They were going to scan to see if her placenta had moved. As far as he knew, she'd had no more problems since that first bleed. Although they weren't exactly on gynecological terms, he figured she would have told him if something further had happened.

"If you're going to be late, head straight to the hospital. I don't mind waiting," he said.

She shook her head automatically, then checked the time again.

"Don't be a stubborn idiot," he said.

"Lovely," she said, but she turned off and started working her way toward the Royal Women's Hospital.

She found a parking spot and turned off the engine, then simply sat behind the wheel, her fingers drumming repeatedly as she frowned out the front window.

"You okay?" he asked after a few seconds.

"Nervous," she said. "The doctor didn't say this, but I read that if the placenta's moved down instead of up, I'll probably have to be admitted to hospital for the rest of my pregnancy."

He nodded. She would hate being bedridden, and she would worry about the business and feel guilty, but she would do it.

"It's unlikely. Really rare. Probably why he didn't bother mentioning it," she said, her fingers beating out a rapid staccato now. "And I haven't had any more bleeds, so the odds are good everything is fine."

"Want me to come with you?" he asked.

She glanced at him, then quickly looked away.

"Thanks, but I should probably go alone," she said. Right.

"I don't know how long I'll be," she said. "Sorry."

The next hour crawled by. He couldn't understand what was taking so long. He got out of the car twice, ready to go inside and track her down to make sure she wasn't sitting somewhere, struggling to deal with bad news on her own. Both times he forced himself to stay put. Lucy had defined the parameters of their relationship. He needed to stick to them.

He couldn't stop himself from getting out of the car when he saw her walking across the asphalt after nearly an hour and a half. She was smiling, and there was a new swing to her walk.

Despite his worry, he couldn't help smiling in return.

"Good news?"

"The best. My placenta is midway, just where it should be. I am now officially a normal twenty-five weeks pregnant woman. No special instructions, no restrictions. Woo-hoo!"

She was practically skipping, and he couldn't help laughing.

"We're going to have to tie a string to you so you don't float away," he said.

She stopped in front of him and her expression sobered.

"Sorry it was so long. They were running late."

He shrugged it off, but she reached out to touch his arm.

"I was thinking while I was waiting. I want you to know I really appreciate everything you've done for me over the past few weeks. The extra work, all the support. You're a good man, Dominic Bianco."

He stared down at her, frustrated. He *was* a good man—he was also a man who desperately wanted to kiss her. A man who felt a fierce desire to protect her and belong to her.

"You make it easy," he said.

She stood on her tiptoes and pressed a kiss to his cheek.

"You make it easy, too," she said. "Too easy, sometimes."

It was just a peck, a kiss between friends, but his body roared to life anyway. Before he could stop himself, his arms came up to stop her from stepping away.

They stared at each other. Lucy's eyes dropped to

his mouth. Four weeks of careful diplomacy flew out the window. He wanted to kiss her. He was going to kiss her.

She sighed as his lips met hers. His tongue slid inside her mouth, tasting her sweetness and warmth. He slid his hands into her hair, cradling her head as he kissed her deeply.

He'd kept a tight rein on himself for so long, but he could feel his control slipping. He wanted to slide his hands beneath her clothes and touch her. He wanted to see her breasts, feel them in his hands. He wanted to feel her legs wrapped around his waist. He wanted to be inside her, part of her.

He backed her against the van and kissed his way across her cheekbone to her neck. She dropped her head back, her breath coming quickly.

"Dom," she said.

He pressed an openmouthed kiss to the tender skin beneath her jaw, unable to get enough of her. She smelled so good, felt so good....

"Dom. We need to stop," she said. "This can't go anywhere."

She sounded reluctant, and her body was still clinging to his. But she'd said it. He stilled, his face pressed against her skin. He was hard and he wanted her, so much. Not just physically. In every way.

Slowly he lifted his head and looked into her face. Her pupils were dilated, her mouth swollen from his kisses. But her eyes were serious. It was enough for him to release her.

They stared at each other for a long moment. There were so many things he wanted to say to her. He understood her reluctance to complicate her life, but life *was* complicated. The feelings between them were very real. She was prepared to risk so much in her professional life, but in her personal life she had all the hatches battened down tight.

"You know I want more from you than just a few kisses in a parking garage," he said.

She shook her head. "I can't risk it."

"I'm not Marcus, Lucy. I'm not going anywhere."

She simply stared at him. He ran a hand through his hair and stared out at nothing for a moment.

"Okay. I understand. We'd better get back to the market," he said.

He slid into the passenger seat. She got into the car and put the key in the ignition but didn't start the engine.

"I'm attracted to you. It's not that I don't want you," she said quietly.

"Yeah, I got that." He sounded like a sulky kid and he sighed heavily. "Look, we agreed to keep things about work, and I crossed the line. I'm sorry. But like Ma always says, we don't choose the ones we love. It's just the way it is."

She stilled beside him and he closed his eyes.

Way to go, Bianco. Why not write some bad poetry and carve her name in a tree while you're at it?

He waited for her to say something, but after a short, tense pause she turned on the engine.

They were both silent for a few minutes. Then she cleared her throat.

"Sorry for keeping you so long from the market. I hope your dad won't be too upset."

"He'll be fine," he said.

So this was how they were going to handle his inadvertent declaration—ignore it and hope it went away.

A pity he couldn't do the same thing with his feelings for her.

Loving Lucy Basso and not being able to have her was turning out to be the toughest thing he'd ever done.

Chapter 9

The day of the Web site launch party, Lucy dropped her silver earrings into her makeup bag and zipped it shut. She threw the whole thing into her overnight bag, then checked to make sure she hadn't missed anything. Her dress was on its hanger, suspended from the top of the bedroom door. She had her shoes and makeup and jewelry and perfume. Dom already had all the brochures and other materials at his place.

She was ready to go.

Lucy hung her dress carefully in the van before tossing her bag onto the passenger seat. It was three hours before their guests were due to arrive, but she'd insisted on helping Dom set up. In return, he'd insisted that she shower and dress at his place rather than return home. At the time, it had made sense. Now, it made her nervous. Somehow, the thought of getting naked in Dom's house, even when he was in a far distant room, made her feel distinctly…edgy.

It had been almost two weeks since Dom had told her he loved her. Two weeks of neither of them mentioning it or referring to it in any way. Her fault—she was the one who'd sat in stunned silence when he'd spoken the words. She was the one who had started the car and changed the subject instead of addressing what he'd said.

She'd gone over and over the moment a hundred times, justifying her response to herself, trying to convince herself that what he'd said had been a generic, sweeping kind of statement and not about her, about them.

But she knew it was. Deep in her heart, she'd known for a long time that the way he looked at her, the way he behaved around her was not just about lust or desire. She understood him so much better now, after all the time they'd spent in the van together, after all the working dinners and spirited discussions.

He was loyal to a fault. He was honest, committed. He cared about everything he did. And he was kind—he'd proved that to her time and time again with his generous, selfless actions.

He was also incredibly sexy and clever and witty.

And he loved her.

The knowledge had been working on her like water on rock. Every time she looked at him she thought about what he'd said.

We don't choose the ones we love.

She pushed the memory away as she parked her van in front of his house. She had no idea what to do with it, so she avoided it, the way she'd avoided responding to him at the time.

"Hey. Let me grab that for you," Dom said when he answered the door. He took her dress and bag from her.

"The caterers will be here soon. I've left the flowers for you. I'm still trying to get the patio heaters working."

She followed him up the hallway but stopped awkwardly when he turned through a doorway into a bedroom. One glance was enough to let her know it was his—his suit and shirt were on the bed and his aftershave tinged the air. Briefly she took in the neutral decor, the wooden bed with a mocha linen quilt and the pile of books on his bedside table before she looked away.

He hung her dress on the hook behind the door and left her overnight bag beside the bed.

"There are fresh towels in the bathroom," he said, indicating the door to what was obviously an ensuite.

"Great. Thanks," she said. Her palms were sweating and she wiped them down the sides of her leggings.

She would never have said yes to this if she'd known it would feel so…intimate.

She was relieved to see the armful of cut flowers waiting on the kitchen counter. Work—that was what she needed right now. Lots of work to keep her mind from going places it shouldn't.

"I'll leave you to it," he said.

He picked up a remote control and clicked a CD into play as he exited the house to the covered deck out the back. The smooth tones of Duffy filled the room in his wake. She watched for a minute as he bent to examine the gas bottle on one of the three large outdoor heaters they'd rented to warm the patio. He was wearing a pair of old cargo shorts and a faded T-shirt, and he frowned with concentration as he adjusted something. She was so used to that look now, his I'm-trying-to-work-this-out expression. It made her want to laugh and smooth away the lines at the same time.

She forced herself to look away and concentrate on her own tasks. Within minutes she was immersed in trimming and arranging great bunches of Oriental lilies, saw grass and birds of paradise into what she hoped would pass as professional displays. Duffy's voice rose and fell around her and she hummed along. She placed the first vase just inside the front door on the hall table Dom kept there. The second she placed on the front corner of the kitchen counter. The third went into the center of the dining table. She kicked her shoes off as she surveyed the living area, looking for a home for the last vase.

She saw that Dom already had his laptop linked to his flatscreen TV. They planned to use it as a giant monitor throughout the evening, with their Web site demonstration repeating over and over, showcasing their new services to their customers.

She decided the living space had more than enough color, so she headed outside. She smiled as she caught

Dom singing to himself as he manhandled the last heater into position. He flashed her a grin, sheepish at being busted. She placed the vase in the middle of his outdoor table and stepped back to assess the effect.

"Perfect," she said.

"Even if you do say so yourself."

They smiled at each other again and she found herself thinking how natural this felt—being with Dom in his house, sharing with him.

She clamped down on the thought. It had no place in the reality of her life, like a lot of other thoughts she'd had lately.

The caterers arrived on time, and she spent another hour checking over their marketing materials and their Web site display.

She looked up when Dom's bare feet appeared in front of where she sat on the sofa, hunched over the laptop.

"You want first shower?" he asked.

She stared at his feet, not surprised that even they were attractive—brown and strong-looking, his toes even and regular.

"Aren't you cold?" she asked stupidly.

He glanced down at his feet. "Nope. First or second shower?"

"Um, second," she said.

"Okay. I'll yell out when I'm finished."

He left. She finished with the laptop and put it out of the way. Then she fidgeted, waiting to hear his voice calling her to the shower, trying not to think about him standing under a stream of water, big and naked and wet. It seemed like a long time before she heard a door open.

"All yours," he called.

"Thanks."

She entered the bathroom from the hall, noting with relief that he'd closed the door to his bedroom. Fluffy towels were piled on the shelf at the end of the bath and he'd left her overnight bag beside the vanity. She closed the hall door and started to pull her top over her head. She froze as she heard movement in his bedroom, then rolled her eyes at herself. Of course he was in there— he was getting dressed.

A wave of totally inappropriate heat swept over her as she imagined him getting dressed. Pulling boxers over his strong thighs. Buttoning his shirt over his broad chest. The image was so clear in her mind's eye she had to blink to dislodge it.

She growled at herself and whipped her top over her head. Within seconds she was beneath the shower, washing herself with soap that smelled like Dom. She tried to get a grip by staring hard at her belly, but all she could focus on was what he would think of her pregnant body. Her belly was taut and smooth, but it was undeniably a belly. Her breasts were full, bigger than they'd ever been, and her nipples were darker and very sensitive to the touch. Her legs were still long and slim, her best feature. And she'd only widened margin-ally in the hips....

Lucy flicked the water off briskly. It didn't matter

what Dom might think of her pregnant body. He was never going to see it.

She pulled on her underwear and did her makeup and hair, taking more care than usual. She'd chosen a sleek, modern maternity dress, but she needed the confidence of knowing her hair and face were at their best. She swept her hair up and left several strands down to tickle her neck. She colored her lips with a deep plum lipstick, then made her eyes smoky with kohl. Lastly she slipped her earrings into place, smiling as they brushed her neck as she tilted her head.

Then, her towel wrapped tightly around her, she tapped lightly on the door through to the bedroom. There was no answer and she opened it carefully. The room was empty, but Dom's aftershave hung heavily in the air. The quilt cover was wrinkled from where he'd sat to put on his shoes. His watch lay curled on the tallboy, the leather band curved to the shape of his wrist.

She stood for a moment, looking around. This was where he slept. His clothes were behind those sliding doors. She was in his most private space.

She was doing it again: fixating on a man she couldn't have. Frustrated with herself, she let the towel drop as she reached for her dress. The dark blue fabric slipped down her body and she smoothed her hands over the fine black beading on the bodice and skirt. It was only when she tried to zip the dress that she remembered Rosie had helped her try it on in the store. She bit her lip. Dom would have to zip her up.

Her heels clicked quietly on the floorboards as she

walked to the living room. Dom was talking to one of the caterers but he looked up when she entered. It was wrong to feel a rush of pleasure at the way his eyes darkened. Wrong, but impossible to deny. As it was impossible to deny the slow burn in the pit of her stomach as she looked at him, tall and gorgeous in his charcoal suit.

"Can you zip me?" she asked.

He stepped forward. She turned her back, and she felt the slow tug as her zipper closed. When he reached the top, he lingered for a moment, his hand heavy on her back.

"You look very nice," he said. She almost laughed at how much meaning four little words could hold. Except the way she was feeling—at war with herself—wasn't very funny.

"Excuse me, but did you want to start with just the champagne or offer all the wines when people first arrive?" the caterer asked.

Dom turned to answer and she tried to catch her breath.

Don't, she told herself. *Don't forget what's at stake.*

But for the first time it hit her that maybe she had more to lose than she had to gain by keeping her distance from Dom.

It was a revolutionary thought. And a very disturbing one.

"Hurry up! We're going to be late," Rosie called as she took one last swipe at her eyelashes with her mascara wand.

"Sweetheart, I've been ready for half an hour," Andrew said dryly.

She turned from the mirror and saw that he was, indeed, fully dressed and reclining on the bed, arms behind his head as he waited patiently.

"Right. Sorry. Won't be long."

"No rush. I like watching you turn yourself into a mantrap." He wiggled his eyebrows suggestively.

She smiled to cover the wave of guilt that swept through her. He was the perfect husband. Her soul mate. Her better half.

She didn't deserve him. Not by a long shot.

Her hand was shaking when she slid the wand back into the tube.

That's what you get for being a liar, she told herself.

Lucy's advice sounded inside her head for the fiftieth time since their heart to heart: *talk to him.*

Simple words but they opened the door to a whole world of doubt and fear.

Rosie and Andrew handled on average sixty divorces a year. She'd sat opposite puffy-eyed men and women more times than she could count, listening to tales of woe and acrimony and disillusionment. She knew better than anyone the kinds of issues that killed marriages. Whether to have children or not was right at the top of the list, rubbing shoulders with money problems and old-fashioned infidelity.

You can't go on like this, a little voice whispered in her ear as she smoothed on lipstick.

She knew it was true, but the alternatives terrified her.

"Want me to call the cab yet?" Andrew asked. They'd decided to catch a taxi to and from Dom's place so they could both drink without worrying about driving.

"Um, sure. I only need another few minutes," she said.

She could hear him confirming their address for the automated taxi service as she checked her hair and slid her earrings into her ears. The pearls Andrew had bought her for their eighth anniversary were cool against her skin as she fixed the clasp around her neck.

"Five minutes," he said as he ended the call. "Just long enough for me to ruin your lipstick."

He crowded into the bathroom behind her, his arms sliding around her waist. He angled his head into her neck and pressed a kiss against her nape.

"You smell so good."

She watched him in the mirror, her love for him so strong inside her it brought tears to her eyes.

I don't want to lose you, I love you so much, she told him in her head.

"Hey, I just remembered. Do you have cash for the cab? I meant to go to the bank earlier but I forgot," he said.

"I'm tapped out, too. We'll have to stop at an ATM on the way to the party," she said.

He grunted his agreement and pressed his face into her neck again.

"Oh, wait. There's a fifty in the zip pocket in my work bag. Lucy's share of the water bill," she said.

"I'll grab it. Your bag in the study?"

"Yep."

He left the room, and she hit her pulse points with one last spray of perfume before moving into the bedroom to collect her coat and evening bag. She wondered how Lucy was doing, aware that a lot was riding on the success of tonight's party. Dom and Lucy had set themselves the target of signing up a quarter of their existing customers to their new Web-based order system by the night's end. Rosie had confidence in their combined skills, but she wished that every hurdle wasn't quite so high and quite so urgent for her sister. Lucy deserved to catch a break.

Then she thought of Dom and corrected herself. Her sister had already scored the biggest break of them all— she just hadn't recognized it yet.

She heard the sound of a car engine out the front and tweaked the curtain aside to check out the window.

"Taxi's here," she called.

There was no response from the study. Which was when she registered how long it had taken Andrew to collect the money.

She'd completely forgotten—

It hadn't occurred to her—

She strode through the house on legs that felt like lead.

His head came up as she stopped in the doorway. She didn't need to see the shiny foil strip in his hand to understand that he knew. It was in his face, in the hurt, shocked disbelief in his eyes.

She felt dizzy. As though she needed to sit down and throw up and scream all at the same time.

"I'm sorry," she whispered.

Andrew fingered the packet of contraceptive pills, his thumb pressing into the little indent where today's pill used to live.

"Did you stop at all? Was there ever a chance?" he asked.

She swallowed, the sound very noisy in the too quiet room.

"The first month. But then I…I filled the rest of my prescription."

A car horn sounded from outside the house.

"That's the taxi," she said lamely.

Andrew stared at her for a long moment, then he stood and walked past her, angling his body very carefully so that they didn't brush against each other in the doorway. As though he couldn't stand touching her.

And why not? She'd betrayed him, made a fool of him. Lied to him every day. Had sex with him and let him hope each time that they were making a child when in fact she'd made very sure they weren't. Commiserated with him when her period came. Talked about what it would be like when it didn't come, the plans they'd make.

She heard the front door click shut and Andrew's footsteps in the hall. She gathered herself and went to join him.

"I'm ready now," she said.

He gave her a disbelieving look.

"I sent the cab away."

Of course he had. They weren't going to Lucy's party, not after what had just happened. Crazy to even think it, but she couldn't seem to think at all right now.

"I can explain," she said.

"Can you?"

She didn't like the way he looked at her, couldn't stand the unfamiliar, angry hardness in his eyes.

"I should have said something earlier."

His eyebrows rose. "*Earlier?* The only reason we're having this conversation at all is because I found the pills in your bag."

She pressed her hand to her throat.

"Just tell me one thing. How far were you willing to go?" he asked.

"Sorry?" Why couldn't she think? All she could see was the anger in his eyes, and all she could hear was the thump of her panicked heart.

"Weeks, months? How long did you figure it would take for me to lose heart and accept it wasn't going to happen for us?"

"It wasn't like that," she stammered. And it was true. She hadn't planned or plotted. There was no method to her madness—she'd been acting on pure, fear-driven instinct.

"You'll forgive me if I find it hard to believe a word you say right now," he said.

She took a step toward him, but he raised a hand to

ward her off and she stopped in her tracks. He closed his eyes and took a deep breath.

"Jesus. I can't believe this, Rosie."

He walked past her to their bedroom. Tears burned at the back of her eyes but for some reason they didn't fall. She took a deep breath, then another. Reason told her to give him a moment to calm down, but instinct drove her to chase him, to throw herself at his feet and explain and beg forgiveness.

Andrew was at the wardrobe with an armful of clothes when she entered.

"What are you doing?" she asked.

Then she saw the open suitcase on the bed behind him.

"Please don't. Oh God. Can't we talk about this?" she begged.

Andrew tossed the clothes into the case.

"Now you want to talk?"

"I'm sorry. I know what I did was wrong but I was so scared and I didn't know how to raise it with you. I just needed to buy some time, that's all."

He didn't stop throwing clothes in the case. Far more than he needed for one night, she noted. Bile surged up the back of her throat.

"You don't want kids," he said flatly.

"That's not it," she said.

He nailed her with a look. God, even now she had trouble getting the truth out of her mouth.

"I don't know," she said more honestly. "I have reservations."

"Right."

He crossed to the chest of drawers and began tossing underwear and socks into the open case. He didn't say anything more, and she watched him with growing panic.

"Please, Andrew, say something," she said.

"I don't know what to say to you right now. I feel like I don't even know you."

"I'm not saying I definitely don't want kids. I just need more time to get used to the idea."

"This is not about whether we have kids or not, Rosie!" he said, anger in every line of his body. "You lied to me. You looked me in the eye and lied to me *every freaking day*. What the hell am I supposed to do with that?"

"I'm sorry," she said, because she could think of nothing else to say. There was no excuse or explanation for her actions. Reasons, yes, but nothing that made what she did more palatable or forgivable.

"I thought you were my best friend. I thought we were going to grow old together, that I could trust you with anything," he said.

"You can. I am," she said.

He shook his head. "No."

She gasped at his stark denial. He zipped the case shut.

"Please don't go. We can work this out. We just need to keep talking," she said.

He hefted the case off the bed.

"Not tonight."

"Please. Please don't go."

They'd never spent a night apart because of an argument. They'd never even gone to bed angry. The thought of letting him walk out the door made her dizzy all over again.

"I can't be with you right now," Andrew said.

He stood in front of her, the case in one hand. She looked into his face, tried to summon the words that would make everything all right. Nothing came.

She stepped to one side and he moved past her. She trailed him to the front door.

"Where will you go?" she asked again.

"Does it matter?"

"Can you at least call me and let me know where you're staying?"

"Fine."

He could barely look at her. She reached for him, needing to touch him. He stiffened as her hands found the lapels on his jacket.

"I love you, Andrew. Please believe that I never meant to hurt you," she said.

He just looked at her until she let her arms fall.

She watched him walk down the path to the carport. He threw his case in the backseat and started the car. Then he was reversing down the driveway. And then he was driving off into the night.

She stood on the threshold well after the echo of the engine had died away.

He'd gone. He'd really gone.

Panic and fear and regret and hurt threatened to choke her. She barely made it to the bathroom before she lost her dinner to the toilet bowl. Her anniversary pearls clanked against the porcelain as she rested her elbows on the seat.

What have you done? What have you done?

And how would she ever make it up to him?

Her mouth bitter with bile, she sank to the floor. She opened her mouth on a soundless cry as the tears came.

What have you done?

The house was filled with savory cooking smells by the time the doorbell rang for the first time. Dom answered it and greeted their first guests and soon the house was filled with the sound of laughter and conversation. Like Dom, Lucy worked the room, talking to her clients, introducing people to each other, making sure everyone had a good time.

One of the last arrivals was Dom's father and mother, both looking uncomfortable in their Sunday best. She saw the surprise on Dom's face when he spotted them. He hadn't expected them to come. She made sure they both had drinks—good Italian red wine—and introduced them to one of her favorite customers.

Vaguely she was aware that Rosie and Andrew were late. Around 9:00, her cell phone beeped with a text message from her sister:

Not feeling well. Sorry. Catch up tomorrow. Good luck.

It was unlike her sister to text instead of call. And Rosie had seemed fine when she saw her earlier in the day. Lucy wondered for a moment if she should call home to make sure everything was okay. Then one of her customers approached her to ask some questions about the site and she pushed her sister to the back of her mind. Andrew would take care of Rosie if she was feeling under the weather.

As the night wore on, the feeling of nervous anticipation in Lucy's blood settled. Their clients were having a good time, and by 10:00 almost half of them had signed up for Market Fresh's Internet-based service, well beyond her and Dom's target for the evening. Dom's father had overcome his social nerves and was holding forth on the patio, and a hum of convivial goodwill filled Dom's house.

They'd pulled it off.

At 10:30, she glanced across the room and caught Dom's eye. He smiled and raised his champagne glass. She raised her orange juice, pulling a sad face to let him know she'd rather have bubbles. He laughed and something undeniable caught her in the chest.

He was so beautiful. So wonderful.

And he loved her.

Unexpected tears stung her eyes as the full import of his declaration hit her. This man—this incredible, amazing man—loved her. He'd shown her in a million different ways how much she meant to him. He'd saved her business, helped save her baby's life, stood by her and supported her even when she pushed him away.

She blinked rapidly. Across the room, he frowned. She watched as he put down his drink, preparing to come to her side. Quickly she shook her head, gesturing for him to stay where he was. If he came to her now, she didn't think she would be able to trust herself.

He stopped, the frown still on his face. She forced a smile and turned to the nearest customer. Slowly, the rush of emotion ebbed. She told herself it had simply been the excitement of the evening. Nothing more.

Her feet were aching by the time they ushered the last guests from the house. Dom's father went smiling, full of bonhomie after an evening of playing the expert. Most of their clients went home happy, full of food and wine, clutching brochures for Market Fresh's Web site.

Dom sighed as he shut the door on the last customer and leaned against it.

"Done."

"Like a dog's dinner," she said.

He rubbed his eyes. "I don't think I have kissed so much butt in my entire life."

She laughed. "At least it was for a good cause."

They returned to the living room and surveyed the damage: glasses and plates of half-eaten food everywhere, platters of finger food on every flat surface. The caterers had left over an hour ago and would only return to collect their glassware and serving platters in a few days' time.

"Oh boy," she said.

Dom shook his head.

"Forget about it. You go home and I'll take care of this tomorrow."

She toed her shoes off. "If we at least do some of it now, it won't be so bad," she said.

She crossed to the kitchen and started to empty wine-glasses into the sink.

"Lucy, go home," he said with a laugh. "What is it with Italian women? They never know when to stop."

He was behind her, and he reached over her shoulder to pluck a glass from her hand.

"I want to help," she said.

The truth was, she wasn't ready to go home yet. She didn't want the night to be over. Which was stupid, because she had to go home. The alternative was…well, reckless, to say the least.

"We've got a ton of stuff to go over tomorrow. You can help by getting a good night's sleep," he said.

She half turned toward him, then turned away again. She couldn't say what she wanted to say while looking at him. She reached for the edge of the counter and gripped it tightly.

"What if I don't feel like sleeping?" she asked.

She closed her eyes, immediately wishing the words unsaid.

She had to be crazy. She was pregnant, huge. Dom may have kissed her once and told her that he was interested in something more and maybe even indicated that he might love her but she'd gone from round to bulging since then.

There was a profound silence. She heard Dom take a deep breath.

"Lucy."

She knew she had to face him. She let go of the counter and slowly turned.

He was standing very close and her stomach brushed his hip. Finally she met his eyes.

"Does that mean what I think it means?" he asked.

"Yes. If you think it means I'm asking if you'd like me to stay the night. If you're still interested, that is."

He went very still. She had no idea what was going on behind his eyes. She could feel heat burning its way up her neck and into her cheeks.

"You know how I feel about you," he said. His voice was very low, very deep.

"Yes. I mean, no. I mean, sort of," she said. Her hands fluttered pointlessly in the air between them. As though he needed more clues that she had no idea what she was doing. Even at the best of times she was no femme fatale. Now, tonight…she felt about as sleek and sexy as a Volkswagen.

His mouth quirked into a little smile.

"Maybe I should repeat myself," he said.

His gaze dropped to her mouth and he leaned forward. She closed her eyes as his lips found hers. Warm and firm, his mouth moved over hers. Then his tongue was in her mouth and she was tasting heat and wine and need. Her hands found his shoulders, curling into his collar in case he tried to pull away before she'd had her fill of him. She angled her head to give him more access, but he pulled away from her and broke the kiss.

They were both panting. They stared at each other across the few inches that separated them.

"This isn't just tonight for me, Lucy," he said.

His voice had a tremble in it. It gave her the courage she needed to take the leap of faith he was asking of her. He'd asked her to trust him. She did. He'd told her he wasn't going anywhere. He hadn't. And he'd told her he cared. That he loved her. Tonight, she chose to believe him.

"I know that. This isn't just about tonight for me, either," she said. "I don't know why this has happened in my life right now. The timing couldn't be worse. I'm not exactly at my best. I'm definitely not a great catch. But I can't look at you and not want to touch you. And I can't stop thinking about you. And I'm sick of trying to be sensible when so much of me wants to believe…."

His face softened and his gaze traveled over her features.

"Believe," he said, then he kissed her again.

This time his arms slid around her, pulling her close. Her belly pressed into his, but she forgot all self-consciousness as need long denied swept through her.

It had been a long time since she'd felt sexy or attractive. A long time since she'd allowed herself to be a woman and not a mother-to-be. A long time since she'd been with anyone except Marcus.

But the way Dom kissed… He made her knees weak, stole the air from her lungs. Brought all the forgotten parts of her body roaring back to life.

His mouth slid from her mouth to kiss a trail up her cheekbone to her ear. She shivered as he circled the curve of her ear with his tongue, then sucked lightly on her neck. She let her head drop back and moaned as he pressed openmouthed kisses to her throat again and again. It felt so good, he felt so good.

She ran her hands over his shoulders, her fingers dig-

ging into the big muscles of his back as Dom began to
kiss his way down her neck. One of his hands slid up
her side to cup her breast, and she shuddered as white-
hot desire raced through her.

Had she ever felt so hungry for a man's touch? Had
she ever been so desperate to feel skin against skin?

His thumb grazed her nipple once, twice. She
grabbed his shoulders, not sure how much longer she
could support her own weight.

"You're so beautiful," Dom murmured as he kissed
his way down into her cleavage. "So beautiful."

She bit her lip as he nuzzled the neckline of her dress
then tugged the fabric to one side to reveal the stretch
lace of her black bra. She closed her eyes as his hand
closed over her, warm and large, then he was pushing
the lace to one side and his hot mouth was on her breast.

"Oh!" she said. "That feels so good."

She felt him smile against her skin. Then he lifted
his head and looked into her eyes.

"Come to bed?" he asked. There was still doubt in
his eyes. She liked that, liked that not for a second did
he take her for granted.

"Yes."

Chapter 10

His hand clasped hers and he tugged her after him as he walked to his bedroom. The bedside lamp was on, the light soft and golden across the bed. He pushed the door shut, then pulled her into his arms again.

Perhaps it was being in the bedroom, or perhaps it was simply the growing knowledge that soon they would be naked with each other and her body would be revealed in all its rounded glory, but she was self-conscious this time, more aware of where her stomach pressed against him.

He kissed her long and slow, then slid a hand onto her breasts again. He drove her crazy rubbing his thumb across her nipples through her dress, but not for a moment did she stop worrying and thinking. After a few minutes, Dom kissed his way to her ear, one of his hands sliding to her nape, the other to the small of her back.

"What's wrong?" he murmured, his question more vibration than spoken word.

She considered lying, bluffing. But she trusted him. If this was going to happen, it was going to be honest, right from the start.

"I'm nervous. I haven't done this for a while. And things are kind of...different."

His hand slid around from her back to rest on her belly.

"You mean this?"

"Yes. That tiny, insignificant little thing."

"You're worried about the baby?" he asked.

"No. No, the doctor said sex was okay. As long as it's not hanging off the chandelier or something," she said. This was so hard. But she wanted him, wanted this.

"I'm worried you won't want me once you see me without my clothes on," she confessed in a rush.

He stilled for a second, then pulled back so he could look into her eyes.

"Never going to happen," he said.

"But still," she said, shrugging one shoulder. "It might."

He smiled slightly.

"You have no idea how long I've wanted you, do you? Since we were kids. And in the past few years, so much that it made me feel guilty even though my marriage was already history. I've been dreaming about getting you naked for years, Lucy Basso. And this—"

he caressed her baby bump "—only makes you more gorgeous."

She nodded. She wanted to believe him. Realistically, there was no way to get past this other than to forge ahead, as it were. If she took off her clothes and he ran a mile, she'd have her answer.

She turned and offered him her back.

"Unzip me," she said.

"Lucy…"

"Please."

Silence for a moment, then she felt the tug as he unzipped her dress. He pressed a kiss onto her shoulder, then her nape as he slipped the dress off her shoulders. She held her breath as he helped the dress slide down her arms. She pulled her arms free and felt the slither of silk against her skin as the dress fell to the floor.

Dom's hands landed on her shoulders as though he knew this was a big moment for her. She closed her eyes and took a step forward. His hands fell away. From behind, she knew, she looked almost normal, apart from a little extra weight she'd put on around her hips and backside. She held her breath and turned to face him. She knew what he was seeing—her breasts stretching out a black lace bra, the matching panties riding low beneath her bump. And in between, her belly, round and undeniable.

"Lucy. You want to open your eyes?" Dom asked, his voice full of gentle amusement.

"I don't know. Do you still want to do this?" she asked.

"More than ever."

She opened her eyes then and saw the naked desire in his face.

"You need more proof?" he asked.

He stepped closer and took her hand. Holding her eye, he slid her hand to the front of his pants. Her fingers curved instinctively around the hard length she found there. He felt very big and very erect.

No chance he was faking that.

"Good enough?" he asked.

"Hell yeah," she said.

He laughed. "I wasn't fishing for compliments," he said.

"Well, you got one anyway." She pressed her palm against him. Soon, they would be naked and all this hardness would be inside her....

"You're wearing way too much clothing," she said.

She wasn't sure where her sudden boldness came from, but she was too far gone to care. He wanted her. She wanted him. He was a man, and she was a woman. A pregnant woman, yes, but still a woman.

"You want to help me with that?" he asked.

There was something about the way he said it, a catch in his voice that made her wonder if her undressing him was something he'd thought about before.

The idea made her smile and suddenly she felt infinitely saucy, incredibly sexy. She stepped closer and hooked her finger into the neckline of his shirt. She'd admired his body so many times. The thought that she was about to lay hand and mouth on him made her a little dizzy.

One button slid free, then another, then another. She pushed the sides of his shirt open and pressed her mouth against the wide triangle of chest she'd uncovered. His skin was very warm, his muscles firm. He smelled delicious—spicy and masculine.

She fumbled the rest of his buttons and pushed the shirt off his shoulders and down his arms. He had a beautiful chest, his pectoral muscles well defined with a silky sprinkling of hair that narrowed down into a sexy trail as it headed below his belt.

"Wow," she said as she smoothed her hands over him. "Lifting boxes of fruit really agrees with you."

He laughed and reached out to draw her close. She shook her head.

"I'm not finished yet."

She undid his belt buckle, then tackled the button and fly on his trousers. Her hands were shaking as she pushed his trousers down over his hips. He was wearing black boxer-briefs, the fabric snug over his impressive erection. He shoved his pants down his legs and toed off his shoes. Then he stepped free of his clothing, naked bar his underwear.

She stared at his thighs. Hard and muscled, they made her want to purr with anticipation.

"You have the best legs ever," she said reverently.

He grinned.

"You're good for my ego," he said. "Come here."

This time she didn't stop him when he pulled her

close. The first press of his bare skin against hers was breathtaking. She made an impatient sound and reached behind herself for her bra clasp, wanting to feel all of him against all of her. Her bra loosened around her rib cage and she shrugged it off. Dom inhaled sharply as her breasts were bared and his eyes got very dark and very intent.

"If you had any idea..." he said, then things got a little crazy.

Soon they were on the bed with nothing between them but heat. All the weeks of watching and secretly wanting him, all the doubt and uncertainty, and now there was nothing but the slide of his body inside hers, the warmth of his skin on hers, the sound of his breath near her ear.

This was right. This was meant to be. This was perfect.

Her climax came quickly, sweeping her away. She cried out, held him to her. And then he was saying her name and his body was shuddering into hers one last time.

He kept his weight on his forearms afterward, always careful. He lowered his head to kiss her, long and deep. Then he withdrew and disappeared for a few seconds into the bathroom.

She kept her eyes closed, savoring the satisfied warmth spreading through her body. The bed dipped as he returned. His legs tangled with her own as he moved close and slid an arm around her.

"Okay?" he asked quietly.

She opened her eyes and stared into his face.

"More than okay."

They stared at each other, suddenly very serious. Words crowded her mouth, but she hesitated to give voice to them. Not so long ago, Dom had been someone she only saw across the trestle tables at the market. In a few short months, he'd become inextricably entwined in her life, her business and her heart.

"Lucy Basso," he said, smiling. "At last."

He kissed her forehead, her cheek, the end of her nose. Then he gathered her close and rested her head on his chest. She listened to his heart beating, slow and steady. And she swallowed the words. There would be other nights, other moments like this. She had all the time in the world to tell Dom that she'd fallen in love with him.

Closing her eyes, she snuggled closer. For now, she had this. It felt like more than enough to be going on with.

Dom woke with Lucy's hair tangled across his chest, her face resting on his shoulder. She was deeply asleep, her chest rising and falling evenly. He smiled as he saw that one of her hands was curved over her belly—even in sleep, she thought of her baby.

Last night had been...well, suffice to say he was a lucky man. A very lucky man. Never in his wildest dreams had he imagined Lucy in his bed. Okay, that was an exaggeration. Many of his wildest dreams featured Lucy in a starring role in just that location. But he hadn't expected her to let him close, not for a long time, anyway. He'd known he'd been paying the price for her ex's faults, that she was cautious and scared and that she had good reason to be.

But last night she'd let him in in a spectacular way. He remembered the way she'd undressed for him, the uncertainty in her eyes, the way her chin had lifted as she stood before him wearing only her underwear.

She had no idea how fine she was, how perfect. She was beautiful, with her big, full breasts, her swollen belly, her long slim legs. She was beautiful and last night had been a gift. Touching her, holding her, being a part of her…

When things had fallen apart with Dani, he'd wondered if maybe he'd had his one shot at happiness and messed it up. Lying here with Lucy in his arms made him believe in an infinite number of tomorrows.

He loved her. Had been half in love with her for years and was now totally besotted with her.

A small frown creased Lucy's brow and she stirred against him. He watched as her eyelids flickered, then opened. He knew the exact moment she remembered what had happened last night, saw the slow smile dawn on her mouth and the warmth in her eyes.

"Morning," he said.

"Morning," she said. Her smile widened and she put her hand on her belly. "Someone else is up, too."

She looked at him uncertainly.

"Do you want to…?"

Hell, yes. It had been weeks since he'd felt the baby's

first movements, and he'd been aching for a chance to share the experience with Lucy again. He slid his hand onto her stomach and she guided his hand to where the action was at.

"Of course, she'll decide to go to sleep now," she said dryly.

It took a few minutes of patience, but at last he felt the strange and wonderful surge of movement beneath her skin.

"Wow. That's pretty full on. Much stronger than last time," he said.

He realized Lucy was watching him carefully, just as she had last night when she'd taken off her clothes and stood nearly naked before him.

"This really doesn't make a difference to you, does it?" she asked.

"Not in the way you mean."

"You know that in about another thirteen weeks, I'm going to be cranky from lack of sleep and I'm going to smell like milk and barely have time to wash my hair, right?"

He pulled a comic face.

"That bad, huh? How soon can you be out of my bed?"

She shoved a hand into his shoulder and he captured it in both of his.

"Lucy, you're going to have a baby. I want to be with you, I want to help you. Caring for you means I already care for your baby. It's not a big deal," he said.

"It would be for some men. It's Marcus's baby, and

he practically ran in the opposite direction when he found out."

"Maybe he never wanted children. Maybe he's never wanted to be a father."

He said the words without thinking. Lucy's face softened and she pulled his hand to her face and pressed a kiss into his palm.

"That's one of the nicest things you've ever said to me," she said.

He stared at her, feeling like a fraud. Not because what he'd said wasn't true—being a father had once been one of his most important dreams—but because it was never going to happen for him. And she needed to know that before their relationship went much further.

Tell her. Tell her now. The longer you put it off, the more it's going to mean. And the harder you'll fall if she decides she can't live with it, the way Dani did.

Lucy slid an arm around his waist and rested her head on his shoulder. He loved the feel of her hair on his chest and the warm rush of her breath across his skin. He loved the feel of her slim, strong arm across his body.

He loved her.

I'll tell her tonight. Not now, tonight.

The moment the decision was made, his body grew tense. He tried to imagine her face when he told her, how she might react. With pity? Disappointment? Anger?

"What time is it?" Lucy asked, lifting her head to look into his face.

"Nearly ten." He was surprised he could speak, his chest felt so tight.

She grimaced ruefully. "I'd better get going. Rosie will be ready to send out a search party. Or she'll be waiting to interrogate me. I'm not sure which is worse, to be honest."

She smiled at him and he pushed thoughts of the future away. Lucy Basso was in his bed, in his arms. That was the important thing. Everything else would follow from that. He had to believe that, or he might as well give up on life and go live in a cave in a hillside somewhere.

Lucy moaned with despair when they walked into the kitchen in search of breakfast.

"Oh my God. I told you we should have put some of this way last night," she said as she stared at the debris from the launch party.

He pulled her into his arms.

"You telling me you'd rather have cleaned?"

She smiled. "No. No way."

"Good."

He made them eggs on toast then washed her in the shower. Saying goodbye took some time, between Lucy's insistence that she help him tidy up and his that she go home to rest and the mandatory bout of kissing that occurred on the doorstep.

Finally he was alone. He put something loud and pumpy on the stereo and started cleaning, but it wasn't enough to distract him from his thoughts.

Lucy had feelings for him. She was attracted to him.

She enjoyed his company. He wanted to believe she'd fallen in love with him, the way he'd fallen in love with her.

More than anything, he wanted to believe that loving him would be enough for her. It hadn't been enough for Dani.

She's not Dani. She's a completely different person.

But he couldn't help remembering the fights, the blame, the rejection. He couldn't help remembering the pain of losing the woman he'd vowed to love and honor for the rest of his life.

This is Lucy. This is different.

He looked around at his living room, still scattered with dishes and glasses. He would clean later. Right now, he needed to run.

He pulled on shorts and trainers and was out the door within five minutes. The pavement was wet, and a fine rain misted his cheeks. He didn't care. He ran past the cemetery, through the university and into Royal Park. By the time he returned home he was soaked with sweat and rain and his legs were trembling. He leaned against the tiles in the shower and let hot water wash it all away.

He would tell her. He would sit her down and explain about getting sick in his early twenties, then he'd tell her about his marriage and how he and Dani had tried everything to have the child they so desperately wanted. And then he would tell her to think about what he'd said for a few days, even a week, then come back to him and give him her answer. Was she willing to live with a man who could not give her more children?

It would kill him to have to wait for her answer, but she deserved the time. He wanted her to go into this with her eyes open. He wanted to love her unrestrainedly, unreservedly, without fear of a later rejection.

The man staring back at him from the mirror was grim as he toweled himself dry. There was every chance Lucy would be angry with him, that she'd think his infertility was something she should have known about before she took the huge step of staying with him last night. His only defense was that he hadn't expected her to proposition him. He'd resigned himself to waiting until after the baby was born and she'd found her feet as a mother before he approached her again. Then she'd looked at him last night and asked if he was still interested, if he still wanted her...

He threw the damp towel to the floor. It was useless to speculate. He'd already made his decision. He was telling her. How she responded was not something he had any control over.

He was shrugging on a clean T-shirt when he saw the blinking light on his answering machine. Lucy had called while he was out. He frowned when he heard the emotional quaver in her voice as she asked him to call.

He grabbed the phone and called her back.

"Lucy. What's wrong?" he asked the moment he heard her voice.

"Can you come over?" she asked. She sounded as though she'd been crying.

"I'll be there in ten minutes, but first tell me what's wrong."

"It's Rosie and Andrew. They had a big fight last night. Andrew stayed at a motel. Rosie's a mess—"

"Okay. I'll be there in ten," he said.

He made it in eight thanks to a little bending of the road laws and some luck with green lights. Lucy didn't say a word when she answered the door, she simply walked into his embrace and pressed her cheek to his chest. He soothed circles on her back and rested his cheek against the crown of her head.

"It will be all right," he said, even though he had no idea what he was dealing with. Rosie and Andrew had seemed like a solid, loving couple to him. Definitely not the type to have the kind of fights where one of them had to find somewhere else to sleep the night. But no one ever knew what really went on in other people's marriages.

"I'm sorry," Lucy said as she finally pushed away from his chest. "I just got myself so upset when I started thinking all this through. I wanted to see you."

He smoothed the hair back from her troubled face. She would never understand how honored he felt to be the person she sought comfort from. She trusted him. Better—she felt safe with him.

She led him to the couch and spilled out what she knew of the story.

She'd come home to find Rosie and Andrew's house in darkness, all the curtains drawn, Andrew's car gone, but Rosie's still in the driveway. She'd waited for Rosie to come knocking with an inquisition's worth of questions about why her younger sister hadn't slept in her own bed last night, but it had never happened. After an hour, she'd gone through the connecting door to the house and found her sister curled on the couch in her study, huddled under a blanket, still wearing last night's cocktail dress.

"I'm really worried about her. I've never seen her like this," Lucy said. "She's always been the fiery one, the bolshy one. But she doesn't want to talk, I can't make her eat. And Andrew isn't answering his phone."

She paused then, and he guessed she was trying to work out in her mind what she was free to tell him and what was too private.

"They've been trying get to pregnant," she said. "For maybe a couple of months now. But I found this on the study floor."

She pulled a strip of foil from her pocket. It took him a moment to understand what it was.

"The pill," he said.

She bit her lip and tears filled her eyes.

"Rosie told me a few weeks ago that she was scared of being a mom, scared she wouldn't be up to it and that she wouldn't be able to bond with her baby because she's never been very maternal. When I found the pills, she admitted she's been taking these in secret. Last night, Andrew found them."

Dom sank back against the couch, imagining his own reaction in similar circumstances. He could understand the other man leaving the house. Being very angry with someone you loved was never an easy thing.

Lucy shook her head.

"They have always been so happy, you know? Perfect for each other. They fell in love at first sight at university. I know that sounds crazy, but it's true. I knew the first moment I saw them together that they would get married. And now..."

"Hey, they're not divorced yet. They've hit a pothole. Shit happens in relationships. There's every chance they can get past this."

She looked at him, her eyes clouded with doubt.

"And sometimes shit happening destroys relationships. Look at us. I was with Marcus for eight years, you've just gotten divorced. There are some things that people can't get past. And I'm scared this is one of them."

Something inside him went very still at her words.

"You don't think Rosie and Andrew can work this out?"

Lucy bit her lip. "I think wanting to have a family is one of the most powerful urges in the world. Andrew has always been gung ho, always. I can't see the compromise in this situation. He either gives up on the dream of having children, or my sister has children just to please him. Not exactly a recipe for success, whichever option they go with."

"You don't think that Andrew might decide that Rosie is more important to him than having children?"

She tucked her head into his neck, and he couldn't see her face when she next spoke.

"Maybe. It's possible. I guess I'm just speaking from my own experience. I've always wanted to be a mother. Believe it or not, my first reaction to learning I was pregnant was happiness, even though Marcus had gone and I was all alone. To me, family is what makes the world go round. I'm going to have a little girl, and I want her to have brothers and sisters to lean on and share stories and memories with when she grows up. I want her to have what I have with Rosie, you know? A sense of belonging. Continuity. Love. I don't think I could deny that part of myself and pretend it wasn't there."

She had to have felt him tense, because she lifted her head and pulled back so she could look him in the eye.

"I've totally freaked you out, haven't I?" she said, and he could see she was only half-joking. "I know exactly what you're thinking. One night with a pregnant woman and she's already lining up the cribs in the nursery."

"You haven't freaked me out," he lied. "Family is important to me, too. I understand."

He did, too. He understood exactly what she was saying. He'd heard it all before, after all, in fights across the kitchen table, arguments in the car, tearful discussions in specialists' waiting rooms. He'd been over and over the same ground with his ex-wife, and he knew exactly how undeniable the urge to be a parent was.

He looked down into Lucy's face, into her warm brown eyes, and he acknowledged a truth he'd been hiding from himself for the past months. Lucy was a lover, a giver. A natural caregiver, a nurturer. She was born to be a mother.

And he was sterile.

Sitting in her flat with her head on his shoulder, he could only see one future for their relationship. He could only see pain on both sides. Anger. Resentment. All places he didn't want to go again. Couldn't. It had taken him a year to drag himself out of the depression he'd fallen into at the end of his marriage. He didn't want to even imagine what it would be like to have to get over Lucy.

But he was going to have to. Because he was holding an impossible dream in his arms.

He tucked a strand of her hair behind her ear, then traced her cheekbone with his thumb. She looked into his eyes, a small frown creasing her face. He lowered his head and kissed her, closing his eyes so he could consciously savor the moment.

I love you. I think you're wonderful. I want you to be happy.

Lucy's eyes remained closed for a few seconds when he lifted his head. He studied her face, wanting to remember her like this—soft and loving in his arms.

Then he reached for his cell phone.

"What are you doing?" she asked.

"Calling Andrew."

"He won't pick up. I've tried already, three times."

"He might pick up if he doesn't recognize the number," Dom said.

"Oh. Good idea. Sneaky, but good."

He smiled tightly. Lucy gave him Andrew's cell number and he punched it into the phone.

As he'd hoped, Andrew answered almost immediately.

"Andrew, it's Dom. Lucy wants to speak to you," he said.

He handed the phone over and listened as Lucy spoke to her brother-in-law, explaining Rosie's state of withdrawal, asking him to make contact with her, wondering when he planned on coming home. It was a short call, and he could tell by Lucy's face that she wasn't satisfied with the answers she received to any of her questions.

"He's still angry. And hurt," she said.

"He'll get over it. He loves her."

"Sometimes love isn't enough, though, is it?"

He shook his head. "No, sometimes it isn't."

No one knew that more than him.

Lucy stood with an effort and rubbed the small of her back.

"I'm going to go check on Rosie again, let her know I've spoken to Andrew. Even if it wasn't very satisfactory."

"Okay."

He glanced toward the door. He wanted to go. Needed to go, because he wasn't sure how much longer he could keep it together.

"Would you mind waiting?" she asked tentatively.

He wanted to reassure her that he would always be there for her, that she would never have to doubt his support. But she was going to hate him enough in the weeks to come without him digging a deeper hole for them both.

"Sure. Whatever you need," he said instead.

She smiled gratefully before turning away.

"Remind me when I get back how lucky I am," she said.

He remained silent as she opened the connecting door to the house and slipped through.

Lucy *was* lucky. She was about to become a mother. And he was about to spare her the pain of choosing between loving him and her lifelong dream.

For a moment, he was so overwhelmed by anger and frustration that he wanted to throw back his head and howl.

He didn't. He took a deep breath, let it out again, and waited. There would be time enough for him to withdraw from Lucy's life over the next few days and weeks. Soon enough she would understand that it wasn't going to happen between them. Today, right now, she needed him, and he couldn't deny her what she needed. Not yet, anyway.

There'd be plenty of time for that later, when she hated him.

Rosie hadn't moved from her curled position on the couch. Even though she was covered with a thick blanket, her hand was cold to the touch when Lucy sat on the edge of the couch and took it in both of hers.

"I just spoke to Andrew. He answered his cell when Dom called."

Rosie opened her eyes and turned her head slightly toward her sister.

"You spoke to him? Is he okay?"

"He sounded angry," Lucy said. There was no point lying.

Rosie's eyes closed again. "Did he say anything?"

"He doesn't know when he'll be home. I told him you were pretty upset. That might make a difference."

Her sister's body tensed beneath the blanket.

"Why did you do that?"

"I thought it might make him come home."

Rosie wriggled around beneath the blanket so that she was facing Lucy and not the back of the couch.

"I don't want him to come home because he feels sorry for me."

"Isn't the important thing that he's here? That you guys start talking again?"

Rosie glared at her, then started pushing the blanket off herself.

"When he comes back I want it to be because he wants to, because it was his decision. Not out of pity or a misguided sense of responsibility."

Rosie swung her legs to the floor and shoved the blanket all the way off. Lucy stood.

"Sorry. I thought he should be here," she said.

Some of the indignation left her sister's face and her shoulders slumped.

"It's okay, Luce. Thank you."

"It's going to be all right," Lucy said.

"Sure it is. I lied to my husband every day for six weeks and he just found out about it, and everything is going to be dandy."

Lucy winced at her sister's acid sarcasm but she figured that fiery, angry Rosie was better than apathetic, catatonic Rosie. Much better.

"God, my mouth feels disgusting," Rosie said. She walked to her bedroom then into the ensuite bathroom. Lucy stood in the doorway as Rosie began to undress.

"What are you going to do?" Lucy asked.

"I don't know."

"Maybe we could go to the hotel so you guys can talk."

"No," Rosie said firmly. "He's angry with me. He has every right to be angry with me. The least I can do is let him have the space he needs."

"You're a better woman than me, then."

"I didn't say it was going to be easy," Rosie said as she turned on the shower. "You think I don't want to go over there and throw myself at his feet? I tried that last night and it didn't work."

Lucy watched her sister sadly. She had no idea what to say, what advice to offer.

"What about counseling?" she finally suggested.

Rosie's head came up.

"You mean, like a shrink?" Her sister looked appalled. Rosie frowned. "I don't think so."

She stepped beneath the spray, and Lucy went to sit on the bed while her sister showered. She wasn't long and soon she came into the bedroom, the towel wrapped sarong-style around her. She was still frowning, her wet hair dripping down her back.

"I mean, I wouldn't even know where to find a counselor," she said. "And what would I say to them?"

"Claire Miller saw someone last year when she was going through her divorce," Lucy said. They'd both known Claire since they were kids, and she knew her sister respected the other woman. "I could get the number from her. And I guess you just tell her what's going on and how you're feeling. She'll take care of the rest."

"It's a woman?" Rosie asked.

"Yep. Claire said she was great. Helped her get her shit together."

"I've got a lot of shit that needs getting together," Rosie said grimly.

Lucy shrugged. "Gotta start somewhere."

Rosie nodded, looking thoughtful.

"I need to do something. I need to show Andrew that I care, that this means everything to me."

"You need to stop giving yourself a hard time for feeling the way you feel, too," Lucy said. "There is no edict from the skies that says every woman must have children. You're allowed to not want them."

Rosie sighed and sat next to Lucy on the bed.

"If only it was as simple as that. It's not like I can't imagine a little baby who looks like Andrew. A little part of him. When I think of a baby in those terms, it seems crazy not to do it. But then I start thinking about everything else…"

Lucy looked at her sister, hating the worry and sadness and fear creasing her face. Her sister had always been there for her. When they were kids, she'd made sure Lucy never missed out on anything, even if it meant sacrificing herself. She'd protected Lucy in the schoolyard and stepped in to take the brunt of their mother's temper or sadness when things were precarious at home. Even as adults, she'd been the stalwart of Lucy's life, the person she turned to before her mother, before her lover. Lucy understood that was partly because deep down she'd always known Marcus was unreliable, but it was also because she trusted her sister implicitly, with any crisis or problem or secret.

"You know," she said slowly. "You say you're not maternal, but you've been looking after me for years. And I've seen the way you fight for your clients, the way you go beyond what's required to support them. You care, Rosie."

"Then why am I so scared of being a mother? So scared I lied to my husband?"

"I don't know. Maybe because you bore the brunt of all the uncertainty when we were growing up. I always had you to turn to, but you had no one when Ma was out working or was too wound up to be there for us. Maybe in your head, you equate being a mom with all of that."

"If that's true, then why don't you?" Rosie asked.

Lucy kissed her sister's cheek and smoothed her damp hair from her forehead.

"Because I had you to be my mom, stupid. I learned from the best."

Rosie stared at her, her eyes filling with tears.

"It's going to be okay," Lucy said.

This time, she meant it.

Dom was waiting when she returned to her flat. He looked up from reading a magazine when she entered.

"Sorry I was so long. She's up, she's talking, I think she's even going to have some breakfast."

"Good stuff. What can I do to help?" he asked.

"Kiss me?" she asked.

He put down the magazine on the coffee table.

"Like that's a hardship."

His arms were strong and warm as they came around her. She pressed her face into his chest and inhaled his smell. It was like coming home. She couldn't believe she'd been so foolish as to deny herself this happiness and comfort. Dom was not Marcus. Dom was…one in a million.

"I think you're wonderful," she said, her words muffled by his sweater.

He squeezed her a little tighter in response. She closed her eyes. That wasn't what she'd really wanted to say. Not even close. She took a deep breath.

"I also think I'm falling in love with you," she said.

He went very still, then she felt his hand on the back of her neck.

"Lucy," he said.

She waited for him to say something else, anything else, but he didn't. She told herself that he'd already made his declaration to her that day in the car, but she'd be lying if she didn't admit to feeling disappointed.

Quickly she pushed the feeling away. They'd had one night together. She trusted him. She knew he felt the same way. It was there every time he touched her or looked at her. She didn't need to hear the words.

That night, Dom collected takeout Indian and she, Rosie and Dom watched an old action movie in the flat. Andrew still hadn't made contact and Rosie couldn't settle in the house, so they made up a bed for her on the sofa when it was clear that exhaustion was kicking in after a day of high anxiety and emotion.

"I appreciate this, Luce. And sorry for cramping your style," Rosie said as she pulled the blankets up to her chin. Her gaze slid over Lucy's shoulder to where Dom waited in the kitchen.

"I'm not sure I know what you're insinuating, young lady," Lucy said primly.

Rosie smiled wearily. "Good night."

Dom turned from rearranging the magnets on her fridge door when Lucy approached.

"Don't worry about deliveries tomorrow if you want to spend the day with Rosie," he said.

"Thanks. Maybe I can start chasing up clients from last night," she said. She had no idea if her sister was planning on going into work, but it was nice to have the option of supporting her if she needed to.

"Let me know if there's anything else I can do," he said. He stepped forward and kissed her gently on the lips.

As always, his touch heated her blood, and she pressed closer and opened her mouth beneath his. He didn't pick up on her cue to deepen the kiss, however. Instead, he pulled back, but not before pressing a kiss to her forehead.

"You know, you don't have to go home if you don't want to. Just because Rosie's on the couch doesn't mean you can't stay," she said.

"Not that it's not very tempting, but I'll be up early and you might as well grab sleep while you can," he said.

She wanted to tell him she didn't mind being woken in the morning, but then she remembered the way he hadn't responded to her declaration earlier. For the second time that day, doubt gnawed at her as he pulled away from her.

She reminded herself of the certainty she'd felt last night, the rightness of being with him. She trusted him.

"I'll see you tomorrow, then," she said as she followed him to the door.

"I'll call," he said.

He kissed her once more, then he was gone.

It wasn't until she'd shut the door and turned out the outdoor light that she realized he'd avoided answering her directly.

Chapter 11

Rosie woke from a restless sleep to the sound of a door opening. She squinted at the glowing digital clock on her sister's DVD player. Three in the morning. She guessed Lucy was going to the bathroom and rolled onto her side, hoping she'd be able to kill a few more of the long, dark hours till dawn with sleep rather than staring at the ceiling the way she had last night.

"Rosie?"

Her heart slammed against her chest as she recognized Andrew's voice, lowered to a whisper.

"Rosie, are you in here?"

She sat up. She could see his tall body silhouetted in the doorway to the house.

"I'm here," she whispered back.

"Thank God. The bed was empty and I was worried…"

She stared into the darkness.

"You were worried?"

Hope flared inside her. Andrew had come home in the middle of the night and he'd been worried when he hadn't found her in their bed.

Maybe he wasn't angry with her anymore. Maybe he was ready to talk.

She started to get off the couch but he was already moving toward her. She settled for pulling her knees in tight to her chest as he sat beside her.

"I was worried," he confirmed.

She could see his face now her eyes were adjusting to the dark. He looked tired and concerned, just like he'd said.

"Don't worry about me," she said, shaking her head. She didn't deserve his consideration.

His eyes searched her face.

"I'm sorry. I shouldn't have left last night. I should have stayed and let you explain—"

She leaned forward and pressed her fingers to his lips.

"No! Don't apologize to me. I *lied* to you, Andrew. I was a chickenshit and I lied to you and I hurt you. Don't you dare let me off the hook."

"Rosie," he said, but again she pressed her fingers to his lips.

"No. No," she said.

His hand came up to pull her fingers away from his mouth.

"You always were stubborn. And tough on yourself."

She swallowed a lump of emotion as he wove his fingers with hers. His hand felt so big and strong and precious. So familiar.

"Do you mind if I finish what I was saying?" he asked.

She just stared at him.

"I'll take that as a yes." His thumb swept across the back of her hand. "I was sitting in my hotel room, feeling hard done by, going over and over it all again. How pissed I was at you for lying to me. How stupid I felt. How I couldn't believe you'd do this to me. I mean, you never lie, Rosie. You're one of the most honest, forthright people I know. You can't even fib on a survey. I've seen it eat you up. And then it hit me. I realized how absolutely terrified you must have been to take those pills and not tell me. What it would have taken for you to get to that point."

She started to cry as he lifted their joined hands and pressed a kiss to her knuckles.

"I've been pushing for us to have a family for so long, and you've been doing everything you can to push back. And I ignored it, because I didn't want to think about it, because I figured it was just cold feet or worry about money or worry about the practice. I didn't give you many options, did I?"

She sniffed inelegantly and wiped her face on the sleeve of her pyjamas. "I could have talked to you. Like any sane, normal person would have. I could have told my husband how I was feeling."

"I know. And the fact that you didn't is what kills me the most, Rosie. Because it means you were so scared you couldn't, and I hate that more than anything. I hate the idea of you being so messed up about something that you couldn't even share it with me."

He shifted his head and she saw shiny streaks on his face. He was crying. It was the final straw. Even though she didn't deserve his comfort or his understanding, she threw herself into his arms.

"I'm so sorry," she whispered as his arms came around her.

"So am I."

They held each other so tight it hurt. She didn't ever want to let go. Andrew kissed her temple, her cheek, her nose, her mouth. She kissed the tears on his face, rubbed her cheek against the stubble of his beard.

"I love you so much," she said.

"I love you, too. Let's never do this again," he said.

She hiccupped out a laugh and he pulled her into his lap. She sniffed back fresh tears and made an effort to pull herself together. Andrew had come to the party, and it was time for her to step up, too.

"I'm going to go see someone," she said. "Lucy knows a counselor. I think maybe I have some things to work out."

She could almost hear him thinking, processing what she was saying.

"Is this something you want to do alone or together?" he asked.

She squeezed him tighter and pressed her face into the angle of his neck.

"Together and alone, maybe. Depending on how screwed up I am."

"You're one of the most together people I know," he said.

"At the moment, that's not saying much."

He tilted her chin up with his finger and kissed her fiercely.

"Whatever it takes," he said.

She stared into his face, so beloved and precious to her.

"Yes. Whatever it takes," she said.

They both blinked as the overhead light flicked on. Lucy stood in the doorway to her bedroom, squinting against the brightness of the light.

"Andrew. Thank God. I thought it was either thieves or Rosie was talking in her sleep," she said.

The concerned look left her face as she took in the way they were sitting.

"Anyway. I didn't mean to interrupt. Sorry. As you were."

"Thanks, Luce," Rosie said. She hoped her sister understood the world of gratitude the single word represented.

Lucy waved a dismissive hand, then flicked off the light and retreated to her bedroom.

"Is there room on this couch for two," Andrew asked, "or should we go back to the house?"

It was a no-brainer. "The house."

She wanted to be in her own bed, with her husband beside her.

She felt his thighs flex beneath her, then he stood with her in his arms. She grabbed at his shoulders.

"Andrew! God, you'll kill yourself," she said.

"Do you mind? I'm having a moment here," he said.

He was smiling foolishly, and she couldn't help laughing. Somehow he managed to get the door to the house open without dropping her, although he did knock her feet against the door frame a few times.

"Sorry," he said.

She rested her head on his shoulder as he made his way through the darkened house. He set her down gently on the mattress and she fell silent as he knelt in front of her.

They stared at each other. Rosie's chest ached with gratitude and love.

"Whatever it takes," he said again.

"Always."

Since she didn't have to babysit her sister for the day, Lucy got up at her usual time and drove into the market. Dom had left her his car and taken the van, and she parked the Mercedes carefully before hunting him down at his father's stand.

He was sorting through a crate of apples when she found him, his head lowered as he selected produce for an order. She smiled to herself as she took in his jeans and steel-toed work boots. She loved him in his suit, all shiny and polished, but this was how she thought of him—a hands-on man, physical and ready for anything.

"Dom," she called as she approached.

His head came up, and his gaze searched for her in the crowded market. He frowned as he caught sight of her, but by the time she was by his side his expression was unreadable.

"Rosie's okay?" he asked.

"Andrew came home last night. Or this morning. It was dark, that's all I know. They're talking and sleeping in the same bed, so I figure they're well on their way."

"You didn't need to come in, though. You must be tired," he said.

"No more than usual. Besides, I wanted to see you."

She stepped closer to greet him properly, but he tensed and all her doubts from last night crashed down on her.

"Is everything okay?" she asked.

She expected him to give a quick and easy affirmative, maybe tell her that he'd just had an argument with his father or a problem with a customer. Anything to explain away his reaction.

But he didn't. Instead, his gaze shifted over her shoulder for a few seconds, then he shrugged.

"This probably isn't the best place to talk," he said.

He took her by the elbow and started to lead her toward the coffee shop. She jerked her arm free.

"What's going on, Dom?" she asked, fear squeezing her diaphragm.

"Come on." He gestured for her to keep walking, but she dug her heels in.

"Tell me what's going on."

He sighed heavily. Then he slid his hands into the front pockets of his jeans and hunched his shoulders.

"I'm not sure this is going to work out," he said.

For a moment she thought she had to have heard wrong. She blinked.

"You don't think this is going to work out," she repeated. "What exactly does that mean?"

"The other night was great, but I think you're looking for something that I can't give you."

Again she shook her head. This was the man who had touched her so reverently, so passionately the other night that he'd made her feel beautiful and shiny and new all over again. This was the man who had moved heaven and earth to help her save her business. This was the man who had held her hand when she'd been afraid her baby was going to die.

This was the man she'd trusted enough to love.

And he was telling her…what?

"What exactly is it that you think I want that you can't give me?" she asked carefully.

Maybe this was all a misunderstanding. Maybe she was reading this all wrong.

"I think you want a husband. A father for your baby. More children. And I can't give you any of that."

His voice was flat. Distant. She stared at his face,

trying to understand what was going on. How did a person go from so much intensity, so much connection, to this... emptiness? In the space of twenty-four hours?

"I don't believe you," she said.

For the first time he met her eyes.

"It's true. Believe me," he said.

"What about the other night? The things that you said. That you wanted more than one night. That you cared for me."

His eyes traveled over her face.

"I meant them at the time."

She gasped. He might as well have slapped her.

"Look, Lucy, I'm sorry. But I didn't realize how intense things were going to get so quickly. I'm fresh out of a divorce. I don't know if I'm up for so much so soon."

She shook her head.

"No. You're the one who wanted this," she said. "You're the one who told me your feelings wouldn't change. You told me I could trust you. You pursued me." She stared at him, at his distant eyes and his tight, unreadable face. "You made me fall in love with you."

He had the good grace to look away then.

"I'm sorry."

He was sorry.

It didn't even come close. Didn't even touch the sides of the pain and hurt opening inside her.

She looked around, trying to find the words or the actions or something, some way of responding to the colossal hurt he'd just inflicted on her. She felt hoodwinked, swindled, cheated. For weeks he'd wooed her, and she'd held him at arm's length because she was afraid, because Marcus had taught her not to trust. And finally she'd taken the leap of faith—and Dom had pulled the rug out from beneath her.

"Listen. I never meant to hurt you. Believe me, that's the last thing I wanted," he said.

"Too late," she said.

She turned on her heel and started walking. After a few feet she stopped and retraced her steps.

"Give me the keys to the van," she said.

He frowned. "I'll do the deliveries today."

"Give me the keys to the van."

"You can't do the deliveries on your own, Lucy."

"Give me the freaking keys!" she yelled.

People stopped to stare. Out of the corner of her eye she saw Mr. Bianco start to move toward them.

"What about the baby?" Dom asked.

She wanted to punch him in the face. Mash his nose, split his lips, pummel him until the rage bubbling up inside her was gone.

"I'll worry about my baby. Give me the keys," she demanded.

"What is going on? Is there problem?" Mr. Bianco asked as he came up beside them.

Lucy didn't take her eyes off Dom. After a long moment he pulled the keys from his pocket and handed them over. Her hand closed around them. They were warm from his body and her hand curled into a fist, squeezing the keys tightly.

"You're an asshole," she said to Dom. She threw the keys to the Mercedes at his feet.

More than anything she wanted to walk away and never see him or hear from him again. But she didn't have that luxury. She had a business to run, and his father was her key supplier. Worse, Dom was her business partner.

She turned to Mr. Bianco. There would be time to work out how to disentangle her life from Dom's later.

"Can you help me fill my order for the day, Mr. Bianco?" she asked.

Tony darted a glance at his son before nodding.

"Of course, of course, Lucia. No problem."

She didn't look at Dom as she turned away. She didn't so much as glance his way as Mr. Bianco helped her load her trolley over the next fifteen minutes. And she kept her head down as she pushed her load back to the van.

Only when she was alone in the privacy of her van did she sit down on a stack of empty crates and let herself howl. Hands clutched to her belly, she rocked back and forth as all her shock and disappointment and hurt streamed down her face. She cried till she was gasping for air and her chest ached.

It had been so hard for her to trust him. But she had. And he'd thrown her trust back in her face, along with her love.

I can't give you what you want.

"Oh God," she said.

How could something so new hurt so much?

Soon, she knew, she would be angry, and that would be a good thing. But right now, she was devastated and she didn't know where to put herself.

A rapid fluttering inside her belly drew her mind back into her body. Her baby was kicking in agitation, clearly distressed by her distress.

She took a deep breath and let it out on a shudder. She needed to get a grip. She had orders to deliver. More importantly, she had her daughter to consider.

There would be plenty of time to brood over her stupidity and gullibility later. All the time in the world.

She wiped her eyes on a wrinkled tissue she found in her pocket, then pushed herself to her feet.

She didn't have the luxury of falling down and staying down. For the rest of her life, she would have to get up and keep fighting on her own. Because there was another life completely reliant on her ability to continually get up and keep fighting.

She set her jaw grimly. She might as well get used to it now, because she would never make the mistake of trusting someone else to fight alongside her again.

Dom couldn't concentrate. Three times he added up the same order incorrectly. Every fiber of his being wanted to chase after Lucy and pull her into his arms and comfort her. But he couldn't offer her comfort when he was the one causing the pain.

He swore under his breath as he fumbled the keys on the calculator for the fourth time. His hands were shaking so much the glowing display shimmered before his eyes, blurring the digits together.

Or maybe that was because he was on the verge of tears.

Damn.

Michael was walking past and Dom shoved the calculator at him.

"Could you take care of this order? I've got to do something," he said.

He didn't wait for other man to reply, just took off.

He barely made it into the darkness of the cold storage before his emotions overtook him. He swore out loud in English and Italian, then kicked an empty orange crate so hard it skidded along the ground and shattered against the far wall.

It wasn't fair.

But life wasn't fair, and he'd done the right thing.

Now he simply had to live with the consequences.

Lucy hating him. The mess of their business partnership. His own guilt and pain. The knowledge that he'd hurt her.

"Goddamn," he said, his voice deadened in the metal-lined space.

He sat on a crate and dropped his head into his hands. He pressed his fingers into his eyes and tried to get a grip. Long moments passed where there was nothing but the sound of his own harsh breathing. Then light streamed in as the door opened.

He shied away and tried to wipe his eyes on the tail of his shirt.

"Dom, you here?" his father called.

"I won't be a moment, Pa. Tell me what you need and I'll bring it back to the stand," he said.

He kept his back turned, praying his father would take the hint and leave him alone.

Dom heard the heavy tread of his father's footsteps before his warm hand landed on Dom's shoulder.

"Dominic. Talk to me," his father said quietly. "What has you so upset? And why is Lucia so upset? What is happening?"

"It's not important. We'll sort it out," Dom said.

He kept his back turned.

"My son," his father said heavily, "when did you stop trusting your papa?"

Dom sighed. After a long pause he half turned toward his father.

"It's not that I don't trust you, Pa. There's just nothing you can do about it. Nothing anyone can do."

His father dug into the pocket on his apron and pulled out a handkerchief.

"Here."

Dom took it and blew his nose, feeling about nine years old. He was pretty sure that was the last time his father had caught him crying. At least that time Dom had had a broken leg as an excuse.

Wood creaked as his father sat on one of the crates.

"You love Lucia?" he asked. He made it sound so commonplace, so matter of fact, Dom almost laughed.

"Yeah, I do."

"I thought so. Your mama not so sure, but me, I see."

Great. His whole family probably knew about it by now—sisters, cousins, relatives back in Italy.

"Lucia does not love you, this is the problem?" his father continued.

"She loves me," he said heavily.

"Ah. You worry about bambino? That you not the father?"

"I don't care. It's Lucy's baby. That's all that matters to me."

He could practically hear his father considering and discarding other options. Dom ran his hand through his hair.

He'd been meaning to tell his father about his infertility for a long time. And it wasn't as though this day could possibly suck any harder.

"I can't have children, Pa," he said. To his everlasting shame, his voice cracked on the final word and he had to blink back fresh tears. "That's why Dani and I broke up. Remember I had mumps when I was twenty? It doesn't happen very often, but sometimes it can make men infertile. I got lucky."

His father was silent for a long moment.

"No bambinos?"

"No. Never. Dani and I tried everything. But it was no good."

"This is why you divorce?"

"Yes."

"Your mother will be very sad for you. This is hard thing."

"Tell me about it."

He wasn't sure what he'd expected from this moment—Recriminations? Guilt? Shame?—but his father's quiet sympathy in the dark was unexpected.

They were both silent for a while.

"And this is why Lucia and you fight?" his father asked eventually.

"Lucy doesn't know."

"So why for you fight?" his father asked, bafflement rich in his tone.

"She wants brothers and sisters for her baby, a family. I can't give her any of that. So I ended things between us."

"I see. You ended things so Lucia could have what she wants?"

"Yeah."

His father exhaled heavily, then pushed himself to his feet.

"I am very sorry for you, my son."

For the first time in years, Dom found himself drawn into the all-encompassing embrace of his father. Tony Bianco's big arms squeezed him tight, his hands patting Dom's back comfortingly. Dom breathed in his father's hair pomade and the smell of his mother's laundry detergent.

"This is big sadness for you to carry. I am very sorry," his father said again.

Dom hugged his father back.

"I am very sorry for you, but I think you make big mistake," his father continued.

Here we go.

Dom let his arms drop to his sides. "Pa—"

"Lucia is not Dani," his father said over him. "Lucia is Lucia. You not give her the chance to make her own decision."

Dom shook his head. "She shouldn't have to make a decision. She should have what she wants—brothers and sisters for her daughter."

"You sound like one of your mother's saints, making the big sacrifice." His father mimed someone hanging on a cross.

Dom shrugged uncomfortably. He hadn't meant to come off as a martyr. "I just want her to be happy."

His father nodded as though he was agreeing with Dom. "And you are scared," Tony said.

"I'm not scared. What have I got to be scared of?"

His father tucked his hands into the waistband of his apron. "What if you tell Lucia no bambinos and she says no matter? What if she says she loves you and one bambino is enough? Then she changes her mind and what happened with Dani happens with Lucia, all over again?"

"What am I supposed to say to that?" Dom said.

"That it is true. That it might happen. That you are afraid."

His father held Dom's eye, waiting.

"I can't give her what she wants," Dom said. "What's the point in starting something that will only hurt her more in the end?"

"This is Lucia's decision to make, not yours."

Dom looked away from his father's knowing eyes.

"You know I right, Dominic."

Dom shook his head. What his father was asking was too much. He refused to set himself up for disaster again. He'd done the right thing. For both of them.

To his surprise, his father stepped forward and patted his cheek, just as he used to when Dom was a very small boy.

"You will work out. You smart boy," his father said. "I want you to know, I very proud Saturday night. The party, the people, all the fancy pictures on the television." Tony nodded his head sagely. "Very impressive. Very smart."

Dom smiled ruefully. "You don't have to throw me a bone just because you caught me sooking, Pa."

His father frowned. "No bone. I go home, I look at the thing, the order thing you buy...?"

"The handheld unit."

"Hmmm. Is not so hard."

Dom stared at his father. "You used the handheld unit?"

His father shrugged, but Dom could see he was proud of himself. Dom snorted his amusement and surprise. Talk about leading a horse to water... Except this particular old donkey had taken his own sweet time in lowering his head for a drink.

His father dusted his hands down the front of his apron.

"You coming back to stand now?" he asked.

"In a minute."

"Take your time," his father said magnanimously.

Dom stood in the dark for a few minutes after his father had left. After months of conflict, his father had finally come around. Unbelievable. Maybe now they could start streamlining the business, making things more efficient and cost-effective.

Any satisfaction Dom felt faded as he remembered the look on Lucy's face when she'd thrown his car keys at his feet.

He'd hurt her. The last thing he'd ever wanted to do.

He leaned against the cool metal wall, forcing himself to remember the passion in Lucy's voice when she spoke of the importance of children in her life. It was all very well for his father to pat him on the cheek and say wise words, but he hadn't been there when Lucy talked about wanting siblings for her daughter. And he hadn't watched the wife he loved turn into a bitter stranger because a harmless virus had taken away his ability to be a father.

Lucy would thank him in the long run.

Lucy spent that night with her sister going through her accounts with a fine-tooth comb, trying to find a way to buy Dom out of their partnership. Between bouts of pacing and ranting and sitting and sobbing, she ate chocolate-chip ice cream and far too many Tim Tam cookies.

"I'm sorry," Rosie said for the tenth time. "I feel so responsible. I practically pimped you out to him. I was so sure that you guys had this spark. The look he used to get in his eye when he was with you… But I guess I was wrong."

"You didn't make me kiss him or sleep with him or fall in love with him. I did that all on my own—with a lot of help from Mr. I'm-Not-Going-Anywhere," Lucy said bitterly. "I'm so stupid. I told myself over and over that I couldn't afford to get involved with someone, let alone my *business partner.* I honestly don't think there is a dumber woman alive. What was I thinking?"

"Falling in love isn't exactly a right-brain function," Rosie said sympathetically.

Lucy looked up from the spreadsheet she'd been studying.

"Do you think if I show the bank the Web site and all the customers who have signed over to the new program and our new marketing plan they might reconsider the loan? It might be different now that I've got the Web site running."

"You can try. But there are clauses in the contract about you and Dom buying each other out. You need to get the business assessed by a small-business broker. He owns half of it now. Any improvement you've made means that his half is worth more, too."

Lucy sank back in her chair and reached for her spoon again.

"Why did I do this to myself?"

"Stop giving yourself a hard time. You fell in love. It's not a crime. He made it incredibly easy for you to fall in love, too. And you had every reason to believe what he said to you. Up until now, he's been the perfect man. Kind. Thoughtful. Always honest and reliable. Passionate. Committed."

Lucy felt tears welling again, and she held up a hand to stem the flow of her sister's words.

"Stop. Please."

Rosie pushed the ice-cream tub closer.

"Have some ice cream."

Lucy sniffed and dug her spoon into the tub, but couldn't summon the effort to pry it out again. She wasn't hungry, she was heartbroken.

"Did you get on to the counselor today?" she asked as she reached for another tissue.

"Got my first appointment next week."

Rosie sounded nervous. Lucy blew her nose.

"You'll be fine. If you don't like her, if it doesn't make sense or feel like something that will work for you, you just don't go again. Simple."

"I know. Just like changing hairdressers."

"Exactly."

"Except we're talking about the inside of my head and not the outside."

Lucy couldn't help smiling.

"I'm so glad you and Andrew are talking again."

Rosie twisted her wedding ring around her finger, studying the single diamond for a moment.

"I'm very lucky."

"He's lucky, too, you know."

Rosie smiled. She looked very wistful.

"There's a stupid part of me that hopes I'll walk in the door of this counselor's office next week and she'll wave a magic wand and everything will be okay. I won't be scared anymore, no more doubts. I know it won't work like that, that it'll be hard. But still…"

Lucy slid the spoon free from the tub and reached for the lid.

"No more doubts. I'd buy a ticket for that," she said. "Who wouldn't?"

They smiled at each other. Rosie took the ice cream from her and crossed the room to return it to the freezer.

"What are you going to do?" she asked when she came back to the dining table.

Lucy stared at her spreadsheet.

"I'm going to endure," she said finally. "I'm going to suck it up and keep running my business and seeing him every day, even though it will be one of the hardest things I have ever done."

Rosie watched her sadly.

"I can do this," Lucy said. "I'm tough."

"Like an old boot."

"Or one of those black box things that survive plane crashes."

They both laughed.

The smile faded from Lucy's lips.

"If only I could stop loving him," she said quietly.

Rosie didn't say a word, simply reached out and rubbed her arm. What more was there to say, after all?

The next day, Lucy sat in the van in the parking lot behind the market for a full ten minutes before she could summon the courage to get out and fill her order. She didn't want to look at Dom, hear his voice, even say his name. But she'd already gone over all of that with her sister. She didn't have a choice. Even if he wasn't her business partner, his father was the best and cheapest fresh produce wholesaler in the city. Their lives were inextricably entwined.

Hands tight around the push bar of her trolley, she walked slowly to the Bianco Brothers' stall. Dom had his back to her as she approached, his head lowered as he talked intently to a tall, gangly young man. She didn't need to see his high cheekbones and strong jaw to know he was a relative.

Her stupid body hadn't quite caught up with the events of the previous day, and her heart gave a ridiculous kick as she stared at Dom's broad shoulders and beautiful backside. For one night, he'd been hers, and it had been wonderful.

Yeah, and you paid a bloody high price for the privilege, her cynical self chastised.

The thought helped her square her shoulders as Dom turned around, almost as though he had sensed her approach.

For a second he simply stared at her. She made a point of holding his gaze. He'd hurt her. She wasn't about to pretend it was any different and she wasn't ashamed of caring for him. He was the one who should be ashamed of the way he'd treated her—like the latest toy, to be played with until the next amusing thing came along.

After a long silence, Dom gestured over his shoulder toward the young man.

"This is my sister's boy, Michael. He's going to help you out with the deliveries until the baby's due," he said. "If things work out, he's interested in the job driving the second van."

Her gaze flicked to Dom's nephew. Michael gave her a little half smile and a wave, then shifted his feet awkwardly. Poor kid. She figured he had no idea what kind of a mess his uncle had dropped him in the middle of.

"You don't think this was something we should have discussed first?" she said, returning her attention to Dom.

"Of course. But I figured you probably didn't want to talk to me last night and that you wouldn't want me doing deliveries with you today."

"Bingo." She crossed her arms over her chest.

"You can't do deliveries on your own, Lucy."

"What I do or don't do is none of your business."

Dom's jaw tensed again.

"Actually, it is. If you hurt yourself on the job, Market Fresh is liable," he said coolly.

She took a breath to argue some more, but she could feel pressure building behind her eyes. She refused to cry in front of him. Owning her feelings was one thing, but blubbering in front of him was a whole other ball game.

"Fine. Whatever. Michael, pleased to meet you," she said, thrusting her hand at Dom's nephew.

"Oh, um, you, too," he said, shaking hands awkwardly.

"Let's go."

She pushed the trolley past Dom and didn't stop walking until she was as far from him as she could get and still be standing in front of Bianco Brothers'. Michael watched her anxiously as she breathed deeply and sniffed a few times.

"It's okay. I'm okay," she said.

"Do you want a handkerchief?" he asked.

He offered her a neatly pressed white square. The sight of it made her laugh.

"I bet your ma made you put that in your pocket this morning," she said as she took it.

"Won't let me leave the house without one," he grumbled.

She blew her nose, then looked him in the eye.

"Don't tell your uncle I was crying," she said.

He shook his head.

"No way."

Dom kept his distance for the rest of her time at the market, and she didn't look his way once. Still, she felt a little nauseous by the time Michael pushed the trolley back to the van.

This was going to be hard—much harder than she'd thought. Seeing Dom every day. Driving around with his look-alike cousin in the van beside her.

But that was what enduring was all about, right? Doing what you had to do, no matter what.

"Okay, Michael," she said. "Let's get this show on the road."

Chapter 12

Eight weeks later, Dom checked his watch for the fifth time in as many minutes.

Lucy was late. He wondered if she'd changed her mind about coming. She hadn't been exactly thrilled when he called to suggest a face-to-face meeting. Not that he blamed her.

It was raining outside, pelting down. Briefly he wondered if he should call her, make sure everything was okay. He quelled the impulse. Probably the weather was slowing traffic.

He pushed his coffee away. He was as nervous as a kid on a first date. Except this was no date. This was almost the exact opposite of a date, in fact—a meeting to dissolve his partnership with Lucy.

He'd cut her free from their relationship, and now it was time to cut her free from their business contract.

She was unhappy. He could see it in her eyes, the dullness of her skin, the downward slope of her shoulders. Being tied to him was difficult. Painful. Once their partnership was dissolved, she wouldn't have to deal with him anymore. Someone else could serve her when she came to the stand. Hell, he'd even make sure he was absent during the times she usually came to collect her supplies. That way, they'd never have to see each other at all. That should make things easier for her.

He rubbed his eyes. He hadn't had a good night's sleep in weeks. He hadn't counted, but he was pretty sure that if he cared to do the math, he'd work out that he hadn't slept a full eight hours since the Sunday he'd realized that he was going to have to give Lucy up.

So his motives weren't entirely selfless in regard to dissolving the partnership. It was killing him having to deal with her all the time, too. He'd tried to make it as easy as possible—hiring Michael to help with deliveries so he could ensure she was looking after herself without physically being there himself, staying away from her when she came to the stand, keeping any business discussions brief and to the point and conducting as many of them as possible via e-mail.

It didn't make any difference. He still wanted her. He still dreamed of her. He still turned automatically toward the sound of her voice. His chest still ached when she laughed. Not that she'd been laughing much lately.

He'd hurt her. But he hadn't had a choice. He'd have

only made her even more unhappy in the long run. This was the lesser evil, the kinder cut.

It was the same thing he'd been telling himself over and over, and he was sick of hearing it. He shoved his cup even farther away and coffee lapped at the rim, almost spilling over.

He knew the feeling. Maybe it was the lack of sleep, or the guilt, or the pain of being a part of Lucy's world but not a part of it, but he'd felt damned close to spilling over a number of times lately. He'd been short with his father. He'd even snapped at his mother. He was pretty sure most of the staff members at Bianco Brothers' were going out of their way to avoid him.

He sat back in his chair and stared blindly out the window.

How long did it take to stop loving someone? To stop dreaming of the smell of their skin, the feel of their hands on your body?

How long did it take to kill a dream?

Longer than eight weeks. But maybe dissolving the partnership would help. He bloody hoped so.

The bell over the coffee-shop door rang and he looked up. Lucy met his eyes as she shook out her umbrella. She looked tired, drained. He'd arranged to meet at the end of her delivery run so they'd have more time to discuss things, but now he wondered if he should have made it a morning meeting.

"You look tired," he said as she joined him at the table.

She didn't respond. She dumped her umbrella under

the table and lowered herself carefully into the chair. She'd grown in the past few weeks, her belly burgeoning into a classic pregnancy silhouette.

"What did you want to see me about?" she asked.

Her gaze was clear, her eyes distant.

Right. Straight into business.

"I want to dissolve the partnership," he said.

"I see."

He shoved a sheaf of papers across the table toward her.

"I had my lawyer draw this up. This gives you full title to the company. Once we sign, Market Fresh will be all yours again."

She scanned the front page, then quickly flipped through the next few pages.

"It doesn't say how much you want. We need to get the company valued," she said.

"I don't want you to buy me out. I'm signing my half over to you," he said.

She stared at him.

"You're *giving* it to me?"

"That's right."

She let her breath out in a rush, then she looked down at the papers in her hand for a long moment. She stood, her chair scraping across the café floor.

"Where are you going?" he asked as she stooped awkwardly to collect her umbrella.

"Home. Where I won't be insulted."

He stood.

"Wait a minute." He grabbed her arm.

"Don't touch me."

"Lucy. Don't be stupid," he said. "Stay and talk it through."

She shook him off. Her eyes were wide with anger. "I don't know what's wrong with you, but I am not accepting thirty thousand dollars of investment in my business because we slept with each other. I don't believe I've sunk to the level of whoring just yet."

"For Pete's sake—"

"What else is it for then, Dom? It's guilt money, pure and simple. And I am not your freaking charity case," she said. Her voice quavered then broke on the final few words, but she kept staring him down.

"That's not the way I think of you," he said.

"What am I, then? A mistake you need to pay off?"

"No."

She threw her hands in the air.

"What, then? You tell me why you want to give me thirty thousand dollars for nothing."

"I want you to be happy. I want to make sure you're all right."

"Neither of those things are your responsibility," she said.

She turned to go. He grabbed her arm again.

"Lucy—"

She swung around on him. "No! You gave up the right to care about me when you cut me loose like some girl you'd picked up in a bar."

"I did you a favor, Lucy," he said.

She laughed, the sound hard and bitter. "Is that how

you sell it to yourself? Wow, what a guy. You should go get yourself measured for a suit of armor. Make sure it's nice and shiny."

She headed for the door. This time he let her go.

She stopped on the threshold to fumble with the umbrella. He was about to head to the counter to pay his bill when she dropped the umbrella and clutched at her belly.

He was at her side in two strides.

"What's wrong?"

"I think I'm bleeding again," she said. "I felt a rush, like last time. Oh God."

She lifted the hem of the stretchy black tunic she wore over a pair of pale gray leggings. They both stared at the damp spreading down her thighs.

"That's not blood," he said.

Her face was pale as she met his eyes.

"My water must have broken."

There was bone-deep panic in her eyes. She was only thirty-four weeks.

His phone was in his hand before he'd even formulated the thought.

"Ambulance," he told the emergency services operator. Immediately he was patched through to the ambulance service. It took only a moment to give their location.

"Two minutes. We're lucky we're so close to the hospital," he said as he ended the call.

"It's too early," she said as he led her back inside the café. "The baby's too small still."

"Lots of babies are born early and survive," he said.

She grimaced and her hand shot out to grasp his arm. Her fingers convulsed around his wrist.

"Oh boy. I think I'm in labor."

She leaned forward, groaning.

"Is she all right?" a voice asked behind them.

It was the shop owner, looking concerned. A crowd of customers was forming.

"The baby's coming," he said. "The ambulance is on its way."

"Oh!"

"It hurts!" Lucy groaned.

The wail of sirens sounded in the distance. One of the customers went out into the street to flag it down.

"We'll be at the hospital in five minutes," he said.

"Rosie! I need Rosie."

"I'll call her."

The ambulance shuddered to a stop out the front of the café, lights circling, its siren piercing until it was silenced abruptly.

Rosie's phone went through to voice mail when he dialed. He left a quick message.

"I'll try Andrew," he said before Lucy could ask.

She nodded her thanks as the ambulance crew entered. While they settled her into the gurney, he called Andrew's cell. Again he got voice mail. He left another message.

"They had a court hearing this afternoon. A divorce," Lucy said as the paramedics began to wheel her out the door.

He grabbed her bag and coat and umbrella.

"I'll meet you at the hospital," he said.

She nodded, but he could see how afraid she was. He hesitated only a second before following her to the ambulance and climbing in after her.

"I'm coming with you," he said.

She bit her lip, then nodded.

"Thank you."

He reached for her hand as the ambulance started up.

"You're going to be okay," he said.

She was about to answer when her eyes rounded and she gasped.

"Oh God!" she groaned, curling forward.

"When was your last contraction?" the paramedic asked.

Lucy was too busy panting to respond.

"Just before you arrived," Dom said.

The paramedic's eyebrows rose. "That's pretty close."

"I guess. Is that bad?" Dom asked quietly.

"It's fast. Her water just broke? There's been no other signs of labor? No backache or any other cramping?" the paramedic asked.

Lucy shook her head and collapsed down onto the gurney.

"Are the pains supposed to be this bad?" she asked, her voice faint.

"When the labor is fast like this, they hit hard."

The ambulance slowed as it turned a long curving corner. Dom guessed they'd arrived at the emergency bay.

Within seconds the doors were open and Lucy was being raced to a cubicle. They transferred her to a bed, and a nurse helped her remove her leggings and underwear. Dom moved to the head of the bed and laid his hand on Lucy's shoulder. He felt utterly useless, but he refused to leave her side.

An older woman with faded blond hair entered the room.

"Hello, Lucy, I'm Julie. I'll be your midwife this afternoon," she said with a warm smile. "How are we feeling?"

Lucy groaned as another pain hit. Dom watched as her belly hardened and her body stiffened. Julie frowned.

"Okay, Lucy, I'm just going to take a quick look and see how far along you are."

Very aware that he had no right to be a part of this experience, Dom glanced away as the midwife checked Lucy's cervix. The midwife was very matter of fact when she straightened.

"Lucy, you're almost fully dilated. This baby wants out, fast. I'm afraid we're not going to be able to give you any pain relief."

Lucy shook her head. "Is my baby going to be all right? It's so early…"

"We have the neonatal team on standby, but thirty-four weeks is very viable," Julie said. "I've called your obstetrician, Dr. Mason, and he's coming in. But I should warn you that you may have delivered before he gets here."

"I don't care. As long as my baby is okay."

She growled low in her throat as another contraction hit. This time she slapped a hand onto Dom's arm and clung on so tightly his skin turned white.

"Hang in there, Lucy. This is going to be fast and furious. The important thing is that I want you to wait until I tell you to push, okay? Pretty soon you're going to want to do that more than anything, but I need you to wait until I give you the go ahead. Okay?" Julie asked.

Lucy nodded. Dom reached out to push the damp hair off her forehead.

"You're tough. You can do this," he encouraged her.

"It's not like I have a choice. I never have a choice," she panted.

Her mouth opened on a silent cry and her fingers tightened around his. He watched her body quiver for what felt like forever, then she collapsed back onto the bed.

"I want my sister," she said, staring forlornly at the ceiling.

"I know. I'm sorry," he said.

She turned her head to look at him.

"You don't have to stay. I know you feel guilty, but you don't have to stay."

"If you want me to go, I'll go," he said.

Lucy's face screwed up with pain and she clutched at his hand as another contraction hit. Over the next fifteen minutes, her contractions came faster and lasted longer. Sweat rolled down her face. Dom offered water, his hand and words of encouragement. He'd never felt more helpless in his life.

"Oh! It's burning," she gasped. She grunted, her chin buried into her chest, tears rolling down her red face.

Julie checked between her legs.

"You're crowning, Lucy. Don't push right now. Give your vagina a chance to stretch. I know you probably want to push like hell, but give your body a chance to adjust."

Lucy tucked her chin down more and panted.

"Right. Go for it, Lucy. Whatever feels good. Give me all you've got," Julie said.

Lucy strained upward, letting go of Dom's hand to clutch at the mattress, both hands fisting into the sheets. Dom moved close, his arm sliding around her shoulders to support her, wanting to take some of the pain for her or help her in some way.

"Good girl. You're doing great, Lucy. I can see the baby's head," Julie said.

"Oh!" Lucy said, her eyes widening suddenly.

And then a thin, high wail sounded and Julie was holding a small, red-and-white bundle in her arms.

"Is she okay? Is she all right?" Lucy asked.

"She's breathing well. Our neonate specialist, Dr. Wilson, is just going to check her over," Julie said.

Dom took Lucy's weight as she relaxed. Not for a second did her gaze waver from the small shape in the doctor's arms. Dom stared down at Lucy's face, damp with sweat, tendrils of hair clinging to her temples. She was amazing. Absolutely amazing.

"Lucy, I need you to stay with me for a bit," Julie said.

Lucy tensed and groaned, a look of utter surprise crossing her face.

"More pain. Isn't it supposed to stop now?" she gasped.

"That's the placenta. Just push when you need to."

The next few minutes passed in a blur as Lucy grimaced and panted and bore down.

"Okay, I've got it. Well done, Lucy," Julie said.

"How is my baby?" Lucy asked for the fifth time.

"She's six pounds three, a good weight for thirty-four weeks," Dr. Wilson said. "Good color. Good movement."

"Can I hold her?" Lucy asked.

"I don't see why not. We'll want to get her into an incubator and check her out more fully, but she's a good, strong, healthy baby for thirty-four weeks," Dr. Wilson said.

He brought the baby to the bed. Lucy held out her arms and the doctor placed her on Lucy's chest. She looked impossibly tiny to Dom, her body curled in on itself, her skin still speckled with blood and a white, waxy substance. Her dark hair was matted to her skull, her tiny face screwed up in outrage as she mewled her objection to the rude awakening she'd just experienced.

"She's beautiful," he said, his voice rough. "She looks like you."

Lucy laughed. Tears rolled down her cheeks. She reached out and ran a finger gently down her daughter's cheek.

"Hello, little one. I've been waiting so long to meet you."

"Congratulations, Lucy. Do you have a name picked out?" Julie asked, a warm smile on her face.

Lucy nodded, never taking her gaze from her child.

"Mariella. It was my grandmother's name," she said.

"That's lovely. Does it mean anything?" Julia asked.

"Beloved," Dom said quietly. "It means beloved."

Lucy looked up at him. There was nothing he could do about the tears on his face, so he just held her eye.

"Lucy, how about we see if she will take the breast?" Dr Wilson suggested. "She may not, but she's so strong I'd like to at least give it a try."

Dom let her rest back against the pillows while Julie helped adjust her hospital gown. Lucy cradled her daughter close to her breast while Julie offered a few quick instructions.

At first Mariella screwed up her face and turned her face away as Lucy brushed her nipple across the baby's mouth. Lucy tried again, and finally the baby's mouth opened. She nuzzled the nipple curiously, then instinct took over and she drew it into her mouth.

"That's fantastic. Wonderful," Dr. Wilson said.

A slow smile spread across Lucy's face as Mariella suckled. She glanced up at Dom, her eyes big and soft.

"Isn't she incredible?"

"Yes."

Emotion choked his throat. More than anything today, the sight of her breastfeeding her child hit him in the gut and the chest.

"I'll go try Rosie again," he said, backing away from the bed.

Lucy nodded, not taking her eyes from Mariella.

"Tell her to hurry. She's missing out."

"I will."

He stepped out into the corridor and strode down the corridor quickly until he could see daylight outside the emergency entrance doors. Then he was sucking in the damp cool air of a wet afternoon.

He had just witnessed a miracle. It was the only way he could describe it. The birth of a tiny new person. Lucy's child. Mariella. Beloved.

He took a deep breath, fighting for control. He would never forget the past hour, ever. It was burned into his memory, the most privileged and precious moments of his life.

For a man in his position, it had been the ultimate gift. A priceless blessing.

And he was well aware that he was the last person Lucy would have chosen to share the experience with if she'd been given a choice.

He pulled his phone from his pocket.

Now that the emergency was over, Lucy would want her family by her side.

Lucy fretted as the nurses cleaned her up and helped her into a hospital gown and transferred her to a ward.

They'd taken Mariella away for a more thorough examination but promised to return her to Lucy for another feed.

A tired smile curved her mouth as she thought of her daughter. So small and pink and angry. She was perfect and fragile and terrifyingly small. The love that had risen up inside Lucy the moment she'd looked into the daughter's face had been so overwhelming, so undeniable it had taken her breath away.

A footfall sounded in the corridor and she tensed. Maybe they were bringing Mariella back to her.

Or maybe it was Dom.

He hadn't come back. Not since the birth. She'd waited for him to come back after calling Rosie and Andrew again, but he hadn't.

She frowned down at the blanket she was pleating between her fingers. She knew better than to expect anything from him. After all, he was the man who "couldn't give her what she wanted." Seeing her give birth wasn't going to change anything. If anything, it would probably make him run in the opposite direction.

Even if he had cried when she held her daughter for the first time.

"Lucy!"

Rosie rushed into the room, Andrew following.

"I'm so sorry. We were in court, it went on and on. We broke the sound barrier trying to get here," her sister said. "Are you okay? Is the baby okay?"

"I'm fine. The baby is good. The doctors wanted to

check her out again, but she's really healthy. Big for thirty-four weeks."

"I'm so sorry I wasn't here for you," Rosie said.

"Dom was here," Lucy said.

"So I gathered." Rosie gave her a careful look and Lucy shrugged.

"That'll show him for dumping me."

"Yeah, way to punish him. Make him witness childbirth," Rosie said.

Andrew leaned forward and kissed Lucy's cheek.

"Congratulations. Do we have a name?"

"Mariella."

Rosie's eyes filled with tears. "Oh. That's beautiful."

Andrew smiled and put his arm around his wife.

"When can we see her?" Rosie asked.

"She's in the preemie nursery on the second floor."

Andrew and Rosie looked at each other.

"Off you go," Lucy said with a rueful smile. "I can see I'm no longer the star of the show."

"We won't be long," Rosie said. "I love you."

"I love you, too."

Rosie and Andrew headed for the door.

"Oh, and your mother's on her way in," Andrew said.

She settled back down onto her pillows as they left and closed her eyes. Her body ached. She had two stitches and some bruising from the rapid labor. She was exhausted. She wanted her daughter.

And she also wanted Dom to come back.

* * *

Rosie stood at the window to the nursery, staring at the rows of tiny babies in front of her. They were all so small, most of them with tubes in their noses and mouths, and drips in their arms.

"They're so tiny," she said.

"Not ours," Andrew said. He gave her a nudge and she saw that the crib closest to the door was labeled Mariella Basso and was playing host to the biggest baby in the nursery.

"Good lord, she's a giant," Rosie said.

Andrew laughed. "Only by comparison."

They moved closer, pressing their hands against the glass. A few dark strands of hair poked out from beneath the baby's bonnet.

"She's got dark hair, like Lucy."

"And she's got Lucy's nose and mouth."

"Thank God. Can you imagine Marcus's nose on a girl?"

A nurse came forward to check on Mariella. Rosie frowned and moved to the doorway.

"Excuse me, sorry. I'm her aunt. Is everything okay?" she said.

The nurse smiled.

"Absolutely. She's a firecracker, this one."

She gestured for Rosie and Andrew to come in.

"Come closer. She won't bite."

"If you're sure…?" Rosie said.

"Of course. Aunts need to meet their nieces straightaway. Makes it easier to ask for babysitting duties later on," the nurse said with a wink.

Rosie moved closer to the clear-sided crib. She glanced at Andrew and he smiled, his eyes soft.

Mariella lay curled on her side, her hands pressed to her mouth. Her eyes worked behind her eyelids, and her mouth opened and closed rhythmically.

"Mariella. It's very nice to meet you," she said quietly, leaning close. "You certainly came in a big hurry, didn't you?"

The baby shifted her head fretfully.

"Hello, little lady," Andrew said. He reached out a finger and ran it over her cheek. "She's so soft."

He smiled at Rosie, and she reached out a tentative hand.

This was her sister's child, her blood. The next generation of her family. A part of Lucy, and a part of Rosie, too.

She stroked Mariella's cheek, then traced a tiny pink ear.

"She's perfect," she said.

Love welled up in her, and she let the tears slide down her cheeks. That was something she'd learned in her once a week therapy sessions—that it was okay to cry, to feel compassion for herself. She'd learned a lot of other things, too, about herself, and her relationships with her mother and her sister and her husband.

Nobody had waved a magic wand. She still had her moments of doubt and uncertainty. But she was starting to understand herself better, and how the patterns of her childhood had impacted on her adult life.

She traced one of Mariella's tightly fisted hands. To

her surprise, the baby uncurled her fingers and opened her hand. Rosie hesitated a moment, then pressed her finger into the tiny palm. Immediately little fingers closed around her finger in a tight, instinctive grip. Rosie swallowed noisily and sniffed. Then she looked at her husband.

"I want this," she said fiercely.

He leaned across and kissed her.

"We'll get there."

Looking into his blue eyes, she could only believe that they would.

"Whatever it takes," she said.

It had become their mantra.

"Whatever it takes."

Lucy woke to the rustle of plastic bags. She'd dozed off while she waited for her sister to return. She opened her eyes as Dom moved quietly toward the door.

"I thought you must have gone home," she said.

He looked caught out.

"Sorry. I didn't mean to wake you. The nurse said you might not have small enough clothes for Mariella since she was so tiny, so I went and grabbed a few things for her."

She pulled herself higher in the bed and saw her overnight bag was sitting on the guest chair, alongside two shopping bags.

He'd gone to her flat to collect her baby bag. She frowned, and he shifted uncomfortably.

"I hope you don't mind. Your keys were in your

purse, and I figured Rosie and Andrew wouldn't have a chance to stop by home on the way in…" he said.

"It's fine. It's lovely, actually. I hate hospital gowns. Thank you. That was…thoughtful."

He was always thoughtful. She'd been so hurt and angry over the past few weeks it had been easy to ignore the many little kindnesses he showed her every day. But the truth was, even though he was no longer interested in her, he still looked out for her. To the extent that he'd actually offered to give her business back to her today.

"Is there anything else I can get for you? Anyone else you need me to contact?" he asked.

She shook her head.

"No. Thank you for looking after me today. You always seem to be there when I need you."

He shrugged again and looked away. She didn't think she'd ever seen him looking so uneasy.

Was it because he felt guilty? Was that why he was so generous and considerate and compassionate toward her, and why he was so uneasy now? He couldn't give her what she wanted—him—so he tried to give her everything else?

The thought made her feel very sad. For both of them.

"I suppose this has put you off babies for life," she said. "All the moaning and groaning."

"No."

He glanced toward the door.

"If you need to go, it's okay," she said.

"It's just I know you'll have all your relatives here any minute."

"It's okay. I understand. This is probably the last place you want to be."

He frowned, started to say something, then shook his head.

"I'll, um, check in with Rosie tomorrow, see how you're doing," he said.

"Sure."

He turned for the door. She struggled to contain the words rising up inside her, but she couldn't help herself.

"For what it's worth, I'm glad it was you," she said before he could go. "I'm glad you were the one who was with me. I know that probably makes you uncomfortable, but it's true. It's crazy, but I can't think of anyone who could have made me feel as safe as you did today."

His step faltered. She could feel heat rushing into her face.

"Lucy," he said. His expression was pained as he turned to look at her.

She held up a hand. "It's okay, you don't have to say it. I don't need to hear how you did me a favor again. You're not the only guy who'd run a mile at the thought of an instant family. The miracle is probably that you even looked twice at me in the first place."

She knew she sounded angry and self-pitying and bitter, but she wasn't a woman who loved easily. And for better or for worse she'd fallen in love with Dom and it was going to take more than eight weeks for her heart to mend. Maybe that made her soft or stupid, but it was just the way it was.

"It's not you, Lucy," he said. "Or the baby. Believe that. No guy in his right mind would walk away from you."

She didn't look up from the blanket. She didn't want to see the pity in his eyes, or the guilt.

"It's not you, Lucy," he said again.

She could feel him watching her. She was very afraid she was about to cry.

"You should go," she said.

She rolled over onto her side so her back was to the door. She waited for the sound of footsteps, but it never came. She sighed.

"Look, I shouldn't have said anything. Pretend I didn't. Just go."

"I can't have children."

His voice was so quiet, his words so totally unexpected, she almost didn't hear him.

She stared blankly at the wall. Then she looked over her shoulder, certain she had to have misunderstood. He stood stiffly in the doorway, his dark eyes steady on her.

"I'm sterile, Lucy," he said simply. "That's why my marriage broke up, and it's why I ended things with you, okay? Not because of anything you did or didn't do, or because of Mariella. You are the most…" He paused and lifted a hand to rub the bridge of his nose. His shoulders lifted as he took a deep breath.

"One day soon, some lucky bastard is going to find

you and give you everything you need and want, and all of this won't mean a thing."

She stared at him. She thought about the way he'd gone quiet the day they discussed Andrew and Rosie's baby problems in her flat, and she thought about the way he'd been so distant the next day. And she remembered what he'd said to her, over and over: *I did you a favor.*

For eight weeks she'd lain awake, sifting through every second of her time with him. The way he'd looked at her, the way he'd talked to her, the way he'd touched her, the way he'd made her feel. For the life of her, she hadn't been able to understand how she'd gotten it so wrong, misread all the signals, been suckered so completely.

And all along…

"You walked away from me because you're sterile?"

"Because I can't give you what you want."

Her hands clenched the edge of the blanket as she understood what he'd done: sacrificed himself—*them*—for her. For what he believed she wanted.

"How do you know what I want?" she asked quietly.

"You want more children. You think family is the purpose of life. You want brothers and sisters for your daughter. That's more than enough to rule me out."

He said it like it was carved in stone, immutable, unchangeable, unarguable.

"How do you know what I want?" she repeated, her voice louder. "Did you ask me? Did you give me the choice? Did you sit down and have a conversation with *me* so that *I* could decide what my future was going to look like?"

He shifted his weight.

"I didn't want you to have to give up your life's dream for me, Lucy. I've played that game before, I know how it ends. I did what I thought was best."

"Then you're an idiot, Dominic Bianco!" she said. "You think guys like you grow on trees? You think people fall in love the way we fell in love every day? I did everything I could not to love you, but it was impossible and you dared to make a decision on my behalf without even consulting me?"

She thumped the bed with her fists, her body vibrating with fury.

"Lucy, calm down," he said.

"I have been miserable for two months, crying myself to sleep, dragging myself through each day, eating my heart out over you! Don't you dare tell me to calm down!"

He took a step forward, but she grabbed the plastic water jug from her tray table and threw it at him. It glanced off his arm and hit the ground with a clatter, water splashing everywhere.

"You should have asked me!" she said. "You should have bloody well asked me and bloody well let me choose. You stupid, stupid idiot."

She was crying, her face crumpled with distress.

"Lucy," he said.

He crossed to the bed and tried to take her in his arms.

"Sweetheart, don't cry," he said. "Please."

She hit him on the chest, the shoulder, the arm but he caught her fists easily and held them to his chest with one hand as his other pulled her close. Then her head was on his shoulder and she was breathing in the warm, woody smell of him.

"You idiot. Don't you know how much I love you? I took my clothes off for you when I was the size of a whale. Surely that must have told you something?" she sobbed into his chest.

She felt him press a kiss onto the top of her head.

"I want you to be happy," he said quietly. "Can't you see that? I want you to have everything."

She pulled back to look him in the face.

"Life doesn't work like that, Dom. No one has everything. And if I get to choose whether I have you in my life to love and laugh with and grow old with and lose my marbles with, I'm going to choose you every time. Every. Time."

He searched her face as though he couldn't quite let himself believe what she was saying.

"You want children," he said.

"Yes. Don't you?"

He sighed heavily, and she could see years of grief and resignation in his eyes.

"More than anything, Lucy. But it's not going to happen."

"Ever heard of adoption? Sperm donation? Fostering? How many ways do you need to have children in your life, Dom?"

He stared at her. "Dani didn't want to adopt. She wouldn't even consider sperm donation."

Lucy reached up and grasped his chin in her hands.

"I'm not Dani, in case you hadn't noticed. I'm Lucia Carmella Basso, and I love *you,* Dominic Bianco. I want *you.* Anything else is a bonus."

For a moment Dom just stared at her. Then he closed his eyes and pulled her close, burying his face in her neck. His shoulders shook and Lucy's arms tightened around him.

He'd been so hurt by his ex-wife's rejection. So wounded. Lucy held him as close as she could, trying to convey with her body how much she needed and wanted and loved him.

"I love you, Dom. You're more than enough for me."

He held her tighter, his arms like steel around her.

"Lucy. God. I love you so much," he said over and over.

"I know," she said, pressing her hand to the back of his head. "You love me so much you were prepared to give me up. I should probably warn you, I'm not that noble. I plan on hanging on to you for the rest of my life. So if you have a problem with that, speak now or forever hold your peace."

He laughed. He pulled back to look into her face and she reached up to wipe the tears from his cheeks.

"My sweet idiot," she said softly, lovingly.

Then she pulled him close and kissed him. It was like coming home after too long away. It was perfect, as good as she remembered.

Better—because this time she understood exactly who she held in her arms and how lucky she was and how lucky he was.

"Hey, Luce, guess who we found in the elevator? Oops!"

"Lucia!"

Dom broke their kiss but didn't immediately turn to acknowledge her sister and mother. He smiled and caressed her cheek. She smiled back.

Later, they would talk some more. He would hold her, and she would tell him over and over how much she loved him—whatever it took to remove the shadows of the doubt he'd lived with for so long.

"Does someone want to tell me what is going on? Why are you kissing Dominic, Lucia? I thought there had been a falling out? Why does nobody tell me anything?" Sophia asked.

Lucy's smile broadened as she looked over Dom's shoulder at her family. Rosie had a smug smile on her face while Andrew was doing his best to look as though he found his sister-in-law in a lip-lock with her estranged business partner after giving childbirth every day of the week. Her mother was flushed and expectant-looking, far more curious than she was outraged.

Lucy took Dom's hand in hers and tangled her fingers with his.

"Relax, Ma. Everything's going to be all right."

And for the first time in a long time, she knew it was true. She knew the weeks and months and years ahead would bring with them their fair share of problems and heartbreak and troubles. But she also knew she could take on anything with Dom at her side.

She glanced at him, and he raised their joined hands and pressed a kiss to her wrist.

She smiled. This was going to be good.

* * * * *

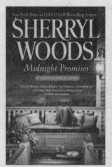

New York Times and USA TODAY Bestselling Author

SHERRYL WOODS

Midnight Promises

"Sherryl Woods always delights her readers—including me!"
—#1 New York Times bestselling author
Debbie Macomber

$7.99 U.S./$9.99 CAN.

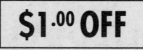

$1.⁰⁰ OFF

New York Times bestselling author

SHERRYL WOODS

draws you into
the emotional journey
of a marriage worth saving.

Midnight Promises

*Available June 26, 2012
wherever books are sold!*

MIRA

H HARLEQUIN®
™ www.Harlequin.com

$1.⁰⁰ OFF the purchase price of MIDNIGHT PROMISES by Sherryl Woods.

Offer valid from June 26, 2012, to July 16, 2012.
Redeemable at participating retail outlets. Limit one coupon per purchase.
Valid in the U.S.A. and Canada only.

Canadian Retailers: Harlequin Enterprises Limited will pay the face value of this coupon plus 10.25¢ if submitted by customer for this product only. Any other use constitutes fraud. Coupon is nonassignable. Void if taxed, prohibited or restricted by law. Consumer must pay any government taxes. Void if copied. Nielsen Clearing House ("NCH") customers submit coupons and proof of sales to Harlequin Enterprises Limited, P.O. Box 3000, Saint John, NB E2L 4L3, Canada. Non-NCH retailer—for reimbursement submit coupons and proof of sales directly to Harlequin Enterprises Limited, Retail Marketing Department, 225 Duncan Mill Rd., Don Mills, Ontario M3B 3K9, Canada.

U.S. Retailers: Harlequin Enterprises Limited will pay the face value of this coupon plus 8¢ if submitted by customer for this product only. Any other use constitutes fraud. Coupon is nonassignable. Void if taxed, prohibited or restricted by law. Consumer must pay any government taxes. Void if copied. For reimbursement submit coupons and proof of sales directly to Harlequin Enterprises Limited, P.O. Box 880478, El Paso, TX 88588-0478, U.S.A. Cash value 1/100 cents.

52610240

5 65373 00007 6   (8100)0 11780

® and TM are trademarks owned and used by the trademark owner and/or its licensee.

© 2012 Harlequin Enterprises Limited

MSW0712CPN

We hope you enjoyed reading

A NATURAL FATHER

by

SARAH MAYBERRY

This story was originally from
our Harlequin® Superromance® series.

*Look for six compelling new romances every
month from Harlequin Superromance!*

Angie Bartlett and Michael Robinson are friends. And following the death of his wife, Angie's best friend, their bond has grown even more. But that's all there is...right?

Read on for an exciting excerpt of WITHIN REACH by Sarah Mayberry, available August 2012 from Harlequin® Superromance®.

"HEY. RIGHT ON TIME," Michael said as he opened the door.

The first thing Angie registered was his fresh haircut and that he was clean shaven—a significant change from the last time she'd visited. Then her gaze dropped to his broad chest and the skintight black running pants molded to his muscular legs. The words died on her lips and she blinked, momentarily stunned by her acute awareness of him.

"You've cut your hair," she said stupidly.

"Yeah. Decided it was time to stop doing my caveman impersonation."

He gestured for her to enter. As she brushed past him she caught the scent of his spicy deodorant. He preceded her to the kitchen and her gaze traveled across his shoulders before dropping to his backside. Angie had always made a point of not noticing Michael's body. They were friends and she didn't want to know that kind of stuff. Now, however, she was forcibly reminded that he was a *very* attractive man.

Suddenly she didn't know where to look.

It was then that she noticed the other changes—the clean kitchen, the polished dining table and the living room free of clutter and abandoned clothes.

"Look at you go." Surely these efforts meant he was rejoining life.

He shrugged, but seemed pleased she'd noticed. "Getting there."

They maintained eye contact and the moment expanded. A connection that went beyond the boundaries of their friendship formed between them. Suddenly Angie wanted Michael in ways she'd never felt before. *Ever.*

"Okay. Let's get this show on the road," his six-year-old daughter, Eva, announced as she marched into the room.

Angie shook her head to break the spell and focused on Eva. "Great. Looking forward to a little light shopping?"

"Yes!" Eva gave a squeal of delight, then kissed her father goodbye.

Angie didn't feel 100 percent comfortable until she was sliding into the driver's seat.

Which was dumb. It was nothing. A stupid, odd bit of awareness that meant *nothing*. Michael was still Michael, even if he was gorgeous. Just because she'd tuned in to that fact for a few seconds didn't change anything.

Does Angie's new awareness mark a permanent shift in their relationship? Find out in WITHIN REACH by Sarah Mayberry, available August 2012 from Harlequin® Superromance®.

Harlequin® *Super Romance*®

Save $1.00 on the purchase of
WITHIN REACH
by **Sarah Mayberry,**

available August 7, 2012,
or on any other Harlequin® Superromance® book.

Available wherever books are sold, including most bookstores,
supermarkets, drugstores and discount stores.

- ✂

Save
$1.00

on the purchase of
WITHIN REACH by Sarah Mayberry,
available August 7, 2012,
or on any other Harlequin® Superromance® book.

Coupon valid until October 23, 2012. Redeemable at participating retail outlets
in the U.S. and Canada only. Limit one coupon per customer.

52610396

Canadian Retailers: Harlequin Enterprises Limited will pay the face value of this coupon plus 10.25¢ if submitted by customer for this product only. Any other use constitutes fraud. Coupon is nonassignable. Void if taxed, prohibited or restricted by law. Consumer must pay any government taxes. Void if copied. Nielsen Clearing House ("NCH") customers submit coupons and proof of sales to Harlequin Enterprises Limited, P.O. Box 3000, Saint John, NB E2L 4L3, Canada. Non-NCH retailer—for reimbursement submit coupons and proof of sales directly to Harlequin Enterprises Limited, Retail Marketing Department, 225 Duncan Mill Rd., Don Mills, ON M3B 3K9, Canada.

5 65373 00076 2   (8100)0 11799

U.S. Retailers: Harlequin Enterprises Limited will pay the face value of this coupon plus 8¢ if submitted by customer for this product only. Any other use constitutes fraud. Coupon is nonassignable. Void if taxed, prohibited or restricted by law. Consumer must pay any government taxes. Void if copied. For reimbursement submit coupons and proof of sales directly to Harlequin Enterprises Limited, P.O. Box 880478, El Paso, TX 88588-0478, U.S.A. Cash value 1/100 cents.

® and TM are trademarks owned and used by the trademark owner and/or its licensee.
© 2012 Harlequin Enterprises Limited

NYTCOUP0612

Based on the popular *Sweet Magnolias* series comes

THE SWEET MAGNOLIAS COOKBOOK

New York Times and USA TODAY Bestselling Author
SHERRYL WOODS
WITH CHEF TEDDI WOHLFELD

The
SWEET MAGNOLIAS
Cookbook

MORE THAN 100 FAVORITE SOUTHERN RECIPES

From The Sweet Magnolias Cookbook!

Fire & Ice Pickles

2 (32-ounce) jars nonrefrigerated pickle slices
4 cups granulated sugar
2 tablespoons Tabasco sauce

1 teaspoon crushed red pepper flakes
4 minced garlic cloves

1. Combine all ingredients, and mix well.

2. Cover, and let stand at room temperature 3–4 hours, stirring occasionally.

3. Divide into 4 (1-pint) canning jars. Seal tightly.

4. Refrigerate up to 1 month.

Note: Best if made at least 1 week before eating to allow flavors to develop.

MAKES 4 PINTS.

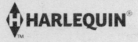